Something
to Talk
About

Other Books
by
Melanie Schuster

Luck in Love
Benita Cochran and Clay Deveraux

Until the End of Time
Renee Kemp and Andrew Cochran

My One and Only Love
Ceylon Simmons and Martin Deveraux

Let It Be Me
Vera Jackson and Marcus Deveraux

A Merry Little Christmas
Angelique Deveraux and Donnie Cochran

Wait for Love
(In the *Candlelight and You* Anthology)

Something to Talk About

Melanie Schuster

BET Publications, LLC
http://www.bet.com
http://www.arabesquebooks.com

ARABESQUE BOOKS are published by

BET Publications, LLC
c/o BET BOOKS
One BET Plaza
1900 W Place NE
Washington, DC 20018-1211

All Kensington Titles, Imprints, and Distributed Lines are available at special quantity discounts for bulk purchases for sales promotions, premiums, fund-raising, and educational or institutional use. Special book excerpts or customized printings can also be created to fit specific needs. For details, write or phone the office of the Kensington special sales manager: Kensington Publishing Corp., 850 Third Avenue, New York, NY 10022, attn: Special Sales Department, Phone: 1-800-221-2647.

First Printing: April 2005

10 9 8 7 6 5 4 3 2 1

Printed in the United States of America

Prologue

The patriarch of the Cochran family held his newest grandchild lovingly and looked into her big, bright eyes. At nearly four months of age, Lillian Rose Bennett Cochran was a beauty, with her mother's dimples and her father's rich caramel coloring. Big Benny Cochran chuckled as the baby smiled up at him and squeezed his forefinger tightly.

"I think you're a keeper, little girl. You remind me of your Aunt Benita when she was a baby," he said fondly.

He was seated in the living room of his youngest son, Adonis Cochran. Donnie and his wife, Angelique Deveraux Cochran, glanced at each other, then looked back at the handsome white-haired man doting on their daughter. Donnie was about to bring up a very sensitive subject. He and Angelique had something of great importance to discuss with his father, which they'd been putting off during the Christmas holidays and the New Year celebration. They had agreed to wait until after they renewed their wedding vows on Valentine's Day to talk about it, and now the time was here.

They were in the middle of unpacking their new home, and the usual array of packing boxes was visible in every room. On Christmas Eve, Big Benny had given the young couple the family home in Palmer Park, as he and his wife, Donnie's stepmother Martha Davis Cochran, wanted to move into a condo. So now the young couple was in the throes of unpacking, Big Benny was in the midst of spoiling his fourteenth grandchild, and Donnie was about to bring up his father's best-kept secret.

"Pop, Angelique told me about the conversation you had with her before Lily Rose was born. I think you know which conversation I mean," he said gently.

Big Benny barely glanced away from Lily Rose, who was making the humming sound she made every time she was completely content. "Of course I remember the conversation, Adonis. Do you think I've suddenly turned senile? I told Babydoll about an episode of my life, one that I'm not particularly proud of." He paused to shift Lily Rose more comfortably in his arms. "I'm not ashamed anymore, but I can't take it to the grave with me. It's time the story was told to everyone concerned."

Angelique's eyes met her husband's and they communicated wordlessly for a moment before she spoke. "Well, Daddy, if you're determined to do this, how do you want to do it? And when do you want to do it? And how are you going to . . ." Her voice trailed off as Big Benny waved aside her questions.

"Babydoll, don't worry your head about it. There're a few details to be worked out, but we can handle them. I agree it's going to be a surprise to a lot of people, but I've always liked surprises. Lily Rose likes them too, don't you, sweetheart?"

Donnie made a skeptical face as his father blew noisy kisses on Lily Rose's cheek, making her giggle with joy. "Uhh, Pop, I think *surprise* is an optimistic understatement. This is more along the lines of a guided missile set to detonate any second. It's going to take a lot of getting used to for a lot of people, not to mention all the attention it's going to attract. A story like this one is going to make a lot of headlines. Are you sure you want to have to deal with all of that?"

His father looked him full in the face and all traces of the doting grandfather vanished. He looked every bit what he was, a man in control of his own fate, a man who would bend to no one and followed only his own rules. "At this point, Adonis, I don't give a damn who gets upset. This is the right thing to do and I'm going to do it. I've taken the easy way out for too long. I'm not about to leave this world without putting this right. And as far as headlines are concerned, who cares? People always have something to say, so we'll just give them something to talk about." He went back to playing with the baby as though they'd been discussing nothing more important than the weather.

Donnie walked across the sunny living room to embrace Angelique, who had stopped unpacking to listen to what was being said. Putting his long arms around her, he kissed her hair, then her face, and murmured, "Well, Angel, at least being a Cochran isn't dull."

She leaned against the comforting warmth of her husband's body and nodded in agreement. Being a part of his family was many things, but none of them were boring. And things were about to get a lot livelier.

Chapter One

"Ladies, we are running out of bachelors. Here it is April and the auction is set for May and there just aren't as many candidates as there were last year," Michaela said sadly. She and her sorors were gathered to discuss the lineup for the annual Bachelor Auction that was a major fundraiser for their group. Her announcement drew noises of protest from her tablemates.

"What do you mean we're running out?" asked Erica, her pretty face creased in alarm. "Didn't you call the ones we used last year?"

Michaela sighed deeply. "Of course I did and the supply is short, I'm telling you. Church bells have been going off like nobody's business around here. Dr. Warren Alexander is now happily married, Vincent Hankins is also married, and Pierre Rollins has moved to Cleveland."

Nicole's expression brightened. "Well, heck, Cleveland isn't that far, I'm sure he'd come back for the weekend. It's a good cause, after all," she said confidently.

Michaela was shaking her head as she put her stemmed goblet of water down. "Pierre moved to Cleveland with his *new bride*," she reported glumly. "And of course we all know that Donnie Cochran got married. Twice!"

"Yes, he did," agreed one of the women. "He eloped last Valentine's Day and then he and his wife renewed their vows on their anniversary this year. I can't get hooked up one time and they did it *two times*. I'm so jealous."

A collective sigh went around the table, broken by the snap of someone's fingers. "Well, what about *Adam* Cochran? He's always glad to do it and he's not married yet." This comment came from the happily engaged Sarita. Her pretty, round face took on a look of extreme surprise at the reaction brought on by her words.

"No, no, no! Not Adam Cochran, anybody but him!"

All eyes turned to the speaker, Katina Warren. Katina immediately held up her hand in the easily recognized "don't even go there" signal. Her sorority sisters didn't have long to wait to find out the reason for her vehemence.

"Adam Cochran is too *weird*. He may be the best-looking man in Detroit, but he's crazy. And there's no point to asking him, because he'll do the same thing he always does. He says sure, no problem, he'll be glad to. Everybody gets all excited about winning a date with him, but he brings that so-called business partner of his and hands her his checkbook. Then, as soon as there's a really high bid, she doubles it, writes out a check, and he disappears into the night. What fun is that? He's disappointed too many women over the years. It's just not fair," she said, pouting.

The women tried to cover their amusement with varying degrees of success. Sarita immediately defended Adam. "Don't say that, he's not crazy. He's different, that's for sure, but he isn't crazy by a long shot. I dated him, remember, and he's a wonderful guy, very romantic and sexy, and he treated me like a queen. And if it wasn't for Adam I might not have met my Derrick," she said, waving her three-carat ring as a reminder. "He's the one who introduced us and look how that turned out."

Michaela smiled in memory. "You must admit that Adam is eccentric. He asked me to go to a concert once and I got all excited, thinking we were going to see Prince, and he took me to see Placido Domingo. Me, who'd never been to an opera in my life," she said fondly.

Katina pointed her finger at Michaela and made a face of triumph. "See what I mean? I told you he was weird. Who wants to hear some stupid aria when Prince is in town?"

"Hey, I didn't say I hated it, did I? I developed quite a taste for opera after that night. And he cooked me a delicious late supper afterward, too. It was a wonderful evening, as a matter of fact." Michaela smiled dreamily and winked at Sarita. "And I ended up meeting my husband at the symphony one night, so he actually did me a big favor."

Katina was on a roll, however. "He's got that horrible long hair, he never commits to anything, and he never does what he's supposed to do. I say forget about him and let's find some real men for the auction."

The other five women at the table stared at Katina and someone said what was on all their minds. "You seem to be taking this all quite personally, soror. What exactly did Adam *do* to you?"

Katina struggled with her response, then it all came out in a heated rush of words. "He asked me to go up north with him one weekend and I'm thinking we're going to the Grand Traverse Lodge or someplace luxurious like that, someplace with a big casino and a fireplace in the room and a four-star restaurant. He took me up north, all right. *Camping,*" she said venomously. "Can you believe it? He actually expected me to sleep in a tent and cook out over a fire!"

The other women burst into simultaneous laughter. "It's not funny," Katina said crossly, her cute little face taking on an unbecoming red hue. "I got my hair done, a manicure and a pedicure, and bought a new Tracy Reese to dazzle him and this joker takes me into the woods where the critters are! It was the shortest camping trip in history because we had to come back to Detroit that very night. I wasn't staying in the wilds with that maniac," she huffed.

Sarita and Michaela winked at each other and spoke in unison. "That's why you're so ticked off; you don't know what you missed out on, girl." They were giving each other a discreet high five when a voice that sounded as rich as one-hundred-year-old cognac cut into the conversation.

"Good evening, ladies. How is everyone this evening?"

Adam Cochran loomed over their table wearing a perfectly fitted cashmere sport coat and a perfectly charming smile. Everyone returned the smile but Katina, who was frozen in a posture of utter horror. *How the devil did he sneak up like that? Dear Lord, he didn't hear me, did he? And why does he have to look so darned good?*

Adam was with a tall, equally handsome man who was also wearing a devastating smile. Adam introduced him as Bryant Porter. Michaela, who was on a mission for her sorority, boldly asked if he was available for their auction. "It's for a wonderful cause and it's a fun event, too," she said persuasively.

Bryant turned his dark chocolate face with the beautiful bone structure to her and smiled with what looked like genuine regret. "Unfortunately, I live in Chicago and I'm only here on business. If my schedule weren't so full I'd love to accommodate you. I'm sure my friend here will volunteer in my stead though," he said with a pointed glance at Adam.

Adam shrugged eloquently. "Sure, I'll do it. You know I always step up to the occasion." He kindly ignored the indelicate snort that issued from Katina. "If you like, I can ask a couple of my associates at the firm to participate. They'd never miss an opportunity to perform a service for the community," he said smoothly.

After he and Bryant left the ladies' table a few minutes later, one of the women looked at Katina with an expression of total disbelief. "And you made that hunk of man bring you home so you could sleep in your own bed? Girl, if that had been me, we'd still be in the woods and we'd *still* be busy. You're not mad at him; you're mad at yourself, fool. And I'm not mad about that long hair, either; that ponytail is *hot.*"

After Adam and Bryant were seated in a booth, Bryant nodded toward the table of women. "Why do these organizations think that auctioning off men is a good way to raise money? There's something really creepy about being 'sold,' even if it is for a good cause," he said with a shudder.

Adam shrugged and gave an expression of indifference. "Yeah, it's kinda whacked in a way, but I never pay it any attention. Some women go crazy for it and they do make a lot of money every year. Me, I go along with it. I get Alicia to bid on me with my money and get me outta there before any real damage is done."

Bryant raised his eyebrows and smiled. Alicia Fuentes was a topic of interest with him. As all three of them were architects, they'd met often over the years, usually at conferences. The reason Bryant was in Detroit was the annual Midwestern Conference of African-American Architects and Urban Planners. After the conference ended, Bryant had offered to take Adam and Alicia to dinner to repay their hospitality, as they had hosted him earlier in the week. But that wasn't the only reason; he wanted to get to know Alicia better. Alicia was brilliant, attractive, and single, and Bryant was quite taken with her. Now he was reconsidering his interest because if he wasn't mistaken, someone else was rather taken with her, too, and the person was sitting across the table from him.

Suddenly Adam rose from his seat, just as Alicia reached their booth. He stepped aside to allow her to enter and made sure she was comfortable before resuming his place. Alicia flashed her usual bright smile and greeted the two men. "Sorry I'm late, but I had to pick up the kids from daycare and drop them at my parents' house. Have you ordered yet?"

Bryant reached for her hand across the table and squeezed it gently. "Absolutely not. We just got seated a few minutes ago. We ordered drinks, but nothing else. You're really not late at all," he said. He looked her over thoroughly, enjoying the intelligence in her long-lashed eyes. "I didn't know you had children," he added.

Alicia returned the squeeze with a friendly one of her one, and then gently took back her hand. "I don't have children, yet. I was referring to my niece and nephew. I live with my sister and we share a lot of carpooling duties," she said as she rapidly skimmed the menu.

Adam hadn't said a word; he was merely observing his dining companions with a neutral expression. Alicia was her usual charming self, understated but beautiful. Her deep bronze complexion was rosy from the cold weather, her shining black hair was in its usual long braid, and she was neatly but casually attired in khaki slacks, a ribbed silk pullover sweater, and a nicely tailored wool sport coat. She had no idea of the effect she had on men. Alicia never seemed to notice when one was drooling all over her, and Bryant was doing just that. For reasons he wasn't willing to examine closely, Bryant's attention to Alicia was getting on Adam's last nerve. Adam was the coolest, calmest, and most self-possessed of all the men in his family, but something about the way Bryant was looking at Alicia was annoying in the extreme. The caress of Alicia's familiar fragrance, coupled with the warmth of her body, created a warm aura from which he was loathe to emerge, but Bryant's constant attention to his partner was jarring him out of his newly found comfort.

The drinks arrived, and Alicia beamed when she saw that Adam had ordered her favorite libation, a mojito, a rum cocktail that originated in Cuba. The server asked if they were ready to order and Alicia was the first to respond.

"Absolutely. I'd like a cup of French onion soup, the petite filet mignon, medium rare, and the steamed vegetables. And may I have extra vegetables instead of a potato? What's the house dressing?" she asked, looking up at their server. Upon hearing that is was a creamy Caesar, she replied, "Okay, that's fine, I'll have that, please, but I'd like my salad after my entrée, and yes, I will be having dessert if you have blueberry pie and vanilla ice cream." She handed her menu to the server. When he told her they did indeed have the pie, she smiled in delight, which charmed Bryant.

"Alicia, I have to confess, I love watching you eat," he drawled. "There's something profoundly sensual about watching a beautiful woman enjoying the pleasure of a good meal, and you, my dear, have perfected the art. I love watching those lips in action."

Alicia's eyes crinkled in a smile and she responded cheerfully, "Well, you'll get plenty of opportunity to watch since I never seem to stop eating, do I, Adam?"

Adam took a deep swallow of his scotch and soda before answering, and when he did it was more of a grunt than actual words. He'd never told anyone before, but he loved to watch Alicia eat too. Her eyes always lit up when she was about to consume something wonderful and she had a habit of giving her bottom lip a dainty little lick before she took her first bite. Then she would issue a heartfelt sigh of repletion and close her eyes in bliss as she savored the morsel. Alicia had really sexy lips, lips that were big and moist and prettily shaped, and the way she used that mouth in eating was, well, *arousing*, that was the only way to describe it. Adam got a secret thrill whenever they ate together. But being her mealtime voyeur, that was *his* thing, something between him and Alicia alone. And that bigheaded, grinning baboon had somehow stumbled onto his private fantasy. Adam abruptly excused himself and left the table.

Something was going on in his head and his heart that was becoming more and more difficult to handle. He and Alicia had been best friends and business partners for over ten years, and somewhere along the line, Adam had crossed the line of friendship. But what was he venturing into?

Alicia took a good long look at Bryant as she sipped her smooth, icy cold mojito. She didn't drink often, but she loved the taste of the Cuban rum cocktail. And she didn't see Bryant Porter often, but she always liked what she saw. He was an intriguing and personable man. And unattached, which was a total puzzle to her. As she often did, Alicia spoke before she thought. "Bryant, you're one of the nicest people I've ever met. Why aren't you married? Are the women in Chicago just nuts or what?" she asked curiously.

Bryant laughed out loud, a deep, sexy, belly laugh. "Well, thanks for the compliment, but I might ask you the same thing about the men in Detroit. How have you managed to evade matrimony? You're gorgeous, smart, funny, and down-to-earth. Why has no man snatched you up?"

Alicia twisted her face in a halfhearted imitation of a smile. "I can cook, too," she said wanly. "And I'm not as, umm, *irresistible* as you might imagine. I was engaged once, to my college sweetheart, as a matter of fact. We were going to get married right after I finished grad school."

Bryant could sense her withdrawal and probed gently. "What happened, Alicia?"

"Oh, the usual. I was extremely busy with a dual program of architectural design and urban planning. One of them is bad enough, but combined it makes for the program from hell. I was studying and working on projects almost twenty-four-seven," she said quietly.

"Well, sure, that's to be expected. So what became of the fiancé?"

"He decided I wasn't giving him enough attention and he found someone else who would," she said simply. "And that's my sad story. What's yours?"

"Well, I was married for a while, I have two beautiful children," Bryant told her while admiring the slight slant of her big eyes. "Apparently my wife was feeling unfulfilled and neglected too, although I wish she'd let me know about it before she found a lover."

"Wow. I'm sorry I asked. I wasn't trying to get in your business," Alicia began.

Bryant waved away her apology. "It's ancient history," he said easily. "I don't want you to think it didn't hurt because it did; it hurt like the devil. That's a blow to the heart and the ego that's almost unbearable, but you know about that, don't you?"

Alicia nodded in agreement. "You're right about that. It's painful and miserable and depressing. But you get over it eventually. I have to tell you, though; your wife was a big fool. As wonderful as you are, I don't know how she could turn her back on you." She took in his perfectly smooth ebony complexion, his deep dimples, his straight white teeth outlined by his impeccably groomed moustache and goatee, the whole package set off by a small gold hoop earring. Once again her well-known candor kicked in before she realized what she was saying. "So why hasn't some lucky woman snatched you up? I can't believe someone as handsome and talented and successful as you isn't taken."

Her remark earned another shout of laughter from Bryant. "Alicia, you're so good for my ego! I'd take you back to Chicago with me, but I don't think your partner would like that at all," he said with a knowing smile.

"Oh, I think you're right," she agreed. "We have so

many projects going, if I was to leave town he'd be a little bit perturbed."

It was Bryant's turn to study her face; he admired her silky skin unadorned by makeup, her high cheekbones, and her wonderfully sensual mouth. He was starting to wonder what that mouth would feel like on his when Adam returned to the table. Adam gave him a quick look without speaking, a look that most people would have missed. It was just a flash, something that could have been dismissed as imagination, but Bryant was wise enough to read the signal and Adam was telling him in no uncertain terms to step off.

Adroitly changing the subject, Bryant announced that he would be spending a lot more time in Detroit. "I was asked to teach a course at Wayne State this summer, so I guess we'll be seeing a lot of each other for a while."

Alicia was enthusiastic in her response, which made up for the total silence from Adam. "Bryant, that's wonderful. This'll be great, there's a lot to do in Detroit in the summertime, and you'll really enjoy it. Will you be here on the weekends, too?"

"Probably some of them, but I'll be going back to Chicago as much as possible to spend time with my kids. I can't stand being away from them. It's hard enough not seeing them every day," Bryant said solemnly.

Alicia patted his hand comfortingly. "That's only natural. Maybe they can come to see you sometime. Adam has a ton of nieces and nephews they can play with; they'd have a ball."

Bryant's sexy mouth turned up in another huge smile. "That's a great idea, Alicia. I have a feeling that this is going to work out just fine, once I have a place to stay."

What Adam thought of the situation was an entirely different matter.

Chapter Two

After following Alicia home to make sure she arrived there safely, Adam drove around aimlessly for a while. Alicia always insisted there was no need to follow her home; she thought he was being needlessly protective. Adam would let her say her little piece, and then he'd calmly follow her Mini Cooper to the condo where she lived with her sister, Marielle. He would wait until she had closed the door and turned the outside light off and on, the signal they'd established over the years. Nothing was ever going to happen to Alicia as long as he was alive to protect her. Besides being his partner in their very successful firm, she was his best friend and companion. He couldn't imagine living without her in his life, although lately he was imagining a lot more.

He couldn't pinpoint the exact moment when he accepted the fact that his platonic love for her was turning into something else, but he could remember three specific instances that had occurred in the last six months that had started his mind working in an unfamiliar manner. First there was the racing incident.

Adam was a true daredevil. Extreme sports were made for him; he loved testing himself in all kinds of ways, including physical endurance. Snowboarding, parasailing, white-water rafting, and motorcycle racing had all taken his fancy at once time or another, but car racing had eluded him until a few months earlier when he decided to give it a whirl. He'd taken racing lessons and decided to enter a Formula Five race to test his skill. All his brothers came to the track to watch, and naturally, Alicia did, too.

It was an exciting race, made even more heart-stopping by the fact that another car had spun out in front of him, causing him to almost lose control of his car. After a brief moment of sheer terror he'd recovered control of the wheel to win the race, to the excitement of his cheering brothers. After the formalities, he'd joined his family, looking around vainly for Alicia. He found her returning from the ladies' room looking as pale as paper and trembling like a leaf. As he walked toward her, concern all over his face, she'd crumpled a little and he had to catch her to prevent her from falling down.

"Alicia, baby, what is it?" he'd asked. She couldn't answer; she stood there mutely with tears running down her face.

"Were you scared? Did you think something was going to happen to me out there? Come on, baby, you know me better than that, I'm made of iron," he'd told her, trying to make her smile. Instead, she burst into real tears as she put her arms around him and he could feel how hard she was shaking. She clung to him urgently, nestling into his neck with a shaky, tear-filled sigh. All he could do was hold her and whisper comforting words into her ear until she began to calm. He'd kissed her hair and her face and promised her he'd never do it again and finally she drew a long, shuddering breath and stared up at him as if he were the center of her entire universe. He had felt himself leaning toward her to seal his promise with a kiss when they were joined by his loud, happy brothers, the ones with no sense of timing at all.

Adam was still shocked by that incident, both by Alicia's reaction and his response. Alicia was a tomboy at heart, she was certainly no sissy, and she enjoyed physical activity as much as he did. They'd parasailed together on a trip to the tropics and had also gone rock climbing and rappelled into the Grand Canyon together. He'd never seen her fall apart like that, certainly not over any of his stunts. And he had no intention of ever getting behind the wheel of a race car again. If it made her unhappy, he just wouldn't do it, that's all. Adam had never compromised on anything in his life and here he had capitulated totally, just to spare her pain.

By now Adam had reached his spacious loft in the Harbortown section of Detroit. He parked his ancient and venerable Range Rover and went into the building, checking his mail as he did so. After entering the loft, he automatically took off his shoes and hung up his sport coat, stopping to turn on a few lights and point the remote at his stereo. Soon he was sitting on his long custom-made window seat watching the moonlight on the Detroit River. He had a bottle of mineral water in his hand, but he wasn't drinking it. He was thinking about the second revelation he'd had concerning Alicia. This one had happened soon after his niece's premature birth last November.

After the race incident Adam was more aware of Alicia than he'd ever been, or so it seemed. He found himself watching her when she was unaware of his observation, drinking in her essence as though savoring a fine wine. When his brother Donnie brought his wife home from the hospital with the newest Cochran, Lily Rose, Adam had taken Alicia over to their house to meet his infant niece. Alicia had been instantly smitten with the baby, as expected. She loved children and was always happy to be around them. While she'd had her turn holding the beautiful baby and cooing at her, someone had teased her about having one of her own. To his surprise, she'd agreed that it was time.

"I do want a baby, more than anybody knows. In fact, I'm going to have one. In two years, I'm having a baby no matter what."

The calm assurance with which she'd uttered the words had shaken Adam. At that precise moment a pain had pierced his heart, a sensation totally foreign to his normal range of emotions. He'd had a primal revelation, a flash of insight that stunned him. *Nobody's putting a baby in her except me. If she wants a baby, I'll give her one. As many as she wants, but no one else is putting their hands on her.*

Adam did take a long swallow of water at that point; the mere memory of that episode still caused him to sweat a little. He'd never considered marriage or children up until that point, and it wasn't as though the many women in his life hadn't tried to lead him that way. He'd been perfectly content to lead the life of a happy, handsome bachelor until the moment he'd seen his best friend cuddling his tiny niece. At that very second his whole world had been rocked and rocked hard.

He stood up quickly and stretched. He took the bottle of water with him and went into his custom-designed bathroom. A long hot shower before bed was just what he needed. In a few minutes he was standing under a forceful stream of hot water lathering his body with the special hard-milled soap with which Alicia kept him supplied. He loved the big oversized bars from Spain and Portugal and France. Even the fact that they were highly scented delighted him because they reminded him of her. And she always got him sandalwood or pine scents, things that weren't too feminine. He didn't want to admit it, but he wished she were in the shower with him. He'd almost gotten that wish two weeks before. It was the third incident that had made him realize once and for all that he wanted more from Alicia than he'd ever acknowledged.

Two weeks earlier

The Range Rover sailed over U.S. 10 W heading to Idlewild, Michigan. Alicia was relaxed and almost completely happy as she checked out the scenery. It was a bright and sunny, albeit cold, day. Frank Zappa was blasting out of the stereo and Adam was singing along with the music. The only thing that was missing to make her day perfect was a pit stop. Adam was determined to make the four-hour drive without a break, something that was making her really uncomfortable.

"Adam, I don't care if you have to pull over next to a tree, I have to *go*. You know I have a bladder the size of a pea; why do you do this to me?" she complained.

"Okay, we'll stop at the next exit," he said. "I don't think you want to be dropping trou by the side of the road; there's a lot of wildlife around here."

Sensing another one of Adam's tall tales, she raised an eyebrow. "Wildlife? Like what?"

"The usual. Deer, raccoons, wild turkeys, bears, coyotes," he said with a sidelong glance at her to see if she believed it.

"You're making that up," she said slowly.

"Oh yeah? Check that out," he replied, pointing out his window.

Alicia's mouth fell open as she beheld a herd of buffalo. They were confined in a corral and were obviously domesticated, but it was a weird sight nonetheless. "Would you look at that? A buffalo farm. Who would believe that?" She continued to stare at the huge, shaggy creatures as the SUV sped past. They passed a Christmas tree farm and then she caught sight of a sign that made her laugh out loud. "Dairy Doo? What kind of place is that?" she asked curiously.

"It's a dairy farm that also sells manure. See? It's all color coordinated and everything," he pointed out. Sure enough, there were towering piles of neatly arranged manure in different shades of brown.

"Adam, you certainly know a lot about this area," she said as she continued to gaze at the unusual array.

"You know me, once I decided to build a summer place for the family, I started doing research. I've been up here a few times looking around and I found out quite a bit about Lake County. My dad was born here, you know."

Alicia pushed the brim of her battered baseball cap up so that she could see Adam's profile better. "No, I didn't know that. Where in Lake County was he born?"

"He was born and raised in Idlewild. We're going there first so I can show you around. Idlewild used to be this fabulous black resort back in the day. From the 1920s to the 1960s, it was *the* place to be. They had camping, fishing, hunting, and boating, and besides all that, there were these amazing nightclubs with floor shows that rivaled the Copacabana and the Las Vegas strip. Everybody who was anybody came to Idlewild. W.E.B. Dubois, Count Basie, Billie Holiday, Duke Ellington, you name them, they were here," he told her.

"Wow. I've heard about it, but I never knew what it was really like," Alicia admitted. "Your sister's movie gave me more insight on it than anything else I've seen." A few years earlier, his only sister, Benita, had written a screenplay titled *Idlewild* that was produced by her husband, Clay Deveraux. "So, Adam, what happened to it? Why did people stop coming to Idlewild?"

Adam raised one shoulder in a gesture of resignation. "Desegregation happened, mostly. People came to Idlewild because the white resorts wouldn't allow them in. When the color bars were raised, people scattered en masse. They didn't want to come here and be treated like royalty anymore; they wanted to go where they were barely tolerated," he said with a hint of bitterness.

Alicia opened her mouth to respond but was distracted by the sight of a gas station ahead. Adam let her out in front of the building and she made a mad dash for the facilities. Adam was pumping gas when she returned a few minutes later drinking from a large bottle of Dasani water. He went inside to pay for the gas and rejoined Alicia, giving her a sardonic smile.

"What?" she asked innocently.

Adam nodded at the water. "You were just complaining about having to go and here you are filling up again. Is that logical?"

She looked from the bottle of water to Adam and gave a short, embarrassed laugh. "Okay, maybe not. But we'll be there pretty soon, right?"

"Yes, we're almost there."

After they arrived in Baldwin, Idlewild's neighboring community, they checked into the Pere Marquette River Lodge, a motel that also offered quaint two-bedroom log cabins. Alicia took a look around the cabin and was very pleased with what she saw. The cabins were comfortable and nicely decorated in a rustic lodge motif that made them homey and inviting. "This is really nice, Adam. When we come back, we'll have to plan on cooking while we're here," she said as she inspected the nicely appointed little kitchen.

Adam knew she was talking about the inevitable trips from Detroit that constructing a house in Lake County would engender, but it sounded like she was talking about little vacations for the two of them. For his own reasons, he liked the way that sounded.

After a day of exploring Idlewild they had dinner at the Village Inn in Baldwin where Alicia, as she put it, made a pig of herself over the homemade carrot cake. It was dense, rich, and moist with the best cream cheese frosting she'd ever eaten and she had two pieces. Adam was satisfied with one slice of chocolate cake with thick fudge frosting, but, as always, he got a charge out of watching her enjoy her dessert. When she licked the last bit of frosting from her fork, he felt a faint thrill of sensation at the base of his spine. Adam was more than happy to get the check and settle their bill; if he had to continue to watch her pretty pink tongue lick her luscious lips, he wasn't sure what would happen next, but he could feel his control slipping.

They returned to the cabin tired, but happy and totally ready for bed. Adam's realtor was coming in the morning and they had another long day to look forward to, so an early bedtime was a good idea. The only problem was that while the living room and Adam's bedroom were warm and cozy, it was still frigid in Alicia's room. Adam offered to trade rooms with her, but she refused.

"Oh, don't worry about it." She yawned. "I'll sleep in my sweats and I guarantee you I'll be out like a light in about ten seconds. I shouldn't have eaten that second piece of cake, but it was so *good.*" She gave another huge yawn and told Adam good night. In a few minutes Adam heard the shower running while Alicia prepared for bed. When it was his turn to shower, his senses were assailed by the warm fragrance Alicia left in the small bathroom. The scent of her perfumed bath gel surrounded him and subjected him to a burst of physical longing that was as unexpected as it was unwelcome. After a quick shower, he toweled off and threw on a T-shirt and sweats in deference to the other occupant of the cabin, then went to bed. The sooner he was asleep, the sooner he'd stop having inappropriate thoughts about his best friend.

Fate was not smiling on him, however. Alicia nudging him in the back broke his slumber. "Move over, Adam; it's like an icebox in there," she said grumpily. He turned on the bedside light and squinted up at Alicia, who was clad in a Detroit Tigers sweatshirt and pants and wrapped in both her blanket and bedspread. "Scoot over," she repeated and he did as she asked. Moments later, they were cuddled up like spoons and she was fast asleep. They slept like small children, innocently and chastely, through the cold northern Michigan night. The morning, however, brought a decided change to their circumstances.

Adam was awakened by a burst of soft laughter from Alicia. "Umm, Adam, I think those are mine," she said with amusement. He realized instantly what she was talking about. At some point during the night the extra bedclothes had been discarded, along with Alicia's sweatshirt. She was now wearing only an oversized T-shirt and her sweatpants. And his hands had somehow found their way under the shirt and were clamped firmly around her breasts. Adam smiled and flexed his long fingers over the warm fullness of her ripe bosom.

"Oh, you mean *these*? They're yours, hmm?" He continued to caress them, moving his hands over the smooth, enticing silkiness of her skin while learning every curve.

Alicia tried to stifle a sigh of pleasure but didn't quite succeed. "Yes, Adam, those are mine," she said breathily. "So why don't you let go of them so I can get up?"

By now Adam was wide-awake and ready to explore more of Alicia's delightful body. "Don't be stingy, Allie. After all, I let you roll all over me last night and I never said a word, did I?"

Alicia shifted so that she was on her back, which broke his hold on her right breast while giving him better access to her left one. "I was not rolling all over you, Adam Cochran. I stayed on my side of the bed like the perfect lady I am," she said primly. She took a quick breath as he rolled on top of her and recaptured her left breast, stroking both of them with his broad, warm palms as he smiled down into her face.

"That's a lie, Alicia, whether you realize it or not. You were all over me, baby. You were rubbing me and stroking me and grinding up against me until I almost lost my mind. Would my body lie to you?" he asked as he positioned his rock-hard member against her most feminine part. "I was hard as Japanese steel all night because of you."

Alicia's eyes closed and she bit her lower lip as her body responded to his with a sensuous movement of her hips. "I'm not saying I believe you," she breathed, "but if it's true, why didn't you wake me up?"

Before Adam could answer, there was a sharp knock on the cabin door. Someone called out, "Yoo-hoo! Mr. Cochran, it's Geneva Williams from Lake County Realtors," in an annoyingly chipper voice

Alicia gasped and whispered, "The realtor! Oh, dang, Adam, we've got to get dressed!" Seconds later he was sprawled across the bed alone while he could hear the sounds of Alicia frantically brushing her teeth. As so often happens in life, he was a victim of bad timing. On the other hand, maybe he was a *victor* of bad timing; if that knock on the door hadn't sounded, it would have been too late to turn back; he would have broken the most sacred promise he'd ever made to the person who meant more to him than anyone else.

Adam lay on his back, staring up at his bedroom ceiling. He'd been trying to go to sleep for some time, but the effort was in vain. All he could think about was Alicia. They had become instant friends in graduate school, since they were seeking the same degrees and were in most classes together. Moreover, they shared a lot of interests outside the classroom. Adam had never met anyone with whom he felt so comfortable. If she hadn't been engaged, he would've wasted no time in letting her know he wanted her. After the breakup of her engagement, things had changed. At the time it seemed the right thing to do, the only thing to do. And now it was too late. Too many years had passed; too many things had developed—like their eternal friendship and their business partnership. If only he hadn't given her his word . . . He groaned aloud and willed sleep to come. It came, finally, but only after a long, lonely, and pointless amount of regret.

Chapter Three

The urban-chic offices of the Cochran-Fuentes Archi-tectural Design Firm were almost empty. The lone occu-pant of the suite of offices on the top floor of the Cochran Building was Alicia Fuentes, who was sitting at her drawing table brooding. She looked vainly around the spacious, ergonomically efficient and tasteful work space to find something on which to focus, but she was failing miserably. She surveyed the long windows with the leaded panes, the gray Berber carpet with the blue saturation, the walls painted in a matching hue, and the black-and-white photographs of the firm's most out-standing work that were displayed on the walls, but noth-ing caught her interest.

Forcing herself to get off her stool, she stood up, stretched, and made a cursory inspection of the huge potted plants that were displayed strategically through-out the offices and the reception area. She was trying to convince herself that she was doing something mean-ingful, but she was just wasting time. The plants were professionally cared for by a firm that catered to the office-bound plants of corporations. They didn't need her attention in the least, something of which she was well aware. She was just mousing around trying to shake off a sense of impending doom. Alicia was in deep trou-ble, and she knew it.

She'd tried her best to ignore the symptoms, but there was no getting around it. She was falling in love with her best friend. It wasn't really a surprise to her, some kind of huge cosmic shock that had just presented itself in a blinding flash of insight; the feelings she had for Adam Cochran had been growing steadily for the duration of their friendship. Adam had been her best friend, her strongest ally, her confidant, and her rock since their days in graduate school. Had it not been for the pact they'd made ten years before, she'd have been trying to get with him. She gave a short, bitter laugh as she acknowledged the total truth, that she would have chased him down like a dog and begged him to be hers. And she'd almost done that very thing on their recent trip to Idlewild.

Alicia wandered into the reception area and plopped down on the big navy sofa with a heavy sigh. A swift shudder racked her body as she relived the sexy scene that unfolded that morning. When she'd awakened, curled on her side with Adam spooned next to her, she'd felt warm, safe, and content, until she realized that his hands had staked a claim on her very willing breasts. Instead of being embarrassed or alarmed, she'd been thrilled and aroused. The way his hands had felt on her body, the feel of his big body on top of hers, even for a moment . . . Alicia covered her face and gave a heartfelt cry of frustration. That real-estate broker had probably saved her life, she admitted, because there was no way that she would have stopped Adam from whatever came next. She'd been waiting for him too long to say no. A decent woman would have felt some semblance of shame at that morning's events. But she felt nothing but frustration that their playful interlude hadn't come to fruition. *Madre de Dios, I'm turning into a big ol' skank,* she thought sadly. *Here I am, a nice Catholic girl, turning into a desperate hoochie. What else can you call a woman who has designs on her best friend?*

Her cell phone rang, startling her out of her reverie.

She pulled it out of her pants pocket and said hello without looking at the caller ID.

"Hello yourself. I know it's the last minute, but how about dinner and a movie tonight?"

Alicia's face split in a huge, genuine smile as she recognized the voice of Bryant Porter.

"Bryant, when did you get into town?" she asked.

"I got in last night. I had some meetings at Wayne State and so forth, plus I need to find a place to live. I'm going to be here through tomorrow at least," he replied. "So how about that dinner?"

Alicia looked down at her khaki slacks and made a face. "Well, I'm not dressed up, but if you don't mind going some place casual, I'm on."

"Casual is my favorite thing," he assured her. "Want me to pick you up?"

"Tell you what, let's meet at the Fishbone's in Greektown. Do you think you can find it?"

After Bryant assured her he could, they agreed on a time to meet. Alicia ended the call feeling much better. This was just the break she needed, a nice evening with a friend to clear her head of all the strange, unsettling thoughts that had been crowding in. She went back to her office to retrieve her purse and leather tote bag and walked back through the office singing a lilting Cuban song as she switched off the lights. She'd reached the reception area when a deep voice made her jump straight in the air.

"Adam, you scared the life out of me," she fussed. "I've told you about sneaking up on me like that." Her words were at war with her feelings, since the very sight of him made her melt inside. He'd been out on a site all afternoon and she was surprised that he'd come back to the office at all. His words, however, were very plainly spoken.

"And I've told you about being up here by yourself. No matter what, I don't want you in the office by yourself, especially this late. If you find yourself working late, you have three choices. Take the work home, call me to stay with you, or call security to come up here until you're finished," he said sternly.

Alicia was torn between aversion and arousal. She didn't like Adam treating her like an infant, but it was hard to resent him when he was so concerned for her well-being. If only he hadn't looked so darned sexy. He was wearing jeans, heavy, well-worn Land's End boots, and a denim shirt with one of his favorite sport coats. He looked like a Ralph Lauren ad in a chic fashion magazine. Alicia took a deep breath and counted to ten before answering. This was old territory with them; there was just no getting around the fact that Adam was overprotective. Willing her heart to stop pounding and her voice to be steady, Alicia told him that she was perfectly capable of taking care of herself.

"I always lock the main door after everyone leaves and it's not like we're in the 'hood, Adam. This building is perfectly safe, as you are well aware. I'm not a little girl, you know," she said firmly.

Suddenly Adam's stern countenance turned playful and he closed the gap between them with one long step. "Yes, *chica*, you are. You're your daddy's little girl and I have no desire to explain anything to him or your two big brothers. Just what do you think they'd do to me if I let something happen to you?"

He had her there. Her father and her two older brothers approved of the close relationship between Adam and Alicia in large part because they knew no harm could come to Alicia with him around. She smiled with resignation and changed the subject.

"So how did it go this afternoon?"

Adam groaned. "Our client is turning into a huge pain in the rear," he admitted. He moved to sit down on the long, comfortable sofa and took Alicia's hand as he did so. Alicia folded her legs under her and Adam leaned back against the pillow-backed sofa. With his eyes closed he recited the list of new demands from Darcy Hamilton, a very wealthy client whose constant input was driving him crazy. They were remodeling a thirties-era Arts and Crafts style bungalow in Grosse Pointe for her, something that should have been a relatively simple job, but since she kept changing her mind about the details, the job was dragging on endlessly.

"Okay, today she decided that a big round window on the stair landing would make her life perfect. It took me two hours to explain to her that what seems like a simple change would cost her ten thousand dollars more. She just wasn't getting the idea that once the design is complete, you just can't go making these little whimsical changes when the mood hits you," he said, disgust evident in his tone of voice. "I should have just told her okay, fine, put in the window and taken her money. Unfortunately, I have too much integrity to do that and she has too much money to care."

Alicia rolled her eyes before commenting. She felt a little heat in her cheeks, even though Adam hadn't seen her make the evil face. She hated admitting it, but she couldn't stand that little Darcy. The woman was Alicia's polar opposite: she was petite, dainty, and ultrafeminine and had more clothes than Alicia could contemplate. She'd never seen the woman in the same outfit twice. And that way the woman ate Adam up with her eyes was just plain sickening. Alicia had no doubt but that the woman made up things like the new window just to get Adam on her turf. Alicia was trying to think of something to say that wouldn't reveal how jealous she was of their client when Adam's eyes popped open and he looked directly at Alicia.

"Get this, no sooner did I finish explaining to her that the window idea was totally impractical than she comes up with another request. She wants the laundry room on the second floor instead of in the basement where it already is. That's only going to involve moving a load-bearing wall and ripping out work that's already been completed," he said angrily. "That woman is a menace."

"Well now, I can't say I blame her about the laundry. That's really the best place to have it since that's where most of the dirty clothes accumulate. Too bad she didn't mention this bright idea a few months ago."

Adam snorted. "Yeah, well, from now on you can deal with her. She asked where you were, anyway. Maybe you'll get along with her better than I do. She just irritates me," he confessed.

Before Alicia's dismay at having to deal with Darcy could register on her face, Adam smiled the lazy, sexy smile that never failed to jump-start her heart. "Let's go get something to eat." He looked down at her with his piercing dark eyes and the long straight eyelashes that made most women swoon and Alicia almost forgot that she already had dinner plans.

"Oh, Adam, I just told Bryant I'd have dinner with him. I'm sure he won't mind if you come, too. We're just going to Fishbone's," she said eagerly.

The warmth went out of his eyes so quickly it was as though she'd imagined it there.

"That's okay, I don't want to intrude. You have a good time," he said offhandedly.

"I will. I mean *we* will. Bryant's always a lot of fun," she said hesitantly.

She looked bemused as Adam abruptly stood up and offered her a hand. "Well, let's not make you late for your date," he said. "Let's get out of here."

In near silence they rode the elevator down to the parking garage and headed for their vehicles. After saying their good-byes, Alicia wondered about Adam's abrupt change in mood as she maneuvered her way to Greektown. As she found a parking space near the restaurant, her slight anxiety left her. She looked out the window and saw Adam nod as he prepared to go on his way; as usual, he'd followed her to her destination to make sure she was safe. She sat there smiling to herself until she could no longer see the Range Rover. At least some of her affection was returned; there was no doubt that Adam cared about her. Was it wrong to want more from someone who was already her best friend? She sighed deeply and went in to meet Bryant.

Bryant could sense that Alicia's mind was somewhere else. She was trying her best to be good company, but the lulls in their conversation weren't filled with comfortable silence. When he wasn't talking directly to her, she was distracted and clearly thinking thoughts that had nothing whatsoever to do with their date. He watched her carefully as she drifted away once more. Her pretty face with its arresting features was still, but he could practically hear the wheels turning in her head. Oddly enough, he had a feeling that he knew what she was thinking about.

"Alicia, I'm going to ask you something that's none of my concern, okay?"

Startled, Alicia met his gaze and nodded without speaking.

"Now, I want you to know that I'm not just trying to get in your business and I'm not just dipping." He smiled and held up both hands to indicate innocence of any chicanery. "I just want to know how long you've been in love with Cochran and what you intend to do about it."

Alicia turned bright red, dropped her head into her hand, and emitted a squeaking sound like a wounded mouse.

"Aw, I embarrassed you," Bryant said gently. "I didn't mean to, but I tend to be a little bit more perceptive than most people when it comes to these things. I notice things that other people don't."

His tone was so soothing and kind, Alicia's discomfort

eased at once. "Bryant, I don't know what to say. I just started admitting to myself that I feel more for Adam than I should. You don't think he's noticed, do you? I don't think I'm ready to deal with that yet," she said ruefully.

Bryant reached across the table and took her hand. "C'mon now, it's not like you're throwing yourself at him or anything. I just happen to be more insightful than your average salivating horny male. I pay attention to small details, that's all. And who says you shouldn't have feelings for Adam? You two are friends, aren't you? So you already care about each other, right?"

Alicia sighed deeply before answering, "That's the problem, Bryant. Adam and I are best friends and have been for years. We have the perfect friendship and a great partnership. I don't want to ruin everything we have now, and if we get involved romantically, that's just what could happen. And besides, Adam thinks of me as a sister, a pal, a buddy. I don't want to make him uncomfortable by letting him know that I think of him as more than that," she admitted. To her utter surprise, Bryant laughed. She turned big puzzled eyes on him and he explained his laughter at once.

"I'm not laughing at you, Alicia, I'd never do that. You may not know this, but I'm a good friend of Clay Deveraux. A very good friend," he emphasized.

Alicia nodded. She naturally knew Clay, who was married to Adam's only sister, Benita. Encouraged by her nod, Bryant elaborated.

"When Clay met Bennie, he went off the deep end. I mean he went totally nuts for her and she felt the same way. But he was hesitant about getting involved with her because he thought they were too much alike and they'd end up hurting each other or some junk like that. And you see how that turned out," he reminded her.

"Yes, they got married and lived happily ever after with five beautiful children. But the two situations are hardly the same, Bryant," she said with a little sigh.

Bryant squeezed the hand he was still holding, and then gave it a little pat as he removed his large, warm hand from hers. "They're very much the same, my dear. You have two people who are perfectly suited for one another and scared to make a move for fear of messing everything up. The only way you can mess this up is to do nothing, Alicia. Trust me. And this is coming from a man who had every intention of hitting on you, so if I'm willing to step aside, you'd better be willing to take action."

Alicia was so enthralled by his words that at first she didn't realize the implication of what he'd said. Slowly it dawned on her and she blushed again. "Bryant, that's the sweetest thing anyone's ever said to me."

Bryant looked at the sincere pleasure on her face and it was his turn to sigh. "Story of my life, all the good ones are taken," he said playfully. "I had to do a little playacting with Benita to make Clay realize he was in love. Am I going to have to do the same thing with you and Cochran?"

"No! Absolutely not, Bryant, thanks but no thanks," she said hurriedly. Despite his words of encouragement, she wasn't ready to do anything about her feelings except feel them. Bryant must have sensed this, because he couldn't resist giving her more advice.

"Look, Alicia, love is too rare to pass up and life is too short to be worried about making a fool of yourself over love. What's that thing that people are always e-mailing to each other? 'Work like you don't need the money, dance like nobody's watching, and love like you're not going to get hurt.' That's pretty wise for pop philosophy."

"Okay, Bryant, once again, why aren't you taken? I can't believe that someone as wonderful and sensitive as you is still walking around unattached."

Bryant made a comical face and clutched at his heart. "Not the S word, please don't label me sensitive, that's like the kiss of death. I'm not sensitive, I'm a big macho doofus. Being called sensitive is worse than being called a nice guy," he said with a shudder. "And everybody knows nice guys finish last."

Alicia laughed delightedly. "Sorry, Mr. Macho, you really are a sweet and sensitive guy. But I'll keep your secret if you insist. I won't let anyone know that you're a wonderful man."

Bryant returned her smile with one of his own, although a tiny, tiny part of him wished that for once he'd been wrong about the attraction between a man and a woman.

"You're a wonderful woman, Alicia. And if Cochran isn't smart enough to realize it, just look me up any time. Any time at all."

Chapter Four

A few hours later, Alicia was sitting in the middle of her big bed thinking about her evening. Her sister Marielle was downstairs finishing some paperwork as usual, and the children were fast asleep. Taking her clothes off to prepare for her evening ritual of brushing her hair and showering, Alicia reflected on her conversation with Bryant. Even though their date took on a dimension she wasn't expecting, Alicia had a good feeling after her dinner with Bryant. She certainly hadn't anticipated revealing her deep dark secrets, but somehow she felt better afterward. She laughed softly, thinking about her Catholic school education. The sisters were right: confession was good for the soul.

Alicia put on a light cotton robe and sat down at the small Chippendale secretary that served as a desk and dressing table. Although her mind was not on her task, she automatically undid the long, long braid to prepare her hair for its nightly brushing. The act of brushing and arranging her hair made her smile, because it made her think of a moment when she was totally aware of Adam as a man and nothing more. Not as her best buddy, her partner, or anything but what he was, a totally desirable man.

One of the many things she and Adam shared was long hair. Adam simply refused to cut his anymore when he turned ten or so, and the result was a long ponytail that he often wore braided. It made him look like the avante-garde creative genius that he was, not to mention the fact that most women found the thick, glossy hair devastatingly attractive. Alicia, on the other hand, had been born as bald as the proverbial billiard ball.

Her mother and her aunts found her infant alopecia somewhat alarming since every other Fuentes child came into the world with a full head of hair. The hairless state remained until she was about three years old, so when her hair started coming in it was a huge relief to everyone. So much so that Alicia was forbidden to even think about cutting her hair. Even though her mother and her sister Marielle wore their hair in fashionable styles, Alicia's by now very long hair was most often worn in a braid. There was so much hair on her head that the idea of wearing it unfettered was just not practical.

Alicia didn't give her tresses a lot of thought until Angelique asked her to pose with Adam. She was a professional photographer about to do a shoot for a hair-care company and she needed some models with beautiful hair. "And who has prettier hair than you two? C'mon, guys, even if the company doesn't go for the idea, these will be some stunning shots," she persuaded.

And that's how she and Adam ended up spending the afternoon half clad with their hands all over each other. Angelique had taken shots of them with their braids over each other's shoulders and with the hair from their respective heads joined in one massive braid. The best ones had their hair loose and wild with their hands tangled in each other's manes. Adam had been wearing worn old jeans and no shirt, while she'd been wearing his old, soft chambray shirt with nothing else on but her best underwear. They'd each had a glass of wine and with the aid of Angelique's enthusiastic instructions and the wonderful Latin music that flooded the studio, they'd had a wonderful time posing.

Alicia's hands stopped while she recalled the intensity of her desire that afternoon. Whether they'd been sitting back to back, or had their arms around each other in a passionate embrace, or had been dancing to the salsa music with abandon, she'd been so on fire for Adam that day that just thinking about it brought back the heat. She could still see the smooth, hard planes of his muscular chest and arms, could still feel the warmth of his body and smell the unique combination of fragrance and pure Adam that ignited her senses like nothing else. The photographs that resulted from that afternoon were so blatantly sexy that she kept her copies locked away in a drawer, but out of sight was not out of mind; all she had to do was think about that afternoon and she was back in Adam's arms. . . . She stopped brushing her hair and caught it up in a hasty knot so she could jump in a cooling shower right then and there.

After she dried off and got into her usual sleep gear of men's boxer shorts and an old, oversized T-shirt, she tackled the hair again. While she was braiding it up, she heard a light tap on the door.

"Come on in, sweets, I'm not asleep," Alicia said.

"You should be," Marielle said sleepily. "And so should I. Got an early day tomorrow, and it's going to be long, too." She sat down on the edge of the bed and yawned widely.

Marielle was the event planner for the Detroit Tigers organization and oversaw every special event held at Comerica Park where the Tigers' home games were played. Besides having a time-consuming and very demanding job, Marielle was also raising two small children alone. Her husband had left her after she announced that she was pregnant with their now one-year-old daughter. Marielle's life revolved around her children and her work and there wasn't a space, even a tiny one, for personal time.

"Did you have a good time tonight?" she asked.

Alicia said she had. "Bryant is a lovely man. We had a nice meal and a good conversation. You know, you should have come with us, you'd really like him," she

mused, looking at her older sister with appraising eyes.
Marielle was a true beauty, with rich, deep brown coloring and a fantastic head of thick, lustrous black hair. She
was tall, like Alicia, but way too slender due to her determination to do everything on her own. She could
have afforded regular housekeeping help and even a
nanny, but she refused, saying that her children were her
responsibility. Marielle worked far harder than she
needed to, as if to prove something to herself or maybe
the world at large. Now she was looking at Alicia with a
slightly scornful expression.

"No, thank you, little sister. I know quite enough men,
I'm knee-deep in macho males around the clock, and
frankly, I'm not impressed by most of them."

Alicia regretted even suggesting that Marielle meet
Bryant. She knew how touchy her sister was on the subject of men. It was her opinion that the reason her sister hadn't divorced her husband was that she was still in
love with him and wanted him back, but she knew better
than to ever utter such a statement. She chuckled at the
thought of Marielle's rage and what she'd do to her for
even thinking such a thing.

Marielle looked at her curiously. "What's so funny?"

"Nothing. Just thinking about something Adam said,"
Alicia said hastily. It was only a partial lie; she and Adam
made each other laugh all the time.

"Oh. Well, sleep well, *chica*, I'm going to bed,"
Marielle said with a yawn.

"G'night." Alicia watched her sister close the door behind her and got into bed. She had every intention of
following her sister's example and going right to sleep,
but sleep was a long time coming, and when it did, it was
full of dreams of Adam.

The next morning, all was right with the world. Alicia
did sleep well, so well that she prepared a treat for the

family and brought some to work with her. The other employees greeted her offering of two fragrant loaves of banana nut bread with enthusiasm.

"Ooh, Alicia, thank you. You did take the carbs and calories out of this, right?" asked Rhonda, the office manager. Her tongue darted into the corner of her mouth, as she looked longingly at the bread, moist, rich, and dense with bananas and nuts.

Alicia laughed and confessed she'd done no such thing. "You're on your own there, Rhonda. Overindulgence could mean extra laps in the pool tomorrow," she warned.

Rhonda sighed, and then shrugged her shoulders. "Oh well, too bad. We do what we must, and right now I must have some of that bread." She sighed as she sank her teeth into a generous slice.

Paul, another architect, cast a surreptitious glance at Rhonda's firm, generous backside and curvy hips before helping himself to a slice of the bread. Her attention to her diet and her firmly ingrained exercise habits showed in every inch of her delightful figure.

"You've got nothing to worry about on that count, Rhonda. By my calculations you could consume quite a bit more and it wouldn't have any effect on your figure," he said with admiration.

Rhonda's look of surprise at the heartfelt compliment went unnoticed as Adam entered the small break room in the rear of the office suite. "What smells so good, and is there enough for me?" he asked.

Alicia flashed him a brilliant smile and assured him there was plenty. "And I was just about to make some coffee, too."

That announcement was greeted with a grin from Adam and looks of horror from Paul and Rhonda. They couldn't tolerate the rich, intense flavor of the Cuban espresso style of coffee that she and Adam favored.

"Ugh, no jet fuel for me this morning, thanks. I'm

hyper enough as it is. Paul, don't forget you have an appointment in Rochester Hills at ten. Alicia, the model maker is coming by to deliver the Garrison project at nine-thirty, and, Adam, you seem to be free until eleven-thirty. I'm going to get ready for the quarterly financials, so if you need me for anything I'll be in my office," she reported as she left the room with another slice of the bread.

Paul's face was full of admiration for Rhonda as she left the break room. "Amazing woman, isn't she? Better than a Palm Pilot," he mused as he departed.

The room filled with the aroma of the Cuban coffee as it began to brew. Alicia took a good look at Adam while she took two small cups out of the small cupboard next to the sink. As always, he looked good enough to devour like a piece of her bread. She tried not to let her appetite show on her face. That wouldn't do at all. But he was pretty hard to resist, she admitted. His hair was still damp from the shower, braided neatly and hanging down his back. He was dressed a bit more formally than usual, wearing khaki dress slacks and a crisp blue oxford cloth shirt unbuttoned at the neck. His navy sport coat was expertly tailored, but she knew it would end up hanging on the back of his office door before long. Adam just couldn't work if his body was too confined by clothing.

He was also observing her closely, and she was relieved to see that whatever coolness had erupted last night had dissipated. He gave her the warm smile that always curled her toes and asked how her dinner with Bryant went.

"Fine. It was a nice evening, good food, you know," she said shyly. "He might stop by today to say hello. He's looking for a place to stay for the summer."

She wasn't looking directly at Adam when she said this, or she would have noticed a quick tightening of his jaw that was over almost at once. She poured them

each a cup of the hot, inky concoction and they both inhaled with deep pleasure before taking their first sip.

"Thanks for the bread, Alicia. Although I don't like
the idea of you having to get up extra early to make stuff
for us, it's really good."

She blushed at his sweet tone of voice and waved aside
his praise. "It was no trouble, Adam. I get up early every
day. It's not like anyone can sleep once the *Princesa Mariposa* arises, as you well know. Once my niece opens her
eyes, everyone else better get up and tend to her every
whim, or else. And I'm glad you like it. I baked another
loaf just for you. It's on your desk," she told him, enjoying the grin he flashed her way.

Just then Rhonda rang her on the office intercom to
inform her that the model of her latest project had arrived early. Adam laughed and said, "You know those
guys are crazy about you, right? That's why their work is
always perfect and always early, they live in hope that
you'll go out with one of them one day."

Alicia felt her face grow hot again and she gave a
short, embarrassed laugh. "Adam, that is so not true!
They're just really professional and good at what they
do, that's all."

She quickly left the break room and went to meet the
Thompson brothers, Troy and Justin, two of the best-
known model makers in the business. They could create
scale models of anything an architect or designer could
conceive and do it with a skill that made the replica
come alive. Being able to present a physical version of a
concept was critical in the presentation process, and the
Thompson brothers were, in Alicia's opinion, responsible for C&F Design winning many of their bids for highly
prestigious projects.

She entered the conference room where the brothers had set up the model, and her face lit up with pleasure. "Oh, guys, this is wonderful." She sighed. "This

is absolutely beautiful, maybe the best one you've ever done for us. How can I thank you?"

Adam entered the conference room and took in the scene with amusement, watching the two tall, good-looking, and obviously intelligent men shuffle their feet and look like pleased schoolboys basking in the warmth of Alicia's praise. He graciously ignored their adoration of his partner and took a look at the model. It was an office tower with an attached atrium that connected it to a pavilion with shops and restaurants leading to a hotel. It was to be constructed in the downtown area of Detroit near the William Clay Ford Stadium and Comerica Park, part of the amazing renovation taking place in the Motor City, as Detroit was fondly known.

"Alicia's right, guys. You did an amazing job on this," he praised, walking around the large conference table on which the model rested.

Troy Thompson, the older of the brothers by one year, looked pleased at the accolade, but was quick to point out that it was Alicia's design that was amazing. Justin was quick to agree. "This is a fantastic design, Alicia. The whole concept and layout are beautiful," he said warmly. Adam looked at the two men reveling in Alicia's aura and for a moment the two strapping six footers with chiseled features set in smooth, darkly brown skin looked like two overgrown puppies hoping for a pat on the head.

I ain't mad atcha, brothers, I know exactly how you feel, he thought ruefully. He continued his walk around the table until he was next to Alicia, who was examining the model with every appearance of rapture on her face. She stopped in her perusal to meet Adam's eyes. Adam reached for her hand and clasped it tightly as he pulled her into a quick embrace. "They're right, Allie. This is some amazing work. You have every right to be proud."

It was as though everyone else in the room disappeared. For Alicia, there was no one there but Adam, nothing but the feel of her body next to his, nothing but the smell of his skin, the warmth of his arms . . . She was dizzy from sensation and content to remain that way, or would have been had Rhonda not stuck her head in the door.

"Umm, Adam, Darcy Hamilton is here to see you," she said slowly.

Alicia sprang away from Adam as if he were on fire and quickly immersed herself in conversation with the Thompson brothers. Adam tried hard not to let what he was feeling show on his face as he nodded to Rhonda and prepared to follow her up front to greet his visitor. He did cast one more glance at Alicia and her admirers before exiting, however. And he was sure that if Darcy Hamilton knew what he was thinking at that very moment she'd have found someplace else to be, because she was certainly not welcome there.

Chapter Five

The only thing that would have improved Alicia's disposition was a miracle. She knew she was really far gone in the Adam department; otherwise she wouldn't have been so irritated by Darcy's little drop-in that morning. She cloistered herself in her office, trying not to grind her teeth, and wished with all her heart that she were the kind of person who could drown her sorrows in drink. She was tense and angry for being that way. She'd always despised jealous, petty women. She had just decided that a nice long run would make her feel better and get rid of the negative energy she'd conjured up. She was preparing to leave the office to go home and get into running clothes when her private line buzzed and her miracle manifested itself.

"Hey, girl, come get me. I'm hungry, I'm tired, and I need to see a friendly face."

"Roxy! Girl, where are you? Are you in Detroit?"

"I'm in Novi. Or Troy, someplace like that. I'm at the Executive Suites Motel, can you find it?"

"Absolutely! I'll be there in fifteen minutes. No, make it thirty minutes, it's construction season. What room are you in?"

After getting the information, Alicia rapidly packed up her briefcase and then decided to leave it at the office. There was no way she was going to be working that night, not with her best friend, Roxy, in town. She let Rhonda know she was leaving and left the building in a much better mood than she'd been in earlier. She hadn't seen Roxy in a few years due to Roxy's schedule and her own and she was looking forward to this evening with all her heart. It was impossible to be gloomy or even out of sorts around Roxy; she was the most lively and effervescent person in the world. Alicia laughed with the anticipation of seeing her old friend again.

In a short time she'd made it to the luxurious suite-styled inn where Roxy was staying and quickly found Roxy's door. She knocked impatiently and heard an "I'm coming!" The door was opened and Alicia almost had the breath knocked out of her by the force of nature that was Roxy Fairchild.

"You look gorgeous, kiddo, now let's go. I'm starving!" Before Alicia could utter two coherent sentences they were back in her car and on their way to J. Alexander for a good meal and a nice long chat. They got seated at once and ordered big glasses of iced tea. While they were waiting for their server to return, Alicia finally had a chance to talk.

"So what brings you to Detroit? You never mentioned that you were headed this way, and we talk at least once a week," Alicia said accusingly. "You could have let me know you were coming so I could plan some things to do. How long are you going to be here, anyway?"

Roxy gave her a smug smile in return. "Well, I didn't tell you I was coming because that's the essence of a surprise, is it not? I wanted to shock you, that's why I never mentioned it. As to what brings me to Detroit, it's a new job. I didn't tell you this, either, but I've had a promotion. You are in the presence of the new vice president of acquisitions for Birney, Pearson and Rawlings Worldwide. I'm going to be working out of the Troy office and as to your last question, I'll be here permanently. Now how's that for a surprise?" she finished proudly.

Their server returned before Alicia could properly express her joy at the news. Roxy scanned the menu one last time and then placed her order. "I'd like the grilled chicken with mixed vegetables and a spinach salad. Do you have a balsamic vinaigrette dressing? I'll have that and no potatoes at all, please. If there's anything resembling fresh fruit, I'd like some for dessert and that's it," she said with finality.

After Alicia gave her order, she looked Roxy over carefully as the server left the table. "Don't tell me you've succumbed to the low-carb craze," she said. "I haven't had a chance to get two words in, but you are looking fabulous, girl." And it was true, Roxy looked like a new woman. Her rich mahogany skin glowed, her fashionably short hair glistened, and she had definitely lost weight. Roxy had always been beautiful, but she'd been a cuddly size twenty-two the last time Alicia had seen her in person. "What are you wearing now, a fourteen?"

Roxy gave her trademark laugh that could rouse the dead from a sound slumber. "Let's not get crazy. I'm about an eighteen and I don't plan on getting any smaller, not really. I met this tall, good-looking doctor who said the three magic words and I had no choice but to change my lifestyle," she said with a mysterious smile.

"What three words? I love you?" Alicia leaned forward, breathless with anticipation.

"No . . . diabetes, hypertension, and cholesterol! My numbers were really funky and I finally decided I had to make some lasting changes. Honey, twenty years from now I am *not* going to be the one at the family reunion rolling up in a wheelchair talking about 'Bring Auntie her pressure pills, baby, and come scratch my stump.'" She paused while Alicia burst into laughter.

"I got real serious about taking off the weight because I've worked too hard for too long to let my health destroy my life. So now I'm following a low-fat, low-carb diet, I exercise four times a week, and I feel wonderful. I'll always be thick, but I'm in great shape and that's what matters most."

"Well, you look fabulous, Rox, and I couldn't be happier about you moving here. This is going to be so much fun! Have you decided where you're going to live?"

Discussing where she might reside took up a large part of their meal. Their intrepid server had indeed found a plate of fresh seasonal fruits to finish their meal, and Roxy was consuming hers with enthusiasm when she noticed a certain look in Alicia's eyes. "Okay, give it up. You've been dancing around it, whatever it is, long enough, so spill it. What's going on in your life that you need to confide to your old friend?"

Alicia smiled gamely. There was no hiding anything from Roxy; they'd been friends since their freshman year at Northwestern, a friendship that continued through grad school with Roxy at the Wharton School of Business and Alicia at M.I.T. She took a sip of iced tea to clear her throat and then set the glass down carefully before speaking.

"Roxy, I've done something incredibly stupid. I've fallen in love with Adam," she said glumly.

Roxy patted the corners of her mouth with her napkin and raised her hand as their server hovered nearby. "Check, please." She gave Alicia a look that dared her to argue and said, "We're getting out of here right now and you're going to start from the very beginning and not leave out a single word. Or else."

A short time later they were lounging in the living room of Roxy's suite. Roxy looked at her long and hard, and then began the inquisition. "Okay, talk. So how long have you had these feelings and when were you going to let me know about them? And most importantly, have you told Adam how you feel?"

Alicia looked horrified at the very thought. "No, no, no! Oh, no way have I told Adam anything, that's not possible," she said fervently.

"Why? Is he married, engaged, involved, gay, what? I've known him for almost as long as you have and he's always seemed like a wonderful guy," Roxy offered. "Why haven't you said something to him?"

Alicia slumped down in her chair staring at her long legs. "Roxy, it's too crazy. Adam and I have been friends forever, since the day we met in grad school. He's almost like a male version of you, if you know what I mean. He's the person I laugh with, confide in, work with, plan with, and we're incredibly close. Outside of my family and you, there is no one on this earth that I share more with than Adam. I love him from the bottom of my heart. I'd take a bullet for him and he'd do the same for me. But this friendship came at a tremendous cost and I can't risk it for anything," she said passionately.

"If we have a fight, or we're getting on each other's nerves, we just walk away from each other for a minute and cool out and we apologize and get on with our lives. Friends can do that. But lovers? There's a big difference between hanging out and shooting pool with each other and being intimate with each other. Once the intimacy starts, there's a whole other dynamic that takes control. When two people are caught up in a love relationship, things take on another dimension entirely. It's much harder to shake hands and make up. Look at what happened to my sister and her husband," she said sadly.

Roxy nodded slowly. "Yes, Marielle did get a rough break. She was married to an idiot. But that doesn't have anything to do with you and Adam, now, does it? I think we're really talking about you and He Who Shall Remain Nameless and Die of a Terrible Disease, aren't we?"

Despite her angst, Alicia burst out laughing. That was indeed how she and Roxy always referred to Preston Chalmers, her ex-fiancé. "It's okay, Roxy, you can say his name. And actually, no, it doesn't have anything to do with Preston. That ship sailed a long time ago, girl. I'm so over him it isn't even worth discussing."

Roxy wouldn't relent, however. "You might be over Preston, as you put it, but I think the fact that you and Adam found him and Adam's girlfriend in bed together might have something to do with your reluctance to get involved with Adam. It was just a nasty, awful thing to have to deal with, and the fact that the two of you witnessed it makes it pretty indelible."

Alicia made a face and shook her head at her friend. "No, that's not it, Rox. It was so long ago and so much has happened between me and Adam since then, that that incident is just part of the past that we share. In a thousand ways I'm truly grateful it happened the way it did. Suppose I'd married that weasel? What kind of life would I have had with him? He was a lying, conniving, cheating rat and my life eventually would have been hell on earth. As it was, they deserved each other, because we all know that if someone will cheat *with* you, they'll cheat *on* you. I'm infinitely better off without Preston Chalmers and I doubt that Adam even remembers what his ex-girlfriend Yvette DeLoach looks like." She picked up a bottle of mineral water and took a deep swallow.

Roxy relaxed fully as she watched Alicia. She smiled to herself as she realized that Alicia was speaking the whole truth, that the sordid way her engagement ended hadn't permanently scarred her. On the contrary, it seemed to have made her stronger. Roxy continued to smile, unaware that Alicia was now observing her.

"Okay, Rox, what are you smirking about?"

"Excuse me, missy, I do not smirk. I hate that word, it sounds so smug."

"That's the point of the word, Rox," Alicia replied.

"Whatever. I was just remembering the time a bunch of us went down to Key West for a week, do you recall that? It was the year after you broke your engagement."

Alicia's eyes lit in a smile. "Of course I remember, it was one of the best vacations I've ever had," she said.

"Alicia, that was the worst vacation I've ever had in my

life. Everyone hated that vacation except you and Adam. Let's start from the beginning, when we flew down to Florida and our luggage flew somewhere else and we had to wait hours and hours before it showed up again. Do you remember that?"

Alicia's brow puckered. "Vaguely. I remember going to the beach," she said slowly.

"That's because you and Adam went to some drug-store and bought these funky shorts and these tacky tie-dye tank tops and eighty-nine-cent flip-flops and went to the beach while the rest of us sat around com-plaining about not having any beach clothes. By the time the luggage got in and we collected it from the airport, y'all were already chilled out and tanned from playing all afternoon."

Alicia had a faraway look in her eyes as she recalled the fun she and Adam had relaxing on the beach. Roxy continued to talk about the trip, bringing up more mem-ories with every word.

"Do you remember when it rained for two days and we were all housebound and snapping at each other like de-ranged Chihuahuas? Nobody could agree on anything and everyone was getting on everyone else's nerves?"

"Not really," Alicia began, only to be cut off by Roxy.

"That's because you and Adam were never around. You two didn't let the rain stop you, you went to every lit-tle grimy bar and restaurant on the island, every tacky lit-tle gift shop and tourist trap you could find, and you came back laughing like you'd had the best time in the world together."

"We did have fun on that trip, Roxy, it was a lot of fun," protested Alicia.

"It was fun for you two because you were in your own little world," corrected Roxy. "You two were so close it was like you were the same person, Alicia. Everyone was pretty convinced that you two were into something real undercover because you were so blissful together. I was watching you on the beach one day and Adam was wringing the water out of your hair and I have to tell you, girl, it gave me fever. He kind of wrapped your braid around his wrist and brought his hand up and squeezed it and whoa, baby! It was like something off one of those late night music video shows." She waved her hand in front of her face to indicate extreme heat. "Very hot, very hot indeed."

Alicia had the grace to blush and look away. "Umm, okay, yeah, well . . ." was all she could manage.

Roxy laughed at her discomfiture. She stood up and stretched, and took off her tailored jacket and went to hang it up in the closet. "I'm going to take this suit off, if you don't mind. I need to get a little more comfortable. Sometimes I think you have the right idea, dressing business casual for work. I'm jealous. I wish I could dress down," she said, glancing down at her expensive shoes and smoothing her hand over the costly fine wool of her skirt.

Alicia shook off the memories of the Key West vacation and frowned. "Believe me, today I wanted to be dressed up. I wish I'd had on something chic and wonderful today, boy."

Roxy stopped and turned around. "Really? Why is that?"

Alicia proceeded to tell her all about Darcy Hamilton and her interest in Adam, as well as her impromptu visit to the office. "She's about five one, a teeny little thing, and she wears these fabulous outfits that you only see in *Vogue* or *InStyle*. She has this reddish brown hair and it's always perfect, one of those haircuts that never seems to move, not to mention perfect makeup. And here I am looking like some sturdy Amish type in my sensible shoes and khakis." She groaned.

Roxy tried not to laugh but was woefully unsuccessful. "I'm sorry, I didn't mean to laugh. But this is so cute, you're actually jealous and getting all territorial and whatnot. I have to say, I like that in ya," she said with another laugh. "I like it a lot because it's going to make my next words much easier to take. You need a makeover, girlfriend. And I'm just the one to get you hooked up."

Alicia looked stunned for a moment, and then set her jaw grimly. "You know what? I think you're right. I've been looking like this since I was sixteen."

Roxy clasped her hands in delight. "You've been looking like that since I've known you, and that's a long time. Same long ol' braid, no makeup, sturdy shoes, and pants for all occasions. Has Adam ever seen you in a dress?"

"Has *anyone* seen me in a dress since my first communion? Yeah, every time I'm a bridesmaid." Alicia laughed. "He's seen me in shorts lots of times, though, and bathing suits, too."

"Not the same thing. A dress is something else, Alicia, it gives an entirely different vibration. So does a skirt, it shows your legs in an elegant, sexy, flirtatious way, not like wearing shorts that just say 'get outta my way, I'm running,' or rock climbing, or whatever."

By now the two women were in the dressing room of the suite staring into the mirrored wall behind the built-in vanity. They were both studying Alicia's reflection and looking objectively at her tall, shapely body covered by serviceable slacks and an unremarkable tailored shirt.

"You're right, Roxy. I can look better than this. I'm *going* to look better than this," she said with determination.

Roxy bounced happily and gave Alicia a big hug. "Now that's what I'm talking about! When we get finished he's not going to be able to resist you. You won't have to do another thing, just let him get a load of you in your new look and he'll be swept off his feet. And maybe you two will get busy at last," she said merrily.

Alicia gave her friend a very private and mysterious smile. "You mean get busy *again*. Adam and I have been intimate before, Roxy."

The look on Roxy's face was well worth the barrage of soaps and shampoos she threw at Alicia in her zeal to get the whole story.

Alicia was laughing as she allowed Roxy to chase her through the suite. "Okay, okay. Get out of your suit and put on your jammies and I'll tell you the whole story. I promise, I won't leave out anything."

"You better not, woman, or I won't be responsible for my retribution. Talk slow, I don't want to miss a word," she warned.

Chapter Six

Ten years earlier

A light rain was falling as Alicia and Adam left the library. They were among the last students to leave, not unusual for the time of year, which was just before finals. And it was certainly not unusual for the two graduate students pursing double degrees.

"I keep thinking that maybe I should've just stuck to architectural design." Alicia yawned. "Why did I think I needed to have a master's in urban planning, too?"

Adam waited until she was in midyawn and thumped her on her chin, something that always caused her to wrinkle her face comically and take a swing at him.

"You need both degrees for the same reason I do, so we can write our own tickets when we get out of here. Don't be so lazy," he chided her.

Alicia narrowed her eyes and made a fist at his temple. "I got your lazy right here, pal. Don't even try it, I'll brain you. Did you bring the wine?"

It was Adam's turn to yawn as he fished around in his backpack to produce a bottle of serviceable red wine. They were on their way to Alicia's apartment where Adam's girlfriend, Yvette, was cooking dinner for the four of them: Yvette, Adam, Alicia, and Alicia's fiancé, Preston. The thought of a cozy dinner for the two couples was very cheering to Alicia.

They reached the doorway of the old brownstone building just as Alicia was saying something about how fortunate they were to have such understanding mates. "If Preston wasn't so caring and supportive, I don't think I could make it through this program. And this is just the first year," she said with a playful shudder. "I'm so glad he's willing to wait until after I graduate to get married," she added, once again inspecting the big diamond ring on her left hand.

Adam held the door open for her without comment, maintaining his thoughtful silence up the flight of stairs to Alicia's front door. He held her books while she fished her key out of her pocket, and they looked at each other strangely when the door opened into a dimly lit living room with no smells or sounds of a meal to be found. Alicia walked into the living room and looked around expectantly, but no one was there. She turned to Adam with her hands outstretched and was about to speak when a noise from the back of the apartment caught their attention.

They moved to the hall and stopped when it became evident that the noise was coming from the bedroom. The door was ajar and Alicia suddenly froze, overcome with fear. On some level she knew what she was about to see, but she couldn't face it. Adam had no such concern; he pushed the door wide open and allowed the sickening spectacle in the room to be seen by both of them.

Alicia turned an ashen gray as she witnessed her beloved fiancé, Preston, having frantic and sloppy sex with Adam's girlfriend, Yvette. They were so involved in their frenzied activity they had no idea they were being observed. Yvette's head was banging over and over against the headboard as she screamed Preston's name out loud. Preston, clad in his fraternity T-shirt and black silk socks, one of which had a tiny hole in the heel, was making the gorilla face that heralded a massive orgasm, as he demanded to know whose body he was savaging. "Whose is it, Momma? Whose is it? Who's your daddy now, huh?"

Despite the sordid scene before him, Adam's dry wit didn't desert him. Flipping on the overhead light, he asked in a monotone, "Are we too late for dinner? Since y'all seem to be having dessert, it only seems right to ask."

Yvette screamed and pushed Preston off her writhing body, causing Preston to lose his balance and fall off the bed. Alicia stared at her faithless fiancé in stark horror until she finally remembered to breathe, then she pushed past Adam to go back into the living room. Adam felt no need to leave, however. "Get dressed and get out and if either of you so much as looks at Alicia while you're leaving, you be leaving here butt-ass naked," he said with true menace in his voice. And to their total chagrin he stayed where he was while they scrambled into their clothes like an amateur porn movie played in fast-forward.

Incredibly the whole thing only lasted about ten minutes. Alicia sat in the living room, her face an unmoving mask of pain, while Adam ushered them out the door, not allowing either to speak a word. When they were gone he went into the bedroom, stripped the linens, and opened the windows to release the fetid smell of illicit sex. Coming back into the living area, he located a trash bag in the kitchen and deposited the soiled and irredeemable sheets into the trash bag and put it in the corridor outside the front door. He knew without being told that Alicia would sooner die than lie on those sheets again, no matter how often they were laundered.

Finally he washed his hands and came into the living room where Alicia sat without moving, staring at nothing at all. His concern was all over his face as he sat down and put his arms around her. At first she resisted, but the strong, sure touch of his warm hands made her melt against him. She allowed him to pull her into his arms and give her the comfort she deserved. "I'm sorry you had to see that, Alicia, I'm sorry that I brought that selfish little bitch into your life. I feel like this is somehow my fault, baby."

Alicia didn't answer at first; she just crawled into his lap and held on to him for long wordless moments. Finally she mumbled something he had to ask her to repeat. She sighed, then sat up and spoke more clearly. "Don't be sorry. Be glad we found out what they really are before it was too late. Just think, I could have married that jerk," she said in a croaky voice that didn't sound anything like her own.

Adam rocked her like a baby for a while, and asked if she wanted to spend the night at his place. Alicia's eyes grew misty and she smiled, a weak and shaky smile to be sure, but it was a start. "Thanks, but I'm not letting him run me out of my own home. I am, however, sleeping on the sofa. After we drink that wine, that is. Open it up and let's get drunk," she said, wiping her leaking eyes.

Roxy's eyes were wide and her mouth was hanging open in amazement. "Girl, no, you didn't! Y'all drank that bottle of wine and in the middle of a drunken fit you started ripping each other's clothes off! I'm . . . I'm stunned. I'm just floored, I really am."

"You're also wrong, Rox. You're completely and totally wrong. We didn't do anything but have a few glasses of wine. I was too numb to do anything else. I was in such a state of shock I couldn't really react at that moment. I couldn't talk, I couldn't think, and I was damned if I was going to cry in front of Adam; I just wasn't going out like that. My brothers would have beaten the paste out of me if I'd ended up a sniveling mess; I had the Fuentes name to uphold. We don't break down in front of anyone; no matter how much it hurts you never let them see you cry.

We drank the wine, we sat there looking stupid for a while, and he left. I made up a bed on the couch and I eventually went to sleep. The wine was good for that at least," she said ruefully.

They were now sitting in the middle of the big bed and Roxy fell over on her side with a groan. "Alicia, quit dragging this out and get to the meat of the story. Did you or did you not do the deed with Adam? And if so, when? Don't do this to me, woman, you know I have immediate gratification syndrome, I need to know *now*."

"My goodness, you are impatient, aren't you? Okay, sit up and listen. I was like an automaton for the next few weeks. I managed to finish my exams, get a new mattress, explain to my family that the engagement was off, and ignore the gossip on campus. I even survived the inevitable confrontation with Preston, who somehow had the shiny brass *cojones* to try to get back into my life and my bed by apologizing. Over and over again, I might add. He sent so many flowers my apartment looked like a funeral home, or it would have if I hadn't given the flowers away to everyone in the building," she said derisively.

"I was miserable, but I made it through all of that mess until Yvette came to me and announced that she was pregnant and if I would just be so kind as to stop clinging to Preston, they could have a life together. That was just too much sugar for a dime, as my grandmother used to say. He didn't want her and had the gall to use me as a reason for not marrying her," Alicia said indignantly. "I went ziggety-boom on that heifer. I cussed her for old and new and told her to go hell. Don't pass go, don't collect two hundred dollars, just go straight to hell and take her Satan spawn with her. I swore for about ten minutes in Spanish and English until her eyes were popping out of her head and she looked like a troll doll. She was standing in my doorway like I was supposed to let her in for tea or something and I shoved her bony butt into

the hallway and slammed the door." Alicia's eyes were
blazing with remembered pain.

"For some stupid reason, that's what did it," she admitted slowly. "That's what made me go all gooey and
head straight to Adam's apartment."

The scent of the spring rain coming in the open windows was a refreshing contrast to Adam's current
mood. The situation with Alicia was eating at him like
a slow-acting poison. He knew he'd never forget the
look on her face when she realized that the man she
was prepared to spend her life with was rutting another
woman in her bed like a boar servicing a breeding sow
in heat. He'd cursed himself over and over again for
pushing open that door, knowing what was on the other
side, but he couldn't undo what he'd done. And he
certainly couldn't take back the set of circumstances
that had led Yvette and Preston to betray the people
they supposedly cared about. It was ironic in a sick way;
he'd been as devastated as Alicia over the incident but
for an entirely different reason. He wanted to rage and
rant and plant his foot deeply in Preston's behind, but
not because of Yvette, because of Alicia.

He and Yvette had been dating, true, but she was like
every other woman in his life, a temporary diversion,
someone to spend time with. She was pretty and mildly
amusing, but finding her in bed with another man affected him only because it almost destroyed Alicia. She
was gaunt and pale and listless, and even though she was
putting on a brave front, she was miserable. He was
frankly amazed that she'd passed all her exams and was
still going to take on a fellowship over the summer. He
smiled wryly, thinking that in many ways, she reminded
him of his sister Benita. She was delicate, true, but she
was also tough and resolute. No one was going to keep
her down for long.

Adam looked around his partially packed apartment and sighed deeply. In a few days he'd be heading off to California for a summer internship and he'd be away from the situation in body, but not in mind. The thought of being away from Alicia was causing him distress he didn't want to deal with. He walked over to the stereo system that was still set up and slipped in a Miles Davis CD. The lush love song that issued from the speakers probably wasn't the best choice, given his mood. He was about to substitute his favorite Roxy Music CD when he heard a knock at the door. He wasn't really dressed for company; he was wearing denim shorts that had seen their best days some years before and he was shirtless. He was also barefoot, but anyone who came to his place unannounced had to take him as he was. Opening the door he was stunned to find Alicia, soaking wet from the rain and trembling.

He ushered her in immediately, asking what was wrong. "Baby, you're wet to the skin and you don't even have a coat on. What's the matter, Alicia? What brought you out in this rain?"

She shook her head mutely and he realized that the moisture on her face wasn't just rain, it was tears. He pulled her into his arms and held her against his chest, his heart breaking as she sobbed against his neck. "Alicia, baby, tell me what's wrong," he entreated her. "What's happened to hurt you so, angel? Tell me."

Her sobs continued as though his soft words only made her feel worse. Picking her up in his arms as though she were a tiny child, he carried her into his bedroom and sat her on the bed.

"I'll get it all wet," she said, sniffling.

"No, you won't. I'm going to get you all dry, how's that?" he said softly. He handed her some big fluffy towels and one of his sweatshirts, plus a pair of thick woolen socks. "Take off those wet things and put these on. I'm going to make you some tea, okay? I'll be right back."

In a short time she was attired in dry clothing and sitting in the middle of the bed looking lost and embarrassed and he was back with a steaming mug of tea that smelled heavenly. It also had a delicious taste as she discovered when she took a sip. She smiled when she realized that he'd laced it with rum. "Mmm, that's nice," she murmured.

Adam didn't answer. He was busy lighting some big scented candles on his dresser. He got in the bed with her and completely surprised her by sitting behind her so he could dry her hair. He wrapped a towel around her shoulders and removed the band from her hair to begin blotting the moisture from it while he talked to her in a soft, soothing voice.

She allowed his hands and the sound of his voice to lull her out of her agitation. Only the occasional hiccup remained of her tears and she felt warm and protected. After the tea was finished she leaned forward to put the mug on the nightstand. Then she scooted back against Adam and sighed raggedly as she felt his arms enfold her.

"She's pregnant, Adam. She came to see me today, to tell me she was having Preston's baby and to ask me to stay out of his life so they could be together," she said, unaware that her voice was shaking. "As if I'd give that louse the time of day. If his head was on fire I wouldn't pour a glass of water on it," she added with as much scorn as she could muster with the tears returning. "I don't ever want to see him again in this life, I don't care what happens to him, or to her, and here I am crying like an idiot and I don't know why," she sobbed.

Adam couldn't stand her anguish one more second. He turned her around in his embrace so that she was facing him and he kissed her tears away, kissed her and held her tightly and assured her that it was okay to cry. "Let it all out, baby, then it'll all be over. Just let it go, Allie, get rid of it."

His arms tightened around her and he continued to

kiss her face and her neck and slowly she began to return his kisses, on his neck, then his cheek, then their lips touched, very slowly and gently, as fleeting as the caress of the rain that fell against the windows. Adam sat up and tried to pull away from her. The softness of her lips, her skin, the satiny smoothness of her long bare legs revealed in the oversized but inadequate cover of the sweatshirt, and the delicate scent of her skin were too much for him to stand.

"Alicia," he murmured, trying to put some space between his yearning and the temptation of her body, "Alicia, angel . . ." He couldn't get out another word because her lips were caressing his and the sensation was too overpowering to deny. He pulled her luscious lower lip into his mouth and sucked on it gently, then sighed with delight as she returned the favor, pressing closer to his body and opening her mouth to allow their tongues to caress each other. The kiss went on and on, sending waves of passion through him like a seismic shock resonating in a desert. The fire continued to build as their hands began to explore their heated bodies, touching each other, caressing each other, demanding more and more.

Adam's big hands encircled Alicia's waist under the bulky garment and found her tight, supple body pliant and yielding to his exploration. Her slim, clever hands were making demands of their own, sliding over his broad chest and smoothing her warm palms against his sensitized nipples until a surge of passion arose from which there would be no turning back.

"Stop, baby, we have to stop this," he murmured, but any fool could tell he didn't mean it.

Alicia pulled away from his embrace long enough to remove the sweatshirt, kneeling in front of Adam with her eyes ablaze with desire and her kiss-swollen lips daring him to resist. "No, Adam, we don't have to stop," she said so softly that he could barely hear her. She looked incredibly beautiful, the candlelight glinting off the dusky bronze of her naked body. She stared at Adam with need and desire pouring out of every pore, smiling a little as she reached back to discreetly remove the big wool socks. She repeated her words in the same hushed voice heavy with longing. "We don't have to stop, do we?"

His only answer was to remove the little clothing that he was wearing and hold his arms open for her willing body. With a sigh of anticipation, she slid into them as though she were born for his pleasure alone. They held each other for long moments, delighting in the feel of silken skin against hard muscle, and then Adam turned her so she was on her back. With great tenderness and devotion, he kissed her face, her lips, her neck, and her shoulders, while his hands caressed her breasts. His lips and tongue pleasured each nipple as his hands began a more intimate exploration of her most feminine attributes, teaching her a kind of loving she'd never experienced before.

Alicia tried to reciprocate but Adam wouldn't allow it. He took complete control of her body as he devoured every inch of it with his hands and his tongue, branding her in a way that her ex-fiancé hadn't come close to achieving. She was sighing his name over and over and trembling with barely suppressed passion when she felt his massive erection against her thigh as he reached for the box of condoms in the nightstand. He was about to rip open the packet with his teeth when she took it from him and pushed his shoulders so that he was lying down and she was in control, if only for the length of time it took to put the latex condom on. The heat of her small hands on his engorged, sensitized member was almost his undoing, but he controlled himself until he eased his thick, straining manhood into her hot, moist opening and joined their bodies in the most intimate embrace possible.

He brushed her hair away from her face and looked

at her with eyes made heavy by the extreme erotic pleasure and was touched to see her looking at him with
such love and tenderness that he knew at that moment
this was the woman without whom life would have no
meaning. Their bodies rocked back and forth in the age-
old rhythm and the primal pressure that was building in
both of them exploded into a shattering climax that
went on longer than anything he'd ever experienced in
his life.

Allie, Allie, my heart, my angel, I love you, I love you, baby,
he thought, and in the trembling, mindless shattering
release that followed he could have sworn he heard her
saying the same words to him.

By now Roxy's eyes were full of tears and she was wiping them away with the sleeve of her expensive pima cotton pajamas. "Oh, my soul, Alicia. That's the most
beautiful story I've ever heard. About two people I actually know, that is. It was magical." She sighed. "So what
happened next? Why didn't you just pick up from there
and go on like two people in love since you obviously
were?"

Alicia had been sitting Indian style for so long her legs
were cramped. She gingerly unfolded them and got up
from the bed for a long stretch. Looking down at Roxy,
who was staring at her expectantly, she shrugged. "That's
a good question. It's just not that simple, Rox."

Alicia put her hands in her pockets and wandered
around the spacious bedroom, taking in the opulent fur-
nishings and freeing one hand to finger the gilt tracery
on the dresser. Finally she looked into the big mirror
and met the reflection of Roxy's inquisitive gaze. "That
night it seemed like the simplest thing in the world. We
connected so profoundly and so intimately, it was obvious that we belonged together. But in the bright light of
morning, it was just all wrong."

* * *

Adam came awake very slowly, reluctant to return to consciousness after a night in paradise. He usually woke up quickly, his eyes would open and he'd get out of bed without any preliminaries. Adam's nervous system was like that of a jungle cat, wary and sensitive and alert to any changes in his surroundings. He'd been so overcome with erotic delirium from his night with Alicia that his normal reactions were affected. Everything was affected; the passion they shared had changed everything. His eyelids were still closed, but he could smell the faint fragrance Alicia had left behind. He knew without moving that she was no longer in the bed with him and he was touched by an undeniable sadness. She'd left him during the night. She'd left his bed, left the apartment, left him alone, and he could understand why, although he wished with all his heart that she were still here.

He finally opened his eyes and threw the covers back, getting up abruptly and heading into the bathroom. After brushing his teeth and attending to a few other needs, he started for the kitchen. A pot of coffee was first on the agenda if he was going to regain any semblance of normalcy. Once he had some caffeine in his system it would be easier to figure out a way to apologize to his best friend for the best night of his life, one that was undoubtedly causing her more pain.

Walking into the kitchen naked as a jaybird, he was stunned to find Alicia wearing her wrinkled jeans from last night and one of his T-shirts that hung midthigh on her. She was stirring something in a bowl and from the array of ingredients on the counter it looked like she was making him a feast. She looked up when she heard him come into the room and smiled when she saw his lack of attire. "My, we are informal this morning, aren't we?"

Adam was too stunned to react at first, then he glanced down and did something he hadn't done since his preschool days. He blushed. He could feel the telltale hot flush racing up his neck as he went back to the bedroom. He returned to the kitchen wearing an old pair of jeans and a denim shirt that could have used some ironing. By now the familiar fragrance of Alicia's strong Cuban coffee was filtering through the apartment and the smell of whatever she was cooking filled his nostrils.

"Sit down," she invited. "I went to the store early this morning and got some groceries. I made you croquetas, little ham croquettes. And I also made you scrambled eggs and tostadas. It's almost ready, but you can start with the fruit, if you like." She placed a small plate with sliced guava, mango, and fresh pineapple in front of him.

Adam ignored the food; his attention was all on Alicia. He was so relieved that she hadn't dashed out of the apartment he hadn't managed to speak a word. She didn't seem to notice his reticence, though; she seemed quite cheerful and composed. Her hair wasn't confined in its usual braid, it was flowing in big waves down to her butt, and she was singing some little song in Spanish as she finished the meal. When she finally turned away from the stove and put the platters on the table, Adam noticed for the first time that her hands were shaking just a little bit. She took a seat and was about to start talking again when he grabbed the hand nearest to him.

"Thank you, Allie." At her questioning look, he elaborated. "Thank you for this, for not leaving last night. When I woke up this morning I thought you were gone," he said simply.

Alicia's face flooded with understanding and she clasped his big hand in both of hers. "I should be thanking you, Adam. Thank you for the love and tenderness and caring you shared with me," she whispered. "I've never felt so cherished in my entire life, and that's the truth. No one has ever made me feel as special as you, no one has ever taken care of me like you, and I love you for it."

Adam's eyes lit up with passion and he leaned over to kiss her. It was supposed to be a gentle kiss, a quick caress, but it turned into something else entirely, a long, sensual promise. This time it was Alicia who said they had to stop. "Adam," she breathed as he stood up and pulled her into his arms. "Adam, no, we can't do this. We can't."

He would not be denied as he scooped her up and took her into the living room, where they cuddled on the sofa, kissing with increasing passion. "Oh, Adam, please stop," she moaned. "You have to because I can't, I can't stop."

Her hands slid down his neck to his broad shoulders as he kissed her throat, and the sensitive spot under her ear. "Why do we have to stop, Allie? We're so good together, baby, just think about how good it was last night. It'll be even better this time, I promise."

Alicia pushed him away with a sob in her voice. "I know that, Adam. Of course it will, but it's all wrong. We can't do this, Adam. We just can't."

Hearing the genuine distress in her voice, Adam stopped the sensual exploration of her body and held her closely for a few moments before looking her in the eye. "What's the problem, Allie? I think we've already proven that we belong together. Why do you think this is wrong?"

Alicia sighed and traced the outline of his beautiful mouth, the mouth that had brought to her to ecstasy so many times the night before. "Adam, not a month ago I was engaged to be married to Preston. If we hadn't walked in on him and Yvette, I'd have married him. I was in love with him and I wanted to spend my life with him. And you would still be with Yvette, the woman you love.

"Even though Preston is a first-class jerk and a liar and I don't love him anymore, I can't be in love with you. It's too soon for me and it's too soon for you. What we did was wrong because neither one of us is ready to start a new relationship, especially not one with each other."

A decent man would have felt his desire waning, but Adam was too far gone to be concerned with propriety. Alicia looked like a slightly bedraggled angel and she felt so incredibly sexy in his arms he wasn't thinking about anything but her and how much he wanted her. She was so adorably concerned with his so-called feelings for Yvette and so determined to do the right thing, he fell in love with her all over again.

Adam pulled her against his heart and held her there, stroking her thigh and tangling one hand in her incredible hair. "I understand what you're saying, Allie, but I don't agree with you. I think I know my own heart, and if you just let yourself, you'll see what your heart is telling you, too. This is right, baby, it's just about perfect," he said softly.

"No, it's too soon," she murmured.

"Too soon for what? For this?" he asked as he kissed her forehead.

"No, that's fine," she whispered.

"How about this?" he asked, as he kissed her lips, very gently, like the wings of a butterfly touching her skin.

"Mmm, that's okay," she admitted.

"And this?" He bent his head to her neck, licking and gently sucking the delicate skin of her collarbones and bringing his hand up under her shirt to explore her breasts, which were by now engorged with sensation and crying for his touch.

Her sighs turned into cries of passion as his mouth and his hands turned her into a molten puddle of need. "Adam, don't . . . stop. Don't stop, Adam, don't stop . . ."

With one smooth motion he rose and carried her into the bedroom to complete their journey to a place where there was nothing but the two of them and their love.

* * *

Roxy grabbed a pillow to stifle her scream. "Oooh, girl, I don't believe you! You mean you did it again the next day? And you still ended up being friends? But how—"

Her words were cut off by the sudden burst of salsa music that heralded a call on Alicia's cell phone. Relieved at the intrusion, Alicia said a breathy hello.

"Oh, hi. Were your ears burning? We were talking about you," she said with a happy lilt to her voice. "Who is we? Me and the love of your life, say hello." Without warning she thrust the phone at Roxy, who swallowed hard before speaking.

"Hello," she managed, cutting her eyes at her friend. "I'm great, couldn't be better. How are you doing, Adam? And how's your family? Really? That's nice," she said inanely. "Okay, well, I'm sure I'll see you soon. Here's Alicia, bye."

Alicia was laughing at Roxy's discomfiture when she took the phone back. "Sure I can meet you there in the morning. You buy breakfast. See you tomorrow."

Roxy was looking grumpy when Alicia ended the call. "You think you're funny, don't you? Well, you're not. And if you think I'm letting you out of here without the rest of the story, you're crazy. You owe me, especially after that phone call."

Alicia was busy putting her jacket on and collecting her purse so she could leave. It was really late by now and she needed to get home to bed. "Okay, we made love like there was no tomorrow, but we finally came to our senses, ate a cold breakfast, and promised each other we'd stay friends first and foremost. If we still felt the same way after the summer ended we'd take up where we left off. If not, we'd stay friends." She looked into the mirror, sighed, and flapped her hand at the decidedly non-glamorous picture she made and turned to face Roxy.

"When I got back from my internship in Costa Rica

and he got back from California he was dating someone and that was the end of it. Except we stayed friends and started our own firm after we finished grad school. And that's the end of the story. I'll call you tomorrow. Don't get up, I can let myself out," she said hurriedly as she left the bedroom.

Roxy was left staring at the space her friend had vacated. "That's right, run. But you can't hide from love and you can't hide from me, either. When I get through with you, you'll be a new woman and Adam is going to be a whole new man. 'Best friend' my aunt Fanny," she mumbled as she got out of bed to turn off the lights in the suite. "You two are meant for each other."

Chapter Seven

The next day Alicia thought she'd feel slightly uneasy or at least a little guilty about baring her soul to Roxy, but she didn't. She and Roxy had been friends for so long she knew she could trust her implicitly. Roxy would have forfeited every pair of designer shoes in her vast closet before betraying a confidence. When Alicia picked Adam up at the dealership where he was leaving his beloved Range Rover for servicing, she felt nothing but the usual enjoyment of his company. He was happy to see that she'd borrowed Marielle's Chrysler Pacifica so he wouldn't have to squeeze his length into her Mini Cooper, so happy, in fact, that he was wearing what she called his twenty-four-hour-Colgate-smile, the one that few people outside the family ever saw.

"You look awfully chipper this morning," she said, returning the smile.

"Why shouldn't I? I'm leaving my baby in capable hands and I have the most beautiful chauffeur in Detroit to squire me around. And I have it on good authority that two lovely women were discussing me last night, so it must mean I'm a hot item," he said confidently.

Alicia cast a quick glance his way and rolled her eyes. "We might have been talking about how conceited you are. Did you ever think of that?"

"Nope. One, I'm not conceited. Two, Roxy likes me a lot and she wouldn't be mean-mouthing me. And

three, you'd never let her say anything bad about me,"
he said smugly.

Alicia blew her breath out loudly as she pulled into
one of their favorite diners for the promised breakfast.
"See? Conceited, that's what you are, Adam."

"Not conceited, Allie, convinced." Adam always had to
have the last word.

While they were waiting for their omelets, Adam asked
about Roxy and how she came to be in Detroit. Alicia explained about the promotion and her subsequent relo-
cation. Adam smiled on hearing the news; Roxy was one
of his favorite people.

"So your running buddy is going to be in town on a
permanent basis. That's cool. And just how did my name
come up in conversation?"

Alicia smiled at Adam and raised an eyebrow. "That's
the worst segue I've ever heard, Adam. Nothing subtle
about it. If you must know, she was talking about the
time we all went down to Key West. She said it was the
worst vacation she'd ever had and that nobody had a
good time."

Adam's brow furrowed as he remembered the days
they'd spent there. "I had a great time, Allie. It was one
of the best vacations I've ever taken."

"That's what I told her, too. I had a ball, Adam, I'd like
to go down there again," she admitted.

"Okay then, we'll go." He said it as if it were a done deal.
No further conversation took place on the matter as their
food arrived and they both began eating with enjoyment.

"So you can drop me off at the dealership this afternoon, right?" Adam was watching Alicia put a last bite of
toast in her mouth before she answered.

"Yes, of course. But I need you to do something with
me today too, if you can," she said with a hint of anxiety
in her eyes.

"That's not a problem, what do you need?"

"I'll tell you right before we get there. Otherwise I

might lose my nerve," she admitted. Adam knew her well enough not to pry; he just nodded and finished his coffee.

The workday passed quickly, too quickly for Alicia, who was sure she was doing the right thing but less sure that she could carry it off without Adam at her side. She was working on her latest project, so submerged in work that she was startled when Adam came into her office.

"Are you ready?"

"Wow. Is it that time already? It's so quiet in here I kind of got lost in work," she said as she noticed the wall clock for the first time in hours. "Where is everyone?"

"Allie, it's Friday and it's payday and everyone is gone except for you and me and we're about to leave now. Let's go, *chica*, before the dealership closes."

"Okay, okay. You want to drive?"

Adam looked at her speculatively, but didn't say anything as he accepted the keys to the Pacifica. In short order they had collected his Range Rover and he was preparing to follow her to her destination. "Okay, Allie, where are we going? What's the big secret?"

"We're going to Gigi's," was all she said.

This time Adam looked surprised, but he nodded and said he'd see her there.

Gigi was her middle aunt, one of her father's merry and charming sisters. Her father's family had escaped Cuba years before and had set out to become successful and productive Americans. All of them had accomplished that goal in different ways. Her father, Jose Ernesto Fuentes, had been picked up by a minor league baseball team in Florida and soon made his way to the major leagues. He'd retired from the Detroit Tigers and was now their batting coach. His oldest sister, Marguerita, had worked as a housekeeper for years to support the family and now owned a very successful employment agency. The middle sister, Juanita, known to all as Gigi, started as a shampoo girl in a beauty salon and now owned five full-service salons in different cities. And the youngest, Graciela, had started working in a hospital as a laundry worker. Now she was a doctor and head of an inner-city clinic. They were all successful, inspiring role models, but for what she needed, only Gigi would do.

She pulled into the parking lot behind the chic Birmingham salon at the same time Adam did, for which she was grateful. She might have turned around and left if he hadn't arrived when he did. As it was she was wiping her hands down her pants legs when he got out of the Rover and came over to tap on her window.

"Are you okay? What exactly are we doing here?" he asked.

Alicia fumbled in her tote bag for a minute and unearthed a pamphlet that she handed to Adam. "I'm fine, Adam. And this is what we're doing. Well, what *I'm* doing. I just need you to hold my hand, is all."

Adam's eyes widened for a few seconds as he read the words *Locks of Love* on the pamphlet. "Are you going to do this?" he asked quietly.

Alicia finally got out of the car and stood next to Adam. "Yes, I am. I think it's time. I just don't want to lose my nerve. I need you to hold my hand," she said sheepishly.

Adam looked her over, seeing her resolute expression with the slight hint of panic around the edges. He took her hand and said, "Okay, let's go." They walked into the cool, relaxing reception area where the receptionist greeted them. She rang for Gigi and then told the couple she'd be out at once. Normally Alicia would have felt her usual appreciation for the warm taupe, peach, and cream décor of the salon with the big palm trees and other tropical plants, but she was too nervous right now. Even the soothing jazz that played continuously was no solace. The salon was busy as usual, with women of all ages and colors getting a variety of services from the competent staff. The sounds of soft conversation and occasional laughter were broken as Juanita Marciela Fuentes made her entrance.

It was easy to see where Alicia got some of her good looks from; her aunt Gigi was a beautiful woman, stunning from head to toe. Her African heritage was evident from the dark richness of her skin, but her Latin blood contributed its fair share of her comeliness. She was wearing a dress in a fantastic shade of tangerine that warmed her skin and flattered her trim figure. Even the smock she put on to protect her outfit was chicly patterned in a small leopard print. The gold bangle bracelets she wore on both wrists tinkled as she stretched her arms out to give her niece a hug.

"Ah, *mija*, it's so good to see you. And you, too, you handsome devil," she added as she gave Adam a hug and a kiss on the cheek. Turning back to Alicia, she grasped her niece's long braid and looked deeply into Alicia's eyes. "So, *querida*, are you sure you want to do this? When you called me last night I thought you were kidding, but here you are. Are you really ready?"

Alicia was pale, but she nodded firmly. "Yes, Gigi. I'm tired of looking like a schoolgirl. Let's do it." The night before she had taken a good long look at herself in the mirror in her bedroom and realized that before she got a new wardrobe the hair had to go. And if she could benefit a child while doing it, so much the better. She just needed Adam to get her through the first cut, that's all.

Gigi dropped the braid and clapped her hands. "All right then. Let's get to it."

Before she could even think about her decision, Alicia found herself seated in a styling chair, draped with a cape to protect her clothing. As he promised, Adam was standing in front of her, holding both her hands. The other patrons and stylists watched with great interest as

Gigi went to work. Gigi had loosened her hair from its braid and combed it straight down. Unbound, the hair almost reached the floor. She gathered it loosely in her left hand and with long barber's shears she quickly cut across the wavy length of hair, shearing it off just above the shoulder. Despite her resolve, Alicia gasped and tightened her grip on Adam's hands. The rest of the salon went into a stunned silence after a muffled shriek from an anonymous observer.

Gigi, sensing distress, quickly soothed her niece. "Don't worry, *mija*, it's going to be beautiful. Locks of Love is a wonderful organization, you know. They need ten inches of hair to make a wig for a child who has lost hers to chemotherapy or disease, and you'll be giving them enough for two children."

Alicia looked at her reflection in the mirror and winced. "Yes, I know, Gigi, but I look like hell, I look like a monster. It's a haystack," she moaned. And it really did look dreadful. Her thick, abundant hair, free for the first time in its entire life, sprang out like a wild bush. Alicia couldn't bring herself to look at Adam; she just wished he were somewhere far away from the debacle. Luckily, Gigi took charge.

"Ah, don't worry your head about this, I'm just getting started," she said bracingly. "You go in the back and I'll be there in just a minute. In the meantime, I think Adam should go have a beer or something to pass the time. Come back in two hours, maybe two and a half, okay?"

He nodded in agreement with Gigi, but he leaned over, brushed the hair away from Alicia's ear, and whispered something that only she could hear. She sighed shakily and gave him an equally shaky smile. The smile turned to a grimace as she glanced in the mirror again. Her eyes grew wide and teary and Gigi urged her to get in the back to a private room so the transformation could be completed. This time she didn't hesitate. With a quick wave at Adam she got out of the styling chair and quickly left the main salon.

Adam waited until Alicia scurried to the back of the salon. He then turned his attention to the massive hank of hair Gigi was still holding in her left hand. Without a word of warning he reached over and took a piece of the hair, gently separating a one-inch section from the rest of the bundle. He wound it around his hand several times, then said good-bye to Gigi. "I'll be back in about three hours. Take care of her," he said softly as he turned to leave.

Gigi stared after his retreating figure. "*Madre de Dios,* where was he when I was young?" she murmured. "That, ladies, is a real man."

True to her word, Gigi worked miracles with what was left of Alicia's hair. First, she applied a mild relaxer to make it easier to style. The hair that was so docile when confined to a braid was lively and vigorous in its new state. Gigi applied the chemicals so expertly that Alicia didn't sense any discomfort through the process, she just sat back and let Gigi do her work. While she was rinsing it out and shampooing with neutralizing shampoo, Gigi asked what had brought about the transition. "*Mija,* I thought you would never cut this hair. What made you do it? I don't think it was just because you wanted to donate it to a worthy organization," she said sagely.

Alicia was so enjoying the smell of the shampoo and her aunt's thorough massaging of her scalp she was almost asleep, but the question roused her out of her lull. "You're right, *Tía,* it wasn't just because I thought Locks of Love is a great organization. I've decided I can look better than I do and it's time I paid more attention to my appearance. I'm a career woman, not a schlumpy college student."

"Hmm," was all Gigi said, but it was plain she didn't quite believe her niece's story.

"And I'm tired of looking like Adam's little sister," Alicia added. "We were out running one day and we both had on sweats and baseball caps and I heard this woman say to her friend, "Oh, look. Twins!" I don't think Adam heard it, but it really bothered me. Adam is a good-looking man, but I don't want to look like him," she grumbled.

Gigi smiled to herself as she rinsed every bit of shampoo out. While she was applying a conditioner that smelled like something delicious to eat, she probed gently. "So would I be wrong to say that you might be trying to catch a certain man's eye?"

Alicia's eyes opened in alarm and the look on her aunt's face was hardly reassuring. Gigi had the dreamy, satisfied look of a *yenta* whose fondest wish is about to come true; she looked like she was about to start planning a wedding.

"*Tia*, it's not like that. Well, maybe it is, but please don't say anything to anyone, at least not yet. He doesn't have a clue and I don't want—" Her barrage of words was cut off by Gigi.

"*Chica*, please, I am nothing if not discreet. Do you have any idea how many secrets I carry around with me? All women confide in their hairstylists and I've been doing hair since I got off the boat, practically. Can't you just imagine how many things I know? Pregnancies, divorces, abortions, affairs, there isn't much that people don't tell me. I know everybody's business, honey, here in Detroit and in Miami, Atlanta, Baltimore, and Chicago, too! *Tia* knows how to keep her mouth shut, don't worry." *But I think your Adam has more than a clue, mija*, she thought.

After Alicia's hair was relaxed, conditioned, and lightly toweled dry, Gigi shaped it into a chic layered style with longer pieces caressing her nape and uneven bangs framing her face. It was shockingly becoming as the style drew attention to her big eyes and high cheekbones and made her sexy mouth even sexier. She looked sophisticated and charming, yet she looked like herself. Best of all, Alicia loved the feeling of lightness when she shook her head. She ran her hands through it and was excited to see it fall right back into place, thanks to her aunt's expert cutting.

"Why didn't I do this years ago?" marveled Alicia. "This feels so good!"

"And it looks fantastic, even if I do say so," Gigi said confidently. "You are so beautiful, Alicia. The boys won't believe it's their little sister," she teased.

Alicia smiled again, thinking about her family's reaction. "You're coming over for breakfast next Sunday, aren't you? *Papi* and *Mami* and the boys will be home, finally. I can't wait to see everyone."

Her brothers both played for the Detroit Tigers and they, as well as Jose, had been on the road for almost three weeks with games in Cleveland, Minnesota, and Arizona. Her mother had naturally gone too because since her retirement Jose didn't like to have his wife too far away and she loved to travel.

"Of course I'll be there, we all will," she said, meaning her sisters. "We're bringing something special, too. Now, just let me tame those eyebrows a bit and put a little makeup on that pretty face to make you glow. Adam should be back soon and you're going to knock him out," she predicted.

The "bit" Gigi did to the eyebrows was a waxing, a process Alicia had never had done and something she imagined would be quite painful. It wasn't at all, thanks to Gigi's skill. The result was amazing, though; her brows were still thick and lustrous but cleaning up the area underneath gave them a sharper arch and made them look very sexy and glamorous. As promised, she applied just a bit of makeup, just enough to give Alicia a healthy shimmer. A hint of gold eyeshadow, a little mascara, and a subtle liner in the outer corners of her eyes and she

suddenly had huge, smoky eyes that beckoned and be-
guiled. Alicia drew the line at lipstick, however.

"I've never worn lipstick, Gigi. You know the boys call
me Patti for a reason," she said wryly. Patti was a twist
on her real nickname, *Pato,* the Spanish word for duck.
Her brothers called her that because her lips were so
prominent, especially when she was little.

Gigi clucked her tongue in disgust. "They call you that
because they are idiots. Your lips are just perfect. Lots of
women pay big money to get these lips, trust me. Now
you just line them very lightly like so," she said as she
gently outlined Alicia's lips with a medium brown pen-
cil. "Then you blend in it like so." And she used her little finger to smooth the color all over the lips. "And then
a nice soft neutral color followed by a gold gloss and see?
Very sexy, yes?"

Alicia had to admit it made a huge difference. Just a
few little touches and she looked dramatic, mysterious,
and undeniably feminine. "Nobody's going to think
we're twins now," she murmured. "Gigi, this is worth
every penny. I can't possibly thank you enough for this.
I love you, I really do."

"Worth what penny? I've never done your hair before,
and you know I always do family for free. I wish you
would try to pay me, I'd tear the check up in front of
your face," she said haughtily. "But there is something
you can do to show your appreciation. Let me plan your
wedding, *mija.* That will be payment enough."

Alicia blushed fiercely upon hearing those words, but
she didn't have time to get really rattled. The receptionist buzzed to let them know that Adam had returned, so
it was show time. She allowed Gigi to give her clothes
one last brushing and straightening before going out
into the main salon to greet him. If she'd been paying
him more specific attention she'd have seen a look on
his face that would have convinced her that Gigi's line
about wedding planning might not be too far-fetched.

She completely missed the utter rapture that took over Adam's face as she reentered the salon, though. She also didn't hear the oohs and aahs from the stylists and the applause from the other patrons as they admired her new look. All she could do was stare openmouthed at Adam, who had a long braid in one hand and a newly shorn, neatly styled head of hair—very short hair.

"Oh, my goodness, what have you done?" she gasped.

Chapter Eight

Angelique watched her brother-in-law playing with her daughter and could tell that something was troubling his heart. Adam was always so cool and self-contained. He was difficult to know really well, but in the months since her marriage Angelique had grown close to him, close enough to know when something was on his mind. She smiled as she watched Adam picking out a tune for Lily Rose on the piano while he held her firmly in his left arm and sang her a little song.

"I think your niece likes your voice, Uncle Adam," she teased. And it was true; Lily was bubbling with enjoyment and patting her hands together as Adam entertained her.

Adam rubbed his cheek against Lily's soft curls and kissed her. "I'm just glad she quit screaming at me," he admitted. Lily Rose was the only member of the family who hadn't thoroughly approved of Adam's haircut. She'd taken one look at her uncle and yelled bloody murder. It had taken a lot of coaxing and crooning on Adam's part to convince her that it was really he, albeit with a new look. A few weeks had passed since the great haircutting and Lily Rose seemed to have adjusted, although Adam wasn't completely sure that she had.

"Do you want me to take her? You seem a little preoccupied," said Angelique.

"No, she's fine, aren't you, sweetie?" Lily Rose cooed and reached for Adam's hand to encourage him to get back to playing. Adam ignored Angelique's remark about him being preoccupied; instead he pretended a sudden interest in the new décor of the living room. Big Benny, the Cochran patriarch, had presented the house to the young couple as a Christmas present, as he and his bride wanted to move into a condominium. They'd made a few changes in the house to suit their taste, but the warmth of the big brick home was the same as it had been when he was growing up in the house.

"It's weird, Angel, but when I look around here I can feel my whole childhood pressing in on me," he said quietly. "You've made some nice changes to the old place. It looks like a beautiful place for my new niece to grow up in."

Angelique blushed with pleasure at his simple remark and was about to respond when Lily's sudden cries announced that she was hungry. "Okay, sweetie, Mommy's here," Angelique said cheerfully. She reached for the baby and said she'd be back soon.

Adam knew that Angelique was breast-feeding and wasn't prone to doing it in front of anyone but her husband, which was fine with him. He wouldn't like Alicia's breasts exposed to anyone's eyes other than his, either. Adam groaned deeply. There it was again, yet another totally inappropriate thought about Alicia. He was supposed to be getting a handle on this obsession, and if anything he was getting worse. His fantasies were getting more frequent, more erotic and fully realized, and he was getting more and more irritable about the whole thing. Ever since Alicia's transformation, Adam had been more aware of her than ever and his fixation was driving him crazy.

To be honest, he wasn't entirely pleased by the change in Alicia's appearance. For one thing, until the fateful day of the haircut, Adam wouldn't have believed Alicia could possibly be more appealing than she already was. He'd always found her beautiful; now she was completely captivating. When she'd come out of the private room at Gigi's salon he was sure his heart had stopped. With her exquisite features finally on display, she looked like a model for an expensive line of perfume or some kind of skin care. It was impossible for him to look away from her eyes, to ignore her flawless skin and those lips that seemed to be dripping honey just for him. He'd been shocked when she decided to cut off her hair, but the result was obviously the right decision. His Alicia had gone from being a pretty woman to an absolute stunner. And the new clothes she had taken to wearing just made her more appealing.

She certainly hadn't been a slob before, but instead of wearing tailored shirts and slacks and neat jackets, she was wearing skirts and dresses and feminine blouses in an array of warm colors that brought out all the deep bronze of her skin. After people got over the initial shock of seeing the change in her, there were unanimous raves about her new look. And the same question was on everyone's lips—"why did you decide to do it?" That was what was bugging Adam, although he wouldn't admit it even to himself. He couldn't rid himself of the idea that Alicia was trying to attract some guy's attention and he had a sinking feeling that the guy was Bryant Porter.

He started playing the piano again, keeping it soft because of Lily Rose, who usually went right to sleep after she was fed. He was playing "Stardust" when his brother entered the room. Donnie's first stop on arriving home had been the baby's room, as usual. After kissing his wife and holding the baby until she went to sleep, Donnie was ready to meddle in his brother's life, something he almost never got to do. He nodded approvingly at Adam's technique before sitting down in the new club chair that accentuated the fresh, updated look of the room.

"I see you haven't lost your touch. That sounds pretty good."

"Yeah, I don't get to play too often but I try to keep in practice. I'm thinking about getting a piano. God knows there's enough room for it in the loft."

Donnie agreed and then segued into the one subject Adam wished to avoid. "Hey, did Renee tell you Bryant Porter is going to be staying in the Outhouse? He stopped by to see her and Andrew and he mentioned that he was looking for some place to stay. The Outhouse will be perfect for him to use for a couple of months. He was really happy about it," Donnie said guilelessly.

The Outhouse was the family name for the apartment over the garage in the back of the Indian Village home shared by Adam's oldest brother, Andrew, and his wife, Renee. The house was filled to bursting with the couple and their four little girls, but the Outhouse was a nice little island of calm. It had one bedroom, a living/dining room, and a nice little kitchen and was just ideal for Bryant. Bryant and Renee had been friends for years and offering him a place to stay was a perfectly nice gesture on the part of a friend. The fact that this gesture made Adam's temples throb with tension was his own little secret. He was consumed by the fact that in a few weeks Bryant Porter was going to be in Detroit for the entire summer with unlimited access to Alicia. The thought was causing him considerable distress. He brought his fingers down on the keys harder than he intended and stopped playing immediately. He rose from the piano and walked over to the big bay with the multipaned windows.

Donnie tried not to let his amusement show, but he'd been in Adam's position not too long ago. He too had been in the throes of passion for Angelique, and their courtship had been stormy to say the least. Donnie had also been intensely aware of every man who ever looked at Angelique and he knew full well that Adam wasn't too thrilled with the Bryant Porter situation. He decided to take a shot just to see where the arrow landed. Looking perfectly innocent, he said, "By the way, Adam, I saw Alicia the other day and she was looking *good*, man. She's always been pretty, but now she's beyond fine. This woman is an absolute fox, bro. You better look out, somebody's going to snatch up your partner and run off with her," he added with a friendly laugh.

Angelique returned to the living room and instantly caught the dark look passing over Adam's face and tried to change the subject. "You know what, Adam? I'd like to take a picture of you with Lily Rose. I want to take a portrait with each member of the family. I think that would be a nice keepsake."

Donnie decided to push a little harder this time. "It's a good thing you've had so much practice being an uncle, Adam. Just think, you could be playing uncle to one of Alicia's babies soon. Because the way she looks, with that beautiful personality of hers, she's going to be married in less than a year, bet on it."

"Adonis, come help me in the kitchen. *Now*, please." Angelique put her hands on her hips as she stared at her thoughtless mate.

No sooner had they reached the kitchen than she turned on her big handsome husband and pointed a finger in his face. "Adonis, you have all the sensitivity of a toilet seat," she scolded. "Can't you see that Adam has real feelings for Alicia? Are you trying to start a fight with him?"

Donnie laughed and embraced his wife. "No, Angel, I'm trying to start a *fire* with him. I'm just trying to get Adam to bust a move, that's all. Cochran men are known for being slow and stubborn and he may not say anything to Alicia for years to come. You know how closed down Adam can be when he tries. So I figure a little push here and there won't hurt," he admitted.

Angelique hugged her beloved man back but she

warned him to lay off his brother. "You keep trying
to start a fire with Adam and *you* could be the one who
gets burned."

Truth be told, Alicia wasn't any more excited about
her big transformation than Adam was. She liked her
new look, especially the easy-care haircut, and she loved
the new clothes Roxy had helped her purchase. After
Roxy had gotten over her shock at Alicia's short hair,
they'd gone off to some of the best malls around: Som-
erset Town Center, Great Lakes Crossing, and several T.J.
Maxx stores, and come home with bags and bags of new
outfits and boxes of new shoes. She now had fashionable
alternatives to her normal work wear and several pieces
that were for evening wear only. Everyone, including her
family, had reacted very positively to her new look and
the fact was she felt much better about herself. It was
amazing the effect a few well-chosen articles of clothing
could have on a person. The only thing that prevented
her from feeling totally pleased with her transformation
was the fact that Adam was acting strangely toward her.

She tired to explain it to Roxy as they shared dinner
at P.F. Chang's. She swallowed the last bite of her lettuce
wrap and followed it with a sip of water. "Roxy, I can't really explain it, but somehow I feel this distance between
us. I think he might have started dating someone," she
said sadly.

Roxy's eyes widened in concern. "What makes you
think he's taken up with some floozy? I thought he'd
been kind of on his own for a while, meaning no serious
entanglements with the opposite sex."

Alicia looked around the trendy restaurant before answering and when she finally spoke, it was with lowered
eyes and a resigned tone of voice. "I can always tell when
Adam has a new lady in his life. For a few days he's kind
of formal with me, kind of businesslike, and then it goes

away. And that's what he's doing now," she admitted. "The day we got the haircuts he was wonderful, just like he always is, and a few days later he starts acting like I'm someone he met at a chamber of commerce meeting. He's polite and well mannered but he acts like I'm his insurance agent or something."

"So did you ever tell him why you decided on the big overhaul? I mean, did he ever ask what was behind the new you?" Roxy sipped her wine while she waited for Alicia to answer.

"Actually, I did tell him. One night we were working late and he went to get Greek takeout. While we were eating he asked me why I felt the need to improve on perfection." She smiled dreamily, remembering the sweetness of the words. "I wasn't trying to be a femme fatale or anything, but I was really flirty while I told him the truth. I told him it was because I wanted to attract the attention of a certain man. I wanted this man to see me in a totally different way and that's why I did it."

Her face grew hot as she remembered the dead silence that had resulted from her statement. She'd hoped for a totally different response, one in which they ended up kissing wildly after he confessed he was already interested in her. She'd prayed that if she made herself more desirable and more sophisticated, he'd respond immediately and they'd be swept away by the kind of passion she remembered from their forbidden night. His reaction was quite the opposite.

"Rox, it was terrible, at least it was for me. It was just like this mask dropped over his face, he changed expressions that fast. He went from smiling and sexy to disinterested and stern in less time than it's taking me to tell you about it," she said with a frown. "Here I was trying to look all seductive and cute and he's looking completely bored with the conversation. It wasn't a pretty sight, believe me," she said with a grimace.

Roxy was about to answer when their server appeared

and cleared the table before putting their appetizing-smelling entrées in front of them. By the time he departed she had something to say. "Alicia, honey, I've always thought you were brilliant. I may have to reassess that evaluation since you obviously have missed the entire point here. Girl, Adam is acting weird because he thinks you're trying to get with some other man. He thinks all this effort to be gorgeous is for the benefit of some other lucky guy, and it's eating him up inside. That's why he's acting like a nitwit," she said sagely as she eyed her plate appreciatively and took a dainty bite.

Alicia's mouth opened, too, but not for food. She stared at Roxy, who was now eating with enjoyment, and shook her head. "Rox, you're way wrong about this. First of all, Adam's not that dense. I practically threw myself at him and he politely threw me back, that's all. I'm telling you, he's involved with someone else and that's why I'm getting the cold shoulder."

Roxy rolled her eyes in despair. "Alicia, men simply aren't as emotionally facile as women. You can't drop a subtle hint on a man; you have to practically club them over the head just to get their attention. You obviously thought that little bit of kittenish behavior was going to delete ten years of programming from his mental hard drive, but it didn't. All it did was put him on red alert that someone else is getting some of your attention. And from what you've told me, he probably thinks that person is Bryant Porter. Mr. Porter sounds quite dishy, by the way. You might want to kick him over this way," she added with a smile.

Alicia was so intent on Roxy's assessment of the situation she missed her last remark entirely. Her forehead puckered in thought, she recalled the last few times she and Adam had been together. They'd gone to the Tigers' opening home game and huddled in the stands bundled up and holding hands against the cold April day. They'd been out to eat several times, to church, to her parents' house for dinner, and to the movies, and he'd been his usual warm, attentive self. She'd always been able to tell Adam anything and he was more attuned to her than anyone else she knew. How was it possible that he would suddenly get stuck on stupid? She finally looked directly at Roxy and denied her words.

"Rox, once again, I have to disagree. Adam isn't your typical thickheaded male. Adam is sensitive and perceptive; he always knows exactly what I mean even when *I* don't know what I mean. He couldn't be so obtuse that he wouldn't understand what I was trying to say. He just wasn't interested, that's all," she said resignedly.

Roxy beckoned to their server. "I need another glass of wine, please." She gave the young man her best dimpled smile and as he retreated, she turned her attention back to Alicia. "Girl, you're driving me to drink, you really are. I know you and Adam have this perfect friendship and you think he's the perfect man, but that doesn't mean he isn't thick as a plank when it comes to romance. Honey, when a man has feelings for a woman, his common sense goes right out the window. He's not capable of normal thought patterns; everything's all jumbled up in his brain and the result is chaos."

"Hold on, now, Rox, I never said Adam was perfect. We're used to each other, that's all. But perfect? Far from it. Adam can be moody and distant and he's much too self-contained. And he definitely has a temper, but most people don't realize it because he doesn't yell. He *seethes*, though, which is much worse. And he's a perfectionist and he's so neat it's like he has OCD. Everyone thinks Adam and I never fight, but we have our share of arguments. We just get over it, that's all. It's because we're friends, pals, buds, road dogs. We're practically brother and freakin' sister and that's how he wants to keep it."

Roxy stifled a groan after Alicia's diatribe. "I think you need this wine worse than I do. And don't tell me the man's not interested in you romantically, because I saw you together last week, remember? When he took us out to dinner and a movie, there was only one thing he was watching all night and that was you. He hardly takes his eyes off you, and the way he looks at you, well, let's just say children under thirteen should *not* be allowed, even with a parent or guardian."

Alicia's doubt was still apparent, although it was clear that Roxy's words had affected her. She was about to concede this to Roxy when the expression on her face changed to one of distaste. "You make some interesting points, but I still think he's dating someone else. As a matter of fact, there she is now," Alicia said dryly.

Roxy almost got whiplash as she tried to turn her head in the direction that Alicia was staring, but her efforts were unnecessary. Alicia moaned and whispered, "*Madre de Dios*, she's coming this way." She said a few other things in Spanish that were undoubtedly impolite and possibly profane, yet she managed to look perfectly composed when Darcy Hamilton stopped by their table.

"Alicia, darling, how are you? I haven't seen you in weeks but you're looking just fabulous! I almost didn't recognize you with that divine haircut," she said in a sweet tone of voice. As usual, she looked beautiful in neatly tailored silver gray high-waisted pleated slacks and a matching shirt. The silvery color brought out her gray eyes and her chicly styled hair was in its normal perfect state.

With a terse thank-you, Alicia acknowledged the compliment and introduced Roxy. Darcy turned her attention to Roxy and gave her an interested look. "Roxy *Fairchild*? Like Fairchild Cosmetics?" she asked curiously.

Roxy didn't even blink. "Yes, like Fairchild Cosmetics, my family's company. Nice to meet you," she said coolly.

Darcy didn't seem to notice the drop in temperature

from Roxy's direction; she turned back to Alicia with a big smile. "You know I'm having a huge housewarming party after the renovations are done. I do hope you can make it. I've been driving poor Adam mad, but the result is so wonderful I'm recommending Cochran and Fuentes to everyone I know." She glanced across the room and waved at someone, her own dinner date, presumably. "I'm being rude, so I've got to dash. Nice meeting you, Roxy, and, Alicia, I just love that outfit. You really are looking wonderful," she added warmly.

It's hard to be nasty to someone when they're being extra nice to you, so Alicia gritted her teeth and tried to be equally charming. Darcy left them to join her friends and Roxy took a deep breath.

"Mmm-*hmm*. So you're telling me that's the little vixen who has eyes for Adam, is that right?"

Alicia nodded glumly. "That would be her. And I think he's acted on that interest, which is why he's acting cool toward me."

To her surprise, Roxy shook her head violently. "Nope, not possible. *You're* wrong about this one and I'm right. In fact, I'm so sure I'm right that I say we make a little wager. The winner has to treat the loser to a day at the spa, and I mean head to toe, sister, from hairdo to pedicure, with a mud bath and salt scrub in between. If you and Adam aren't a couple by Memorial Day, the treat's on me. But since you're going to lose, I'ma go ahead and make reservations at the most expensive spa I can find. I plan to bankrupt you, Miss Alicia."

Alicia laughed at her friend but she had to clarify something. "Okay, Rox, if that's how you want to waste your money, fine. But why Memorial Day? What's so significant about that particular date?"

"This is why I'm going to win, girl, you don't pay attention to detail. That Bachelor Auction is that weekend, remember? The one where you always go along and bail Adam out so he doesn't have to be bothered with some nitwit trying to push up on him just because she had the high bid. Well, this is your perfect opportunity to bust a move and it's gonna be the deal breaker. If you don't get your point across then, you never will," she said calmly.

Memorial Day was just a week away. If Roxy was right, she had a lot to do between now and then. Just getting her nerve up was enough. How was she supposed to do something to let Adam know she meant business when her simple flirtation had failed?

"And just to make it really interesting, if you go through with it, I'll throw in a week at my time share in the Caymans to sweeten the deal," Roxy purred.

Alicia raised an eyebrow and she stuck her hand out at once. "Done." The gauntlet was thrown. Now she just had to figure out a plan.

Chapter Nine

After a weekend of thinking about the Bachelor Auction the last thing Alicia wanted to do was hear more about it at work, but since two other associates from the firm were involved, conversation was inevitable. One of the newer architects, a tall, slender man named Hannibal Brown, was participating, as was Paul LaBruglia. Paul's inclusion was a surprise move since he was an Australian of Italian descent, but he'd charmed the selection committee with his warm personality and undeniable sex appeal. He wasn't overly tall, only about six feet. And he didn't have the perfect looks of a movie star, either, although his thick curly black hair and dark green eyes were sexy enough to make one forget his large Roman nose. What made Paul so appealing was his frank appreciation of the opposite sex, his piercing intelligence, and his wicked sense of humor. When he suggested they bill him as the Vanilla Thunder from Down Under, the selection committee had all burst into laughter and agreed that he would make a most interesting addition to the group of men.

With three representatives from the firm participating in the auction and practically all of the staff attending, the daily comments about the festivities were beginning to grate on Alicia's last precious nerve, the one she needed intact in order to stay sane. Fortunately, though, Adam was as low-key as ever about his role. All he said was, "I can count on you, right?" She'd said yes and that was it. He would pick her up and they'd attend together, she'd wait until the fateful moment and whip out his checkbook. Then they'd go some place and get take-out food and finish the evening watching samurai movies or playing Scrabble. At least, that's how it had always gone before. This time it would be totally different, that is, if she could find something to wear.

Roxy had been driving her crazy about finding just the right thing to wear, and her enthusiasm was beginning to get to Alicia. They were at the condo with Alicia's new evening wear spread out on the bed. There were lots of sexy things to pick from, but Roxy wasn't convinced yet. The fact that it was a black-and-white ball was a nuisance as far as she was concerned.

"Black-and-white is so boring, so safe! And it's been done to death, too. You need to wear something fresh and lively, like that little orange number."

The dress in question was an intense, vibrant orange strapless dress in a silk and cotton blend, made with a short full skirt that would be perfect for dancing, but as Alicia pointed out, it wasn't formal enough. "It's actually kind of casual when you think about it," she mused. Her seven-year-old nephew agreed with Roxy, however.

"I like that one, *Tía*. It's sexy," he said with a grin.

"What did you say, Paco?" Roxy asked. The family always spoke Spanish at home and Paco sometimes forgot that not everyone understood the language.

"I'm sorry, *Tía* Roxy. I said she should wear the orange dress because it's sexy."

He laughed at the shocked look on Roxy's face, his long-lashed dark blue eyes lighting with glee. Roxy ruffled his curly golden brown hair as she chastised him. "What do you know about sexy, little boy? How did you get to be so mannish?"

"We have cable," he said innocently. "*Tía*, wear this one, this is pretty, too."

This dress was certainly sexy; it was a fitted sheath with

a slit up one side and a daringly cut bodice with one long sleeve. It was also a shimmering shade of violet.

Alicia sighed. "It's pretty, *mijo*, but it's the wrong color. It has to be black or white."

"Who says? You're grown, wear what you want," Marielle said from the doorway. She had her one-year-old-daughter, Gabriella, on her hip and was obviously about to put her to bed. Gabriella squealed and reached for her *tía* Alicia when she saw all the colorful dresses scattered about the room. Playing in her mother's clothes was one of her favorite things to do, and her aunt's room looked like a fantasyland at the moment.

Alicia smiled and took her chubby, curly-haired niece from her sister. "Oh, no, you don't, *Princesa Mariposa*! I know what you're capable of and you're not wrecking this room." Ignoring the child's wriggling, she turned to Roxy. "I guess we'll just have to go shopping tomorrow."

Marielle inspected the dresses lying on the bed and the other furniture and disagreed. "Not really, I may have something for you. Let me get these two into bed and I'll be back. Tell them good night, Paco," she instructed as her son ran to bestow hugs and kisses. "Kiss *Tía* so we can go to bed," she instructed Gabrielle, who immediately produced big fake tears as her mother took her from Alicia's arms.

In a little while the room was restored to order and Marielle had accomplished her goal of bedtime for her children. She returned to Alicia's room with a garment bag, and while she was unzipping it, Roxy commented on the sweetness and beauty of Marielle's little ones. Marielle smiled modestly although she admitted that Gabrielle was a miniature tyrant who ruled the house with a will of iron. "I may never forgive *Papi* for starting that Princess Butterfly thing. She really does think she's royalty, the way the men spoil her. Okay, now this is what

I think you should wear, Alicia. This is the most fabulous dress I've ever owned and I have yet to wear it in public."

She whipped the garment out with a flourish and Roxy and Alicia both sighed with pleasure. The dress was amazing; it was made of a supple matte silk jersey with wide-set straps that joined behind the neck and led down to a plunging back. The open sweetheart neckline was sexy but decorous, as it didn't offer a lot of cleavage. The dress was formfitting and daringly short, stopping at midthigh. There was an overskirt of sheer silk georgette that lay in flat panels until the dress moved. Then the panels parted gently to give tantalizing glimpses of leg. It was a dress designed to tempt, to provoke, to startle a man into submission. Alicia was stunned. Roxy prodded her to put the dress on at once, and she did, going into the walk-in closet for privacy and emerging like a siren.

The dress was a perfect fit and when she moved the skirt rippled around her gently so the flashes of leg revealed were sensual and not blatantly sexual. She whirled around in the dress and for a moment she could see the look in Adam's eyes when he saw her dress, the moment when he took her in his arms. . . . She looked at her sister and her best friend, who were applauding with gusto and pointed something out to them. "Um, I have to ask if anyone has noticed that this dress isn't exactly black *or* white."

The dress was, in fact, *red*, a deep true-blue red with a crimson saturation so deep it tricked the eyes. The color was so profound when one looked away from it everything had a pink cast for a few seconds. It was the reddest red Alicia had ever seen and it looked incredible against her skin. She'd never find anything this fabulous and she knew it. But still, she had doubts. "Come on, are you actually suggesting that I wear a red dress to a black-and-white affair? That's such a cliché: the maverick strolling into the ball wearing something that gets all the attention, yadda, yadda, yadda. For heaven's sake, they did that in *Jezebel*, that ancient Bette Davis movie," she pointed out.

Marielle laughed in her sister's face. "I'm not suggesting you wear the dress, I'm *insisting* on it. When did you get to be such a goody-goody? Who cares if it's a black-and-white ball, a pink-and-purple ball, or a green-and-gold ball? You're not a member of the sorority, you're paying good money to attend this shindig, and you can wear any dratted thing you want. Besides, you look fabulous. I say wear it and to heck with them."

Roxy agreed wholeheartedly. "Who cares if it's a cliché? Clichés become clichés because they're tried and true. If they didn't work, people would stop doing them and they'd be random oddities. That's not the case here, sister. You need to make an entrance no one will ever forget, and that's the dress to do it in," she said dramatically. "I'm not mad at a cliché, they have their place in life. That's why writers use them in chick flicks and romance novels, they get the job done. Just like when you put lemons, water, sugar, and ice together you get lemonade. It always works if you work it right, and you, Alicia, are working that dress. You have to wear it, it's amazing. Marielle, how come you never wore it in public?"

Marielle smiled as she looked at her younger sister modeling in the full-length mirror. "Roxy, I bought that dress to take on my honeymoon. I put it on and my husband went insane. *Dios*, he was so excited with me in that outfit we never made it out of the suite. I tried again when we got home. I tried so many times to wear that dress and the result was always the same. Once he saw me in it, we didn't make it out of the house. We tried, we really did, but that dress just did something to him." She sighed. "So if you intend to rope in Adam Cochran, that's the dress you need to be wearing, little sister."

Before Alicia could react to the fact that her pathetic

cover had been blown, Paco gave a low wolf whistle from the doorway.

"*Tía esta muy caliente,*" he said with a comic wiggle of his eyebrows.

Marielle jumped up from the bed laughing and went to take him back to his room. "Paco, we need to have a little talk about men and women," she told him.

"Oh no, *Mami,* my *tíos* told me everything," he was heard to say earnestly.

Alicia and Roxy burst out laughing. "If that's the case we're going to have to deprogram the poor child. Who knows what my brothers put in his head?" Alicia said.

"Yes, but he knows his auntie is hot in that dress, child, and you're going to wear it to that auction if I have to drug you to make you do it. In fact, I'm going with you to make sure you don't chicken out," she said firmly. "Of course, now we have to go shopping for real because *I* don't have a thing to wear."

Adam was backstage, wishing with all his heart that he were somewhere else. The other bachelors who were waiting for their turn at the block were equally fitful, pacing around, talking stuff, and expressing the idea that this was without a doubt the dumbest thing they'd ever done in their lives. One poor man was talking frantically into his cell phone, begging his girlfriend to please make a high bid on him. "Look, Sheila, I can't go out looking like a chump. Just make it a real high bid, baby, and I'll pay you back tonight. We'll go straight to the ATM and I'll give you cash. C'mon, Sheila, don't do this to me," he moaned. All that could be heard was her high-pitched laughter as he held the phone away from his ear. "Okay, Sheila, if that's how you want to treat me," he mumbled as he snapped the phone shut.

He turned to his fellow bachelors for support and spread his arms wide. "She's sitting out there in the front row and she's gonna look so mean nobody else will dare bid on me and I'ma end up going out for a buck two ninety-eight, just watch and see." The fact that he was a big overgrown Detroit Lions linebacker made his plight all the more pitiful.

Adam just wanted it to be over. He'd planned on picking Alicia up the way he always did, but she informed him that she was riding to the Athenaeum Hotel with Roxy and she'd meet him there. It would serve him right if she didn't show up at all, the way he'd been acting. He fully intended to apologize and throw himself at her feet to beg for mercy. He knew he'd been behaving badly, but he couldn't reconcile himself to the idea that his Alicia was making herself gorgeous for some other man, Bryant Porter to be exact. True, Bryant was back in Chicago for the moment, but he'd be back in Detroit any day now and with the warm summer months approaching there was no telling what they'd get up to. He clenched his jaw and his fists, realized he was being ridiculous, and relaxed. He looked over at Hannibal and Paul and decided they had the right idea; they seemed pretty cool about the whole thing.

He walked over to the two younger men and commented on their demeanor. "You two seem calm and collected. No nerves at all?"

Hannibal assured him he was perfectly calm. "I have a secret weapon," was all he would say.

Paul sighed deeply and shrugged. "This could be the single most stupid thing I've ever done in me life, mate. Of course, I took a page from your book and gave Rhonda a wad of money to bid on me so I wouldn't look like the most pathetic man on the stage. I also have to provide her with a ride to and from work for the next month as well as lunch, but it's a small price to pay, right?"

Adam stopped listening the moment Paul mentioned giving Rhonda money, because it was at that moment he realized that he hadn't given Alicia his checkbook. As snarky as he'd been behaving it would serve him right if she just left him dangling or worse, let some serious manhunter drag his carcass out of there as her new possession. He was about to lose his much-vaunted composure when it was Hannibal's turn onstage. He and Paul went to the wings so they could give their colleague silent support. The support wasn't needed after all, since Hannibal wasn't kidding about having a secret weapon.

After Michaela, acting as the mistress of ceremonies, introduced Hannibal, giving his vital statistics and a brief background, she asked if there was anything he wanted to share with the ladies before the bidding began. He nodded and took the microphone from her, dropping a brief kiss on her hand. He then said he had a dedication for all the beautiful women in attendance and began to sing the immortal R&B classic, "A Song For You." It was enough that he was over six feet tall, slender, and nicely muscled under his tuxedo, that he had deep brown skin and perfectly cut hair to go with his neat moustache and goatee, but the voice that was coming out of him was so beautiful it would make angels weep to hear it. The bidding started immediately and by the time the song was finished, it was up to twenty-five hundred dollars. Rhonda even got caught up, much to Paul's chagrin.

"Hey, that's my money she's bidding with, that twit!" he said in outrage. With a resigned look he turned to Adam. "I'm dead meat, you know."

"Don't worry about it, man. Just be yourself and smile and it'll be over before you know it," he advised.

Soon, it was Adam's turn onstage and he had to take his own advice. He'd opted for a classic look: his father's custom-tailored white silk dinner jacket with tuxedo trousers and the traditional pleated shirt with onyx studs. He couldn't stand wearing ties, however, and the shirt was open with the tie undone as if it were waiting for the soft hands of his woman to tie it for him. Although Adam was far from a hermit, there were a lot of people, particularly women, who hadn't seen him since the haircut, so when he walked out onstage there was quite a hubbub. He looked so incredibly handsome and debonair no one could tell that he was wishing he was somewhere in a remote Himalayan village where no one had ever heard of bachelor auctions, sororities, or formal balls.

He took center stage with his normal aplomb and hoped against hope that Alicia was out there and would have his back. The mistress of ceremonies went into her spiel and Adam braced himself for what would come next.

"Ladies, this is Adam Cochran, a partner Cochran and Fuentes, a leading architectural firm based right here in Detroit. Adam enjoys all kinds of music, especially jazz and Latin; he likes to ski, loves to ride horseback and swim, and has a passion for excellent food. So if there are any cooks out there, this might be your chance to impress him with a really good meal," she said with a sultry wink.

Before she could ask if Adam had any comments the bidding began. "Five hundred dollars," a voice rang out.

"Six hundred!"

"Seven hundred and fifty! And I can *cook*, too, honey," a loud woman informed the audience.

The bidding was getting more and more frantic and Adam was starting to feel distinctly uneasy because he still couldn't see Alicia in the crowd. All at once a flash of color in the tedious sea of black and white caught his eye. A sudden hush fell over the audience as everyone else could see what he was seeing; it was Alicia, walking toward the stage as though she had nothing else to do for the rest of her life. She was wearing the most incredible smile he'd ever seen and a dress that defied all description. Her shining hair was artfully arranged off her face and her sensual beauty radiated through the entire ballroom. In a clear voice she placed the bid that people would be talking about for years to come.

"Five thousand dollars. Cash," she said confidently, fanning the crisp new bills out with one sure move of her right hand.

A collective "Ooh" rippled across the room as her words resonated.

Adam didn't hesitate; he went to the edge of the stage and descended the stairs, walking out to meet her. He took the red rose from his buttonhole and kissed it before putting it in the V of her neckline. Then he cupped her face in his hands and kissed her slowly and gently.

Michaela recovered from a near-swoon at the romantic scene and finally reacted like a proper emcee. "All-*righty* then, I guess that's a done deal. I don't think we'll be seeing Mr. Cochran up here next year. Somebody please go get that money from her before she drops it," she said briskly.

Adam and Alicia were making a hasty exit from the ballroom when Darcy Hamilton stepped directly in front of them. She had a hand on one slender hip and a quirky grin as she looked at Adam and said, "Well, I guess the best man won."

Roxy distracted Alicia's attention from Darcy by handing her the long silk evening coat she'd worn. "I'll get your car back to you tomorrow, honey. In the meantime, you have a good night. Looks like you've got a spa day coming—on me."

In a very short time they were in Adam's loft. They hadn't really spoken a word on the way there, but Adam hadn't let go of her hand during the ride. They rode the elevator to the top floor of the building in silence, but it was a silence full of meaning. When they were finally in the cavernous loft, Adam took her wrap and looked her over as if she were a rare work of art, taking in every nuance of her beauty from her glossy hair to her slender feet. She was wearing dangerously high stiletto-heeled red sandals in silk shantung with silk ribbons that wrapped around her slender ankles, and he had a sudden urge to see her in those shoes and nothing else. "Alicia, you look incredible. I don't know enough words to tell you how beautiful you are."

"Thank you, Adam. So are you," she said shyly.

Adam put her coat away and took off his dinner jacket while he was caressing her with his eyes. "Allie, walk for me, please. I have to see you move in that dress again," he said in a deep sexy voice that was much more revealing than his normal tone. He leaned against the door and prepared to watch her graceful body move just for him. She surprised him, though, when she made a half pirouette and stopped.

"I do my best work with music," she said seductively.

"Then music you shall have," he agreed. He quickly used the remote to find the right CD among those in rotation and soon Norah Jones's raspy, sexy voice was serenading them. He also lit several scented candles and opened the custom-made French doors that led out into the roof garden. Then he turned to Alicia and asked her to walk again and this time she did, moving seductively toward him with the skirt's panels swaying around her long, shapely legs. She sashayed across the cavernous living area of the loft like something out of one of Adam's most erotic fantasies, letting the seductive skirt do its work. Suddenly she spun around again and held her slender arms out to him.

"Dance with me, Adam, we didn't get a chance to dance tonight."

"Anything you want, baby."

He pulled her into his arms and had to catch his

breath as she melted against him. She felt so good in his arms, so right. Her scent surrounded him and created a cocoon of desire he never wanted to leave. There was nothing in the world outside of the loft, no one in the world except the woman in his arms. If all life had ceased to exist at that moment, he would have known total satisfaction, but life had something better in store for him. The song on the CD changed and he could feel Alicia smile against his chest. It was one of her favorite songs by Norah Jones, "What Am I to You?" The song was a conversation between lovers wherein a woman is asking her man what she means to him and she describes what he is to her.

Alicia pulled away from him far enough to look into his eyes and with a playful smile and sweet eyes she asked, "What am I to you, Adam?"

"Everything. You're everything to me, Allie, you're my whole world." His eyes were heavy with passion and his skin was on fire with desire as he watched her eyes fill with sudden tears.

He kissed her tears away and followed the soft caress of her cheekbones with a deep kiss, the kind of kiss he'd been burning to give her for so long. Their mouths opened at the same time, the better to intensify the explosion that was building. The dancing stopped but another dance began as they started tearing each other's clothes off. Adam could vaguely hear the onyx studs landing on the hardwood floor as Alicia pulled the shirt away from his body, but his mind was on getting her out of the red dress. He found the single hook at the back of her neck and was delighted to discover that the stretchy dress slipped down her body like the peel of a ripe banana.

When he realized how little she was wearing underneath the dress, he picked her up and carried her into the bedroom while their lips were still locked together. The frantic striptease continued as he pushed the dress down her slender hips and watched it gently puddle around her feet. She stood before him clad only in those dangerous shoes and a seductive pair of red-lace boy shorts that exposed her perfect rear end. He laid her down on the bed and removed his shirt, then the rest of his clothing so when he joined her on the bed, he was naked and magnificently aroused. They held each other closely for a moment, kissing and caressing each other with their eyes wide open to fully savor their desire. He stroked her shoulders and her breasts, then bent his head to her aching nipples and caressed them with his tongue while sliding his hands down her torso. As sexy as she looked in the incredible underwear, right now he wanted it off. He wanted nothing touching her except his hands.

He stopped the passionate kisses long enough to remove her delicate shoes, followed by the panties. Alicia was beside herself with desire; she was shaking with the need to be one with Adam. He kissed his way up her body until their lips were almost joined, stopping only long enough to retrieve a foil packet from the nightstand next to the bed. He slid the latex condom on, then pulled Alicia back into his arms, rolling over on her gently so she could get used to his full weight on her body. She sighed with happiness as she felt the warm weight of him on top of her. She opened her legs and wrapped their silken length around him, helping him to enter her love-moist body and make them one.

He pushed slowly, to give her time to become accustomed to his length. With excruciating tenderness he joined their bodies until the sensual movements of her hips proved too much for him and their rhythm quickened in mutual urgency. His powerful thrusts increased until their bodies were rocking at the threshold of a sensation so powerful it shook them into spasms of ecstasy at the same time, the sweet torture giving way to a hot climax that left them shuddering, sweaty, and complete.

Adam held Alicia tightly as the aftershocks continued to rock them. Their bodies continued to move against each other, the sensual twisting and writhing that increased the pleasure they were feeling and presaged more of the same. Adam could feel his body renewing its need for Alicia. The sinuous movements of her hips, the silken tightness of her vaginal walls clutching him, and her cries of satisfaction were starting him on another passionate plunder of her treasures, but first he had to tell her, he had to let her know. He placed one hand under her chin and kissed her hard, then whispered, "Open your eyes, Allie. I love you, baby, I love you." He repeated the words until the sensations made speech impossible.

With every word he stroked harder and deeper and together they rode another convulsive climax to a shuddering completion that left them bathed in sweat and shaking from release. Gradually, the pulsing slowed down; their heartbeats regained a more normal pattern and their pants of pleasure slowed to more normal breaths. Alicia loosed her long legs from their grip around Adam's body and slid them down so they were entwined with his, although neither one of them moved to break their most intimate connection. They smiled ravishing smiles at each other and kissed very gently, once, then twice.

Adam smoothed her hair away from her face and kissed her brow. Shifting gently so she was on top of him, he cradled her against his big chest. They held each other without saying a word for a long time, just loving the intimate embrace and reveling in the warm closeness. Adam kissed her hair, stroked her back and arms and softly said her name. "Allie?"

Without realizing it she pushed closer to him, stroking his arm and rubbing her head against his neck for the sheer enjoyment of feeling his skin next to hers, loving the scent of him, the taste of his sweaty skin as she ran her tongue across his collarbone. Finally she whispered a response. "Yes, Adam?"

"Everything okay?"

Alicia smiled and buried her face in his neck. She kissed his neck and shoulder, and then rose up so she could look into his eyes while her hands clung to his shoulders. "Everything is better than okay, Adam," she said softly. "I haven't felt like this since . . . ever. This is better than I remembered, Adam. Better than I imagined, better than I dreamed." She cuddled into his shoulder again and ran her hand over his free arm, the one that wasn't holding her against him.

"You know I love you, right?" he asked quietly, bringing his other arm around her and holding her even closer.

She smiled sleepily at his words. "Yes, I do. And I love you right back, with all my heart. I've been in love with you for a long time, Adam."

"Yes, but I loved you first," Adam said softly.

Alicia moved so she was straddling him, looking down into his eyes with a mischievous, sexy smile. "Prove it, Adam. Love me again so I'll know for sure," she whispered.

Adam tightened his grasp on her and reversed their positions so quickly she gasped. "Your every wish is my command, my love." And he began to love her all over again until they were both too weak to move. They fell asleep in each other's arms, sated, completed, and one.

Chapter Ten

A few hours later they had slept in each other's arms, made love several more times, and had a long, sexy shower together, which led to more passionate interplay. Now they were relaxed on Adam's huge bed, Alicia in one of his T-shirts and him wearing a towel around his waist. He was feeding her slices of kiwi fruit with his fingers and she was holding an icy bottle of spring water from which she was taking sips between bites of the cold, sweet fruit. She said she'd had enough and Adam popped the last piece into his mouth, watching her as she looked around his room.

"I like this room, Adam. Although it might be difficult to have overnight guests," she teased.

The sleeping area of the loft was separated from the rest of the loft by a wall of glass bricks. There was no door per se, and the area could be entered on either side of the wall simply by walking around it. The wall didn't extend all the way up to the high ceiling, either; it was ten feet high and about twelve feet long. The bed that he'd designed occupied the unconventional space. It was a platform bed and the platform was also made of glass bricks wired for illumination, so that with the throw of a switch the base of the bed would light with a soft glow that emulated candlelight. The mattress was a California king, a huge expanse that was like floating on a giant raft.

There was very little furniture in the room, just a nightstand to one side of the bed and a long dresser against the wall. A beautiful wool carpet with a subtle abstract pattern in muted tones provided the only color in the room; there weren't even paintings on the brick walls. There were tall palm trees in each of the huge industrial windows that were across the back wall of the bedroom, but those were at Alicia's insistence. She'd forced him into having plants by sending them over as a housewarming gift. Left to his own devices, he wouldn't have had one bit of green anywhere, but he conceded that they made the space more eye appealing.

She stared brazenly at Adam as he rose to remove the black lacquer tray from the bed and return it to the kitchen. She loved looking at his long, muscular legs and torso. His body was like a huge, glistening sculpture in motion. A sudden burst of giggles made him return her look with one of his own. "What's so funny, Allie?"

"I was just thinking about last night at the auction. I'll bet people are still talking about it," she said with a smile. "Especially Miss Darcy Hamilton." Sitting straight up, she suddenly looked puzzled. "What did she mean about the best man winning, anyway? She said that to you last night. Was she calling me a big ol' horsy broad or something?"

Adam gave a wry snort as he went over to the dresser to retrieve a large leather chest from its center. He placed it on the end of the bed in front of Alicia and sat down behind her, spreading his legs wide so they cradled hers and pulling her flush against his bare chest. "She was referring to me, sweetie. Darcy wasn't interested in me, she was after *you*, Allie."

Allie was perfectly still while she strove to understand what Adam was saying. "Oh. *Ohh,*" she said as light finally dawned. "Well, I never . . ." she muttered as she handed Adam the bottle of water to put on the nightstand.

"And you never will, not as long as there's breath in

my body," he vowed as he inhaled the traces of her delicate fragrance.

"Adam, what's in the box?" she asked curiously.

He was so preoccupied with stroking Alicia's hair he didn't answer her question. He loved burying his hands and face in it and inhaling the sweetness that was hers alone.

"You can never run away from me," he whispered. "If you were in a dark forest and I was blindfolded, I could still find you, Allie. Your smell is imprinted on me."

Alicia sighed with pleasure as she felt his warm, sweet breath on her neck and his big hands on her shoulders. She closed her eyes and arched her back against him, her breathing becoming erratic as her desire grew. "Adam," she whispered.

"Yes, Allie?" His tone of voice was innocent, as though he was unaware of the effect he was having on her. He could see her nipples pointing through the thin cotton of the T-shirt and he knew she was more than aroused. He slid his hands under the loose shirt and captured her breast with his left hand. With his right, he searched her feminine recess to find her wet and yearning for his touch. He fondled her breast, squeezing and manipulating the now blossoming nipple, and with the other hand he found her most sensitive spot, the place that would bring her the most pleasure. He used his long fingers to stroke and coax the hot wet jewel until he could feel the gush of moisture that signaled a nearing completion.

Alicia's breathing turned into rapid pants as the sensations he was creating turned her body into a pulsing fountain of desire so keen it was almost painful. She turned her head to the side and he bent to her, capturing her lips and imprisoning her mouth with his tongue. Her moans turned to cries of heated passion as his two middle fingers entered her canal and his thumb continued to bring her to a shattering orgasm that had her screaming with pleasure.

As the tremors subsided Alicia was a little embarrassed. She tried to avoid his eyes as she gently pulled away from his embrace, but Adam would not be denied. He tightened his arms around her to prevent her escape.

"Where are you going?"

"To bathe and to hide my face," she mumbled.

He turned her around to face him. "What's wrong, Allie? I hope you aren't embarrassed. There's nothing we can do together that should ever cause you any shame, just pleasure."

She could feel her cheeks heating up at his words. "I've never done anything like that before. It was different for me. Wonderful," she added hastily, "but different. It was . . . I just felt so, so *exposed*, I think that's the word I'm looking for."

"Exposed because I was watching you and I could see how much you liked it?"

"Yes," she admitted.

"Well, I *was* watching you. It's extremely arousing to watch your pleasure; it's beautiful and very sexy. Is that embarrassing to you?"

She leaned forward and kissed him very softly. "No, actually it didn't embarrass me and that's *why* I was embarrassed. Because I should have been." To her surprise Adam enfolded her in his arms and laughed very gently.

"It's that Catholic school upbringing, baby. We have years of conditioning to undo," he teased.

Alicia turned around completely so she was facing him in a kneeling position. "Oh yeah? So you think I'm an uptight little schoolgirl, do you?" She whipped the T-shirt off and stared at him boldly, letting her eyes roam all over his bronzed body. With a sly smile she divested him of the towel and released his massive erection, taking it in both her hands.

Adam watched her with a lazy smile and eyes half closed from enjoyment. His long lashed lifted in surprise as he realized what was about to happen.

"We repressed schoolgirls like to watch too," Alicia purred.

No more words were spoken except his voice calling her name, hoarse with ecstasy.

The morning was waning into afternoon when they finally managed to get dressed. After a short nap, a long shower, and a quick meal, Alicia was attired in some old sweatpants of Adam's, rolled up several times, and another T-shirt. Adam was similarly dressed and they both looked like bums, but neither of them cared what they looked like, they were too pleased to be together. Now it was time to discover what was in the mysterious chest. This time Adam carried it into the portion of the loft that was outfitted as a study, announcing he couldn't trust her in the bedroom. A broad window seat upholstered in gray Ultrasuede ran the length of a wall under the huge industrial windows in the brick wall. There were a huge antique oak desk and big oak bookcases salvaged from a library that served as a wall to separate the area from the rest of the living space.

Alicia sat cross-legged on the window seat and Adam put the chest in front of her, as he sat Indian style across from her. "Open it."

She smoothed her palms over the supple, polished leather and admired its beauty. "This is incredible. Where in the world did you get it?"

"I had it made. I needed something very special for the contents of this box and I couldn't find anything unique enough. So I designed it and had someone make it for me. Open it," he said patiently.

She lifted the lid and was struck by the exquisite construction of the box. It was burnished golden brown leather on the outside and the interior was ostrich skin, except for the lid and the bottom, which were lined with rich brown velvet. Whatever she was expecting it to contain was certainly not what was resting in the chest. There were a packet of postcards tied with a red ribbon, a stack of letters held with an orange ribbon, a small bundle of what looked like ticket stubs confined with a peacock-blue band that looked like one she used to wear in her hair, and a plethora of other items including a leather-bound book of some kind. Alicia blinked slowly and stared at the unusual arrangement.

"Well, I'll bite. What is all this, Adam?"

He smiled and handed her the packet of postcards. "That's every postcard you sent me from Costa Rica and every other place you've ever been since I met you," he said quietly. "This is every movie we've ever been to." He handed her the thick little bundle. "And every concert and play." He gave her another stack of tickets with a rose ribbon around them. He reached into the box and pulled out a smooth stone. "Remember the time we went to the Grand Canyon? You gave me this for some reason."

Wiping away tears, Alicia nodded. "I gave it to you because it was pretty and it looked like gold in the sunset. I just wanted you to have it. I didn't think you'd keep it."

"I keep everything you give me, Allie." He handed her a parchment document envelope fastened with a thin black ribbon. She opened it with shaking fingers to find every silly note she'd ever written to him, on notebook paper, paper napkins, takeout menus, and one that was on a small paper bag. There were also small neatly cut pieces of wrapping paper, each inscribed with a date and an occasion written in Adam's precise handwriting.

Amazingly, there was a slight redness along his cheek-bones as she stared as him. "Your gifts are always wrapped so beautifully I hate to open them and I never want to forget them," he said sheepishly.

"That's where all the ribbons came from, too." Alicia sighed. By now she was crying freely as she recognized the box for what it was, their entire life together. Adam removed the box from the window seat and put it on the floor. He extended his legs out in front of him, holding his hands out to Alicia, who promptly went into his arms.

"That was supposed to make you smile, you dope. Why are you crying?" he asked tenderly.

"I am smiling," she said through her tears. "I'm so happy I can't express it. That's the sweetest thing I've ever seen, I've never even heard of anything so romantic." She snuggled closer to him, loving the feel of his hard, strong body against hers.

"Yeah, that's me, Mr. Romance," he said mockingly. "Let me show you the best part," he said, reaching down into the chest for the leather-bound book.

Alicia sniffed and wiped her eyes as she took the book from him. Then the tears started again as she saw page after page of pictures, all of her. There she was laughing, smiling, looking serious as she pored over her studies, in ridiculous poses on trips they'd taken together. There were a few shots of the two of them together and some with other family members, but for the most part it was just page after page of Alicia, a ten-year span of her life captured for his eyes only. There were even a few sketches he'd done of her, when and where she couldn't imagine.

"Adam, I don't know what to say," she whispered.

"Say you love me. I like the way that sounds," he told her, kissing away her tears. "Say you'll come away with me, right now."

"I love you. I'll go anywhere with you." She sniffed. She kissed him back, little nibbling kisses on his jaw and chin and lips. "Where are we going?"

"Idlewild. Let's get going before you try to have your way with me again. For a repressed schoolgirl you're pretty scandalous."

"You taught me everything I know," she assured him. "Let's go now, because I feel the urge for another lesson coming on."

Within a few hours they were on their way to Idlewild for the weekend. After Adam packed the things he would need, they drove over to the condo Alicia shared with Marielle. As Roxy promised, the Mini Cooper was in its usual parking space when they pulled up. Marielle was lounging on the patio with a stack of magazines and a pitcher of iced tea when they arrived, but she rose to greet them with a smile.

She took note of Alicia's incongruent outfit of giant sweatpants rolled up so she wouldn't trip over them, the scandalous sandals, and the oversized T-shirt of Adam's. "Someone's been up to something, I'd say. Where's my dress?" she asked with a wicked grin.

"We dropped it at the dry cleaner's on the way over here. Where are the kids?" Alicia looked around for her niece and nephew, who were normally gamboling around like puppies.

"They're spending the weekend with Gigi, bless her heart. I'm doing absolutely nothing but sleeping for the next three days." Marielle sighed.

"Come help me pack," Alicia begged. "That way I'll be out of your hair quicker."

Marielle agreed but couldn't resist a dig. "Speaking of hair, what happened to yours? It look's like a sheep's butt."

Leaving Adam on the patio to take advantage of the chaise longue, the two women went to gather a few things for Alicia. Marielle was also kind enough to bump a few curls into Alicia's hair to tame it a bit. "I was kidding, it didn't look that bad. But you need to get in the habit of keeping a few hair products over at the loft so you can repair the ravages of passion. I vaguely remember what a night of good hot sex can do to a hairdo." She looked at Alicia closely and smiled. "And it was *good* and hot, wasn't it? It's about time," she said carelessly.

Alicia tried to be shocked at the frankness of her sister's comments, but Marielle had never been one to pull her punches. She'd always been a straightforward, earthy woman, much like their mother. "You don't seem surprised, I must say. And you don't seem to disapprove."

Marielle looked at her younger sister and her face softened. "*Chica,* just because my own marriage was a total disaster doesn't mean I've turned into a bitter old broad. There's nothing wrong with being in love and being happy. It was just a matter of time before you and Adam realized you were meant for each other," she told her. "You guys go off and have a wonderful weekend together. The real fun will start when you get back and the aunts start planning your wedding." She laughed.

Adam had more than one occasion to wonder what she was smiling at as they drove north out of the city. As usual on any holiday weekend, the expressway was bumper to bumper with folks heading to northern Michigan where campgrounds, summer cottages, and cabins awaited them. The traffic didn't bother Adam with Alicia by his side, looking adorable in nicely fitting, well-worn jeans, running shoes, and a man-tailored white shirt. He loved the way she would stroke his arm when she made a comment, the way her hand rested on his thigh when they were silent. He just loved being with her, period.

"And you're sure your family isn't going to mind you not being there for the cookout?" Alicia asked for the third time. His father, Big Benny Cochran, hosted a legendary Memorial Day cookout every year, and the tradition had passed on to Donnie and Angelique since they were now living in the big Palmer Park home. Alicia had voiced her concern about him being a no-show, especially since his only sister, Benita, would be in town with her husband and children and they didn't get to visit often. Adam appreciated her concern but didn't share it. Lacing his fingers in her hand, he brought it up to his mouth and kissed it before reassuring her.

"Allie, that's one of the advantages of belonging to a large family. There's so many of you no one's sure if you're there or not. We won't be missed, trust me. And there's no place I want to be more than right here with you. If it's a choice between a long weekend with the woman I love and a horde of screaming Cochrans, what do you think I'm going to choose? Besides, Benita and Clay will be here for a week. We'll have plenty of time to see her and those BLKs. We'll have a party at the loft later in the week and have everyone over. That should make up for my absence. If anyone notices I'm gone, that is."

Alicia was satisfied, although she had a question. "What are BLKs?"

"Bad Little Kids, that's what. I love 'em to death, but those twins are a mess. So don't worry about this weekend, let's just concentrate on each other, okay?"

She smiled. "It sounds like a perfect plan."

Chapter Eleven

Martha Davis Cochran looked at her husband with worry in her eyes. She was always concerned about his health, especially his blood pressure. Andrew Bernard Cochran Sr. was in good health but he had a volatile temperament that could leap out of control at a moment's notice. He was already nervous about what he was about to do, and Martha didn't like the effect it was having on his blood pressure.

"Ben, honey, are you sure you want to do it this way? Maybe there's another way it could be handled," she said quietly.

They were sitting in the sunny breakfast room off the kitchen of their former home. Big Benny had an announcement to make and he wanted all his children present when he did. He was already irritated that Adam, his next-to-youngest child, wasn't present, but he was determined to get it over with. The cookout wasn't until Monday, but everyone was having brunch together on this Saturday morning and he wanted to get it over with before the weekend really got under way. He looked at his lovely wife and patted her hand in reassurance.

"Martha, it needs to be said and be done. I've waited long enough to handle my business and it's not like I have a whole lot of time left to get my affairs in order. I can't think of a better way to do it and that's a fact. I just figured it was better to have everyone in one room and tell them all at once. The only reason I told Donnie's wife anything was that I needed a way to get the ball rolling, so to speak. And she was a good person to confide in. She only told her husband, and that's what I wanted her to do, anyway." He looked over at Martha and smiled. "Not sorry you married me, are you?"

Martha took his hand in a tight grip. "Absolutely not and don't you ever ask me that again. You know how much I love you, Ben. Marrying you was the best decision I've ever made. The past five years have been the joy of my life. As for your announcement, it was something that happened a long time ago and it doesn't affect how you feel about any of them, so they will understand. This could be a wonderful thing, in fact, for everyone concerned."

Big Benny squeezed her hand in return. "I just hope you're right, because it's going to happen whether they like it or not. But I could wring Adam's neck, I really could. Of all the weekends for him to go wandering off, he had to pick this one. Well, it's just too bad, I'm getting this over with today."

"Adam, that lady is following us. I swear she is," Alicia whispered. They were sitting in Jones's Ice Cream Parlor in downtown Baldwin eating the best ice cream she'd ever tasted when she noticed the older woman. Adam glanced in the woman's direction and raised an eyebrow at Alicia.

"Baby, why on earth would someone be following us? Unless she mistook us for someone else."

"Oh, I'm just kidding, you know that. But I've seen her at least three of the places we've been today, and we've been a lot of places," she said. "I saw her at the grocery store, I saw her when we went to Patti's Drugstore, and I swear she was at Road Runners, too." Alicia had been totally taken with the venerable store that had served several generations of Idlewilders. The selection of goods available was amazing in the small store, everything from beverages to imported African clothing and hair-care products. Alicia pulled down the brim of her new Negro League baseball cap, bought at Road Runners, and harrumphed as she went back to eating her ice cream and looking at some of the pamphlets she'd picked up at the chamber of commerce.

It had been a long and wonderful day. She was surprised at all the changes that the spring weather had made in Idlewild. The trees were in full leaf and wildflowers were blooming and she could see the true beauty of Lake County all around her. "Adam, it's so beautiful here," she marveled. "All these trees, all the lakes, it's so fresh and peaceful. I've never seen anything quite like it."

They had driven slowly through Idlewild, looking at the houses and cottages that dotted the heavily wooded resort town. The thing that amazed her were the houses that encircled the lakes. You could be driving down a path that looked like it led to nowhere and suddenly there you were in a lane with a row of houses. The backs of the houses looked like normal, everyday cottages with an occasional two-story thrown in here and there. But the fronts of the houses faced the lake and there was usually a long set of steps that led down to a pier that extended out into the lake, a lake that was clear and inviting and serene.

"There's a lot more water this year than in years past," Adam informed her. "I heard a couple of men talking about it this morning when we were having breakfast."

After checking into the Pier Marquette Lodge the day before, they had gone to the site where the house was going to be built and Alicia was thrilled to see that the ground had been cleared for construction. Adam had designed a beautiful home, a two-story frame house with a stone foundation and fireplaces and a huge veranda that spanned the entire back of the house with a deep roof to take advantage of the fantastic Lake County summers. There was also a front porch big enough for summer entertaining. He was having three cottages built for guests, since the Cochran family was big and the growth showed no signs of flagging. "I think we'll be spending a lot of time up here, even in the winter," he said carelessly as they walked around the site, imagining what it would look like when it was completed.

Alicia got a special thrill when she heard him say those words. It seemed as though he was planning their future together. Not wanting to spoil the moment, she just smiled and marveled at the wonderful view of the lake from the property.

After their long walk around the lake, they decided to have dinner out and get groceries the next day. Neither one of them felt like cooking anything, both too eager to enjoy their private getaway. They'd had dinner in Baldwin and driven back to the motel holding hands in anticipation of the passion they knew would explode in a very short time. And like the times before, their lovemaking was intense and intimate, increasing their closeness and affection for each other. Now, as she was spooning the last bit of homemade black cherry ice cream out of the dish, she met Adam's sultry gaze across the table. The heat that he could generate in one glance was enough to melt the old-fashioned ice cream parlor chair in which she was sitting.

"Stop that," she murmured, lowering her lashes.

"Stop what? Looking at you like I wish you were that ice cream so I could lick you all over?"

Alicia's eyes widened, and then crinkled at the corners in a smile. "You shouldn't be saying things like that to me in a public place. What would someone think if they overheard you?"

"They'd think the same thing I think, that we're very lucky to have found each other," he said quietly.

He held out his big hand and she laid her small one

on top, resting it in a gesture of love and trust. She looked into his eyes and felt her heart melt at his expression, so tender and adoring.

"Adam, why didn't you say something before? Why didn't you put me out of my misery? You must have known I had feelings for you." She sighed.

Adam brought her fingers to his mouth and kissed the palm, then licked the tip of her little finger, sending a thrill up her arm that radiated all over her body. "Because, my sweet Allie, I made you a promise. I couldn't go back on my word, could I?"

"Yes, you could," she said instantly. "Mmm-mmm-*mmm*, if this is the result, you could've broken your word the next day, buddy."

Adam smiled back at her. She was teasing him and he loved it because it meant she was completely comfortable with him. "Yes, but if I'd gone back on my word the next day we might not be here now," he reminded her. "We were young and impulsive then. Now we have years of friendship and trust between us. We know each other, we respect each other, and we're ready to be in love with each other." He paused, loving the beautiful smile she was giving him. Her smile was so warm it lit him up from the inside, but it didn't prevent him from asking a question of his own. "So why didn't you say anything to me? You had to know how I felt about *you*, Allie."

She sighed deeply and laced her fingers through his, admiring the way her much smaller hand looked entwined with his. "I made a promise, too, Adam. And, like you, I consider that to be sacred, I couldn't just ignore it. And besides," she added, so low that he had to lean in close to hear it, "I was so crazy about you I couldn't stand the thought of losing you. I didn't want to risk chasing you away by coming on to you, so I made myself believe we could be friends forever. I took all those feelings and put them in a box in my head with a big padlock on it. And then I put it behind a door marked 'do not open—*ever*.'"

Adam rose from the small table and pulled her up with him. They gathered their belongings and headed out into the afternoon sunlight. He draped his arm over her shoulders and pulled her closer to him while he smiled down at her beloved face. "So what made you change your mind? What made you decide we should be together?" he asked as he kissed her cheek.

"Because I couldn't stand not having you anymore," she said honestly. "I just wanted to be with you so much I would have risked anything to make it happen."

Adam's throat constricted with emotion and he was about to drag her back to the cabin for a demonstration of how much her words had affected him when a sharp tap on his arm interrupted him.

"Excuse me, young man, but what is your name?"

An older woman put the question to him. She was dignified and attractive in appearance and obviously determined to get a response. It was impossible to determine her age. She could have been anywhere from fifty to eighty years old. Her medium brown skin was unlined, although her short, nicely styled hair was white. Her posture was erect and she was a tall, handsome woman, almost as tall as Alicia with the same kind of athletic grace about her. Adam tried not to let his surprise show as he graciously answered, "I'm Adam Brantley Cochran, ma'am."

To his utter shock the woman turned pale and covered her mouth. She rallied at once and said, "You come with me, right now. My car is across the street. You just follow me, please."

Adam and Alicia looked at each other for a few seconds before doing exactly what the woman said. It wasn't until they were under way in the Range Rover that Alicia reminded him of her earlier remark. "I told you she was following us."

He conceded she was right, but asked rhetorically, "Yes, but where is she *leading* us?"

* * *

Adam's question was answered in a very short time. The woman led them into Idlewild, through a densely wooded area, turning into a neat lane with a cluster of small houses on either side of the road. She deftly steered her car into the driveway of a small robin's-egg-blue cottage with bright blue trim. There were flowering shrubs and a neat border of flowers all the way around the house. The woman led them up the stairs to a glassed-in front porch that was rather like a sun parlor with two comfortable-looking settees, well-tended green plants, and magazines displayed on a small table. Stepping over the frantically barking schnauzer who accosted them in the doorway, she ushered them into a cozy parlor and instructed them to sit. She turned on the anxious dog, who was sizing Adam up as if to decide which limb to take a bite out of first.

"Dusty, you little ring-tailed baboon, sit down and at least pretend to be civilized," she said sternly as she left the room.

The dog sighed deeply and hung his head for a second, then seemed to brighten up as he realized he had company. Adopting a winsome grin, he trotted over to Alicia and sat down with his paw out to shake. Alicia laughed and shook his paw before taking a seat as she was bid, although Adam continued to stand. The room was utterly lovely and homey, warm and sweet with the fresh, earthy smell scent of houseplants and potpourri.

There were two side-by-side wing chairs separated by a lovely mahogany table with an antique lamp on its shining surface, a large television, a plump sofa with inviting pillows, and a beautiful wooden bench with ornate scrolling and Florentine-finished leather padding on the back and seat. Two tall bookcases flanked the large window and were filled with family pictures, shelf after shelf of memories. Adam and Alicia could hear the woman's voice as she left the room, calling to an unseen person. "Mother, Geneva was right. Come here, Mother, I want you to meet someone," she said, her voice shaking with emotion.

Alicia stared at Adam, who was looking around the charmingly decorated room with an unreadable expression on his face. She was about to say something to him when the woman returned, accompanied by the unmistakable scrape-roll, scrape-roll of a walker. The woman stopped dramatically in the wide doorway of the living room and gestured to the smaller woman at her side. "Adam Brantley Cochran, this is your great-*great*-aunt Emmaline, your grandmother's sister. And I'm your great-aunt Reba," she added. "Welcome home."

Chapter Twelve

Adam couldn't have been more surprised if he'd been told that the elderly woman was the Dalai Lama. He tried to cover his shock as Aunt Emmaline scrape-rolled across the carpet to stand in front of him. The look on her face was so naked with elation it was hard for him to react, but she made it unnecessary. Clasping her small wrinkled hands together, she stared up at him as though she'd been awaiting his arrival for years.

"Well, bless my soul," she breathed. "You look just like your daddy did when he was a young man. I thought I'd never see any of my family again and here you are." She sniffed and wiped away a tear, then turned to Reba. "Let him sit down, Reba, him and his wife. My goodness, they must think we have no manners at all," she fussed.

Reba quickly got Aunt Emmaline situated in one of the wing chairs, and Alicia moved to the couch with Adam preparing to follow her. "Oh, please, sit over here." Aunt Emmaline indicated the other wing chair. "I want to take a good long look at you, son. It's been so long I thought I would make my transition before I ever saw Andrew or his family and here you are!" The joy in her voice was evident and Adam had no choice but to take the seat she indicated.

Reba sat on the sofa and gave Alicia a comforting look that said she understood their confusion. "I think an explanation is in order," was her understatement. "My sister-in-law Francine was Andrew's mother. An-

drew left here years and years ago after a terrible dis-
agreement and he hasn't been back since. There were
three girls and one boy in our family. My brother,
Calvin Cochran, married Francine Brantley and had
Andrew Bernard. There was another child who died
in childhood and so it was as if Andrew was an only
child. Francine doted on him so it was a wonder he
could breathe," she said ruefully.

"Anyway, when Andrew came of age, something happened to drive a wedge between him and the family and
I'm sorry to say it made him leave town, never to return.
He came back only once during all this time. We always
heard he had family somewhere in Detroit, but we never
knew how to contact them and never knew if we *should*,
frankly. A few weeks ago Geneva Williams, a busybody if
ever one lived, told us that she'd sold some lake property
to a young man named Cochran, but we thought it was
a coincidence. There wasn't any real resemblance,
Geneva said, the man had a long ponytail or some such
and we knew he couldn't be Andrew's child."

She paused and took another long look at Adam, who
was staring at his aunt Emmaline in shock. "But when I
saw you in the grocery store today, I knew it had to be
you. You look so much like your father it's amazing.
There was no way you could be anything but a Cochran,
the son of my only brother's only child." She stood up
and went to the bookshelf nearest her and took a pho-
tograph from the middle shelf, handing it first to Alicia, who gasped aloud. It was Big Benny, taken years and
years before, and from the tilt of his head to the rakish
grin on his face, the young man in the picture was the
very spirit and image of Adam.

"Oh, my goodness. You really do look just like Big
Benny," Alicia said as she stared at the picture, then at
Adam.

"Like who, dear?" asked Reba.

Adam finally found his voice. "My father, Big Benny

Cochran," he said quietly. "No one ever calls him Andrew, he's known as Benny Cochran. In fact, my sister
Benita is also called Bennie as a nickname."

Emmaline smiled happily and reached for Adam's
hand, which he extended over the small lamp table.
"How many children does he have, dear?"

Adam rubbed his thumb against the delicate warmth
of the older woman's hand. "There are six of us, Aunt
Emmaline. Benita and Andrew are the oldest, they're
twins, just like Alan and Andre, who come next. Then
there's the youngest, my brother Adonis, and me," he
told her. He almost hated to impart the information
since it was painfully obvious that until this day he had
no idea his father had any relatives. Emmaline was delighted with the news, however.

"*Six* children? My goodness, he made up for being an
only child, didn't he? Any grandchildren?" she asked
hopefully.

Adam smiled at her eagerness. "He has fourteen
grandchildren. Benita and her husband have five children, Andrew has four, Alan and Andre each have two,
and Adonis and his wife have a six-month-old baby."

Emmaline's old eyes glowed with delight at the news.
"And you and your lovely wife, when are you expecting?"

Reba put one hand over her mouth and laughed
heartily. "My heavens, your wife is going to think we
are true barbarians! Child, forgive us, we're just so excited at seeing our kin again we forgot ourselves. What
is your name, dear?"

Alicia patted the older woman's arm to show she
wasn't offended in the least. "My name is Alicia Fuentes,
but Adam and I aren't married, we're, um, business partners," she finished lamely with a look at Adam, who was
enjoying her discomfiture.

He didn't do anything to help the situation by giving
her another blazingly hot smile and caressing her with

his eyes. "Alicia and I are architects and we have a firm in Detroit," he informed his aunts.

Aunt Emmaline seemed possessed of the kind of insight that only very elderly women seem to have, for she just nodded and turned her gaze from Adam to Alicia. "Business partners. Is that what they're calling it down state these days?" she asked archly. "Down state" was how people who lived in northern Michigan referred to the rest of the state. She gave Alicia a good look-over and commented that she'd heard the name Fuentes before. "There was a wonderful ballplayer named Jose Ernesto Fuentes who played for the Detroit Tigers back in the day. My goodness, that was a good-looking man!"

Alicia beamed so brightly that all thirty-two of her perfectly white teeth showed. "That's my daddy," she said proudly.

Reba laughed out loud. "Oh, well, now you've started something. Mother loves her some baseball. So you mean those two pretty Fuentes boys that play for the Tigers now, those are your brothers?"

"Yes, ma'am, Raphael and Carlos are my brothers."

"Well, my goodness, isn't that something? Please, let me get you all something to eat," Reba suggested.

"Only if you let me help," Alicia said quickly. They stood up and Reba led the way to the spacious kitchen followed by Alicia, who heard Aunt Emmaline tell Adam that he'd better hurry up and marry Alicia because they were certainly going to have some pretty babies. Given the oddness of the day, it was an entirely appropriate remark.

The Saturday brunch was a huge success, as was any meal shared by the Cochrans. All the men loved to eat and were lucky enough to have found wives who loved to cook. Angelique Cochran, the newest bride, was a fine cook, but today she had plenty of help from her sisters-in law and her mother, Lillian, who was visiting from Atlanta. Working together they had prepared a southern feast of scrambled eggs, bacon, sausage, fried chicken, cheese grits, hash browns, tossed salad, fried corn, squash casserole, asparagus tips, fruit salad, hot biscuits, cinnamon rolls, and muffins. Everyone ate until they were satisfied and the men cleaned up the kitchen afterward with fulsome praise from the women. The children were playing in the family room; the smallest children were napping in the bedroom with the exception of Lily Rose, who was taking a nap on her uncle Clay's shoulder. The adults had assembled in the living room at Big Benny's request.

He looked at his family scattered around the big living room of the Palmer Park home. He'd always taken great pride in his children, although he had his own ways of showing it when it came to his only daughter, Benita. He'd been too possessive of her, too controlling, and he'd almost lost her as a result. Thank God he'd learned that loving meant letting go, and she was the one who'd taught him that. Benita was seated next to her husband, Clayton Deveraux, and it was obvious to anyone who saw them that they were more deeply in love than they were when they met and married. She hardly looked a day older although Clayton had a generous amount of gray hair now, due, he always said, to their lively boys.

He proudly surveyed his other children: Andrew and his wife, Renee; Alan and Andre with their wives, Tina and Faye; and his youngest child, Adonis Cochran, with his bride, Angelique. Everyone was there except Adam, his maverick son. It was annoying that he was a no-show, but that was Adam for you; there was never any use predicting what he was going to do. Benny wanted them all together, but too bad. He had to get it said while the resolve was there. Despite his bombastic and brusque approach to life, this was one announcement he wasn't looking forward to. It could mean the destruction of his family or signal a new beginning.

In addition to the family, his oldest and best friend, Bill "Bump" Williams, was present with his wife, Lillian Deveraux-Williams, who was Clay Deveraux's mother and Benita's mother-in-law. Bump was one of the five people in the room who shared Benny's secret; another one was Ruth Bennett, sister to his late first wife, Lillian Bennett-Cochran. He was grateful for their presence and only hoped that the repercussions from his words wouldn't affect them negatively. He glanced at his watch and gathered his thoughts; it was time.

Clearing his throat, he went to stand beside the big brick fireplace and smiled when Martha joined him. "I know you're wondering what in the world I could possibly have to say that's so important that I dragged you all in here. I have something to tell you all that's going to change all of our lives permanently. You know me, I'm not good at being diplomatic or saying things in a nice way, so I'm just going to say it outright." He paused and took his wife's hand.

"A long time ago I did something that to this day I regret because it was something that never should have happened. I loved your mother very, very much, but I wasn't always the best husband to her. I was not, I regret to say, the kind of husband that my sons are to their wives, the kind of husband that Benita has in Clay. I violated her trust in me by having an affair. And that affair led to a child, a son whom I've never acknowledged," he said quietly.

No one moved after he uttered the words, no one said anything. As the full weight of what he was saying began to sink in, the faces of his children reflected shock, surprise, and incredulity.

Big Benny looked at each of his children in turn before speaking again. "I don't think there's anything any of you can say that can make me more regretful of my behavior, but I can't spend time wallowing in guilt. What's done was done years ago and what I want to do is set the record straight and try to make up for the sins of my past. My only hope is that you can forgive me and try to understand why I did what I did, which was keep this a secret for all these years."

Alan and Andre were the first to recover their ability to speak. "Pop, are you saying we have a brother out there somewhere?" It was impossible to say which one asked the question; their voices were as identical as their faces.

"That's exactly what I'm saying, son. You have another brother. Before you ask, let me explain. His mother died shortly after giving birth to him and I arranged for the baby to be given to a couple in a private adoption. As far as I know he has no idea that he was adopted, has no idea that I'm his birth father. He's never made any move to contact me, nor has anyone else ever contacted me regarding the matter. He has no clue, no clue whatsoever that he has any tie to this family."

The siblings looked at each other and at their spouses and it was plain that all of them were trying to think of something to say. Clay's arm was around Benita's shoulders and unconsciously he pulled her closer to his side in a protective gesture. On the other end of the sofa, Renee clasped Andrew's hand in hers and squeezed it tightly, giving him all her support and love. Alan and Andre were staring at each other while communicating silently, something they'd been doing since they were children. This was a moment for the archives; the normally voluble and expressive Cochrans were temporarily struck dumb.

It was the uncharacteristic silence that roused Big Benny's legendary temper. "Have you people all gone deaf or something? I just told you all the deepest secret of my heart and you're sitting there acting like you're watching TV! Doesn't anybody have something to say?"

he asked angrily. Martha tried vainly to calm him down, but it was useless.

Andrew raised his eyebrows and said calmly, "Well, Pop, what is it that you want us to say? Do you want us to jump up and run out of the room screaming or something? You just told us that we have a brother out there somewhere. That's a lot to get used to in the what, *thirty seconds* since you dropped the bomb? Give us a minute to absorb it, why don't you?"

Alan and Andre spoke in unison, something they always did in moments of crisis. "Look, Pop, we appreciate you leveling with us about a part of your past, but we don't really know how we're supposed to react." Alan added, "It's not like he's here in front of us. That would be an entirely different set of circumstances." Andre agreed. "If there were a possibility of locating him and the necessity of forming some kind of association, that would be different. Your telling us this, it's kind of conceptual, really."

Instead of Benny's being relieved that they were taking it so calmly, the children's air of sophisticated acceptance pushed the button they all had learned to avoid over the years—the button that pushed the emotional elevator in Benny's head directly to the floor marked *rage*. "What are you babbling about? I know *who* he is and *where* he is, and as soon as I tell him who *I* am, I'm bringing him here. And then your concept becomes reality, Mr. Harvard Law Review," he snarled in the direction of Alan and Andre. "What the hell did you think, I was just going to pass a little information on to you and let it go? Of course not, you knuckleheads! I'm bringing my son home and you'd better get used to the idea."

By now his face was bright red with rage and he was definitely getting the reaction he'd anticipated. Everyone was talking at once now, hands were waving, voices were being raised, and chaos ruled. Martha sighed deeply and shook her head as she insisted that her husband sit down. Aunt Ruth dispatched someone for a glass of water, ignoring Benny's suggestion that it contain bourbon. Meanwhile Lily Rose woke up from her nap and expressed her dislike for all the yelling with some high-pitched yelling of her own. Clay nuzzled her neck and crooned to her in his deep, gravelly voice and she calmed down immediately. Lillian merely looked sideways at her husband, Bump, who was pinching the bridge of his nose and shaking his head. Finally Benita got everyone to quiet down so she could address her father.

"Daddy, I'm not even going to comment on your announcement. My brain isn't working well enough for that. But just how do you plan to approach this man? You say you arranged for him to be adopted and he doesn't know anything about it. This is going to be a huge shock for the man. What makes you think he's even going to give you the time of day? That's assuming a lot, even for you," she said pointedly.

Benny took a few grateful swallows from the icy glass Ruth handed him, frowning when he didn't detect the bracing taste of his favorite libation and handing it back to her. "That's where you come in, daughter. You're going to help me with this," he said with the benign, fatherly smile he employed only when he was trying to pull a fast one on her.

"*Me?* What have I got to do with all this? Why on earth do you think I'm going to help you approach this man and turn his life upside because you've started feeling guilty about your past?" she asked with growing heat.

Benny sat back in the leather armchair and gave her the coup de grace of smiles, the one she referred to as his "jackass eating briars" grin. "Because you know this man, Benita, and he thinks the world of you. His name is John Flores."

She instantly went pale with shock and couldn't utter a sound.

* * *

Adam was quiet on the way back to the Pier Marquette Lodge, too quiet for Alicia's comfort. When Adam was upset about something he withdrew from the world and internalized his anger, a process Alicia had become accustomed to over the years. She wasn't looking forward to a long night of silence and brooding, especially after the day they'd had. His aunts were lively, funny old ladies and they seemed to be born storytellers. They told them about Idlewild back in its heyday, about Benny Cochran when he was a child, and about their lives in general, and Alicia was simply riveted. What Adam thought about the afternoon was a mystery since he'd barely opened his mouth from the time they left the little blue cottage.

She eyed him speculatively as they entered the cabin. If he was going to sit and mope all night, she wanted no part of it. She wanted to talk to him, to verbalize her wonder at all that had happened today, but she knew him well enough to know that he was overwhelmed by the unexpected reunion. Her best course of action by far was to leave him to his thoughts.

While he sprawled out on the sofa in the living room, she announced that she was going to take a shower and went to do just that. She undressed in the bedroom they were sharing and donned a pale green terry cloth wrap before entering the spotlessly clean bathroom. After adjusting the water temperature, she put on a cute little green shower cap, took off the wrap, and got into the shower with her bottle of Algemarin bath gel. The clean scent of the gel rose as the hot water cascaded over her body and she began to relax in her enjoyment of the bathing ritual. Closing her eyes, she turned her face into the stream of water and sighed with pleasure, a sigh that turned into a yelp of surprise as Adam stepped into the tub to join her.

"You scared me," she protested even as she was admiring his long naked body. He traded places with her so that he could get wet all over, looking deeply into her eyes as he did so. "You left me," he pointed out. He reached for her and pulled her into his arms, kissing her hard and fierce. "You know I'm a moody idiot. You're supposed to love me out of it," he growled, "not leave me alone in my misery."

Alicia giggled madly as their soapy bodies rubbed together, then protested as he pulled off her shower cap. "Thanks a lot, my hair's going to be a mess tomorrow."

"I like it messy," he murmured as the water slicked her hair back and filled her lashes with big drops. "You look so hot, baby, so incredibly sexy with your hair like that." His big hands stroked her back, making firm circular motions on her bottom and anchoring her against his growing erection. She returned the favor, grabbing his hard, muscular rear end and treating it to the same caresses she was receiving. She looked up into Adam's face and melted against him. The look of love he was giving her was so profound she forgot how to breathe. He leaned down and kissed her again, this time with tenderness and passion. As he gently parted her willing lips with his tongue, Alicia trembled with delight and slid her sudsy arms up around his neck. He pulled her luscious lower lip into his mouth and groaned with pleasure as she did the same. They continued to kiss, sucking gently on each other's lips and gorging in the sheer taste of their passion.

When they finally pulled away, Alicia sighed. "I love the way you kiss me." She gently removed her arms from around his neck and kissed it, then his collarbones, and began licking her way down his chest while the water continued to flow over their bodies.

"I love the way you love me," Adam countered. "And I want it right now, so we'd better get out of here before we welcome a little bundle of joy in about nine months.

Emmaline's right, you know, we're going to make some pretty babies."

Alicia's tongue was circling his nipple with unerring erotic precision while her hands caressed his hips. His knees buckled under the twin assault and without another word he scooped her up and prepared to leave the shower with her in his arms.

"The water, Adam, turn off the water, *querida.*"

He did so with a grumble, not caring about the stupid water at a time like this. Carrying her into the bedroom, he threw a large towel across the bed before placing her on it like a precious work of art.

Alicia was about to ask for another towel when it became apparent that Adam had another idea. He turned to the small bag that contained her toiletries and pulled out her blow-dryer, something that Marielle had insisted she take although Alicia had no intention of using it. He turned off the overhead light of the bedroom, leaving them in semidarkness with only the light from the bathroom showing. After plugging it in, he adjusted the stream of air so it was on a warm setting with medium force. With a smile Alicia was beginning to understand very well, he began to direct the warm air over her waiting body, which was already beginning to tingle with anticipation. The warm stream of air played across her arms, her neck, and her stomach, making her nerves dance with delight.

When he started the soft stream over her breasts, she gripped the bedclothes and trembled from the unusual sensation, but he didn't relent. Using the blower he stroked her entire body over and over, letting the heated air caress her like a lover, gently igniting a fire everywhere it traveled. When he let it play at the apex of her thighs, she gasped aloud, calling his name.

"Adam, stop, that's not fair," she moaned.

He knelt on the floor beside the bed and turned the blow-dryer off. "What's not fair, my love? Doesn't that feel pleasant? Don't you like it?" he teased and turned her so that she was crossways on the bed with her legs hanging down. He picked up one of her long, slender feet and began kissing it, licking it across the sole and making his way up to her toes, which would have curled in appreciation if she hadn't been so limp from sensation. He continued up to her ankle, licking and kissing his path up to her knee, then the tender flesh of her inner thigh, all the while pulling her closer to the edge of the bed.

By now her breath was coming in fevered little pants, she was so aroused at the sensual onslaught to which she was being subjected. The warmth of his hands, coupled with his hot tongue, was conspiring to make her start to lose herself in ecstasy. She felt as if she were being swallowed up in a starry sky. When his seeking mouth delved into the moist opening between her thighs, the stars exploded all around her as his tongue imprisoned her, bringing her to a level of release she didn't know existed. Her hips moved in undulating circles as he plundered the honeyed sweetness he craved in an unending kiss that went on and on so long that she thought she would die from the pleasure.

After, giving her too many orgasms to count, Adam relented and began to kiss his way up her body, rising from the floor and finally arriving at her mouth, leaning over her and lifting her body so that he could join her on the bed. When they were wrapped in each other's arms and she was able to speak again, her first words were "I love you."

He grinned in the semidarkness of the room and hugged her even closer. "I know, isn't it great? Because I happen to love you, too, with all my heart," he said softly. After a few more kisses, he turned them so that they were spooned together, a position he loved. He liked the feeling of warmth and protectiveness it gave him. He planted a wet kiss at the nape of her neck and sighed.

"Allie, this has been the damnedest day of my life. I come up here to be alone with the woman I love and plan our future, and I find out that I have kinfolk here, that my father, who always said he had no relatives, has family up here. A family that he's ignored for years and years, that he's never mentioned even once. That's deep, Allie, it really is."

"Your dad never mentioned any family at all? Not once?"

Adam said no. "He never really talks about his past and we've never really asked him, to be honest. I mean, if someone says they have no family, you don't figure they're lying; you just feel kinda bad that they're all alone. We knew my mother's family, all her aunts and cousins and sisters and brothers, but no one has ever mentioned a living soul on the Cochran side of the family. And yet, there they are, two of the sweetest old ladies you ever want to meet," he said with wonder.

"*Four* ladies," Allie reminded him. Before they left that evening, Reba and Emmaline made them promise to come to church with them the next day. "You have to meet the sisters. They're on their way home from a day in Grand Rapids and they'd be crushed to miss you," Reba said. When they agreed to attend, she consulted the colorful calendar on the kitchen wall and announced that it was Church of Christ Sunday.

It seemed the ladies went to all the churches in the area on a rotating schedule. From an ecumenical standpoint, they liked to be on speaking terms with all denominations. Reba had inquired about Alicia's religious preference and nodded brightly when told she was Catholic. "I was a Catholic for a while," she approved, "but the Baptists lured me back." The older woman went deep in thought for a moment, then sighed. "That's why we go to all of them, they all have something to offer."

Adam and Alicia continued to cuddle and talk, stopping every so often for a mind-altering kiss. "So are you going to tell you family about your relatives?" she asked.

"Of course I am, but I've got to talk to Pop first. I've got to try to understand why he did this, why he acted like these people didn't exist," he said reflectively. "I've known the man all my life and for most of that time he was the biggest thing in my life, especially after my mother died. And now I feel like I don't know him at all. Not at all, Allie. This is truly the weirdest thing that's ever happened to me. I feel like I stepped into the twilight zone or something."

"Dee-dee-dee-dee, dee-dee-dee-dee," Alicia piped in a poor imitation of the theme from the cult favorite and laughed as Adam tickled her.

"Very cute. Seriously, Allie, I'm glad you were here with me. For one thing, you're a witness, so when I tell the rest of the family, they won't think I'm nuts. And for another, I'm always more grounded when you're around. You keep me sane, baby," he admitted as he nuzzled her neck.

Touched to her heart, Alicia turned in his arms so they were facing each other. "You keep me happy," she said softly. "Very happy, Adam."

"My work here is done," he said lightly, then took a sharp breath as Alicia took him in hand to provel otherwise.

"Oh, no, baby, your work has just started. It's my turn now," she said with a sultry look.

"As you wish, my love. Whatever you want, whenever you want it." He stopped speaking abruptly and his voice grew hoarse with emotion. "*Allie*," he gasped and the sounds of his passion filled the room.

Chapter Thirteen

Leah Ross Fuentes looked up with a smile when her youngest child entered the family room. She and her husband were relaxing on the sofa, watching a movie when Alicia called and said she was on the way over. Judging from the look on her daughter's face, something was amiss. Right after greeting her parents, Alicia flopped down in the nearest chair with a loud sigh of despair. Even Molly and Pansy, her mother's cheerful little West Highland terriers, seemed to sense her distress and jumped off Jose's lap to see what was ailing her.

"Darling, what's the matter? I can see that something's bothering you, tell us about it," she said warmly.

Jose looked concerned. His entire world revolved around his beloved wife and their children. Baseball was just a paid hobby as far as he was concerned. He loved the game but his family came first. He looked at his daughter's face full of anxiety and wanted to know who or what was troubling her. "*Mija*, what's troubling you? Has someone done something to you?" he asked gruffly.

"No, *Papi*, it's not that. Forgive me for being so melodramatic but I've just had the strangest weekend of my entire life and I have no idea what to do next," she said. She sighed again, then began to explain the events that had occurred over the past few days. "It started when Adam and I went to Idlewild." She patted her thighs to let the dogs know they were welcome and they jumped into the chair with her, scrambling for her lap.

As concisely as she could, Alicia told her mother and father about being followed by the older woman and being taken to the home of the relatives Adam had never heard of. "They were incredibly sweet ladies, *Mami*. And they were wonderful storytellers and so funny! We went to church with them on Sunday and met the other two aunts, and they were really something else. They're the ones that told everything, only they told *me* and not Adam, and now I don't know what to do with it all."

Leah looked perplexed. "With what, darling? What do you mean?"

It wasn't an easy story to tell. On Sunday morning she and Adam had joined Emmaline and Reba for service at the Baldwin Church of Christ, then gone home with them for lunch. It was then that they met the other two aunts, Daphne and Dahlia, the most eccentric ladies she'd ever encountered. They lived next door to Emmaline in a pale green cottage with yellow trim. Like Reba, it was hard to judge their age, for despite their white hair, their caramel skin was smooth and unlined. They were identical twins, exactly alike from their fashionably short hair to the outfits they wore, neat denim skirts with soft cotton knit twin sets, one in violet and the other in blue, with comfortable-looking loafers on their feet. Their voices were just alike, too, so that you had to be looking at them to know who was speaking, and as they routinely finished each other's sentences, it meant the listener's eyes were constantly going from one woman to the other.

The really confusing thing was their refusal to admit that they were twins. "We're not twins, dear," one of them said. "People insist that we are, but it's not true. Sister, when is your birthday?"

"August first, of course."

"And I was born on July thirty-first, so there you have

it. We are not twins, because we were not born on the same day," said Daphne triumphantly. "Our mother went into labor late in the afternoon and if God had intended us to be twins . . ." She paused.

"We would have been born on the same day. We don't even share the same month," Dahlia pointed out. "We may have shared a womb for a time . . ."

"But we are not twins," Daphne said emphatically.

Or maybe it was Dahlia, Alicia wasn't sure. She was sure, however, that these were the two most talkative women in all of Lake County. After meeting Adam and exclaiming over him and shedding identical tears of joy, the ladies cornered Alicia in the kitchen where she had come to help them get dinner on the table. She was making a salad while the sisters gave her the real story about Big Benny leaving Idlewild. With one on her right and the other on her left as they talked, it was like hearing in surround sound.

"Francine was a sweet woman, she really was. But she was weak, don't you think, sister?"

"Yes, I think she was, sister, because, after all, losing a child is the worst kind of tragedy, but the poor thing never got over it. Never did. And they way she hung on to poor Andrew was terrible, wouldn't you say so, sister?"

"It was terrible, I have to say it. She couldn't bear to have him out of her sight, she treated him like he was made out of glass, she really did. And he was such a jewel, too. He was never a bit of trouble, he didn't do anything to worry her or cause her any anxiety, he really was a good boy, wasn't he, sister?"

"He really was, and he loved his parents, too, especially his daddy. Now he might have been good to his mother, but he idolized his father. Andrew thought the sun rose and set in our brother Calvin, didn't he, sister?"

By now Alicia's head was spinning from the back-and-forth delivery of the aunts. She thought she'd better interject something to break up the flow and asked what Calvin was like.

"He was a pistol, that's what he was!" Both ladies laughed out loud. One of them took up the story. "He was a man before his time, he really was. He owned and operated a beautiful supper club back when Idlewild was a real resort. It was known all over the country, it was called the Hacienda and it was just wonderful, first class all the way. Beautiful crisp white linen tablecloths, fresh flowers on every table. It was all black and silver and white and had these fabulous mirrors on all the walls. Calvin was the kind of man who could take a lump of coal and have a handful of diamonds in no time. He was smart and popular and got along well with everyone. He had so much charisma and charm it was no wonder he was a success."

As soon as Daphne, or maybe it was Dahlia, stopped speaking, her sister began. "Of course, his life wasn't easy, because after Aaron died, Francine about lost her mind. Aaron and Andrew were twins, you see, and Aaron drowned in Lake Idlewild when they were eight years old. Francine blamed everyone for his death, but especially Calvin, which was ridiculous because Calvin was in Grand Rapids on business that day. She lashed out at everyone, almost went crazy, she did. And she was never quite right after that. She was so beautiful and he loved her so much that he treated her like a delicate doll, and, of course, we did, too. We were so fond of her and so sorry for her loss that we all tended to give in to her every whim, and, of course, that's what caused all the trouble."

Both women sighed deeply and looked at Alicia with their piercing black eyes. "We've always regretted what we did and if we could take it back, we surely would. But at the time we thought we were doing the right thing; we had no idea it would blow up in our faces the way it did. No idea at all," said the one Alicia decided was Daphne.

Dahlia looked troubled and wiped away a quick tear as she nodded in agreement. "It was the worst thing we could have done, sister. But Francine was so desperate and we just didn't think there'd be any lasting harm, we really didn't. You see, the year Andrew turned eighteen a lovely young girl came to work at the Hacienda as a hostess. The club had hostesses and dancers and singers. There was a regular floor show every night. Honey, it was just like Las Vegas, it really was. Well, this young girl was named Cassandra and she was just as pretty as she could be, sweet, too. Andrew took one look and fell head over heels for her and she was the same way about him.

"All summer long when you saw one you saw the other, and it wasn't just puppy love, either. He was truly in love with that girl, even though we didn't recognize it at the time. Francine was convinced that the poor child was a floozy, a nasty little shake dancer who was going to lead her baby astray, and she came to us for help. She was so desperate to break them up she was going to tell him that the girl was no good, but she knew that he wouldn't believe her unless she had someone to back her up," Dahlia said with a deeply heartfelt sigh of regret.

Alicia's eyes were wide and despite herself she was completely absorbed in the story. "So what did you do?" she breathed.

It was Daphne's turn to sound regretful. "Francine concocted a tale that she thought was sure to keep her son away from the girl. She told him that he couldn't be involved with Cassandra because the girl was his father's mistress."

At Alicia's gasp both women lowered their eyes for a moment. Daphne recovered first and went on with the story. "I'm ashamed to say that we went along with the lie. To this day I have no idea what would make us tell a whopper like that on our own brother, other than the fact that we really feared for Francine's mental health

and we truly didn't understand how deeply Andrew
loved this girl. We all went along with the lie, including
Reba, I'm sad to say. And that's what made Andrew leave
Idlewild and never return."

Alicia's mouth was open and her heart was pounding.
Madre de Dios, what a story!

Both Leah and Jose were listening with rapt expressions on their faces. "Well, I guess you did have an unusual weekend, *chica.* What did Adam say when you told
him all this?" her mother wanted to know.

Alicia made a mournful face and scratched the Westies in the special spot behind their ears. "That's the
problem, *Mami.* I didn't tell Adam. I didn't know how
to tell him, for one thing, and for another, they made
me promise not to and you know how I am about a
promise. And there's more; when Benny left town, his
mother got so distraught that she committed suicide
right in Idlewild Lake where her son drowned. Her
husband was so broken up over it he sold the club and
moved to Grand Rapids where he died of a heart attack a couple of years later," Alicia said in a sad voice.

"And what's more, Big Benny finally found out about
their deception years later, and he found out in the
worst possible way. He ran into that Cassandra woman
and he couldn't forget how heartbroken he'd been, so
he let her have it and she told him it was all lies. It was
terrible because he was now married to Adam's mother
and had four children, so it wasn't like they could pick
up where they left off. And she'd never married anyone.
Benny was the one love of her life and she never had another one. Isn't that the saddest thing you ever heard?"

Jose looked puzzled and asked how the aunts knew
this. "Because Benny confronted them about it. He went
to Idlewild and told them to their faces that he never
wanted to see them again and he no longer considered

them family and he never went back after that. A mess, isn't it?"

Leah looked at her husband and back at Alicia. "That's an understatement, dear. What does Adam plan to do with the information he does have about the family? Is he going to talk to his father about it?"

"That's the plan. He's not going to say anything to the rest of the family until he's talked to his father, but he knows how those old ladies would love to meet them. They were so excited, *Mami*, you would have thought Denzel Washington had dropped in for tea. They were so happy to meet him, and so eager for news about the rest of the children. And you know, Benny may have talked a good show about never wanting to see them again, but he sends them money every month so they don't want for anything. He's taken care of them in some ways for years, even though he can't seem to forgive them."

Alicia continued to stroke the Westies while she mulled over what she'd told her parents. "I don't know if I should say anything to Adam or not. It's really not my place to bring it up, after all. But on the other hand, I think it's something he should know. What should I do?" she asked helplessly.

Her father grinned and said, "It's not your cat, *mija*, leave it alone."

Alicia laughed in spite of her distress. When she was a small girl, she had been pestering her mother for a Barbie doll or some such and her mother was staunch in her refusal to buy it for her. Leah was driving down a busy street and Alicia was pouting with a vengeance when suddenly a cat fell out of a tree into traffic. The cat looked dazed for a second, then leaped up and started racing across the road avoiding two cars and dashing under a moving semitruck, emerging unhurt on the other side. Leah had gasped and said, "Alicia, did you see that, wasn't that something!" To which Alicia replied with a small child's disdain, "It's not *my* cat." The phrase had become a family joke.

Jose stood up and leaned over to give Alicia a kiss on the forehead. "It will be fine, *mija.* You'll know the right thing to do when the time comes." He clapped his hands to let the dogs know it was time for their walk, leaving Alicia alone with her mother. She got out of the armchair and went over to the sofa, dropping down next to her for a comforting hug. Leah put a finger under her chin and looked at her full in the face.

"It's not so easy to say 'not your cat' when it's someone you love, is it?" she said quietly.

Alicia didn't try to be coy and deny her mother's words, she just nodded unhappily. "I do love him. I love him so much I couldn't stand it if he got hurt because of this. I just hate the thought of him being upset over all this, and I know that at some point he will be."

Leah kissed her on the cheek and gave her another hug. "You always were my sensitive child, the one who would cry when someone else was hurting. I had to stop you from giving away all your toys, you were so soft-hearted and generous. But you can't prevent the pain, sweetie. Pain is part of being human, part of being an adult; you know that just as I do. He's going to get hurt, bet on it. But he'll have you there in his corner to comfort him and give him support and he'll be just fine."

Suddenly her face turned mischievous and she asked a pointed question. "So when did you two decide you were more than friends, hmm? I'm assuming that this feeling is quite mutual," she teased.

Alicia smiled happily and leaned comfortably against her mother. "Very, very mutual. I'm in total bliss. It's so wonderful, *Mami*, I can't wait to see what happens next."

Leah surmised that a wedding would be in the works very soon, but she didn't mention it. "So how did you leave it after the weekend? What are your immediate plans?"

"Well, Adam took me home and said he needed to talk to his dad, so I guess that's next."

After taking Alicia back to the condo and seeing her in, Adam had kissed her sweetly and told her he'd call her later. He went to the loft first, to take his belongings in and plan his next move. Despite the unsettling weekend, Adam was a creature of precise habit and he had to take his things in, unpack, dispatch his dirty clothes to the laundry, and put everything away. His orderly mind couldn't tolerate disorder, and the routine helped him think. He did more talking than thinking on the way home, which was unusual, especially since Alicia was uncharacteristically quiet. The drive home was much longer than the ride up to Idlewild due to the horrendous traffic on I-75 South. Everyone was headed back downstate after the long weekend and the cars were lined up for miles, barely moving. Adam didn't mind the traffic, because his mind was so completely on the last couple of days.

He had brought with him a big manila envelope of pictures that he promised to have copied and returned. "Go ahead, dear," Reba told him. "I'd scan them for you but my scanner isn't working. I'm going to have to get a new one this week." It still knocked him out that his great-aunts were savvy in computer matters. When he told her he'd send pictures of the family, she said he could e-mail them if he had them downloaded to his hard drive. At his look of amazement she'd just laughed. "Yes, dear, we have all the modern conveniences up here, although I know your cell phone stopped working before you got here. There's only one tower up here and it's owned by our local company."

True enough, as soon as they'd reached Chase, Michigan, no cell signal was available or he'd have called home on the spot when Reba found him. As it was, he had to wait until he returned to Detroit and now here he was. He finished the last of his compulsive straightening and consulted his watch. The gala cookout should be over, but there were still two things at the Palmer Park house he needed. One was an amazing array of leftover food, and the other was his father. No, make that three things; Benita was sure to be there and he would definitely need to talk to her and his brother Andrew at length. They were the oldest children and he had always conferred with them about anything of importance. He picked up the keys to the Range Rover and headed out the door.

He laughed to himself on the way over, thinking about how easily he'd driven Alicia to the loft when they returned to town. She had looked at him with a puzzled expression when he announced that they were home. "Um, Adam, this is *your* home. My home is on Chateau LaFontaine, or did you forget that?" The fact was, he had forgotten. He'd been in love with her for so long and she was such a vital part of his life that the new passion they'd shared over the past few days had just served to imbed her more deeply in his heart. It didn't seem logical for her to be going somewhere else, sleeping some place other than his arms. He'd rallied at his gaffe, but he knew then and there that they would have to make other living arrangements and soon.

As expected, everything was put away except for the big white tent in the backyard that would be collected the next day from the rental company. He knocked on the back door and then entered, calling out as he did so, "It's not a prowler; it's just me." Sure enough, the house was still full of relatives, as he'd surmised from the number of cars in the big circular driveway. In short order he was attacked by the BLKs, his nephews Malcolm and Martin, holy terrors belonging to his sister Benita. They were adorable sturdy little boys with curly black hair and deeply bronzed skin that bore a deep tan all summer long from their endless roughhousing in the outdoors. Their long eyelashes and deep dimples didn't fool him for a minute; he knew them to be domestic juggernauts whose exploits were legendary. As he wrestled with them in the kitchen, their older brother, Clayton III, known as Trey, joined them. Trey was the image of their father and showed the same kind of laid-back demeanor that was his father's hallmark.

"What's up, Uncle Adam?" he said with a smile.

"What's up yourself? You've grown about a foot, man," Adam said admiringly.

They went into the family room, Trey leading the way with Adam following, burdened with Martin on his back and Malcolm riding one of his long legs. Adam was surprised at the level of intensity he felt in the room. Benita and Clay were there, as well as Andrew and Renee and Donnie, and they all looked serious. Trey sensed the mood immediately and bullied his brothers into going upstairs to watch a movie with him. They obeyed him instantly as they were well acquainted with his older-brother methods of ensuring acquiescence.

"What's going on?" Adam asked.

Benita was the first to respond and she didn't answer his question, she got up from where she was sitting to give him a big hug. "Adam, sweetie, it's been too long since I've seen you. And you cut your hair! You look so handsome, but I have to say it's a shock. What made you do it?"

Clay gave a deep laugh and said, "He probably got tired of looking like a hippie, that's all." He rose to give his brother-in-law a brief, manly embrace.

"Aw, here *you* go. Don't even try it, I still remember the mullet you were wearing when you met Benita. You better be glad she gave you the time of day, bro."

After exchanging greetings all around, Adam took a seat and repeated his earlier question. "So what's going on around here? From all the long faces it looks pretty serious. Is someone going to fill me in?"

Odd glances passed among the siblings and finally Benita spoke. "Daddy gave us some interesting news about his past on Saturday and we're still trying to decide what to do about it. Apparently there's a lot about his history we weren't aware of and it's all coming home to roost," she said with a wry twist of her mouth.

"That's a coincidence. I found out some very interesting things myself over the weekend and I wasn't sure how to bring them up. Looks like this could be as good a time as any."

"So where were you this weekend anyway? Pop wasn't too pleased you weren't here; he wanted to hit all of us with the same bomb at once," Donnie said.

Adam smiled, a private smile that was generated by his memories of the erotic, passion-filled parts of the weekend. "I was with Alicia," he said quietly.

Donnie's eyebrows lifted and he laughed out loud in happiness.

Benita looked from one brother to the other, wondering what they were talking about. "Okay, so you were with Alicia. As I recall, most of your waking hours are spent with her, so what's the big deal?"

Donnie corrected his sister. "He was *with* Alicia, Benita. The scales have fallen away from his eyes and the shackles from his heart. He and Alicia, if I'm not mistaken, are an official couple now," he gloated.

Adam raised an eyebrow but didn't deny what his youngest brother was saying. "Yes, we are. We're completely committed to each other, as if it was any of your business, you nosey buzzard," he said with affection. Turning to Benita he said, "We went up north this weekend. They cleared the ground at the lake and construction in going to start in a week or so. I told you I was building a summer place, Benita, some place where we could vacation together."

"Yes, you did tell me that. I'll bet it's going to be lovely."

"Wait until you see it. You're all going to love it up there. But wait until I tell you what I found out in Idlewild," he said.

A sudden noise made them all turn toward the doorway of the family room. Big Benny stood there stock-still, his face ashen and sweaty. "What did you say? Where did you go, Adam?" The hoarseness of his voice was as alarming as his face.

Adam replied slowly, "I said I went to Idlewild, Pop, and I think you know what I found out up there."

Everyone reacted in horror as Big Benny slumped to the floor. Andrew reached him first, immediately starting CPR. "Donnie, get me some aspirin, Renee, call 911. Clay and Adam, get the cars out of the way so the ambulance can get in, Benita, get me my bag out of the car," he barked. Thanking God he was a doctor, he leaned over his father and whispered, "Hang in there, Pop, it's gonna be okay."

Chapter Fourteen

Alicia was totally out of sorts when she reached the Cochran Building the next morning. Not only had Adam failed to call her last night, but he didn't answer his cell phone or his house phone and she was through guessing why. She had tried not to fret all night but it was impossible. Her thoughts raced from him having second thoughts about their relationship to him having a terrible accident on the expressway. She couldn't seem to stem the tide of bizarre notions that were tumbling around in her head. One thing she wasn't going to do and that was turn into some drama queen who went careening over to his loft in the middle of the night. She had a key already. They both had keys to each other's places for emergencies, but this wasn't an emergency as far as she knew.

It was probably just cold feet. He probably realized that it was impossible for them to maintain a good working relationship in the face of all that passion and he bailed out, that's all. She wanted to slap herself for being a nincompoop, but there were other people in the elevator. *Why are you doing this to yourself? You're like someone who hits herself in the head with a hammer because it feels so good when it stops. Stop being such an idiot,* she thought fiercely.

The night before, she'd tried not to let her feelings show while Marielle was unpacking her things and putting them away for her. Marielle was the resident neat freak; Alicia had a strictly live-and-let-live policy when it came to clutter. If it didn't bother her, she wouldn't bother it. They survived their adolescent years of sharing a bedroom because Marielle would clean the bedroom while Alicia would do things that Marielle despised, like laundry, cleaning the kitchen, and maintaining the flower beds.

Alicia nibbled her cuticles while watching her sister whip the bedroom into shape. She listened to her comments too; her sister could always make sense out of nonsense. She'd told Marielle about the epoch-making weekend. She saw no reason not to since she'd always confided in her sister. And Marielle didn't let her down, either.

"*Chica,* stop chewing your fingers, that's disgusting. Adam hasn't called because his head is too full of information right now. He had to talk to his family, right? Well, who knows how that went? So give him some space to deal with it. He'll talk to you about it when he's ready," she said as she closed the closet door. She leaned against the door and gave her little sister a dazzling smile. "I'm not sure about what makes men tick; I think they really are from Mars somewhere. But I'm sure of one thing and that is Adam's love for you. He loves you passionately, madly. I've never told you this, but sometimes when I see the way he looks at you, *I* have to take a cold shower. Try not to worry about his family problems; after all, it's not your cat." Marielle smiled wisely and gave her little sister a kiss on the forehead.

The thought of that conversation put a faint smile on her lips as she entered the offices of Cochran & Fuentes. She was glad she had a pleasant look on her face because Rhonda was waiting to pounce on her as soon as she walked in the door.

"Okay, this is none of my business, Alicia, but I have to

know if we're going to be changing the name of the firm any time soon."

At Alicia's look of surprise she elaborated. "How about to Cochran and Cochran? People couldn't stop talking about your 'bid' the rest of the night. I was totally impressed," she said, her eyes shining with admiration.

The stupid auction. So much had happened Alicia had forgotten all about it. She adroitly sidestepped Rhonda's inquiry with one of her own. "So how was the rest of the evening? I hope Paul got a few bids at least; he was so nervous about it."

Amazingly, Rhonda's smooth brown face promptly turned deep red from emotion. She ran her hand over the back of her hair, which was cut close to her scalp in a sleek, sexy cap, and made a sound of annoyance. "Oh, Mr. Paul did just fine. Better than fine, in fact. There was actually a little bidding war going on for a minute. He's now the toast of the town, if you can believe that," she said acerbically and enlightened Alicia about the events of the night.

Lacking Hannibal's magnificent voice and Adams's sheer sexual magnetism, Paul took the stage and started cracking jokes. He openly begged for bids and had the audience laughing so hard that the women were vying for him and he ended up on the arm of a very lovely woman who was openly intrigued by the handsome Aussie. Alicia was deeply amused by the fact that Rhonda seemed to have her nose out of joint about it; Paul had adored her for months and she wouldn't give him the time of day. Now it looked like things were about to sway in Paul's favor.

The ringing phone distracted Rhonda and Alicia escaped to her office. She decided that the best course of action was to act as if she were in total control of the situation, as though there were nothing to be bothered about. Marielle was right, Adam was probably preoccupied with his family drama and he'd get in touch with

An Important Message From The ARABESQUE Publisher

Dear Arabesque Reader,

I invite you to join the club! The Arabesque book club delivers four novels each month right to your front door! It's easy, and you will never miss a romance by one of our award-winning authors!

With upcoming novels featuring strong, sexy women, and African-American heroes that are charming, loving and true… you won't want to miss a single release! Our authors fill each page with exceptional dialogue, exciting plot twists, and enough sizzling romance to keep you riveted until the satisfying end! To receive novels by bestselling authors such as Gwynne Forster, Janice Sims, Angela Winters and others, I encourage you to join now!

Read about the men we love… in the pages of Arabesque!

Linda Gill
PUBLISHER, ARABESQUE ROMANCE NOVELS

P.S. Watch out for the next Summer Series "Ports Of Call" that will take you to the exotic locales of Venice, Fiji, the Caribbean and Ghana! You won't need a passport to travel, just collect all four novels to enjoy romance around the world! For more details, visit us at www.BET.com.

SPECIAL OFFER!
4 BOOKS FREE!

BET☆ BOOKS
www.BET.com

A SPECIAL "THANK YOU"
FROM ARABESQUE JUST FOR YOU!

Send this card back and you'll receive 4 FREE Arabesque Novels—
a $25.96 value—absolutely FREE!

The introductory 4 Arabesque Romance books are yours FREE
(plus $1.99 shipping & handling). If you wish to continue to
receive 4 books every month, do nothing. Each month, we will send
you 4 New Arabesque Romance Novels for your free examination.
If you wish to keep them, pay just $18* (plus, $1.99 shipping &
handling). If you decide not to continue, you owe nothing!

- Send no money now.
- Never an obligation.
- Books delivered to your door!

We hope that after receiving your FREE books you'll want to remain
an Arabesque subscriber, but the choice is yours! So why not take
advantage of this Arabesque offer, with no risk of any kind. You'll be
glad you did!

In fact, we're so sure you will love your Arabesque novels, that we
will send you an Arabesque Tote Bag FREE with your first paid
shipment.

* PRICES SUBJECT TO CHANGE.

YOU'LL GET
4 SELECT
ROMANCES PLUS
THIS FABULOUS
TOTE BAG!

ARABESQUE

Visit us at:
www.BET.com

THE "THANK YOU" GIFT INCLUDES:

- 4 books absolutely FREE (plus $1.99 for shipping and handling).
- A FREE newsletter, *Arabesque Romance News*, filled with author interviews, book previews, special offers, and more!
- No risks or obligations. You're free to cancel whenever you wish with no questions asked.

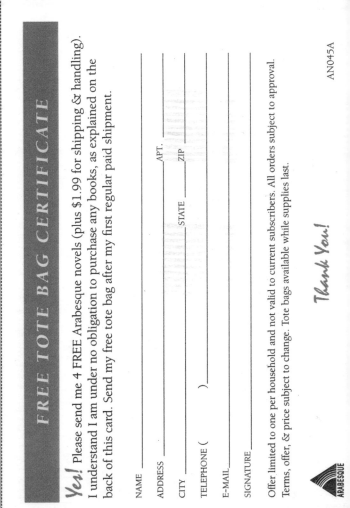

FREE TOTE BAG CERTIFICATE

Yes! Please send me 4 FREE Arabesque novels (plus $1.99 for shipping & handling). I understand I am under no obligation to purchase any books, as explained on the back of this card. Send my free tote bag after my first regular paid shipment.

NAME _____

ADDRESS _____ APT. _____

CITY _____ STATE _____ ZIP _____

TELEPHONE ( ) _____

E-MAIL _____

SIGNATURE _____

Offer limited to one per household and not valid to current subscribers. All orders subject to approval. Terms, offer, & price subject to change. Tote bags available while supplies last.

Thank You!

AN045A

ARABESQUE

Accepting the four introductory books for FREE (plus $1.99 to offset the cost of shipping & handling) places you under no obligation to buy anything. You may keep the books and return the shipping statement marked "cancelled". If you do not cancel, about a month later we will send 4 additional Arabesque novels, and you will be billed the preferred subscriber's price of just $4.50 per title. That's $18.00* for all 4 books for a savings of almost 30% off the cover price (Plus $1.99 for shipping and handling). You may cancel at any time, but if you choose to continue, every month we'll send you 4 more books, which you may either purchase at the preferred discount price. . . or return to us and cancel your subscription.

THE ARABESQUE ROMANCE CLUB: HERE'S HOW IT WORKS

THE ARABESQUE ROMANCE BOOK CLUB
P.O. BOX 5214
CLIFTON NJ 07015-5214

PLACE
STAMP
HERE

her when he could. In the meantime, there was work to do as she meticulously worked on a proposal. It was almost noon when her already ajar office door opened and Adam entered. Against her will, she felt her stomach constrict and her nerve endings start to thrum. He looked way too handsome in a medium blue Polo shirt and tight-fitting jeans. His hair was still damp and he looked freshly shaven. To her utter surprise and joy, he didn't hesitate; he walked over to her and pulled her up from her seat. He brushed his hand over her cheek before taking her lips in a hot, juicy kiss.

"You taste so good, Allie. I need more, but I've got to get back to the hospital," he said by way of explanation. "Pop had a heart attack last night. It wasn't severe, but at his age any cardiac disturbance is pretty bad. I should have called you last night, but things happened so fast and it got so late I didn't want to upset you. I just went home a little while ago to shower and change and I'm on my way back." He stopped speaking to look her all over before continuing.

There was something so comforting about seeing her face. Her hair was different; it was smoothed behind her ears and the top was a tumble of shiny tousled curls instead of the chic style Gigi had given her. She was wearing a nice peach-colored linen blouse with the sleeves rolled back and a matching slim-fitting skirt with open-toed tan sandals. A gold necklace he'd given her some years before was around her heck, and she was also wearing a pair of gold hoop earrings with a tiny topaz dangling from them. He recognized these as another gift and the memory made him smile. "You look wonderful, as always," he said, tightening his hands around her waist. "I missed you last night."

"I missed you, too. And I'm going to the hospital with you. What do you think this is? Do you think I'm just going to sit around here and twiddle my thumbs while you're having a crisis?" She frowned at him as she took herself out of his embrace and looked around for her purse.

"Allie, you don't need to come," he protested. "I'm just going to be sitting around with the rest of the family while we wait to hear what the doctors have to say. I appreciate the offer, but—"

"Well then, let's go," she said firmly. "We'll talk about your failure to call me later," she threw over her shoulder as she approached the door.

Adam bowed to her insistence, secretly glad that she was coming. He wasn't looking forward to whatever was awaiting them at the hospital.

Benita's weariness showed all over her face, to her husband's displeasure. Anything that affected her, affected him and he wasn't one to tolerate any discomfort in her life. She was holding her father's hand, coaxing him to take a sip of water before continuing to attempt to speak. He lifted his head tiredly and took a few sips from the straw in the glass she held out to him and smiled weakly.

"Find him for me, Benita. Bring John to me," he whispered hoarsely. His eyelids fluttered closed and Benita set the glass on the bedside table with shaking hands. Clay's arms went around her at once, giving her the support she needed.

"He looks so weak," she murmured. Clay led her out of the small room in cardiac intensive care and had her sit down in a chair in the family lounge.

"He'll be fine, Peaches. Your dad is the toughest man I know, he'll get through this just fine."

Adam and Alicia, along with Martha, who had met them in the lobby as she was returning to her husband's side, arrived just in time to hear Clayton's assurance to his wife. Both of them kissed Benita on the cheek as they greeted her. She in turn was amazed at Alicia's transformation. "Honey, I might not have known you if I passed you on the street! You were always lovely, but just look at you now, you're beautiful," she said warmly.

Alicia thanked her with a blush and a smile, and Adam wanted to know at once what was going on. "Did we hear anything from the doctor yet?"

Andrew entered the area just then, wearing his scrubs and white coat, looking every bit the outstanding physician that he was. "Yes, we have all the lab tests back and it's not nearly as bad as we thought. Come on, let's go to a conference room so we can talk," he said, indicating they should follow him.

When they were all seated around the big conference room table, Andrew glanced at the chart in his hand and shook his head. "Pop didn't have a heart attack. He was in some distress from angina, but basically he had *gas*. The darned fool ate too much yesterday."

Benita protested, "I saw the plate Martha fixed for him; he had grilled chicken and vegetables, green salad with oil and vinegar dressing, and fresh fruit salad for dessert. He was following his usual diet. Andrew, are you sure it was gas that made him so sick?"

"You might have seen him with that plate, but you know how he is. That plate was a decoy. He finally admitted that he'd eaten ribs, chitlins, a couple of brats, baked beans, potato salad, garlic bread, jalapeño cornbread, and greens with hot sauce and raw onion. He also had homemade ice cream and two pieces of pecan pie. His gall bladder had better sense than he did, that's why he was in such distress. A gall bladder attack can mimic a heart attack; it's just about that painful. We're trying to decide whether or not to remove it. Pop is in pretty good health overall because Martha rides herd on him constantly," he said, patting his stepmother's hand, "but at his age any kind of surgery is nothing to play with."

"Are you absolutely sure, Andrew? He looked so frail and he sounded so weak," Benita insisted.

"C'mon, sis, I know you're worried but let's not forget

what a fine actor he can be. He might still be uncomfortable, but if I know him he's making a play for sympathy to avoid the lectures he so richly deserves."

Everyone relaxed noticeably, especially Adam. "That's good news, Andrew. I have to tell you I was feeling guilty as hell after last night."

That got Alicia's attention immediately. "What do you mean? What happened last night?"

"Pop heard me say I went to Idlewild and he got all weird. I said something like, 'You know what I found up there,' and he passed out cold. I thought I'd given him such a shock he'd collapsed with a cardiac arrest," he admitted.

Alicia took his hand under the table and held it tightly.

Andrew assured his brother that he'd done no such thing. "Believe me, Adam, the way Mr. Bottomless Pit was chowing down yesterday, he'd have made it to the hospital with or without a shock to his system. All the caterers know him from doing the party every year and they were all fixing him this and that and he was stuffing his face like it was the last time he'd see food."

"And it *was* the last time he'll see some of that kind of food," Martha said with spirit and resolve. "Scared us all to death because he was too greedy to control himself. Just wait until I get him home," she vowed. "I'll have him on the strictest diet he ever heard of."

Everyone laughed, which released some of the tension in the room. Benita looked at Adam curiously and asked what it was that he found in Idlewild that might be upsetting to Big Benny.

Adam drew in a deep breath, saying he hadn't intended to tell them about it until he talked to their father. "Now that doesn't seem like such a hot idea. I'm glad you're all sitting down because you're not going to believe what I've got to tell you."

It didn't take long to tell the tale. Beginning with encountering Reba outside Jones's Ice Cream Parlor to meeting Emmaline and the sisters, Adam told them all of the past that he'd uncovered. As he spoke, their faces went from surprised to shocked to utterly stunned. Adam managed a wry grin and said, "Yep, that's about the way I reacted, only I had to keep it on the down low because they were right there in front of me. You have to meet them; they're amazing. These are the sweetest, nicest little old ladies you ever want to meet and why he turned his back on them I'll never know. They were so happy to see me and Alicia, it was truly humbling."

"Did they say why Daddy left town and never came back?" Benita asked.

Adam shook his head. "All they said was something happened to cause a rift between him and the family and he left. They never did get around to saying what it was, did they, Alicia?"

Alicia hoped the sudden heat in her face wasn't evident as she mutely shook her head. It was childish, but as long as she didn't actually say the words, it wasn't like she was really lying to Adam. She was just withholding, which was bad enough. Thankfully, the conversation rolled on without her input although it rolled in a most unexpected direction.

"Andrew, maybe it has something to do with what Daddy told us on Saturday," Benita said.

"You could be right, Benita. They could be connected in some way," he mused.

"You want to clue me in or are you having too much fun being cryptic," Adam said mildly.

The twins looked at each other briefly, and then turned to Adam. "We didn't want to tell you this way, Adam. I wish you'd been there to hear it from Daddy," Benita began.

"And we tried to call you on your cell "phone several times to prepare you," added Andrew, "but we got no response."

"Yeah, once you get past a certain point there's only

one tower and it only works with the local service. I had the cell turned off. I saw all those messages, though. So what did Pop tell you that might be related to what happened in Idlewild back in the day?"

As gently as she could, Benita repeated the words their father had used to announce that he had another son. "I can only imagine how you're feeling right now, Adam; we were all stunned too. And what's more, Daddy insists on telling him that he's his birth father and bringing him into the family, although why anyone would want to jump on this circus train is more than I can fathom," she said wryly.

Adam seemed frozen in place. He hadn't moved or spoken since Benita began her story, and with good reason. He couldn't trust himself to speak. A wave of white-hot anger rushed over him and his sister's voice was starting to sound like *blah, blah, blah* in his ears; he wasn't able to discern individual words anymore due to the rushing sound that was crashing through his head. Another son? *He cheated on my mother and had another child?* He really couldn't focus on anything that was being said because his thoughts were so jumbled. But it suddenly registered with him that Benita was saying something about finding the man and bringing him to Detroit. That made him react at last and he had something to say. He looked at his oldest brother and sister and said a single word. "No."

When they gave him a look of surprise, he shook his head firmly and reiterated his statement. "I said no, and that's what I mean. That's the worst idea I ever heard of. What could you be thinking about?" Before anyone could reply he got up from the conference table and left the room, leaving everyone staring after him, including Alicia.

Alicia felt totally awkward after Adam left the room. She was getting up to leave, too, when Benita stopped her. "Alicia, I know this is some hard news for Adam to take, but we've all got to deal with it somehow. On top of everything else, my father tells me that the man he says is his son is someone I know. His name is John Flores and we've been good friends over the years. You remember when I had the terrible accident in California and lost the baby; well, John is the person who kept me sane.

"He's a very skilled and compassionate psychotherapist, and if it wasn't for John I have no idea what would have become of me or my marriage," she added, looking at her husband with loving eyes. "We stay in touch by e-mail and telephone and whenever he's in Atlanta he comes to dinner. In fact, he lived in Atlanta for a while and taught at Emory University. That was before he moved back to California a few years ago." She stopped speaking and looked thoughtful for a moment. "Everyone always said he favored Adam, but I thought it was because they both had long hair and thick moustaches. Now, well . . ." She looked around the table and everyone looked as deep in thought as she. She turned to her husband and spoke quietly but everyone could hear her.

"Clay, I know you don't want me to be embroiled in this, but I don't see how I can stay away. John is a good friend to us and if all this is true he's going to need a buffer between him and Daddy. You above all people know how Daddy can be. Besides, I happen to know where John is and if Daddy wants to see him, I can bring him here."

"What do you mean, Benita?" Clay looked at his wife intently.

"I mean I got an e-mail from John a few weeks ago. He's taken a faculty position at the University of Michigan. He's right down the road in Ann Arbor."

Clay looked at Andrew and Andrew said aloud what both men were thinking. "Yeah, well, he's gonna wish he was in Timbuktu before this is all over."

Chapter Fifteen

Adam made it all the way out to the parking lot before he realized he'd left Alicia behind. With a heartfelt groan, he opened the door of the Range Rover and got in, driving around to the front of the hospital. Hoping fervently Alicia was calm enough to have followed him, he looked at the big glass entrance and was relieved to see her exiting the main doors. He stopped the vehicle and got out to open the passenger door for her. Without a word, she got into the Rover and was calmly fastening her seat belt when he returned to the driver's seat. "I'm sorry, Allie," was all he said.

They drove in silence for a few minutes, neither looking at the other. Alicia was the first one to speak, looking over at Adam and telling him they had to talk about it. "You can't just stash this away, Adam. This time we have to be able to talk about it, really talk about how you're feeling," she said quietly.

Adam's jaw tightened and his hands gripped the steering wheel so tightly that his knuckles paled. "That's just it, Allie. I don't know *how* I feel about it. This is . . . this is just too much to take in. In the space of a weekend I found a bunch of family I had no idea existed and now my father announced that he has another child, a child none of us ever heard of. And since he admits that he did it when my mother was still alive, we're talking about an adult son, Allie. Someone we know nothing about and who knows nothing about us. I told you before I felt like I didn't know my father. Well, now I know I don't know him, I don't know him at all." Adam's voice was low and intense with anger.

Alicia said a prayer for guidance before speaking. "Adam, I know this is a lot to take in, but maybe there's more to the story than you realize. Maybe there were extenuating circumstances that made your father—"

Her words were cut off by an angry gesture from Adam. "Allie, that's crap. My father, by his own admission, cheated on my mother. There aren't any extenuating circumstances; he couldn't control himself, that's all. He didn't have enough regard for my mother to honor his commitment to her and now he has the twisted idea that somehow we're supposed to form some kind of bond with this guy. The whole thing is just crazy, Allie. And my family is crazy to even think about going along with it," he ended in disgust.

"But, Adam," she began, only to be cut off by him again.

"Alicia, I can't talk about it now. Maybe later, but not right now," he said tightly. He brought the Rover to a stop and looked at her expectantly.

She looked out the window in surprise and realized that they were in the parking garage under the Cochran Building, right next to her car. She blinked at Adam, who was getting out to open her door. He held out his hand to her and she took it, gracefully exiting to stand next to him. She reached in her purse for her keys and Adam took them, opening the car door and handing them back. Alicia was about to get into the car when Adam suddenly hugged her tightly, pulling her into his arms and murmuring her name. "I'll call you later, I promise. I just can't think right now," he said, his voice thick with tension.

Alicia couldn't reply, her throat was clogged with unshed tears and guilt. As she started the Mini Cooper the tears threatened to overflow but she refused to let them. She just drove away, giving Adam his wish to be alone.

Benita and Andrew were sitting in the living room of Andrew's house, the house Benita had lived in for years before she moved to Atlanta. When her best friend, Renee, married Andrew, Benita gave them the house as a wedding present. It was a big, imposing house full of love, laughter, and children, although there wasn't much laughter to be found right now. Bennie was leaning against her twin brother on the sofa looking spent, and Renee was sitting on the matching loveseat looking concerned. Clay was sitting in a big armchair, not saying anything, but his eyes were trained on his wife. As always, his first concern was Benita's well-being.

Renee was still expressing amazement over the whole issue. Her dark skin was flushed with emotion and her golden eyes flashed as they usually did when she was excited. "Bennie, I'm just stunned that your father was able to keep all of this under wraps for so long. And how did you not find out about it when you were making *Idlewild?* It seems like the whole story would've come out then, at least the part about the family."

Bennie laughed wearily. "It's ironic, isn't it? I wrote a movie script about Daddy's hometown, I even went up there and looked around, I did all kinds of research, and I uncovered not one word about my father's family. I guess I'm pretty lousy at research, huh?"

Clay responded automatically. "Peaches, you had no reason to uncover anything," he pointed out. "First of all, when you wrote the screenplay you were pregnant with Trey and you and your father weren't even speaking then. You weren't in communication with him at all, remember?"

It was true, Bennie and her father had been feuding over his treatment of Clay. Big Benny considered him a threat to his relationship with his daughter and had moved heaven and earth to break them up. Clay continued in his deep voice. "You were writing a fictional story that took place in 1922, three years before your father was born. The research you did was on that era of Idlewild, not the time when your grandfather's club was at its peak."

Bennie nodded in agreement. "I did see the Hacienda in pictures, though. I went through as many historical documents as I could and I do remember seeing pictures of the Hacienda and even a couple of pictures of Calvin Cochran, but there was nothing about his personal life. I knew he was Daddy's father, but who knew about all his sisters? Even when we decided to make the movie and we went up there, we didn't really talk to anyone. It was the dead of winter and we just cruised around, remember, Clay?"

"Yes, we did. Didn't even spend the night. If we had, we might have uncovered something," he replied.

"Well, what about when you were actually making the movie?" Renee asked. "How did you manage to not meet your family when you were shooting? It had to attract a lot of attention from the community."

Clay laughed, with Bennie joining in. "It did, Renee. Lots and lots of people turned up every day to watch. Everyone in Cassopolis, Michigan, was thrilled," Bennie said. "We did the exterior shooting in a few weeks and we did it all in Cassopolis and Killarney Beach, which is near Bay City. Our location scout was looking for places that looked like Idlewild looked in the 1920s and that's what he came up with. Most of the film was shot in Atlanta, remember, so there went another golden opportunity for our paths to cross."

She sighed deeply and leaned into her brother's shoulder. Andrew gave her a hug and spoke for the first time. "Yes, it's ironic that you guys made a movie about Dad's hometown and managed to not meet his relatives while you were doing it, but the fact that the man he claims is his long-lost son was also your therapist is the wildest freaking coincidence I've ever heard of. It's so wild I'm beginning to believe it's not a total coincidence."

"What do you mean, Andrew?" Her face puckered in puzzlement as she asked the question.

"I'm just saying, out of all the therapists in the state of California, the one who shows up to treat you just happens to be our long-lost half brother. I just think it wasn't so much a coincidence as a deliberate act. I mean, think about it. Pop couldn't have pulled this off by himself. He had to have had help from someone, someone who was uncharacteristically quiet during the whole exposé, someone who was with you in California after the accident and who probably knows a lot more than she's letting on. Someone who could probably fill in a lot of gaps for us," he said slowly.

All four people spoke at once. "Aunt Ruth," they said in unison.

"Yep, I think Aunt Ruth can probably answer a lot of questions for us." The others agreed, but Clay added something that no one else had considered until that moment. "I have the idea that Bump knows more than he's saying, too."

Andrew looked at his wife and smiled. "So, Renee, you feel like having company for dinner in a couple of days?"

Adam was covered in sweat and his breathing was just returning to normal. After leaving Alicia in the parking garage he'd driven home and changed clothes for a run. He'd run down Jefferson Avenue through Harbortown, past Indian Village, past Ojibway Island, all the way downtown to the Renaissance Center. He ran around Cobo Hall and headed back down Jefferson to home. By the time he neared Harbortown he was considerably calmer than he was when he left the loft. He still couldn't articulate the total rage that overtook him at the thought that he had a half brother, but he wasn't blinded by that anger anymore. Now he thought that the best course of action was for him to talk to his father, something he hadn't had a chance to do. Seeing his father's face and hearing his explanation would go a long way toward helping him make sense of the whole situation. But before he did that, he needed to talk to Alicia, to apologize again for his behavior.

The one thing he never intended to do in this life was to hurt her or disrespect her. And if they were going to be together for the rest of their lives, as he planned, he would have to learn how to communicate with her without resorting to his usual silent, solitary brooding. He slowed his run down to a walk for the cool-down necessary to prevent muscle strain and when he entered the loft he went for the phone immediately to call her. Frowning when he got her voice mail, he left her a brief message with a request to call him. He stripped off his wet, smelly running clothes and tossed them into the washer before going off to shower. The hot pounding water cleared his head even more than the long run. He used lavish amounts of the Algemarin bath gel he'd appropriated from Alicia, lathering his hard body over and over while thinking again how very lucky he was to have Alicia in his life.

When he finally turned off the shower, he wrapped a thick towel around his waist and left the bathroom. A sound from the other part of the loft made him turn his head in surprise. He went into the living room and was surrounded by the sound of Celia Cruz coming from the stereo. With a smile on his face, he followed the aroma that was coming from the kitchen and his heart was warmed at what he beheld. There was Alicia, singing along with the CD and adding a bit of seasoning to the big pot on his huge six-burner range. She was wearing a short, red cotton-knit tank dress with cute little red sandals and she looked wonderful.

"What's all this? I don't think I deserve it, whatever it is."

Alicia turned around with a playful smile. "It's your get-out-of-jail-free card, *querida*. Everyone is entitled to act like a jackass when they have earth-shattering news to deal with. I made you arroz con pollo and empanadas and I'll have a *mojito* for you in a few minutes. You are planning to get dressed, right?"

Adam didn't answer; he danced his way over to her and grabbed her, starting a seductive merengue right there in the kitchen. Adam was a fantastic dancer and one of the things they loved to do on Saturday nights was go dancing, especially salsa dancing. Alicia laughed but had to point out that he was hardly dressed for dancing. "Put some clothes on so we can eat, you crazy man!"

Adam stopped moving and dropped the towel. "We can eat naked, Allie. In fact"—he leaned over her and whispered in her ear—"having no clothes on makes it easier."

Alicia pretended to be shocked and tried to run away from him, which only made him lock his arms around her. "Adam, if we do this now what's going to be dessert?" She laughed.

"Good point," he conceded and kissed her hard before departing to put something on. She smiled at his retreating figure, knowing she'd done the right thing by coming over. All the way to the condo she kept repeating *it's not my cat, it's not my cat,* but she couldn't just leave things the way they were. As Adam had told her in Idlewild, she was supposed to love him out of his bad moods and not let him sit around and mope. So she decided to make him dinner and take it to him. The empanadas were in the freezer and just needed to be heated up. The chicken with rice was something any Cuban cook could make in a matter of minutes and it was always tasty. She'd made enough for Marielle and the children, too, and brought it over to the loft where it just required a little reheating and serving. The look of joy on Adam's face told her that her mission was successful.

In a few minutes they were eating at the work island in the kitchen and Adam was effusive in his praise of Alicia's cooking. "Allie, I still haven't figured out how you can take something as basic as chicken and some rice and make it taste so exotic. You're an amazing woman. You turned this from the worst day of my life into one of the best," he told her. He leaned across the island to give her a kiss on the cheek.

She turned her face so that the kiss landed on her lips, a sweet soft smack that made her smile. "I'm glad, sweetheart. I want to make all your days happy," she said artlessly. Then her eyes widened as she realized her words could be interpreted in several ways.

Adam didn't seem to have noticed, though, he merely stood up and began clearing their dishes off the island and rinsing them to put into the dishwasher. In minutes he had the kitchen as spotless as it was when she arrived. He turned around to find the kitchen empty and went in search of Alicia. She had opened the French doors and was standing out on the roof garden, sipping the last of her drink. The roof garden was what made the loft spectacular. It was bordered with evergreens in pots and there were two glass-topped tables with umbrellas and matching chairs as well as a couple of comfortable chaise longues. Alicia made sure that the big pots of flowering plants were kept well watered and clipped and in the summer it was a magical place for stargazing and relaxing. Adam came up behind her and wrapped his arms around her, rubbing his face in her hair.

"I truly am sorry about what happened this afternoon, Allie. I had no right to go storming out of there and leave you with my family. I shouldn't have let my emotions get the best of me like that."

She turned around in his arms so she could look at

him directly. "Adam, your emotions are yours and no one, even me, can tell you how to react to something. It's your right to respond to something the way you see fit, you're not a machine. I can handle that. You know I come from a family who believes in expressing its feelings at the top of its collective lungs." She laughed. "But when you won't talk to me about it, I don't know how to help you. Or *if* I can help you . . ." Her voice trailed off and she was obviously thinking about something important. "You know before we were . . . involved I used to know what to do, I'd just leave your evil butt alone until you were over it. Now that doesn't seem like the right thing to do. Isn't that funny?" she mused.

Adam didn't respond immediately, he just held her tighter. His deep voice seemed to resonate through her body as he spoke with his mouth close to her ear. "I resent that 'evil' comment. I may be aloof at times but I'm never evil," he said loftily. "I do know that I'm not the easiest person to talk to at times, and I don't mean to shut you out. But damn, Allie, for the life of me I can't figure out how I feel about this. So much happened this weekend I'm still trying to get a handle on it. I think when I talk to Pop in person, I can sort things out better. Right now, though, I really don't want to talk about Pop or Idlewild or the phantom half brother," he whispered.

Alicia sighed with pleasure and asked him what he wanted to talk about. He turned her around in his arms and slid his big hands down her back until they were firmly around her derriere. He lifted her up and she helped him by locking her legs around his waist. "I don't really want to talk about anything except us, Allie." He kissed her and they reentered the loft with their arms looped around each other and their mouths joined together by the sensuous movements of their tongues. When they reached the bedroom, Adam reluctantly let her go long enough to lower her to the bed. He took off his shirt and jeans before getting on the bed with her. When she started to remove her own clothing, he stopped her. "Let me," he said as he reached for her and made short work of the red dress.

They lay in each other's arms, gently stroking each other and reveling in the feel of their bodies pressed close together. Adam reached over to the nightstand for the inevitable condom and while he was doing so, he also picked up the remote for the stereo system. With a flick of his thumb he selected something that made Alicia smile. The incomparable voice of Marvin Gaye floated out into the bedroom. She pulled away from Adam and straddled his body, taking the foil packet from his fingers. "So this is for medicinal purposes, is that it?"

"Absolutely, baby. 'Sexual Healing' is just what the doctor ordered," he agreed. The lighthearted tone soon turned passionate as Alicia deftly slid the condom over his hardened sex. Adam slid his hands up her smooth thighs to her hips, then held her while he entered her, loving her soft sighs of pleasure. Alicia moved up and down slowly at first, until their rhythm was established and their ascent to ecstasy began. She looked down at Adam, not realizing how incredibly sexy she looked to him as the passion overtook her. Her skin was gleaming, her face wore a look of total abandon, and her nipples were huge and erect with fulfillment. Alicia braced her hands on his broad shoulders and loved the profound look of love and desire he was giving her. The strong, sure thrusts brought the quivering explosion that bound them together in a powerful orgasm, so powerful that Alicia could feel hot tears coursing down her cheeks.

As she collapsed on top of Adam he stroked her over and over. "I love you, Allie. You're mine, baby, you're the one God intended just for me. I'm going to spend the rest of our lives making you happy," he said softly.

Alicia sighed in repletion but before she could answer he spoke again. "You're going to marry me, right?" She smiled against his neck and didn't answer at first. She was too happy to speak just then and would have been content to bask in his love for a little longer, but he wasn't having it. Adam gave her a squeeze and a little shake, repeating his question with just a hint of anxiety in his voice.

"Alicia, did you hear me? I just asked you if you were going to marry me."

"Of course I am, you dope. Who else is going to love me like you do? And who else is there in the entire world I could love like I love you?" She kissed him then, with all the love she was feeling. "You're mine, Adam, all mine. Of course we're getting married."

"Good. As soon as all this mess is resolved we'll pick out a date. I just hope Pop comes to his senses soon so we can all get on with our lives," he murmured.

Chapter Sixteen

The next morning Alicia knew she couldn't wait any longer. If Adam was going to talk to Big Benny, she had to make sure he had all the facts. After their long, hot shower, made even hotter by their affectionate water play, she put on a short cotton robe of Adam's that was much too big for her, but it at least covered her body. She went into the kitchen where Adam was already making breakfast for the two of them. His eyes lit up when he saw her. She just looked too adorable for words in the oversized robe. She sat on one of the tall stools by the work island and forlornly tried to roll up her sleeves. He could tell instantly that something was bothering her.

Going over to her, he completed the task of getting the overlong sleeves out of the way and tilted her chin up for a kiss. "What's bothering you, baby?"

She couldn't put it off any longer. Urging him to sit down next to her, she repeated to him what the sisters had told her over the fateful weekend. His face didn't change expression as she talked, telling him about the death of Big Bennie's twin brother and the love affair that was destroyed by Francine's lies. Finally she finished the story and took both his hands in hers. "I'm sorry I didn't tell you right away. I hope you can forgive me and not be too angry about it. I should've told you right away, but you'd had so much to deal with, and then your dad collapsed and that whole thing about his other son came out and . . ." She stopped talking abruptly and looked deeply into his eyes. "I'm just making excuses, Adam. I should have told you immediately. I apologize."

Adam held her hands for long moments, then bent his head and kissed each one. "Allie, I just realized what a jerk I am. If I wasn't it wouldn't have been so hard for you to come talk to me and you wouldn't have put yourself through what was obviously a lot of turmoil. Sweetheart, you're the one person in the world who can tell me anything, anytime, anywhere. How could I ever be angry with you for telling me the truth? Come here," he coaxed, pulling her off the stool and into his lap.

"Alicia, *chica*, you're the best thing that's ever come into my life. You make my life have meaning, structure, and pure happiness. We've always been able to communicate about everything. We can't let that change, baby. I understand why you felt you couldn't talk to me before, but let that be the last time, okay?"

"Okay," she said gravely. "Can I ask you something? Is this going to make talking to your father easier? I mean, now that you know more about his background?"

Adam thought a minute and rubbed his right earlobe between his thumb and forefinger. "Who knows, Allie? It should make it easier, but this is Pop we're talking about. It all depends on how cooperative he wants to be." He glanced at the kitchen clock. "We'd better eat fast and get out of here."

Alicia agreed, saying she had two appointments that morning.

"Then it's a good thing you brought your work clothes with you last night," Adam reminded her. "In fact, why don't you just move in with me?"

The only sound that could be heard was her fork hitting the thick pottery plate in front of her.

Adam greeted Martha with a kiss on the cheek and a sheaf of brightly colored spring flowers. "For putting up with my dad and making him happy," he told her. "Where is he?"

"He's out on the deck," Martha told him. "I was just about to bring his lunch to him. Can I bring you something, too?"

Adam assured her that he was fine and went through the sunny living room of the condominium to the deck where his father was relaxing on a chaise longue. He had a glass of iced water with lemon slices at hand, and a copy of *Black Enterprise* on his lap. He looked like he was entertaining some very deep thoughts, but he heard Adam's entrance and turned around to smile at him. "Come on out, son, and have a seat. It's been a long time since we had a talk," he said with dry understatement.

Adam leaned over and gave his father a kiss on the forehead. "How are you feeling, Pop? You gave us all a scare the other day. All that forbidden food, was it worth it?"

Big Benny didn't have the grace to look the least bit embarrassed. "Probably not, but it was good going down. I won't be doing it again, though. Martha swears she'll leave me if I do." He sighed deeply. "I'm going to have to toe the line from now on, I guess." He glanced up at Adam and asked him to sit down again. "Quit hovering, you act like you're about to fly out of here," he said with a touch of his usual saltiness.

Adam pulled a chair next to the chaise and sat down, his long legs stretched out in front of him. He looked at his father intently, observing him carefully for the first time in a long time. They were so much alike physically, with their high cheekbones, sculptured lips, and firm, stubborn chins, that they could have been brothers if it weren't for Big Benny's snow-white hair. He still wore a thick moustache and neatly trimmed goatee and despite his occasional forays into forbidden foods, he'd kept his physique trim. The years had diminished very little of the man who was his father. This was the man he'd loved and respected his entire life, yet right now he felt as if he didn't know the man at all.

"If you don't feel up to talking about this right now I'll understand. But you know I met the family when I went to Idlewild. Your great-aunt Emmaline, your aunts Reba, Daphne, and Dahlia, you know I met them. Why did you lie? You always said you had no family and we believed that. So now I want to know why, Pop. Those are the sweetest, funniest old ladies I ever met," he said

Big Benny didn't respond for a long moment. He smiled suddenly and said, "Dilly and Daffy."

"What, Pop?"

"Dahlia and Daphne. I called them Dilly and Daffy because they were so sweet and silly. Did they try to tell you they're not twins? They've been doing that as long as I can remember and the sad thing is, they really believe it. You know they're only two years older than me? Yeah, and Reba is three years younger. There were a bunch of kids in my father's family. He was one of the middle children and when he married my mother, he had a brother who was a just a kid. His name was Richard but we all called him Buddy. Uncle Buddy started his family late, so I had aunts who were like my sisters." He smiled fondly. "Great-aunt Emmaline, now, *she* must be a hundred by now," he mused. She was a lot younger than my grandmother; she was the baby of the family. That was a big family, too."

"What happened, Pop? You obviously have fond memories of them. What happened to make you leave?"

After another long pause, Big Benny started talking and the story he told wasn't that different from the one Alicia had told Adam that morning. "After Aaron drowned, my mother was never the same. She was always nervous, always afraid to let me out of her sight. I tried my best to never cause her any worry. In fact, I became the ideal son, hard as that is to believe. I was actually kind of a sissy-boy, if you can imagine that. No sports, no school activities of any kind, I came straight home every day and did whatever she wanted me to do, which was mostly sit and keep her company. I didn't mind too much, because I wanted to please her, to make her happy. I guess I felt guilty for being alive when my brother wasn't, who knows?

"My father told me my most important job was to keep her happy and that's what I did. Up until the summer I graduated from high school, that is. That's the summer I met Cassandra." He sighed, lost in memories. "Cassandra Hightower was from Indiana and she came to Idlewild to work as a hostess in my father's club, the Hacienda. I knew from the minute I laid eyes on her that she was the one for me. She was a sweet girl: tall and pretty with this long coal-black hair and great big eyes. She had a smile so adorable it could break your heart. She wanted to be a teacher and she was earning the money to go to school. Her father knew my father and that's how she ended up coming to Idlewild.

"Cassandra was a good girl, too, a church girl. All the hostesses did was greet people, seat them, and make them feel at home. She wasn't a waitress or a shake dancer, now, they were older and more exotic. A lot of the dancers and waitresses dated the customers, of course, but the hostesses tended to be younger and more innocent, especially Cassandra. Nobody would have dared say anything to her anyway, because I was a big guy even back then and it was understood that I was her boyfriend."

Benny paused and drank some water before continuing. "I was the happiest I'd ever been in my life, son. When she wasn't working and I wasn't working, we were together. We rode horses together, we went for long walks, we spent a lot of time on the lake, and we did just about everything together. Everybody thought it was so cute, the two of us. My father liked her a lot, thought she was a sweet little thing. My mother, well, she hated her on sight. Hated her so much she concocted this huge lie about Cassandra being my father's mistress. I wouldn't have believed her, but Dilly and Daffy and Reba all swore it was true. Adam, they might as well have taken out a gun and shot me dead, because it just about killed me.

"I left Idlewild that night and never went back. I never wanted to see any of them again, especially my father, the man I idolized. I couldn't believe that he could be so low as to cheat on my mother and to do it with someone as young and innocent as Cassandra. Everything just seemed to go to hell after that. I went into the army and after basic training I got shipped off to the Philippines, and when my mother killed herself, I was in a hospital with dysentery. Couldn't come home to see her buried and I knew I was the reason she did it. After she died, my father sold the club and moved to Grand Rapids. He just couldn't stand to be there without her, I guess. I've always felt bad that I never contacted him again, that he died without one decent word from me."

His voice was thick with emotion and Adam was almost sorry that he'd begun the conversation. Maybe it would have been better to leave everything the way it was, but it was too late for that. He was about to suggest that they talk about it later, but his father continued to talk.

"I was sorry for the way I'd treated him, even though I never forgave him for what he'd done. I just couldn't forget what he'd done. I couldn't let it go. Cassandra was everything to me, Adam. She was my whole world, Adam. She made every day wonderful. And with a few words, everything was destroyed. I had a long time to think about it, about how she and my father betrayed me. I never wanted to see that town again and none of those people. I just acted like I had no family, and as far as I was concerned, I didn't. After what I'd found out about my father and Cassandra, they were dead to me. I was a bitter man for a long time until I met your mother. Your mother saved my life, son. She taught me how to live again, how to love again."

Adam stared at his father with the intensity of someone straining to understand a foreign language. "Okay, Pop, that was a pretty raw deal. You loved this girl and you lost her because you were told things about her that weren't true. You turned away from your family and went out on your own. Then you met Mom and you say she taught you how to love again. That's pretty huge. So how did the rest of this happen, if you loved Mom so much? This is what I don't understand: how could you cheat on her?" he asked tightly.

Benny fell silent and stared at the backs of his hands for a long time before answering his son. "Lillian Bennett was one of a kind. She was the kind of person who drew people to her. Everyone loved her; they just couldn't help it because she was so sweet. *I* couldn't help it; it took about two minutes for me to fall in love with her. She was everything a woman should be; she was the best friend, the best wife and mother anyone could hope for. I'll go to my grave regretting being unfaithful to her. It wasn't because of anything lacking in her, she was a wonderful woman and I loved her dearly." He looked Adam in the eye defiantly when he said this, and Adam was shocked to see a hint of moisture in his father's eyes. It wasn't enough, however, to stop him from asking the inevitable question.

"I hear what you're saying, Pop, but you still cheated on her. If you loved her so much, how could you do that?"

Bennie fell silent again, taking another swallow of water and directing his gaze off to the side. After a long, uncomfortable silence he started talking again although his voice was noticeably weaker. "Lillian and I had been married for a long time and they were without question the best years of my life. We had beautiful children, healthy children. Nobody could ask for a better family.

I was out of town on business, over in Gary, Indiana, and I went into a little restaurant. There she was, just like I remembered her. Cassandra Hightower was having dinner in that same restaurant and she looked up at me at the same time I saw her.

"I should have turned around and left when I laid eyes on her, but I couldn't. I went over to her table and she asked me to sit down. I had my speech all planned. Hell, I'd been rehearsing it for twenty-five years. I told her what I thought of her for what she'd done, and took great pains to let her know just what a wonderful life I had. But it didn't end up like I planned. She had no idea what I was talking about, son. She looked at me with those great big eyes full of tears and asked me why I hated her so much since I was the one who didn't want anything to do with her. I was the one who'd run off without a word to her and she never knew what she'd done to deserve that from me."

"It took about ten minutes to get everything out on the table, but the bottom line was I'd been had. My mother, my *own mother* made up a pack of lies and my aunts backed her up. I'd fallen for the oldest trick in the book and ruined my life and Cassandra's life as a result. Oh yeah, her life wasn't what she wanted it to be either. She was so torn up after I ran off that she came back to Indiana and never left again. She finished school, she became a teacher, but she never did get married. Never had another boyfriend after me, she said she couldn't face that kind of heartbreak again."

Adam's eyes never left his father's face during this recitation. He could see that Benny was in another place, another time, reliving the past as he remembered it. It just wasn't enough to sway Adam.

"Okay, so the both of you got a raw deal. You were what, eighteen at the time? By the time you saw her again you had a new life, you had a family and a wife who loved you and trusted you and deserved a faithful hus-

band. What about her, Pop? How did you get from regrets to paternity?" he asked, none too gently.

"I made a mistake, that's how," Benny answered angrily. "We kept talking until the restaurant closed and I
took her home. And I stayed. Just that one night, one
night to make up for all the time we'd had stolen away
from us. I'm not trying to justify what I did, I was a grown
man and I knew when I was doing it I was wrong as two
left shoes. But it wasn't about right and wrong, it was
about something over which I had no control.

"We said we'd never see each other again after that
and she kept her end of it. I never heard another word
from her until she was about to deliver our child. And
the only reason she got in touch with me then was that
she was dying. She knew she didn't have much time left
and she wanted to make sure that the baby was taken
care of. I went to see her then, and I helped arrange for
the baby to be adopted. She died a few days after the
baby was born and the boy was adopted. And that was
the end of it," he said with finality.

"The end of it? Pop, if that was the end of it we
wouldn't be having this conversation now. Why did you
dig all this up? What possible good can come out of confronting this man and bringing him here? What are you
trying to do, atone for your sins?"

"I don't like your tone, Adam. Let's not forget who the
father is here. Who the hell are you to judge me, boy? I'm
doing what I have to do, not what I want to do or what's
going to be convenient for the family. All of y'all are
grown, educated, you have good careers and good lives,
and I'm the one who made that possible. You never lacked
for anything; you had everything you could possibly want.
So don't make it out like I was a terrible father, somebody
who abused you and mistreated you." His face was taking
on a familiar red hue and his breathing was growing
harsh. "Name me one thing you did without when you
were a child, one thing!"

Adam's jaw was so tight he could barely get the words out but he managed. "One thing? Since you ask, I'll tell you. The one thing I did without was my mother. You couldn't make that right." Pale with rage, he left the deck without another word.

For the first time in many, many years, Benny felt real tears sliding down his face as he sat alone on the deck.

As summit meetings went, this one wasn't bad. After Benita and Andrew assured Ruth they weren't trying to crucify her, she came to lunch willingly. All of the Cochrans were there, with the exception of Adam. Bump Williams was also present, along with Renee and Angelique. They had all convened at the home of Andrew and Renee and after a buffet lunch, they were ranged about the living room talking quietly and listening expectantly. Aunt Ruth looked around at her niece and nephews and had to swallow hard to conquer the lump in her throat. Ruth Bennett was an absolute original. She was a career soldier, an army officer who'd resigned her commission when her only sister was killed in a car accident. She'd stepped in as best she could to help raise the children, and the results of her love and devotion were now strong, admirable adults. She'd done everything she could for them; she only hoped that what she had to tell them wouldn't destroy the loving relationship they'd always had.

Clearing her throat, she began. "I don't know how to explain this to you, other than to say that what I did, I did to protect my sister. When Benny called me and told me about the baby, I was the one who found a family to take him. I had a very dear friend, Consuela Flores, who wanted a family more than anything in this world. She and her husband, Nestor, were so happy to have the baby, being parents meant everything to them. We arranged a private adoption and they moved to California. I had a chance to help my friend and keep my sister from finding out her husband had lost his mind and I did it. I didn't see any other way out," she said with a catch in her voice. She paused and pressed her fingers to her temples, trying to maintain her composure.

"I'll understand if you hate me for it, I really will. Everything happened so quickly; I just reacted to the situation at hand. Your father had done something incredibly careless, something that he would regret for the rest of his life. I could compound the situation by telling my sister and destroying her life, or I could make it all go away, and I chose the latter. My sister's happiness, your happiness, was all I cared about. I don't know if it was the right thing to do or not, but it was done a long time ago. I was frankly amazed when Benny told me what he was planning to do, but I understand it, to some extent," she said in a quiet voice so unlike her normal brisk speech.

Donnie was sitting next to Aunt Ruth on the love seat and he put his arm around her protectively. He'd always been her favorite, according to his siblings, and his actions proved it. "Aunt Ruth, look, none of us could ever hate you. At this point it's not a question of who did what or when. That's all over. But there is something we'd like to know, and that's how John Flores came to be Benita's therapist in California. Did you . . . know anything about that?"

Ruth leaned against Donnie and bowed her head briefly. She raised her head almost defiantly before answering. "Yes, I did. I knew where John was and who he was because I'd stayed in touch with his mother. Consuela wrote me and I wrote her. She sent me pictures of John as he was growing up, so I would know what had become of him. I knew he was one of the best psychotherapists in California and Benita had to have the best. Her depression was so profound . . . Well, I don't have to tell you that, you all saw her. I asked for John and he was available and he came."

"Aunt Ruth, Donnie is right, we couldn't possibly hate you. I know you did it out of love for my mother and compassion for my father," she began.

Ruth grimaced and gestured with her hand. " 'Compassion' might be stretching it, Benita. I was in panic mode, quite honestly. I just didn't want Lillian to find out."

"So you knew who John was," Benita marveled. "It's so funny, everyone always says how much he favors Adam, and I thought it was just because of their height and their ponytails. I never really saw that much of a resemblance. Of course, even if I'd seen a true similarity it wouldn't have occurred to me that he was a relative," she added with a half smile.

Bump spoke for the first time. "As long as we're confessing, I have to tell you that I knew, too. Benny told me about it, not too long after the boy was adopted. When I saw John with you and Clay at the airport in L.A., I knew who he was immediately," he said, rubbing the bridge of his nose. "I've always felt bad about not telling anyone about it, but how could I?" Angelique was sitting closest to Bump and reached over to take his hand.

"You couldn't. No one blames you for anything," she said fiercely.

Alan and Andre concurred. "Maybe we're just too cynical for our own good, but this isn't the first time something like this has happened in a family and it won't be the last," Alan said.

"Yeah, it's pretty much time out for all the who did what and when and why. If Mom was still alive it would be a lot different, but since she's gone, God rest her soul, it's up to us to deal with this. We all know what Pop wants, but the question is, what do we want? Are we ready to deal with a new sibling, a half brother? Do we just let it go or do we do as Pop wants?" Andre asked the group at large.

Andrew spoke then. "Benita and I think it would be pretty impossible to ignore it. We want to meet with John and break it to him as gently as possible that he comes from a nest of cuckoos."

Everyone laughed gamely at his lame joke. Donnie agreed with his oldest brother, though. "Yeah, I think that's the general consensus. We can't pretend like this never happened, we have to move forward. Gently, of course, because this is going to be really awkward," he said thoughtfully. "Even on a good day we're pretty unruly. We don't want to scare the guy half to death."

Benita smiled, thinking about John. "It's amazing that none of you ever met him. Renee did because she was with me every step of the way, and of course Aunt Ruth and Clay and Angelique, when she came out to see me. But none of you men ever did, you were just never around when John was visiting. That's really odd," she said, more to herself than anyone else.

"I'm very relieved that you all are so accepting of this," Ruth said, "but there's something you're not thinking about, or someone, I should say." When all eyes turned to her, she elaborated. "There's one person who isn't here right now, and that's Adam. This is going to be very hard on Adam, for a number of reasons, not the least of which is John's birthday."

Everyone looked blank until Ruth explained. "I'm sorry, I keep forgetting you all don't know these things. One of the reasons I ran to help Benny was that my sister had just given birth to Adam. He and John were born five days apart."

No one could think of a thing to say to break the silence.

Alicia was in her office working on an intricate plan when her door opened and Adam walked in. She stopped what she was doing at once and looked at him. "How did the meeting with your father go?" she asked softly.

Adam didn't answer at first. He shoved his hands into his pockets and his jaw tightened. Finally he answered. "It was fine. I just stopped by to let you know I'm leaving. We have that project out west, remember, and I'm flying to Seattle this evening."

"You're going to Seattle? Why do you have to go now, Adam?" Alicia didn't care that her voice sounded demanding and anxious, that was how she felt. Adam was standing in her office looking like they were talking about the weather when in fact, he'd just announced that he was leaving town.

"Alicia, I've been planning this for three weeks. You've known about this project for a least a month and a half, you knew I was leaving this week," he said. He was looking at her with eyes so devoid of expression they looked dead.

"Yes, of course, I knew about it," she said hastily. "But with everything that's going on, I thought that you'd want to stay here. Hannibal or Paul can go in your place, you don't really have to go *now*, do you?" Her anxiety made her sound harsh, not understanding, and she was about to try again when the ice in his eyes melted just a little.

He crossed the short distance between them and put his arms around her. "Believe me, Allie, this is for the best. I need to get out of here for a while and clear my head. Staying around here and having to deal with all this drama is the worst thing for me. I'll call you when I get there," he said quietly.

Alicia stared at him with unhappy eyes and he leaned down to take her lips in a long and tender kiss. "I'm not leaving you, Allie. You're my heart. But I've got to put some space between me and this whole mess. I'll call you." Before Alicia could say anything else, he turned and left the office.

Chapter Seventeen

John Flores sat behind his desk in a big swivel chair dutifully putting away the files he was taking from a corrugated box. He glanced up and realized this one box barely made a dent in the sea of cartons all waiting to be unpacked before the place would resemble an office. He was bone-tired and this was the last place he wanted to be, but the job had to be done. Thank God he had a helper, albeit a rather unwilling one. He pulled open the drawer in the center of the desk and located a small glass container of paper clips. With a smile on his handsome face he began pitching them into the very perfect updo of the woman who was kneeling next to a partially unpacked box, taking out books and arranging them in the floor-to-ceiling bookshelves that made up one wall. A small tightening of her lips was the only indication that she was aware of his activity.

"Do you know how irritating that is? How childish?" she said in her ultraprecise diction.

"Yes, Miss Parker, I do. That's why I'm doing it."

She rose, and with a toss of her head, dislodged all the clips. "If you want me to get this office in some kind of order, I suggest you stop it now. And can you please explain to me what this is doing here?" She held up an oddly shaped piece of sporting equipment with a look of forbearance. "There's a whole box full of this sort of thing, whatever it is."

The apparatus in her hand was a long metal stick with

an oval ring attached to the end of it, a ring that was strung with heavy cords like a misshapen basketball hoop. John smiled as he looked at the device.

"Careful with that, that's my favorite lacrosse stick. I've been playing lacrosse since I was a kid and some of those sticks, the wooden ones, are antiques. I was planning to mount them on the wall."

Miss Parker leaned the stick against the wall and dusted her hands together briskly. "Moderation is pleasant to the wise," she murmured. "Wouldn't a couple of nice diplomas do for decoration instead of these . . . *things?*"

Before John could reply, he was rescued by the ringing of his cell phone. With a grateful grin he answered it. "Hello?"

His grin turned into a real smile as he recognized the friendly voice of Benita Cochran-Deveraux.

"Well, this is a pleasant surprise. How are you, Benita?"

"I'm just fine, John, and yourself?"

"Couldn't be better. I'm just trying to get acclimated to your Michigan weather and get settled into the new office."

"Sounds like you could use a break, like a nice meal," she suggested. "I'm in Detroit with Clay and the children, would you like to meet for dinner tomorrow?"

"That sounds like a great idea. What time and where? Do you want to meet in Detroit? I'm still not too familiar with the area but I think it's pretty close, right?"

"Yes, it is, but I haven't been to Ann Arbor in a billion years, so let's meet there. I think my brother Andrew is coming, too, if that's okay."

"Sure, the more the merrier," he replied.

They agreed on a restaurant and a time to meet and John ended the call with a happy look on his face.

Belatedly he remembered there was someone else in the room and asked if she had plans for dinner the next day.

She looked at him over the top of her severely chic designer glasses and sniffed. "No, thank you. There's a track club here in town and I'm going to see about joining. If I'm going to be here in the back of beyond for the next couple of months, I don't want to get out of shape," she said crisply.

Wouldn't you have to get *a shape in order to lose it?* John thought uncharitably and was immediately ashamed. It was just that Miss Parker was possibly the skinniest woman he'd ever seen apart from Olive Oyl and some truly emaciated models who'd participated in one of his therapy groups for eating disorders. She was rail thin, tall, and very fashionable, but she normally had the disposition of a pit viper. Always polite, always professional, but as cheerful as a funeral procession most of the time: that was Miss Parker. To be honest he was glad she'd turned down the invitation he'd offered out of politeness.

They left the office shortly after the phone call, each going in a different direction. John smiled to himself on his way to the temporary housing provided by the university. He was looking forward to seeing Benita again; he always enjoyed seeing her. Ever since their first encounter years before, she'd held a special place in his heart. He was too honorable and practical to waste time railing against fate for bringing her into his life, but he had to occasionally laugh at the irony. There was something about Benita that he couldn't ignore, couldn't forget.

He knew in his heart that if she'd been single he would've tried to get to know her on a much more personal level, but her marriage made that impossible. He'd never seen two people more in love than Benita and Clay. Still, he couldn't deny the way she affected him. There was something there, something he'd never found in another woman. He laughed bitterly, thinking about his new circumstances. God knew what he was doing after all. Even if she'd been free, they wouldn't have a future together. The news he'd received two months before made that a certainty. *If you want to make God laugh, make plans.* He laughed again at the painful irony.

Roxy took a deep swallow from her glass of chilled mineral water with the slices of lime floating in it. She and Alicia were getting pedicures after a long day of pampering, as Alicia made good on her promise to treat Roxy to a day at the spa. "So I was right and you were wrong," Roxy gloated. "And aren't you glad I was right?"

Alicia tired to look indifferent, then coy, and then gave up. "*Yes*, a thousand times yes, Rox. I've never been so glad to be wrong about anything in my life. Adam and I, we're just . . . it's just wonderful. I had no idea it could be like this between a man and a woman. My life feels like one of those juicy novels you always pretend you don't read."

Roxy raised an eyebrow. "Don't be hatin' on me. If you ask me, *all* Janice Sims novels should be required reading for all couples. Her books are an education, honey. And you read them too, you know you do."

Alicia gave her a very satisfied smile. "You'd better believe it. You're going to be my maid of honor, you know."

Roxy wiggled her toes in excitement, something that didn't thrill the nail technician who was caring for her feet. "Sorry," Roxy said winsomely, "but it's not every day your best friend gets the man of her dreams. I'll be still, I promise."

Claudia, the nail tech, just smiled and waved away her apology. "I feel you, girl. When my sister got engaged I screamed so loud I lost my voice for three days, so you go ahead. Just let me know when you want to holla so I don't snip you with these nippers," she said, brandishing a sharp and ominous-looking tool.

In a short while they were ready to leave the spa, although Roxy confessed that she'd like to move in. "Can you imagine getting a massage like that every day?" She sighed.

Alicia agreed absentmindedly and her lack of attention didn't escape Roxy's keenly observant eye. "Your mind is a million miles away, isn't it? You're all caught up thinking about Adam and the lost Cochran, aren't you? You have to take a step back, Alicia; you can't let this consume you. If you go all mushy in the head you won't be a bit of good to Adam. He's going to need you to have a cool and neutral perspective. This is a lot of drama for any family, even one that's used to the limelight like the Cochrans."

"Drama is probably the right word." They were in the Mini Cooper, driving in no particular direction. "Are you hungry?"

Roxy laughed. "Is fat meat greasy? Have you ever known me to not be hungry? What do you suggest?"

"My mother's house. *Papi* is off the road for a couple of days and I know she has something wonderful to eat; she always does when her boys are home."

Alicia was right, her mother indeed had a wonderful spread, succulent baked chicken, succotash made from peaches-and-cream corn and lima beans with sweet onions and okra and tomatoes, a luscious cucumber salad with a tart vinaigrette and sour cream, and best of all, collard and turnip greens and hot-water cornbread. Roxy sighed with repletion.

"Mrs. Fuentes, I haven't had food this wonderful since the last time I ate at your house. Can you adopt me?" she asked, completely serious.

Raphael and Carlos, Alicia's big handsome brothers, were sitting on either side of Roxy at the long dining room table. Both of them said "no" in loud resounding voices. "Can't do it, Foxy Roxy. That would make you our sister," Raphael explained. "And as soon as I get through sowing my wild oats I intend to marry you, so sorry, adoption is out of the question."

Everyone laughed except Carlos, who frowned at Raphael. "Excuse me, but I've had my eye on Roxy for years and you know it. I told you years ago that she was the woman I planned to marry. This," he said possessively, putting his arm around Roxy, "is the mother of my future children, so you can forget it."

Roxy looked from Raphael to Carlos and smiled widely. They were both well over six feet, big, dark brown muscular men with thick shoulders and huge arms. They looked a lot like their father, Jose, with wide, handsome faces, thick black hair, thick eyebrows, and big pouty lips. "You two need to quit. I have witnesses and I plan to hold you both to those proposals. You won't find it so easy to wriggle out of them in a court of law," she said demurely.

While her brothers flirted outrageously with Roxy, Alicia helped her mother clear the table and clean the kitchen. Leah waited until they were alone in the kitchen and took both her daughter's hands. "What is it, sweetness? You must want to talk to me about something; you know the boys would have cleaned up the kitchen for me. Come and sit down, let's talk," she said, drawing Alicia over to the breakfast table.

"Adam is closing me out again. After he went over to talk to his father, he packed his bags and left town," she said sadly.

Leah's pretty face creased into a frown. Alicia looked very much like her mother, even more so since she'd cut her hair. Leah looked much the way she did when she was a college student at Spelman in Atlanta, where she swept a certain brash minor league baseball player off his feet with one look. She had the mature sexiness of a woman who is completely loved and completely happy, while still maintaining a youthful charm. But she also had the wisdom her daughter needed at the moment.

"He left town? Without a word to you, *mija?*"

Alicia explained that this was a scheduled business trip, but under the circumstances Adam could easily have delegated someone else or rescheduled the trip. "He needed to be alone, *Mami*. He had too much too deal with and he needed to put some space between him and his family. It's all just too much for him to take in." She sighed.

"Alicia, *mi corazon*, it seems like you already know what's going on in his heart. You can't torture yourself like this, you have to let him come to you in his own time and his own way," Leah counseled.

"*Mami*, Adam asked me to marry him. I can't see how a marriage can survive if he's going to keep doing this. He gets cold and distant and uncommunicative and I can't imagine living in the same house with him when he does it. I've known him for ten years and I know he's this way, but we haven't been living under the same roof twenty-four-seven. When he'd be brooding about something, he'd go one way and I'd go another and we'd hook up again when he was over his mood. How am I supposed to live with that distance all the time? How am I supposed to handle it without driving myself crazy, or him?" she asked passionately.

Leah smiled gently. "Honey, do you think your father is a good man?"

Alicia looked startled. Her father was the sweetest, most considerate, attentive husband in the world. What was her mother asking? "Of course he is, *Mami*. *Papi* is wonderful," she began, only to be cut off by a roll of her mother's eyes.

"You don't think I got him like that, do you? He didn't come from the factory in that condition. His current behavior is the result of years of effort on both our parts. Honey, love will find a way. You and Adam love each other dearly. He's your grand passion and you are his. Let Adam find his own way through this, *mija*. Love will find a way."

Leah spoke with such quiet assurance that Alicia wanted with all her heart to trust in what her mother was saying. But with Adam across the country in Seattle, it seemed very close to impossible.

Benita's fingers drummed repeatedly on the table in a rhythmic pattern that finally caused her husband to take her hand and enclose it in his. The warmth and comfort of his big hand wrapped around her own was just what she needed to calm down. He moved his chair closer to hers and put his arm around her shoulder. He leaned over and brushed his lips against her ear, whispering, "It's going to be fine, Peaches. Try to relax a little, sweetheart."

She smiled at his words and the comforting feel of his lips on her skin. The slight thrill she always felt when he kissed her warmed her, and she did feel a little more relaxed. "I love you so much, Clay. I'm so glad you're here with me."

Clay smiled and kissed her again. "Where else would I be but here with you?"

"Get a room, why don't you? Isn't it about time y'all started acting like a respectable married couple?" Andrew joined the couple in the upstairs outdoor dining room of Paoli's, a fine Italian restaurant in Ann Arbor. He gave them a comic look and elaborated on his remark. "You got five kids already and this is how they come about. Can't you keep your hands off each other for five minutes?"

Benita and Clay smiled at each other and kissed again. "No, we really can't," she said with a lingering glance at her beloved. "And you aren't the one to talk about being an old married couple. I seem to have walked up on you and your wife several times in the past few days and you were doing much more than we're doing right now."

Andrew grinned and made a great flourish of straightening his tie. "Well, you know, what can I tell you? I just got it like that," he said with a leer. He glanced at his watch and asked what time John was supposed to meet them.

"I told him to be here at seven-thirty," she began and glanced up with a look of nervous anticipation. "There he is now." She waved at John, who was standing in the entrance to the patio. Without realizing it, she tightened her hand on Clay's and held her breath as he approached the table.

He looked the way he always did, tall and handsome with a ready smile. He was thinner than usual, but still an imposing figure of a man with his nicely chiseled features, thick black moustache, and the wavy black hair that came past his shoulders and was confined in a thick braid. He was wearing a casual outfit of a black linen shirt with a band collar and black pleated slacks, catching the eye of several female diners as he walked to their table. He looked relaxed and glad to see Benita and Clay. He shook hands with Clay and Andrew and gave Benita a quick hug and kiss on the cheek. Taking a seat, he looked around the patio and smiled.

"It's really good to see you two. How long has it been, a year or so?" he asked.

Benita was finding it difficult to speak, but she nodded. "About that long," she said finally. "It's good to see you, too. And I'm glad you and Andrew finally got to meet. We were just saying the other day how odd it was that you've never met any of the boys in the family." She blushed, hoping that her words hadn't betrayed the secret she wasn't yet ready to reveal.

John hadn't detected anything amiss, however. He rubbed his chin and glanced at Andrew, agreeing with Benita. "You're right. I met your aunt Ruth, of course, and Renee and your sister-in-law Angelique. And I've met Clay's brothers, too, when I was in Atlanta. But this is the first time I've had the opportunity to meet a Cochran man."

Andrew spoke for the first time. "It's a privilege to meet you, John. In a way I feel like I know you, since you and I talked on the phone while Benita was in your care in California. And she's told me some wonderful things about you over the years. This is a real pleasure," he said sincerely and quickly lowered his eyes to the menu, fearing he'd said too much.

To Andrew's and Benita's relief the server showed up then, extolling the virtues of the nightly special and taking their orders. Everyone had a glass of wine except John, who stuck to iced tea. Conversation flowed more smoothly after that, and the evening was quite pleasant. The meal was superb and the mood was lighthearted and happy. Benita regaled John with the exploits of their children and John talked about the projects he was working on.

"Right now I'm working on a book about new techniques in therapy. Of course I can't write worth a darn, but the publisher took care of that by sending me the greatest cowriter in the world. She's a big, big help to me in a lot of ways, although she's a bit salty from time to time. We manage to get along, though, and she agreed to come with me to Ann Arbor to finish the book. So in addition to teaching and writing, I'll have a pretty full agenda. I've put my practice on hold for a while because I seem to prefer teaching right now."

The talk faded away as the evening shadows lengthened. Benita tried hard not to stare at the man she now knew was her half brother, but it was an almost impossible task. She was searching his face for similarities between John and the rest of her brothers. Oddly, they were there in the line of his jaw, his hairline, the shape of his nose, the crooked smile . . . Why hadn't she seen them before? Because she hadn't been looking for a resemblance, because there was no reason to think there was a connection between the two of them other than as patient and doctor. And now she had to tell him, she had to say the words that would change his life, the words that might shatter their friendship forever. She took a deep breath and looked at her twin brother before speaking.

Andrew always knew what his sister was thinking, and tonight was no different. He reached across the table and took her hand, giving it a reassuring squeeze. He was looking at Benita and not John when he started talking. "John, one of the reasons Benita asked you to dinner tonight was that we have a story to tell you. It's about our father and something that affected his whole life. In turn, it affects all of our lives now and we thought you should know about it. It's not really a long story, but it's complicated. Would you like to hear it?"

John looked interested and said of course he would. This time it was Benita who spoke, beginning with the simple words "Our father was born in Idlewild, Michigan."

Chapter Eighteen

Long after the dinner at her parents' house, Alicia was still feeling restless. She'd said good night to her parents and brothers, taken Roxy back to her car, which she'd left parked at the spa, and returned to the condo, all with the same uneasiness plaguing her. Her niece and nephew were asleep and Marielle was going over her schedule for the next day. They exchanged a few words before Alicia went up to her room. She got ready for bed, cleansing her face taking a hot shower and slipping into a short, feminine peach silk gown, courtesy of her shopping spree with Roxy. Somehow her old collection of T-shirts and boxer shorts no longer had any appeal as sleepwear. She liked the feeling of sexy sophistication the pretty lingerie gave her.

She said her prayers before climbing into her four-poster bed, praying as always for the health and well-being of her family and friends, but especially for Adam's peace of mind. The rest of his family seemed remarkably sanguine about the revelations about his long-lost relatives from Idlewild and his father's long-denied son. They were accepting the news extremely well, given the circumstances, but Adam's anger was taking over his life. He was remote and reserved, even though they talked on the phone every day. Alicia tossed back and forth restlessly while wondering what she could do to help Adam, and while her thoughts were in turmoil, she fell into an uneasy sleep.

Some time later she awoke, her eyes popping open like one of those wake-and-sleep baby dolls. She sat straight up in bed and with one sure movement threw back the covers and got up, going to her closet and taking out an overnight bag. She tossed in underwear, a couple of tops and a pair of casual flats, and rolled up two pairs of slacks to add to the bag. She was taking out a matching tote bag for her toiletries when a soft tap sounded. Marielle, still fully dressed, entered the room with a puzzled look on her face.

"*Chica*, what are you doing? You just went to bed an hour ago. Now what are you up to?"

"I'm going to Seattle, Marielle. Adam needs me. I know it's not my cat, but he's my man and he needs me," she said resolutely.

"Oh. Okay, well, call me when you get there," she said with a yawn.

Alicia stopped her packing to stare at her sister. "Aren't you going to tell me this is crazy and I shouldn't interfere? Aren't you supposed to tell me to let him come to me if he needs my help?"

Marielle sprawled across the foot of the bed and laughed gently at the look of shock on her sister's face. "Alicia, sweetie, you're a grown woman and you make your own decisions. You've done pretty well so far. The only serious error in judgment was getting engaged to that idiotic pretty boy Preston, and you were smart enough to get rid of him. As far as you and Adam are concerned, well, you two seem to be doing just fine. You know him better than anyone and you know yourself. Who am I to be putting my two cents in? This is not *my* cat, *chica*; this time it's all yours. Do you need me to call the firm tomorrow and let them know you won't be in?"

Alicia told her no as she quickly dressed in jeans, a black scoop-necked sweater that buttoned with tiny jet-black buttons, and black leather ballet flats. "I was taking tomorrow as another personal day anyway, I'm just putting it to better use. She put her small leather purse over her shoulder and picked up the two bags. "I'll let you know when I get there. Just keep us in your prayers, okay?"

Marielle rose from the bed and gave her sister a fierce hug. "You never have to ask for that, you're always there."

She went downstairs after Alicia, ready to close the door behind her. Alicia opened the front door and gasped as she looked into Adam's face. His hand was raised to ring the doorbell and he looked just as surprised as Alicia. "Where were you going?"

"I was coming after you," she said breathlessly.

Adam took the bags from her hands. "Then let's go." With a nod to Marielle, he transferred both bags to one hand and put his arm around Alicia's slender waist. In minutes they were in the Range Rover, driving through the night-swept streets of Detroit.

John lay on his bed, fully clothed. He'd left the restaurant and driven around Ann Arbor for a while, then returned to the university-provided housing that was his temporary home. He took off his shoes and socks and piled the pillows at the head of the bed and just lay there, staring into space. Finally he picked up his cell phone and punched in a familiar number. He was relieved when the line was answered after three rings.

The voice on the other end said hello, and John responded in kind. "Abe, it's John Flores. I've just found out something that will solve part of a mystery. I had dinner with an old friend tonight and she told me a pretty amazing story. It seems that besides being a good friend of several years, she's also my half sister. I was adopted as an infant, can you believe it?"

Abraham Gold, besides being a good friend of John's, was a physician to whom John had turned in recent months. He was rendered speechless by John's words, but he soon found his tongue. "Damn, John. We knew something was off, since your father's blood type made it impossible that he fathered you, but this explains it all. It also explains a few other things. So how are you taking the news?"

John laughed, more from the need to relieve tension than from mirth. "I'm still pretty stunned right now, to tell you the truth. Benita's family lives in Detroit and she's visiting up here with her husband and children. Her father decided to make this big announcement that he'd fathered a child outside of his marriage, and I, apparently, am the bastard prince."

"Whoa. That's pretty deep, fella. So this guy, your friend's father, well, your biological father, I guess . . ." Abe's voice faded but quickly regained its composure. "So the father told you all this? What did you say to him?"

"No, Big Benny wasn't the bearer of the glad tidings. He coerced Benita into doing it. He's always had a huge influence on her and he can still wrap her around his little finger, I guess. Anyway, she and her husband and her twin brother were the messengers. They did it quite nicely, as a matter of fact. They told me the story their father told them and it just so happened I was the punch line to this huge cosmic joke."

"Actually, John, that doesn't sound much better. How did you react? It must have been pretty uncomfortable with all three of them sitting there with expectant looks on their faces. On a scale of one to ten, with ten being remarkably shocked and upset, what number did you register?" Abe's customary dry humor came through loud and clear.

John laughed bitterly. "Probably about a fifteen."

He'd been fascinated by the story Benita and Adam told him about Benny Cochran, his growing up in

Idlewild and the rift that caused him to leave town. To a large extent it explained the determination that propelled Benny into the seat of power he'd occupied until his retirement, and the influence he still wielded over his family. It was actually a poignant story until Benita got to the part about her father's chance encounter with Cassandra that fateful night in Gary, Indiana. At that point, Benita's voice had faded and she'd become distinctly uneasy. She had turned to her brother Andrew, who quietly explained the rest of the tale.

"So, Pop and Cassandra had one night together. It was a mistake, they both realized it, but the love they'd once shared was too powerful to be put aside. They gave in to the memories they shared and they came together for one night, just one night to assuage all the loneliness and the love they'd lost. And the result was a child. John, according to my father, that child was you."

A thick silence fell over the table, silence that John couldn't have broken if his life depended on it. It was up to Benita to start the flow of words again. "Cassandra kept her word and she didn't contact my father again until months later. She was about to give birth, and she also knew she didn't have long to live. She wanted to make sure her baby, *you* were taken care of and she didn't have any family to turn to. So she called Daddy, who enlisted the aid of our aunt Ruth, my mother's younger sister. Aunt Ruth knew a wonderful couple who couldn't have children, a couple she knew would give a baby the best possible life. And she got her friends Consuela and Nestor Flores to adopt you," she said in a hushed voice. "It was, she said, the fulfillment of a dream for them, they were deliriously happy to have you."

John felt as if he were watching a movie. He was completely detached from the reality of the situation, as though he were observing the table with the three good-looking people from far away. So far away that he couldn't hear their words, he could only see their lips moving. It was as if the volume were turned down or they were speaking a language with which he was unfamiliar. His ears were buzzing and his chest was tight; he couldn't breathe properly.

He could feel three sets of eyes staring at him, watching for a reaction, waiting for him to speak. Finally he found his voice, but what he said wasn't what he meant to say; it was all he could get out.

"I don't mean to be rude, but you'll understand that I need some time to put this all together. The meal was excellent. It was nice meeting you, Andrew, good to see you again, Clay." He rose, and leaning across the table, he kissed Benita on the cheek. "I'll call you, Benita. Good night."

Abe's low whistle resonated through the phone. "So you basically just got up and left?"

"Yeah, basically. I couldn't think or focus on anything. It was surreal, man. I've been lying here thinking about everything and trying to understand all of it and in a very weird way, it does make sense. My mother was killed outright in the car accident. When my father was in intensive care and I tried to give blood, it was obvious he couldn't be my father because of the difference in our blood type. I kind of wondered then if I could be adopted since you can't make me believe that my mother was ever unfaithful to my father. Those two were so much in love it was unreal, Abe. They lived for each other and for me and that's the truth. In fact, that's what lets me know that there's probably no doubt that the story is one hundred percent true."

"What do you mean, John? How does that play into anything you were told tonight?"

John sat up and swung his legs over the side of the bed. "My parents were the most incredible people in the world. They were kind and loving and they were so proud of me. Anything I did, they supported me. I once heard someone ask my mother why they didn't have more children and she said they didn't need any more, that they had the best child any parents could ask for and I was more than enough for them. I think that I really was the answer to their prayers for parenthood. On one level hearing the story tonight was a very humbling experience, Abe. Very humbling, to know that my accidental birth was the best thing that happened to my parents."

Abe probed deeper with his next question. "And on another level, what was it like, John?"

"It was freaky, man. I've never told anyone this but for years I've had like a huge crush on Benita Cochran Deveraux. From the first time I met her there was something about her that got to me. I've always thought she was the most beautiful, the most brilliant, the sweetest woman I ever met and if I thought I had a ghost of a chance of getting her away from that husband of hers, I would've made a complete fool of myself over her years ago. And it turns out she's my *sister*, Abe. How sick is that? This is like an episode of one of those really twisted late night talk shows. It's just sick and wrong, man, sick and wrong."

Abe chuckled and acknowledged that it was a unique situation. "But it's not like you knew she was related, c'mon now, give yourself a break. Look at it this way, I'll bet you don't have a crush anymore."

"You got that right. It was better than having ice water poured down my pants; whatever little vestiges of inappropriate affection were there have vanished permanently. All gone, my man. *Poof*, they all disappeared."

"Well, John, all kidding aside, this could be the answer to your problems. Instead of being a huge cosmic joke, as you put it, this could take care of everything," Abe said in a voice serious with concern.

"Abe, I can't go there, man. Can't do it," John admitted.

"At the very least it could be another big part of the puzzle. Did they say what your birth mother died from?" Abe groaned as he realized what he'd said. "I'm sorry, John, I'm not trying to be crass, but you know . . ."

"Yeah, Abe, I know. But I can't go there right now," John said solemnly.

"So what's your next move?"

Sighing deeply, John curled his bare toes into the carpet and stared at his long feet. "My next move? Buy my sister some flowers, apologize for being a jerk, and make plans to meet the family. Seems like the mature thing to do and I've got to grow up sometime, I guess."

"I never thought I'd hear you admit that," Abe said delightedly.

"Aw, you're just jealous of my youth, you old goat. Kiss your wife for me and tell the kids I said hello. I'll keep you posted."

"Do that. And, John, don't forget what I said. This could be your only hope."

Without any conversation, Adam drove Alicia to the loft. They entered in silence and stood facing each other, waiting for the next thing to happen. The next thing was them reaching for each other, embracing tightly and fiercely. "Allie, I missed you so much," Adam breathed into her hair.

"I missed you, too. I was worried about you," she said, pulling away from him far enough to be able to look into his eyes. "And it looks like I had a reason to be worried; you look terrible."

Adam gave her a last tight squeeze before reluctantly letting her go. He didn't want to stop touching her; the sight of her, the smell of her filled his senses. Alicia's hair was tousled, her face was makeup-free, but her skin was dewy and moist and the slight scent of her usual fragrance enticed him. He kissed her forehead and rubbed his cheek against her skin, marveling once again that anything so soft could exist. "I'm okay, Allie. I've been doing a lot of thinking over the past few days, that's all. A lot of thinking and a lot of remembering."

Something about the tone of his voice made Alicia take a step back and look at him intently. He looked tired, almost haggard. The strain of trying to deal with his father's revelations showed all too clearly. She knew what she needed to do, what he needed more than anything right then. She took him by the hand and told him to come with her.

"Where are we going?"

"We're going to the spa," she replied.

In a very short time, Alicia had drawn a bath for Adam in his bathtub. *Bathtub* was hardly the right word for the edifice; it was a huge, custom-built structure of black marble. Round, with whirlpool jets all around, the tub was easily big enough to hold four adults, which meant it was just the right size for two people who were madly in love, something Adam pointed out to Alicia as she leaned over the side of the steaming, fragrant bath. The huge tub wasn't built-in, only the part where the faucets were was flush to a wall and the rest was freestanding, which allowed Alicia to kneel at the side of it, which she was doing now. The room was dim, lit only by exotically scented candles, and flooded with the exquisite sound of *Love Songs* by Miles Davis. A feeling of utter peace filled Adam, except for one little detail.

"You know there's enough room for both of us, right? You're not going to make me stay in here all by myself, are you?"

"Yes, *mi corazon*, I am. You need to relax and this is a good way to do it," she said firmly. "I'm just here to help in that process."

She filled a small pitcher with the bathwater and poured it down his back, followed by another pitcher over his head, smiling as the rivulets streamed down his face. Then she picked up a bottle of shampoo and began to apply it to his hair, massaging it into a fragrant mass of lather. He moaned with contentment as her clever fingers lulled him into a euphoric state. She rinsed his hair with water from the bath and fresh hot water from the bathroom sink, saying that he might have to rinse it again in the shower. He murmured a barely audible response, and she took it as a cue to continue her ministrations.

Picking up a bottle of lightly fragranced Italian bath gel, she poured some into her palm, sniffing it appreciatively before she began smoothing it over Adam's big shoulders. He smiled and suggested she stop what she was doing before it was too late.

"Too late for what, *querida*?"

"For you to stay dry," he answered. Suddenly he sat up straight, turned around, and pulled her, fully clothed, into the tub with him. She screamed in surprise and then started laughing helplessly. He looked so pleased with himself and so much more at ease that she couldn't be angry. She stood up with difficulty, fussing the whole time. "Do you know how hard it is to take off wet clothing? You so owe me, Adam Brantley Cochran. You owe me big time for this one. And it's a good thing I didn't have on my cute little shoes or I'd have to beat you up."

Adam was laughing as he watched her unbutton her little black sweater and drop it on the floor, then start to take off a soft ivory half-cup bra whose delicate cups had become transparent after getting wet. His laughter stopped at once and he suggested she take off her jeans first. Alicia was softly muttering uncomplimentary phrases in Spanish, but she stopped messing with the bra and peeled out of the jeans. "You are taking me shopping tomorrow and buying me an outfit to replace this, a *whole new outfit*, Adam." She was sitting precariously on the edge of the tub while he helped her out of the heavy wet denim. Free from the cumbersome pants, she rose, clad only in the now transparent bra and equally transparent bikini panties that barely covered her bottom; moreover, the enticing black triangle of curly hair that shielded her femininity was quite visible.

Adam looked his fill at her beauty; she looked incredibly erotic clad in bits of foamy spray and glistening with moisture. She was about to exit the tub when his voice stopped her. Holding out his hand, he said, "Come here, Allie. Come be with me, baby."

His voice, low and sexy, gave Alicia no choice but to comply. He looked so handsome and seductive it was as though her legs had no will of their own. She slid down into the warm soapy depths with her beloved. He settled her in his lap, turning her face to his for a long, lingering kiss, while his big hands roamed over her body. She sighed raggedly while his lips pleasured hers and his tongue melted against hers in a rhythm as sexual as it was tender. He caressed her breasts through the thin wet silk, kneading the firm globes until her nipples stood out in hard relief against the flimsy fabric.

"I need to take this off, Adam," she whispered.

"No, you don't. You look so sexy, baby, leave it on for a while," he coaxed. By now he'd turned her so that she was cuddled next to him and he had full access to the center of her womanhood. The ivory silk panties were no barrier at all to his skilled fingers as he pushed past them to cup warm, yielding flesh. Her legs parted to allow him more access and she had to bite back a scream as he gently savaged her nipple, licking, sucking, and teasing it with his teeth. As her moans became more passion-filled, Adam moved the wet silk aside with his unshaven cheek and rubbed the bristly skin across her breast several times, loving the sounds of pleasure she was making. His fingers continued to explore her, massaging her hot, pulsing jewel until she was on the brink of a shattering release. He turned back to her erect, engorged nipple and began a sweet torture, sucking her with the same rhythm he was applying with his fingers until her body was a continuous pulsing mass of sensation. Her release was long and intense. The shudders that racked her body rendered her mindless with the most profound pleasure she'd ever felt, but at the center of it all was Adam; it was Adam who made her feel like a creature of light and energy and love. It was Adam whose strong arms cradled her and brought her back to earth to rest gently in his embrace as he whispered her name.

Some time later they were lying in his big bed, the only light coming from the platform of glass bricks. Now the music was *Warm and Tender* by Charlie Watts. The incredible vocals of Bernard Fowler floated through the scented air while Adam caressed Alicia. She was murmuring something he had to ask her to repeat. "I said, who knew that the drummer for the Rolling Stones was a fantastic jazz artist? I love this CD."

"I love you," Adam said softly.

"I know, isn't it wonderful? I love being in love with you. This night was supposed to be all about you, you know." She kissed his neck and rubbed her face against his shoulder. "It was all about making you feel wonderful. I was going to give you a massage and all kinds of things I learned at the spa."

"We can do that anytime, baby. And what makes you think I wasn't having just as much fun as you were? Sex isn't just about tit for tat or who got off and who didn't. And by the way I did get off, way, *way* off. I've told you before that watching you is arousing in the extreme. I love it. But when I'm making love to you I'm communing with you, joining my soul with yours for a brief eternity. It's not just about having an orgasm, my love."

A long kiss put a stop to further conversation for a time, followed by a comfortable silence in which they just relished being in each other's arms again. "Thank you for washing my hair, Allie. That was kind of special to me. No one's washed my hair since my mother died," Adam said quietly.

"You're welcome, Adam. You can get a shampoo from me any time you want." Alicia snuggled closer to his warmth and yawned delicately. She was about to say something else when Adam's voice cut through her lassitude.

"Did I ever tell you about my mother?"

Suddenly Alicia was wide-awake. "A little bit. I know she was very pretty and very smart."

"She was the most incredible person I knew. I was a real mama's boy, believe it or not. I was the youngest until Donnie came along. I had her all to myself for three years because all the other kids were in school all day. Even after Donnie was born, I was her helper. I used to fetch and carry for her all the time, just so I could be around her as much as possible. Mama was so funny, she used to teach me little crazy songs and we played all kinds of games. We used to play catch every day. She was a great pitcher. Mama was also pretty handy on the basketball court. She was a den mother for our Cub Scout troop and she was absolutely fearless. She'd take us camping and fishing, she wasn't afraid of snakes or worms or anything. I think that's where Benita got it from, she's tough like that, too."

Adam's deep voice went on, talking to Alicia so quietly she could feel the vibrations from his chest as he spoke. "I loved my dad, he was a great father, loud and boisterous and fun, but my mama was my heart. I was crazy about her. Even when I was in kindergarten, we were still running buddies. Kindergarten was only a half day back then, so I'd come home from morning kindergarten and there was always something great to eat and something fun to do. I don't think anyone realized how close we were. It was like that right up until the day she died. That was the worst day of my life, for a lot of reasons.

"Everyone else had gone off to school and Donnie

was asleep. I had a doctor's appointment and Mama was getting me ready when Daddy came home for some reason. I was upstairs but I could hear every word. They were having an argument, something that didn't happen very often. They were screaming this time, though. I'd never heard Mama yell like that. She sounded like her heart was breaking, she was crying and screaming at the same time. All I can remember is that she kept saying, 'He looks just like Adam, Ben. Just like Adam! How could you do this to us?'"

Alicia's arms tightened around Adam and she tried vainly to stop the hot tears she felt forming in her eyes. Adam stroked her body and kissed the top of her head before continuing. "I don't remember exactly what happened next, but I do remember that Daddy left. Mrs. Johnson, the lady who helped Mama clean, came over and Mama asked her to watch Donnie while she took me to the doctor. She also had to take Benita's science project to her school. We got into the car and she was still mad, I could tell, but she wasn't saying anything. We hadn't gone too far when there was this huge explosion, well, it sounded like an explosion to me. A truck had plowed into Mama's side of the car. Everyone thinks she died on impact, but she didn't. I was holding her hand and she was talking to me until the ambulance came."

A voice that didn't sound quite like Alicia's asked, "What did she say, Adam?" She winced, thinking it was a truly insensitive thing to ask, but Adam didn't seem to think so.

"She told me how much she loved me, how much she loved us all. And she told me to be good always. Then her eyes closed and they didn't open again, even though I begged her to please open them, just once. And that was the end of the sweetest woman who ever lived."

Alicia was weeping openly now, her head cradled on Adam's shoulder. Adam kissed her forehead and lifted her chin up to kiss the tears away. "Don't do that, baby.

I've never told you this but I hate to see you cry. It feels like someone is tearing my insides out when you do that. Don't cry, Allie."

"I'm sorry, Adam, it's just so sad. I'm seeing a sweet little boy left all alone and confused and my heart just breaks."

"Confused is the operative word, baby. I was convinced that something I did had caused the argument and it was somehow my fault that Mama was killed. Someone who looked like me had done something awful to her and it was therefore my fault she was dead. So I really had no choice."

"No choice about what, Adam?"

"About doing what she said and being good always. I was terrified that my family would find out that I had done something to cause my mother's death and I became the best child you ever saw. I think that's why I'm so neat now; I was determined that no one would ever have to reprimand me for anything. I got straight As in everything; I was polite, punctual, and organized. I never broke a promise or a curfew. In a lot of ways I was like the invisible child. I was quiet and well mannered and never did anything to upset anybody. I tried to be superchild and in some ways I succeeded."

"But at what cost?" cried Alicia. "Adam, surely there was someone you could talk to about this. Your father or Bennie and Andrew, wasn't there someone for you to confide in?"

Adam shook his head. "Not really. Pop kind of fell apart after Mama died and Benita and Andrew took over the household until Aunt Ruth got there. We were all pretty busy trying to fill the gigantic hole Mama's absence made. It was easier as I got older, I went to camp a lot and I was on the lacrosse team and the swimming team so I had ways to 'sublimate my conflicted emotions.' That last part is a quote. I've read a lot of books about displaced guilt and adolescent anxieties," he said with a dry laugh.

"But that's why this is so hard for me, Allie. I've finally concluded that Mama must have found out about Cassandra and the baby. She had to, that's what the argument was all about. That's something Pop neglected to mention in his pretty little sad story about his lost love," he said bitterly. "Everybody else might be able to handle this, but I don't know if I can because I know how much it hurt my mother, I know it made her last hours on this earth miserable, and I don't know if I can find a way to deal with it. I don't care what Benita and the rest of them do; I'll never be able to accept this John Flores as a brother. Never," he said with finality.

Chapter Nineteen

Benita Cochran Deveraux was curled up in the big bed that occupied the guest bedroom of her brother's home. When she and Renee shared the house, this had been Renee's bedroom. Now it was used as a guest suite. The twins, Marty and Malcolm, were asleep on the convertible sofa in the sitting room of the suite and the babies, Isabella and Katerina, were in cribs brought down from the attic for them. Only Trey was still awake and he was sprawled across the bed talking to his parents. Clay was propped up against the head of the bed, waiting for Trey to wind down so he could be alone with his wife. Trey, however, showed no signs of sleepiness.

"What are we doing tomorrow, Mom? Are we going to the zoo or are we hanging out at the house? When do we get to go to Uncle Adam's loft? Uncle Adam has a cool loft, Mom."

Benita smiled at her son. He was so identical to his father it was eerie. He was so much like a miniature Clay; he always tugged her heart in a special way. She was about to answer him when her cell phone rang and she grabbed it hastily, hoping it was John. "Hello?" she said breathlessly.

"Benita, it's John. I apologize for the way I left things tonight, but it was a bit overwhelming. Can we get together later and make some plans? You and Andrew and Clay, if they're available."

Benita couldn't conceal her joy. "That's a great idea,

John. How about we get together for lunch on Saturday if you're free? Or breakfast or dinner, it doesn't matter to me. Clay will definitely be with me and so will the imps, probably. I think Andrew and Renee are free, too, but I'll check with them to make sure. Thanks for calling, John. I know this isn't easy for you."

"Or for you and your family, Benita. I'm not ignoring the fact that this is pretty cataclysmic for everyone involved. What time shall we meet?"

"Why don't we play it by ear? I'll give you a call at nine and we'll take it from there, is that okay?"

After ending the call, Benita turned to Clay, her eyes alight with excitement. That was Clay's cue to encourage Trey to vanish. Clearing his throat, he stared meaningfully at his oldest son. Trey turned over and propped himself up on one elbow. Looking as grown and dignified as his summer Spongebob pajamas would allow, he said, "Yes, Dad?"

"Isn't it about time for bed, son?" Clay was wearing a short navy blue cotton pique robe, the mate to the oversized pajamas Benita was wearing. He hated wearing nightclothes of any kind; he did it only because Bennie insisted on it when the children were still up or they were visiting someone. Trey could hear the edge in the question his father was asking, but he excelled in ignoring all hints.

"Why, no, Dad, I'm not sleepy in the least. I could probably stay up for another five or six hours," Trey said cheerfully.

Clay raised one eyebrow and stroked his thick moustache with his forefinger. "Suppose your mother and I are sleepy, son. What then?"

"There's lots of room in this bed, Dad. You could just close your eyes and be asleep in no time and I can still be in here watching television. See how that works?"

"How about I might want to be alone with your

mother, who happens to be my most beloved wife, for a change? How does that work?"

Trey grinned mischievously. "You just want to be alone so you can kiss and stuff," he said knowingly.

"Yes, that's right. But I can also do that with you sitting here," Clay answered with a steely glint in his eye. He then grabbed Benita and pulled her into his arms, planting a big juicy kiss on her very willing lips, which made Trey go, "E-w-w-w-w-w!" and flee the room. "Good night, Mom and Dad, I love you," he threw over his shoulder.

"We love you too, baby. Good night and God bless," Benita said fondly.

"Alone at last, Peaches. Can I get out of this thing now? I can't stand being in the bed with you with clothes on. I have to be able to feel every bit of you," he confessed.

Benita gave the sultry giggle that always stirred her husband's blood and agreed they had on way too many clothes. "Just check on the children and make sure the door is closed and you may have your way with me without a single stitch on, I promise."

Clay stood up, preparing to make sure the children were all settled. "I take it that call was about meeting with John. So he's okay with this? I mean, he's willing to talk about it, at least, right?"

Benita nodded and reached up to him for a kiss. "It's a beginning at least. I can't ask for more than that."

Alicia and Adam slept surprisingly well, considering the emotional depths they had plumbed the night before. They awoke refreshed and happy to be in each other's arms. Adam looked down at Alicia and smiled. "This is why you need to move in, Allie. It would solve all our problems." He grinned.

"What problems? I didn't know we had any problems," she said with a smile.

"Any time I wake up without you in my arms, it's a

problem. I say we solve it permanently by sharing the same abode. What do you say?"

"I say not without benefit of clergy, that's what I say. When no man can put us asunder, then we can live together. Until then, no way," she said firmly.

Adam surprised her by whipping the sheet off their heated bodies in one swift motion. "Okay then, get up. We've got a ring to buy and a wedding to plan, because I can't put up with this much longer. Get up, woman, let's hit it!"

They had a wonderful morning together. First on the agenda was grocery shopping, which they accomplished by going to the Nino Salvaggio on Orchard Lake Road. It was a huge gourmet store with the most amazing produce in Michigan and lots of it. There was a butcher counter, a cheese shop, a bakery, a deli, and every kind of imported staple imaginable, all grouped by nation of origin. After eating breakfast at the counter of the restaurant area, they were ready to tackle some serious shopping. Alicia took her time in the produce section because she hated to miss anything. "Adam, what in the world is that? They have things in here that look like they came from other planets," she said happily.

After the groceries were purchased and stowed away at the loft, they ventured back out, this time to replace Alicia's clothes, although they weren't actually ruined. "They're okay, Adam; they were just wet. I wasn't completely serious, you know, I was just giving you a hard time. You don't have to buy me a new outfit," she protested.

"Yes, but I want to," he said reasonably. "I want to buy you something intimate and personal and extremely sexy, so just accept graciously."

"Only if I can buy you something," she insisted.

"We'll see," was all he'd say.

Hours later, Alicia surveyed the results of his noncommittal "we'll see." The sight of so many things just for her was positively embarrassing, but at the same time, totally endearing. Adam had gone nuts in the mall. One thing that Nordstrom's specialized in was capable sales staff who catered to the customers' every whim and they were more than thrilled to assist the tall, devastatingly handsome man outfit his blushing companion. Adam had bought her a beautiful black silk sundress with a full circle skirt with incredible ivory gardenias all over it. It had a tight bodice and a halter neck and with it he bought a sexy pair of black open-toe shoes with ivory flowers on the sides.

He also selected a fabulous pair of high-waisted wide-legged pants in a silk and linen blend that had deep cuffs and looked like something Kathryn Hepburn would have worn in an old movie. To complement this was a delicate ivory silk blouse with a matching camisole. The blouse with its wide lace portrait collar was sheer with tiny pindots and deep cuffs trimmed in the same Belgian lace as the collar. It buttoned with tiny pearl drop buttons and it was ethereal and sexy at the same time. He also insisted on buying a magnificent skirt made by the same designer as the blouse, a full skirt that came to mid-calf with deep pockets and was made entirely of the same Belgian lace as the blouse. He selected a pair of delicate ivory T-strapped shoes with princess heels to go with this confection.

She begged him to stop but he wasn't satisfied until he'd gotten several sets of underwear and a couple of truly scandalous nightgowns. Now she surveyed the bags from Neiman's and Nordstrom's and Marshall Fields and wondered what she'd gotten into. There was also a bag from Sephora where he had personally selected a Philosophy fragrance for her to wear. Since he'd also picked out the fragrance she wore now, Sugar Blossom, it was easy for him to pick another. She sniffed her wrist and sighed. The scent was perfect for her. Adam was smiling at the dazed expression on her face.

"You know me too well, I think. Adam, thank you from

the bottom of my heart, but don't ever do this again. This is too much!"

Adam was touched and amused by the picture of Alicia surrounded by the evidence of his indulgence. She looked adorably flushed and happy despite her protests. "You're not one to talk, Allie. You got me pretty good in the end," he reminded her.

She brightened immediately, agreeing with him. "Yes, I did! Can we set it up now?"

She had managed to get a sweet form of revenge on Adam by buying him a magnificent telescope, something she knew for a fact he'd always wanted but never got around to purchasing. That, with a couple of beautiful books on astronomy, was her gift to him, although Adam had told her she'd already given him the most precious thing in the world. "Allie, you've given me your heart, I don't need anything else. Except maybe a few babies, that would be nice."

Alicia sighed with happiness at his sweet declaration. She was so light and airy with elation she didn't think anything could bring her down. She and Adam were happily engrossed in setting up the telescope of the roof garden when he made another declaration that warmed her heart. "Baby, I think it's time we got the ball rolling on the wedding. I think we should make an announcement to your parents and to my family, don't you?"

Her heart caught in her throat for several seconds before she answered yes. "That sounds like a wonderful idea, Adam. I'll call them and see if they're free tomorrow."

Adam grinned. "I already did and they are. We're going to have breakfast over there tomorrow."

The next morning was a study in the fine art of delicately balanced domestic chaos as Benita and Renee were getting breakfast for the family. The twins were

chasing each other through the house in their Spider-
man underwear, Trey was teaching himself to juggle with
apples, and Isabella and Katerina were getting a bath
from their father with close supervision by Renee's little
dogs, who thought all babies were their personal responsibility. Meanwhile, Andrew was trying to get ready
to leave the house aided by his identical triplet daugh-
ters, Benita, Ceylon, and Stephanie, who were all trying
to help him, slowing his progress considerably. The most
composed person in the group was Andie, Renee and
Andrew's oldest daughter. She was trying to get his attention while he was trying to get his keys from one of
the triplets.

"Daddy, Grandaddy is here," she said calmly.

"What? Hey, don't play with that, sweetheart, that's
Daddy's Palm Pilot, he needs that," he admonished Ceylon gently.

"Granddaddy came to visit, Daddy, and he brought
some ladies with him. Lots of them." Andie leaned
against her father's desk and observed him with her
big golden eyes, so much like her mother's.

"Granddaddy did what, honey? With whom? Did you
tell your mommy, sweetheart?"

Andie sighed deeply and left the room to go to the
kitchen with the terriers, Patti and Chaka, hot on her
heels. They'd decided Clay was capable of giving a bath
and left to find other entertainment. Her mother and
her aunt Benita were deep in conversation as they prepared breakfast. It didn't look too promising, but Andie
tried again. "Mommy, Granddaddy came to visit and he
brought some ladies with him. Lots of ladies. Can I have
an orange?"

"*May* I have an orange and no, you may not, we're
just about to have breakfast, honey, it'll spoil your appetite," Renee said automatically, then realized what
her daughter had said.

"Granddaddy did what? Where is he, baby?"

"In the living room," Andie replied.

Renee and Benita looked at each other with surprised eyes and of one accord they moved through the dining room and into the living room, where an most unexpected sight greeted them. There, like a potentate surrounded by loving subjects, sat Big Benny, with his forbearing wife, Martha, and four women who could only be Emmaline, Reba, Daphne, and Dahlia. As Benita and Renee stood there with their mouths hanging open, Big Benny looked up with his most familiar grin and Patti and Chaka skittered in to see what was going on.

"What are the chances of us getting some breakfast? We left mighty early this morning and we could all use a bite." This last remark was punctuated with a sharp bark from Dusty, Emmaline's schnauzer, who wasn't a huge fan of auto travel even if it was in a luxury limousine like the one Benny had procured for the trip. He also didn't like the looks of those sassy little dogs and was raring for an opportunity to teach them a few things.

Renee recovered first and graciously said that breakfast was in preparation and asked if anyone would like something to drink in the meantime. Benita finally found her tongue and introduced herself to each aunt, giving them each a big hug. The need for further conversation was negated as the children made their way into the living room. Like all children, they always sensed where the action was and wanted to be in the thick of it. Soon Andrew and then Clay joined the happy crowd and everything was hugs and kisses and exclamations of joy until Andrew had to excuse himself.

"I have surgery this morning so I've got to go. I'll see you all this afternoon though," he said as he waved goodbye to everyone and kissed his wife soundly.

Aunt Emmaline was concerned. "He's having surgery? But he looks so healthy!" she said sadly.

"Oh no, Aunt Emmaline, he's not having surgery, he's

performing it. Andrew is a reconstructive surgeon," Renee explained.

Aunt Emmaline smiled in relief. "That's wonderful, dear, I was concerned about him." She took another sip of tea and looked around the huge dining room table, smiling at the beautiful children who were, for the most part, behaving beautifully. "I can't tell you how happy this makes me, to see my nephew's family. You're all just lovely, so very lovely." She sighed.

Benita followed her gaze around the table. "Oh, Aunt Emmaline, you haven't seen anything yet! Just wait until the whole gang of us is here together," she said with a smile. Then she turned to her father and her smile transformed to a look of total frustration. "Daddy, how in the world did this come about? Couldn't you have let anyone know you were going to do this?"

Big Benny was perfectly happy with little Isabella on one knee and Katerina on the other. He looked up with an expression of perfect innocence on his face and said simply, "No."

He shifted the babies so he could reach for a piece of bacon, which got him an ugly look from Martha. "Touch it and you'll snatch back a nub, Ben. You may have some more fruit and another piece of dry toast if you like, but you've had your allotment of nitrates and sodium for the day."

Big Benny tried to look hurt but failed miserably; he was having too much fun. "Well, daughter, I had a little talk with Martha and we decided it was high time I introduced her to our kinfolk. So I hired a car and we went on up to Lake County for a visit. It didn't make sense to prolong the process, so we invited them to come back with us. And we got on the road this morning and here we are. The rest of the family will be here soon," he added casually. "That is, if I can find Adam. He's not answering his phone or he has it turned off or something."

Just then the doorbell rang, but it was strictly a courtesy. The back door opened and Donnie walked in with Lily Rose and Angelique, all of them wreathed in smiles. Daphne, or maybe it was Dahlia, promptly took Lily Rose from his arms for a better look at her.

"My goodness, we do make pretty babies in this family, don't we? And such a handsome young couple! Now which ones are you?" she asked with a smile. It was a phrase to be heard often as the house became crowded with Alan and Andre, their wives and their children. Angelique volunteered to host dinner that night since there was more room in the Palmer Park house. "We also have the most guest rooms available. We have three bedrooms up for grabs if you ladies would like to stay with us."

Only Emmaline declined as she was staying with Big Benny and Martha in the guest room of their condo. The other women were quite happy to accept Angelique's gracious invitation. "We can also help you make dinner; we're quite good cooks; Adam can tell you that," Reba assured her. Then she scanned the crowd of relatives with a question in her eyes. "Where is Adam? He's the only one who hasn't made an appearance," she mused.

Benita looked at Clay and made a face. "I'm sure he'll be here later, Aunt Reba." In truth, she wasn't sure about any such thing.

Chapter Twenty

While Renee and Andrew's house was filled to bursting with both well-known and little-known Cochrans, Adam was miles away at the Southfield home of Leah and Jose Fuentes. Alicia's whole family was there and it could have been a moment of supreme discomfort for Adam, but it didn't bother him a bit. He didn't care if his fiancée's entire family heard him ask her father for permission to marry her. He was perfectly calm and composed, holding Alicia's hand as though this were an everyday event with him. Alicia was his wife now, as far as he was concerned. This was all a mere formality.

Looking at a recent portrait of her mother and father on the wall of the living room, Alicia acknowledged that they were a stunning couple whose longevity had surprised many members of her mother's family. Leah Ross Fuentes was from a socially prominent family of educators who were stunned when she brought home Jose Fuentes, a big, brash Cuban baseball player with no education and a thick Spanish accent. Leah had been working on her bachelor's degree when his sisters introduced her to him. She was studying at Spelman College in Atlanta and he was playing for the Atlanta Braves farm team when they met and it was love at first sight, to her parents' complete dismay.

No amount of dismay was about to interfere with their courtship, however; Leah stood her ground and the result was a very happy marriage, which produced a large and loving family. Carlos Fuentes was the oldest son, followed by a daughter, Marielle, and another son, Raphael. Alicia was the baby of the family, something she felt keenly from time to time. Even though she was a grown woman who had a successful business, she wasn't grown up to her brothers, who alternated between teasing her unmercifully and treating her like a doll. Today she knew it would be unmerciful teasing from her brothers and she was ready for it.

When Adam and Alicia had arrived at the Fuentes house in Southfield for the big elaborate breakfast buffet that her mother loved to prepare, her mother greeted them at the door with hugs and kisses and a long, appraising look at Adam. "My goodness, Adam! I always knew you were good-looking, but you're really something, aren't you, dear? Turn around and let me get a good look at you," she instructed.

"*Mami*, don't embarrass him," Alicia protested, but Leah waved her off. Leah Fuentes was vivacious and outspoken and charmingly frank with everyone. Alicia had a lot of her mother's characteristics, although at the moment she would have denied it. Leah was very fond of her daughter's best friend and was always especially attentive to him.

"I'm not trying to embarrass him, *mija*, I'm paying him a compliment. I liked his hair long, you know, but he looks so polished and sexy this way. You two look quite beautiful together, you really do."

As she spoke, Leah was walking off with Adam with her arm linked through his, chattering away about this and that. Alicia shook her head. Her mother, for all her flighty ways, was a distinguished academician with several degrees in anthropology and social psychology. People and how they related to each other was her mother's passion. She found the structure of society and its evolution absolutely fascinating. Even though she was now a professor emeritus from the University of Michigan, she continued to write and was at work on her twelfth book.

Alicia sighed happily as she trailed through the house, beautifully decorated with artwork from all over the world, especially African and Caribbean art. The spacious modern home was filled with colorful and fascinating things and the walls that served as a backdrop for the art were bold and bright in warm tropical colors. Leah certainly put her mark on everything, Alicia mused. She finally made it into the great room, a huge family room that opened into the kitchen. This was where most of the entertaining took place in the Fuentes house since both Leah and Jose were passionate about eating well and took great pleasure in cooking elaborate feasts for family and friends.

Adam was sitting on a tall stool drinking a glass of what looked like guava juice while Leah stirred a huge pot of grits. "What can I do to help, *Mami*?"

Her mother looked up and smiled. "Not a thing, *mija*. We're having a traditional southern breakfast and everything is done. The boys set the tables for me and as soon as everyone is here we'll be ready. You can relax with Adam," she said with a smile.

Alicia went to stand next to Adam and gave him a kiss on the cheek.

Adam kissed her back and then addressed her mother. "Actually, Mrs. Fuentes, I have something I need to talk to you and Mr. Fuentes about. Maybe now would be a good time," he said quietly.

Leah handed the wooden spoon to Alicia in a flash while taking her apron off. "Here, baby, stir this. Come on, Adam, Jose is in the garden," she said in a fluttery voice so unlike her normal speaking tone. She took him out to her husband, leaving Alicia with an apron in one hand, a spoon in the other, and a very goofy look on her face, or so Raphael claimed when he found her standing there.

"You look really stupid, *Patti*. Are you daydreaming about some man or something? If you're not going to stir that, let me do it."

Alicia gladly handed him the spoon but denied any such stupid look. "I'm not thinking about 'some man,' I'm thinking about my man. For your information, he's out there talking to *Mami* and *Papi* right now so we can announce our engagement."

Raphael made a face of shock and horror, pretending to gag. "Somebody actually wants to marry you? Better him than me." He laughed as Alicia twisted the apron into a snake and popped him with it. "You just better hope *Papi* doesn't scare him half to death."

There was little fear of that, as Jose had been expecting this particular announcement for a long time. He was sitting on the patio doting on Gabrielle while Paco was eating the slices of lemon out of his grandfather's iced tea. "*Mijo*, don't do that, it will ruin your teeth," he scolded gently. Jose tried to be gruff and tough, but when it came to his grandchildren he was an absolute softie. He looked up as Leah led Adam out onto the spacious deck with its big pots of flowers. He tried to hide a smile but was only partially successful. "Paco, take the baby inside. We need to have a talk with Adam," he said as he set Gabrielle on her feet, to her displeasure. She was protesting the whole time, but soon it was just Adam, Leah, and Jose on the deck. Adam looked at the beautifully landscaped garden that surrounded the deck and the house and took a deep breath.

He shook Jose's hand quite formally, then wasted no time in getting to the point. "Mr. Fuentes, I don't think it's a real secret that I'm very much in love with your daughter. I'm asking your permission to marry her, sir, because we want to build a life together," he said simply.

Jose considered letting him twist in the wind for a while, just to see what would happen, but one look at

Leah told him this was a bad idea. He'd always liked Adam, even more since he'd gotten rid of that stupid ponytail. The important thing to him was he knew that Adam would take care of his daughter and make her happy for the rest of their lives and that's what he wanted for her. He dragged his response out as long as possible, trying to keep a stern look on his face. Leah finally shot him a look of pure exasperation and poked him in the arm. "Fine, son. I will give you my daughter's hand in marriage under one condition. That you understand this is a permanent gift, this is not a loan, you got it?"

Adam laughed and said he understood completely. "There's no chance whatsoever that I will ever want to give her back, sir. She's mine for life and I'm hers."

"So what took you so long to figure it out? I could have had four or five grandbabies by now," he said grumpily.

"We'll do our best to fill your order, sir," Adam said with a grin.

The biggest surprise of the morning came a little later when everyone was sitting around the table digesting the excellent meal Leah had prepared. Adam stood up and took Alicia's hands, bringing her up with him. He kissed her on the forehead and took a small box out of his pocket. With a smile of total love and adoration on his face, he asked her again for her hand in marriage as he opened the box. She could barely get out her breathless "yes" when she saw the ring it contained.

It was an oval cabochon stone surrounded by two bands of unusual-looking stones set in a heavy gold band. She thought that one ring of the smaller stones were rubies, but Alicia had no idea what the middle stone was, she'd never seen anything like it. "I hope you like it, baby. That's a champagne tourmaline and the other stones are red diamonds and pink tourmalines."

"I love it, Adam, and I love you. Where in the world

did you find this?" she breathed, staring at her hand with utter amazement.

"I had it made, Allie. I knew I couldn't find anything as special as you in a store."

A clamor from around the table made Alicia realize where she was and what she was doing. She immediately went around the table so everyone could get a good look at her hand. She was laughing with happiness when her father's sisters suddenly entered the kitchen.

"So, *mija*, you do remember your promise, right? This is a wedding I'm looking forward to planning from start to finish," Gigi said, rubbing her hands together in glee.

Alicia's eyes went to Marielle's, whose were alight with laughter. She raised her glass of guava juice in a toast. "Better you than me, *chica*."

Adam's arms went around her waist and she relaxed into his embrace realizing that nothing could possibly upset her as long as they were together. "I hope you don't have any more surprises up your sleeve," she whispered. "I don't think my heart can stand the strain."

"No more surprises, Allie. One per day is my limit."

John was seated across the table from the formidable Miss Parker. They were just about finished putting his office in order thanks to her highly efficient nature. She'd agreed to come to work on Saturday to get it finished, and as a thank-you he had taken her out to lunch. He'd had a phone call a little while before that had rattled him more than he wanted to admit and he was sincerely glad of her company right now. He looked at her appraisingly as she perused the menu. Without any preliminaries he asked her a question.

"Miss Parker, what would you do if you suddenly found out you were adopted?"

"A happy dance," she said dryly, still looking at the

menu. When she finally met his gaze she saw something unusual in his eyes.

"Is this a personal revelation of some kind? Are you sure you want to share this with me?"

Not really, but you have the advantage of being here, John thought and was once again ashamed of himself.

"Yes, indeed it is, Miss Parker. A very personal revelation." He filled her in on the past few days and was grateful, for once, that she showed virtually no reaction. "We were supposed to get together for lunch today and talk, to make plans to meet my, um, to meet Benny Cochran and the rest of the family, but plans have changed. Big Benny went trotting up to Idlewild and came back with the estranged aunts and now they're having a big family dinner to which I'm invited," John reported glumly.

"Are you going?" she asked crisply.

"Yeah, I seem to have agreed to show up. For one split second it seemed like the easiest thing to do, just face them all at once and get it over with. Now I've had a moment of clarity, the thing we shrinks are so fond of when it comes to our patients. My moment of clarity is telling me that this was the worst idea I've ever had and now I can't get out of it without (a) prolonging the inevitable and (b) looking like a schmuck. The schmuck thing is winning, by the way," he said and stared out the window, lost in thought.

Miss Parker was silent as she inspected her silverware, making sure it was absolutely spotless. She slowly took the deep, gusty breath of the martyr and said, "Well, I guess I'll just have to cancel my run, although I have to tell you I wasn't planning on having this assignment encroach on my social life. What time are you picking me up?"

"Picking you up?" John asked blankly.

"Oh, so I have to come with you and drive, too?" she

said in disgust. "I really need to renegotiate my contract. I'm ready to order now, where did that waiter get to?"

John was speechless with gratitude. As hard as it was to believe, Miss Parker was his very own special miracle for the night.

Adam and Alicia finally left her parents' house, glowing with love and happiness. She couldn't stop looking at her ring and telling Adam how much she loved it. "Adam, this is the most amazing ring I've ever seen," she said with her hand extended for better viewing. "I love you so much, Adam, I can't wait to marry you."

Adam reached for her hand as he drove the Range Rover toward Andrew's house. "I feel exactly the same way, baby. And from the looks of it, so does your aunt Gigi. She was pretty excited about the prospect of a wedding," he said with a smile.

"Ha! That's because she has her heart set on planning it. Honey, you need to get ready for this because it's going to be a production, trust me. Remember that movie I'm so crazy about, *My Big Fat Greek Wedding*? Well, this is going to be My Big Fat Cuban Wedding, so brace yourself," she said with amusement.

They talked about the upcoming wedding, about the reactions of her family, which ranged from total joy on the part of her parents, to calm happiness from Marisol, and affectionate teasing from her brothers. Adam didn't tell her that Carlos and Raphael had taken him aside while everyone was talking and laughing and made him a promise that for every tear their sister shed, he would shed two. They said it with pleasant smiles on their faces, but he knew they were completely serious and he knew it was because of how Marielle's husband had treated her. He had a sister of his own as well as sisters-in-law and dearly loved nieces, so he couldn't blame them for being protective.

It didn't take very long to reach Indian Village, but when they approached Renee and Andrew's house Adam was puzzled by all the cars. "What in the world is going on here? Where'd that limo come from?" Built just before the turn of the century by the lumber barons of the era, the huge homes in Indian Village didn't have driveways. Most of the houses were relatively close together with only paved walkways between them. People either parked their cars on the street or used the garages that were behind the houses and accessed through the alleys that intersected most blocks in the community. Now the street was lined with cars, most of which he recognized. It looked like his entire family was in attendance. He and Alicia had to park a block and a half away and walk back to the house. When they reached the house, they went around to the back and were shocked into silence by what they beheld. Almost the entire family was there, Big Benny and Martha and all his brothers and their children and most surprising of all, the aunts from Idlewild.

After greeting everyone and giving the aunts special hugs and kisses, Adam had to ask what was going on. Alan was happy to explain. "Well, Pop just decided to go get the aunts and bring them to us, so naturally we've found a way to turn it into a party. Our wives are out shopping for food right now and we're having a big cookout at Donnie and Angelique's house."

"What a coincidence, us having a party and something to celebrate," Adam said with a grin. "Alicia and I are officially engaged."

Alicia blushed pink while the aunts all admired her ring and wished her well. Big Benny added his congratulations along with a big smacking kiss on the cheek. "Well, it's about time you two got together. I was beginning to think we were going to have to work some roots on y'all to make you see sense." He beamed down at her with pride and affection all over his face. Alicia hugged him and returned the kiss on the cheek. He was a demanding, manipulative, and totally exasperating old man, but she loved him, if for no other reason than he'd fathered the man she would love forever.

She and Adam decided to go over to Donnie and Angelique's to see what help they could be in putting the party together. All of Adam's brothers congratulated them in turn and admired his taste in wives as well as jewelry, and the atmosphere was full a love and happiness until Andre stopped them as they were leaving. "Yeah, this is definitely going to be a big night. All of us together with our newfound aunts *and* our newfound brother. This is going to be a night we won't forget," he said with a big grin.

"Allie, I'm not going and that's final. There is nothing you can say that's going to make me change my mind. I can't do it; I'm not going to do it. If they want to have him in their lives it's fine, but I can't do it." Adam was out on the roof garden with his back to Alicia, looking at the Detroit River but seeing nothing.

Alicia would have felt a lot better if Adam was yelling or screaming, but he wasn't, he was speaking in the calm, dead voice she'd come to know and dread over the years. This was the Adam who could shut the world out and keep it there indefinitely. They'd been having the same conversation for hours, going around and around about his flat refusal to go anywhere near the party if John was going to be there. Alicia had just about given up the fight; there was no point in trying to persuade him to do something he so obviously didn't want to do.

"Okay, fine, Adam. If you don't want to go there's no sense trying to make you. Just drop me at home and you can have an evening all to yourself," she said quietly.

That got a reaction from him; he turned around and

looked at her with something akin to panic in his eyes. "You're leaving me," he said hoarsely.

"Adam, don't be ridiculous, I'm not leaving you, I just need to go home. I haven't been there for two days and I need to put my things away, I need to read my mail and check my messages and just chill. You're not the only one who can use some time alone, you know." She tried not to sound angry but she was so close to tears she couldn't seem to help it.

They gathered her things and drove over to the condo without saying a word. Adam turned off the ignition in the parking lot and they sat there for a minute or two, the silence thick between them. Finally Alicia spoke and her words were exactly what she'd been trying to tell him all along. "Adam, it's not important to me that you and John become best friends or whatever. It doesn't matter to me that your father wins this round, whatever that means. Yes, you might be doing something that he wants you to do, but so what? What's important to me is that you not lose your family. Family is all we really have; it's all that's left when everything else has fallen away. Businesses fail, the things we possess get lost or stolen or just become obsolete, but family is everything.

"I just don't want what happened to Benny to happen to you, Adam. I don't want you to go through life lonely and bitter because you can't forgive your father. A life filled with regret isn't a life worth living, if you ask me." She stopped talking, both because she was afraid she'd said too much and because there was a huge painful lump in her throat.

"Just remember, baby, I'm your family too and I'm not too easy to lose. I'll be here for the long haul, nagging and complaining and telling you what to do until we're both older than Emmaline," she said with a shaky laugh.

Adam gave her a wan smile in return but couldn't manage to say anything. It took next to no time to get all her things in the house and Alicia was genuinely sorry when everything was put inside the condo. She didn't like leaving things this way, but what else could she do? They hugged each other tightly and Adam gave her a quick kiss before saying he'd call her later. She didn't want to, but she stood in the doorway and watched him as he walked away.

A few minutes later her cell phone rang and she answered it eagerly, but it was Bryant Porter. "I just got into town and what do you think I found out?" he said playfully. "You two have been real busy since I left, haven't you? I just saw you a few weeks ago and before I can even start my summer teaching gig you two are engaged. Well, congratulations are in order but I'll be giving them to you tonight. You know I'm invited to the party, right?"

Alicia closed her eyes tightly and prayed for deliverance. How could things possibly get more complicated?

Chapter Twenty-one

John couldn't help it, he knew his mouth was hanging open, but there was nothing he could do about it. Miss Parker had just knocked on his door and her appearance was nothing short of amazing. She was wearing a white dress with a short full skirt and a wide belt that served to emphasize her tiny waist. The dress buttoned down the front with red buttons that looked like cherries and she was wearing a pair of flirty-looking red backless shoes with a sexy heel. The sleeveless dress had a wide collar that set off her face with its chestnut skin, skin that John just noticed was absolutely flawless, poreless and soft like a child's. Her hair was swept up into a high ponytail that hung down to her shoulders and now that she wasn't wearing those intimidating glasses he could see that her eyes were a soft golden brown. She was wearing big gold hoop earrings that accentuated her pretty face and seemed to given her a sensual gleam.

"Are you ready? You're not going to make me drive *and* keep me waiting, are you?"

Yes, it was the same Miss Parker. She might look completely different, but she still had the same cranky disposition. He said he was ready to leave and she turned on her heel so he could see the dress had a halter top, which displayed her tautly muscled back to its best advantage. For some reason the words to "Sun Dress" by the Phat Cat Players started echoing in his head.

They took off at a fast clip; Miss Parker was apparently

an honors graduate of the Jeff Gordon School of Driving. She tossed a piece of paper at him and tersely remarked that it was driving directions she had downloaded from Mapquest. "You have one job and that's to keep us on course," she said in her usual charmless tone of voice.

John knew he was risking his life, but he felt compelled to ask as he watched her jazzy ponytail flipping in the breeze from the open window, "Is all that your hair?"

"What are you, the hair police? Of course it's mine, you want to see the receipt?" She looked at him and, incredibly, flashed him a wicked grin. John was floored. Miss Parker had dimples! In minutes they had reached the expressway and his only thought was to stay alive as she demonstrated a talent for fast driving that was also life-threatening in his opinion. At least he didn't have time to worry about what awaited him at the party; his only concern was getting there in one piece.

Alicia was also trying not to worry, but she was trying not to worry about her man. She had taken a shower and was painting her toenails while she talked to Roxy on the phone. "Rox, it's just too deep for me, it really is. On the one hand I completely understand how Adam is feeling, but on the other, I don't want him to end up estranged from his family like his father did. But I can only go so far with the advice and support, you know? At some point it gets to be nagging or mothering or something and I can't do that. What would you do, Rox?"

"For once I have no advice to offer, sweetie. This is one of the reasons I'm never getting married: true love is way too complicated for me to cope with. If I ever get that close to a man it would have to be a totally drama-free situation. You know me, I can't handle all that stuff. I think you're doing the right thing by stepping away from it for the moment. Why don't we take advantage of your free evening and go to the movies? We can watch something hilarious and stupid and just forget our woes for the night."

That sounded like a great idea to Alicia and they discussed which movie to see. The doorbell distracted her and she went to answer it while still talking to Roxy. She looked out the peephole and made an exclamation of surprise. "Roxy, you're not going to believe it, but Adam is at the door. Hold on for just a second, okay?"

She put on what she hoped was a nonchalant expression and casually opened the door. Adam looked wonderful in a pair of black pleated slacks, black closed-toe sandals, and an off-white linen shirt with no collar. He tried to look cool and collected, but he gave it away with a sheepish grin. "You're not ready. Should I wait or come back for you?" he asked as he handed her a sheaf of highly scented gardenias with white roses, freesia, and baby's breath.

"Roxy, my fiancé is here and he's brought me a bribe. I'll call you later," she said, but the phone was plucked from her hand before she could end the call.

"Hello, Roxanne," Adam said formally. "My family is having a party tonight. Would you like to come? We can pick you up if you like."

Alicia suddenly realized that she was wearing a truly ratty pair of drawstring pants and a paint-spattered MIT T-shirt and those funny little rubber things separating her toes so the nail polish wouldn't smear. "I'll be right back," she said as she sprinted out of the room. In a record twenty minutes she was ready to rejoin Adam and she had the air of a woman who knew she was looking her best. The look on Adam's face said that he agreed with that assessment entirely.

He was sprawled on the sofa waiting her return but stood up as soon as she entered the room. He felt a huge surge of desire as she slowly turned around for his approval. She was wearing the beautiful sundress he'd bought for her with the sexy shoes and she looked fresh and sexy, too sexy to be going to a family party. Her eyes sparkled with the addition of some kind of shimmery stuff that made them look bigger and brighter, and as always her lips looked like an invitation, glossy and delicious. Her small diamond studs were her only adornment other than her engagement ring, and her smile was for him alone.

"Will I do?" she asked coyly.

He crossed the room and put his hands around her waist. "If I didn't know you," he said slowly, "I'd fall in love with you tonight. Sometimes I look at you and wonder what I ever did that was good enough to win your love."

Alicia's pulse began to race as she tilted her head back for his kiss. "You were my friend, my shelter, and my heart. You didn't have to do anything special, Adam; you just had to be yourself. And you're awfully pretty." She smiled. "How could I not love you? You're the best person I know, Adam, and I'm honored to be with you."

"Let's stay home, Allie. Let's get some champagne and just stay in together," he said softly.

"Not on your life. We look good and we're going to show out, so get to stepping, *Papi*." She executed a perfect pivot turn and flounced toward the door with him following. "We'll go put in an appearance and if it gets really rocky we'll leave early. Promise."

"I'm going to hold you to that," he said glumly.

John's calm demeanor evaporated as they pulled into the circular drive in the front of the big brick house. It had suddenly dawned on him what a bad idea this was. He must have been out of his mind to agree to meet the entire Cochran family at once. He didn't move from where he was seated in the car, he just stared at the front door of the house and felt his stomach plummet to the vicinity of his ankles. Miss Parker, however, wasn't in an understanding mood.

"I see that look on your face and you can forget it. I invested valuable time to get this dressed up, it took me a good fifteen minutes to hook up this phonytail, much less the rest of this ensemble, and if you think we're going to skulk back to Ann Arbor without meeting these people you've got another think coming," she said in a voice that would tolerate no nonsense.

He was watching her face while she told him off and was struck again by how pretty she really was. For some reason the words slipped out of his mouth before his common sense had a chance to catch up. "Miss Parker, you amaze me, you really do. Where have you been hiding all this beauty? You're quite lovely, you know that?"

"How utterly charming," she said in a disinterested deadpan voice. "Now get those long legs out of this car and come open my door so we can go into the house. That woman is going to die of anticipation if we don't. You have a choice of socializing for an hour or two or listening to me bitch all the way back to Ann Arbor. Which do you prefer?"

In two seconds he was out of the car and opening her door like the perfect gentleman he'd been raised to be.

The woman Miss Parker was referring to was Bennie, who'd stationed herself by the front door so she could watch out for John. The first thing on the agenda was to introduce her father to the son he'd never acknowledged, and that would require privacy. She opened the door as soon as John rang the bell and stood there smiling for all she was worth.

"Welcome, John." She extended her hands to him and he took them, smiling down at her. "I'm so glad you were able to come," she said warmly, accompanying the words with a kiss on the cheek. John couldn't seem to stop himself; he gave her a hug, a safe, brotherly hug.

Bennie was the first to recover herself and smiled at

Miss Parker. "Your friend is going to think we're terribly rude," she said apologetically. "I do apologize, I'm Benita Deveraux but almost everyone calls me Bennie," she said winsomely.

John had the grace to flush at forgetting his manners. "I'm sorry, too. This is Miss Parker, Benita. She's been ghostwriting my book and doing just about everything else she can to help me get settled here in Michigan. I wouldn't be here without her," he said with an honesty that only he and Miss Parker recognized.

"It's nice to meet you, but don't pay him any attention. My name is Nina, Nina Whitney. Miss Parker is an invention of his," she said, giving John a look devoid of any expression.

"Well, Nina, it's nice to meet you," Bennie said, extending her hand. As they shook hands, she added that she'd love to hear the story behind the Miss Parker moniker.

"John will have to be the one to tell you that," Nina said demurely. "I'm sure you two have things to discuss. May I be of some help in the kitchen?"

Bennie glanced at John and smiled at Nina gratefully, pleased that she was making the situation a little less awkward. "I'm sure my sisters-in-law would love some help. I'll take you into the kitchen and introduce you," she said.

Nina waved her suggestion aside. "Just point me in the right direction, I can introduce myself," she said in a cheery voice totally unlike her normal means of communicating. "See you soon." She gave John a look that he would have sworn was meant to comfort him if he hadn't known her better.

Now it was he and Benita, something that should have made him uncomfortable, but didn't. He was too curious and she was too disarming to let the moment become strained. "John, Daddy's in the study. I thought you'd want some privacy so I asked him to wait there.

She took his hand again and looked into his eyes. "Are you ready for this?" she asked with a tremulous smile.

"Never more ready. Let's go," John said with more assurance than he was feeling. They crossed the big living room and approached a wide paneled double door. Bennie knocked softly and released John's hand to slide the doors apart. They entered the room and John was face-to-face with the man who'd given him life, Andrew Bernard Cochran, Senior. Benita quietly made the introductions, saying, "John, this is my father. Daddy, this is John."

The two men shook hands silently, each taking the measure of the other. John was struck by the resemblance that even he could see: the height, the coloring, the nose and mouth were just like his. So this was what he'd look like in his seventies. The thought made him smile a little. Taking that as a show of relaxation, Bennie asked if the two men needed anything. When both said no, she said, "Well, then, I'm going to leave you alone for a while," and quietly left the room.

Benny sighed deeply as he looked at John. Even if he wanted to he couldn't have denied that this was his son. He looked as much like Benny as any of this other sons. They looked at each other for a long moment, the silence broken by Benny, who gestured to the sofa. "Why don't we sit down? I'm sure you want to ask me a few questions," he said with a sad irony.

Miss Parker, or Nina as she was properly named, had made herself useful when she got to the spacious kitchen. She introduced herself as Nina, a friend of John's, and asked if she could be of any assistance. Angelique had gratefully welcomed her and introduced her to the other Cochran wives, Renee, Tina, and Faye. "We could really use another hand," Angelique admitted. "We didn't get much notice for this, so it's going to be pretty haphazard.

Not that this crew will mind much, our husbands are known to eat anything. If it's smaller than they are and can't get away, they'll eat it," she said with a laugh.

Nina looked at the array of food in amazement; if this was a casually haphazard gathering she could only imagine what the holidays were like. The women had set up a huge buffet of potato salad, coleslaw, green salad, three-bean salad, fruit salad, and crudités with three kinds of dip. There were two smoked turkey breasts, a spiral-sliced ham with a brown sugar glaze, and a vast assortment of sweets, including a German chocolate cake, pound cake, and a huge array of cookies, all of which looked homemade. As Nina's eyes roved the incredible spread, Renee shrugged. "Alan and Andre are grilling the chicken and steak and all the drinks are set up out there. This isn't much, but it's such an impromptu evening I think it'll be okay. As long as there's plenty of food no one will really care what they're eating. Do you mind helping me get the tables set up outside?"

She indicated a stack of colorful cotton tablecloths on a serving cart, along with packages of disposable plates, cups, and cutlery. They wheeled the cart outside where two long tables were set up on the patio, as well as several smaller tables. Folding chairs were also available, a huge row of them leaning against the garage. Nina's eyes grew huge as she beheld more Cochrans; Alan and Andre were efficiently manning a huge grill and Andrew and Adonis were just finishing the arrangement of the last tables. Renee directed a couple of teenagers to get the chairs set up. "Prescott and Drew, when you get done with that I've got a couple of other things for you to do. You're such a big help," she said warmly. "And where is your sister?" She looked around in vain.

"I think she's with the aunts," Drew replied.

Renee nodded absently and began spraying the top of each table with an antiseptic cleaner and wiping it down with paper towels. Nina followed suit and soon each table was ready to be covered with a bright cloth, lending the backyard a festive air. The women worked quickly and efficiently, placing a large, heavy candleholder in the middle of each table to keep the tablecloths in place. Renee was saying something about lanterns that mystified Nina completely until Andrew and Donnie appeared with a couple of strings of large illuminated paper lanterns, which they strung up in next to no time. Nina watched in amazement. "I take it you folks entertain a lot. You seem to have this down to a science," she remarked, waving her hand to encompass all the activity going on around them.

Renee smiled and agreed. "We do a lot of entertaining at home because there's just too many of us to do otherwise. There aren't too many restaurants that really enjoy seeing this horde descend upon them. Sometimes we go out to brunch after church or to celebrate a birthday, but not often."

Nina looked around at the tall handsome men and asked curiously, "So which one of these is yours?"

Andrew overheard the question and joined the two women, putting his arm around his wife and kissing her soundly. "That would be me, I'm Andrew Cochran," he said. "Renee, I can't believe you didn't introduce us. We can behave in front of company, you know."

"I'm so sorry, " Renee said hastily. "Please don't think we're savages, I was just so happy to see another pair of willing hands I forgot myself. Guys, come and meet John's friend Nina."

In seconds Nina was shaking hands with Donnie, Alan, and Andre and trying not to gape as a tumble of children surged out of the house. Renee gamely tried to put a name to each child, but they were moving so fast it was all a blur. "My goodness, are there any more of you?" Nina murmured as the backyard filled with Cochrans, many of whom seemed to look just alike.

"There's one more son, Adam, and he should be here

any minute with his fiancée," Renee told her. "Oh, wait, here he is now."

Adam and Alicia came around the corner of the house with two big bags. A roar went up as nieces and nephews surrounded the couple. Alicia took the bags from Adam and came over to Renee. "These are empanadas, right out of the freezer. They just need to be heated up for about twenty minutes. Are there some big trays we can use?"

Renee said of course and they were about to go to the kitchen when Alicia noticed Nina and smiled. "Hello, I'm Alicia Fuentes, Adam's fiancée. Nice to see you," she said. Nina nodded and was about to speak when Adam joined them. She stared up at the tall man and was struck by his resemblance to John. All of the men favored John to some degree, but there was something about this man that was unmistakably similar to the man she'd come to know over the past few months. A weird little tremor passed through Nina as she stared at Adam, but she tried to cover it up.

"I'm Nina Whitney. Nice to meet you," she said casually, hoping that her face didn't betray her. She watched closely as Adam retrieved the bags from Alicia and took them into the house. This was the reason she'd come, and it looked like her instincts were right. *This could be the one*, she thought.

Adam watched his sisters-in-law and stepmother with affection and admiration; no one could top them when it came to pulling something together at short notice. Alicia was putting the little meat-filled turnovers on a large baking pan before putting them into the oven. "Where are the aunts?" he asked of no one in particular.

"They're upstairs getting ready," Tina told him. "They should be down any time."

Martha turned to him and asked for his assistance. "Adam, honey, I think I left a serving tray by the front door. Can you go see if it's in there? It should be in a big

Marshall Field bag leaning on the umbrella stand in the foyer," she told him.

Adam went off in search of the missing tray. He located it quickly and was about to pick it up when the doors to the study opened. Adam turned in that direction and felt his blood congeal in his veins. There in the doorway stood his father with the man he now claimed as his son, John Flores. Adam could hear his heartbeat resonating in his ears, but nothing else. For the first time he completely understood the meaning of time standing still as an eternity seemed to pass while he looked into the face of the man he would never call brother.

Chapter Twenty-two

Everyone was on his or her best behavior and the gathering wasn't nearly as awkward as it could have been. After being sequestered in the study, Big Benny and John joined the family in the spacious backyard. John was formally introduced to everyone from the youngest, Lily Rose, to the oldest, Aunt Emmaline, and received genuinely sincere greetings from all. The Cochrans managed to be welcoming without being overwhelming, no mean feat for a family as close and demonstrative as they were. It was a warm and celebratory evening and Adam seemed to be tolerating it, even to Roxy's observant eye. She commented on this to Alicia when they were alone in the kitchen.

"Adam seems to be handling this pretty well. From the way you were talking I thought he'd be sweating bullets and swinging from the chandelier right about now. He seems fine," she said.

Alicia made a small face. "He's doing okay, Roxy, but he's shutting down, I can feel it. You should have seen him about an hour ago when Angelique introduced Lily Rose to John. She'd just awakened from a nap and you know how cranky babies are when they wake up. She was fussy and when Adam reached for her she screamed and wanted to go to John." She sighed unhappily at the memory. "She saw his ponytail and thought for a second he was Adam. As soon as he took her she realized he wasn't Adam and started crying again, but, honey, that hurt Adam to his heart." She made a sad face, remembering how Lily had gladly turned to her uncle Adam's arms but kept looking from John to Adam with puzzled and teary eyes.

"Aw, that's so sweet," Roxy said sympathetically. "He's a big softie, isn't he?"

"When it comes to his nieces and nephews he's a total marshmallow, but he'd never admit it. I hope he's able to laugh about it one day, but this ain't the day, Rox. We'll be cutting out of here pretty soon."

"Not too soon, I hope. I barely got a chance to say hello to you," a deep voice said.

Alicia turned around and gave an exclamation of joy. "Bryant, it's so good to see you! When did you get here?"

"Not too long ago. I've been outside talking to Benita and Clay and checking out the kids. They have some beautiful children," he said admiringly. The admiration turned toward Alicia as he beheld her new look. "Alicia, I just saw you a month ago and now look at you! I didn't think it was possible for you to be any more gorgeous, but this new look just floors me. You are one incredible woman and Adam is the luckiest man on this earth," he said sincerely. He walked all the way around the blushing Alicia, making a low sound of approval. "It's a good thing I never saw you in a skirt before this, I'd have fought Adam for you."

Alicia was pink with pleasure and laughing at Bryant's nonsense when she remembered that Roxy was in the room. "Bryant, please stop being silly and meet my best friend, Roxy Fairchild. Roxy, this is Bryant Porter." As the two of them said hello and shook hands, Alicia's eyes brightened. "Hey, you two are homies! Bryant, Roxy is from Chicago, too."

Bryant's eyes lit up and he turned his sexy smile on Roxy. It was evident that he liked what he saw because the smile lingered. Roxy was looking exceptionally pretty in a pair of gauzy deep rose palazzo pants and a matching long-sleeved formfitting top that came down to her hips and showed off her trim waist and luscious curves. The top had a deep scoop neckline and was worn off the shoulder so the sexy line of her neck was on generous display without being vulgarly exposed. Her shining hair was styled to perfection and the glow of her warm brown skin was accentuated by the soft makeup she was wearing, especially the glistening watermelon-pink shade on her generous lips. And she smelled wonderful, something else that wasn't lost on Bryant.

He immediately moved in to get acquainted with Roxy, something that was made easier by Alicia excusing herself and leaving the room. She wanted to make sure that Adam was okay. Roxy gave Bryant a cool and slightly disinterested look, even when he asked what part of Chicago she was from.

"The North Side," was all she said in response.

"Hmm. You know, Fairchild Cosmetics is based in Chicago. You wouldn't be related to those Fairchilds, would you?" he said teasingly.

"Unfortunately, yes, I am," she said tersely. Adding a very insincere "Nice to meet you," she turned and left him alone in the kitchen.

Alicia rejoined the outdoor party, her eyes scanning the crowd for Adam. She was only slightly relieved when she saw him; he was sitting with Daphne and Dahlia and wrestling with Malcolm and Marty, who were showing off for the aunts. To anyone else he looked relaxed and at ease, but Alicia could tell he was wound as tightly as a coiled spring. Big Benny, on the other hand, was having the time of his life. He was sitting at a table with Andre and Angelique while holding Lily Rose, who looked like she was about to fall asleep. Alicia knew she'd have to get Adam out of there soon and started looking for a tactful way to do it. Her eyes suddenly fell on Clay, who nodded in her direction. He walked over to her casually but he seemed to know what was on her mind.

"I think he's had about all he can take tonight. I'll go get my hellions and you can tell him Benita's looking for him. Then you two run for your lives," he said drolly.

Grateful for his perception, she did just that. Adam looked relieved for about a second, then his normal neutral expression returned. He rose and went with Alicia into the house, taking refuge in the large butler's pantry off the kitchen. Alicia put her arms around his waist and almost had the breath knocked out of her when he hugged her so tightly she couldn't move. "Are you ready to leave, baby? Because we can, we've been here long enough."

Adam leaned into Alicia's loving warmth and agreed it was time to go. They left the pantry and said their goodbyes as they made their way to the Range Rover. Once inside Adam took a deep breath and leaned forward, resting his forehead on the steering wheel. Alicia reached over to take his hand, which he gripped tightly. She brought their joined hands up to her lips and kissed the back of his hand before rubbing it against her cheek.

Adam smiled at her and started the engine. "Let's get out of here, Allie. Let's go home."

John could have echoed Adam's sentiments; he was being swallowed up by sensory overload. He had taken refuge in the living room to get away from the sea of oddly familiar faces. His solitude didn't last long, however, as two little girls joined him, one on either side of the armchair in which he was sitting. He looked from one face to the other and had to smile. They were completely identical. "Hello," he said softly. "What's your name?" he asked the one on his right.

"Benita," she answered shyly.

"And what's your name?"

"Ceylon," she said. They stared at John with the unrepentant curiosity of small children. One dainty little hand patted his knee as Benita asked him a question. "Are you ours?"

John raised his eyebrows in surprise. "What do you mean, sweetheart?"

"My daddy said you was our uncle. Are you really ours?" she asked innocently.

John's surprise showed on his face, but it went unnoticed by the girls. "Yes, I guess I am. Is that okay with you?"

Ceylon assured him it was. "Yes, we like our uncles. We like you, too."

Nina entered the living room in time to overhear this exchange. "Well, well, look at this, another set of twins," she said briskly.

"No, we're not," they said in unison.

Oh, great, the whole family is psycho, not just the old ladies. Nina had already encountered Daphne and Dahlia and heard their version of why they were merely sisters. She gave them a tight little fake smile and went along with it, figuring it was the easiest way. "I'm sorry, I thought you were twins, since you look exactly alike," she said in a saccharine voice. Whatever else she was about to say was forever lost as Stephanie entered the room and joined her sisters.

Ceylon turned a kindly eye on Nina. "See?" All three of them burst into giggles, joined, unfortunately, by John.

Nina raised an eyebrow and shot him a look that would have caused fear in a lesser man. "I'd cut that out if I were you, Ann Arbor is a long walk from here."

For some reason, that amused John even more and as it was with most small children, the sight of a laughing adult made them laugh even harder. Even Nina flashed her amazing dimples at the sight of the four of them collapsed in giggles. "Don't test me, John. This could have a detrimental effect on my normally sunny disposition. Remember, I have the car keys," she added.

"Yes, ma'am," he said meekly, only to have the girls echo him.

"That's it, I'm taking you home now before you giggle these three to death. Tell your uncle good night, ladies."

They surrounded the chair and crawled up on its arms to give John wet, noisy kisses and lots of good-byes. As they ran out of the room to find their mother, Nina looked at John, who was slumped back in the chair looking totally wiped out.

"How do you feel?"

John didn't answer for a moment, and then he smiled. "Immortal."

Nina walked over to him and held out her hand. "Well, come on, Zeus, I need my beauty sleep."

John was almost completely silent on the way back to Ann Arbor. His mind and his heart were too full; he was too emotional to trust himself to speak. He was glad Nina wasn't the kind of woman to rattle on and on. She seemed to sense his mood and refrained from conversation; she simply let him be. She'd asked one terse question when they got into the car. "Are you okay?" When he answered he was fine, she let it go and treated him to another thrill ride on the expressway. So much had transpired he couldn't begin to sort out his thoughts. He was so still in the passenger seat Nina thought he'd fallen asleep until he began to speak.

"Thank you, Miss Parker. If you hadn't gone with me, I might have missed one of the best days of my life. This was by far the damnedest day I've ever experienced, but I wouldn't have missed it for the world," he said quietly.

They were back at the university now, and Nina was easing the car into a parking space in front of John's temporary home. She turned off the ignition and waited for John to exit the car, but he continued to lean back against the headrest and talk quietly.

"A couple of weeks ago I knew exactly who and what I was. I was the only child of a beautiful, loving set of parents who were killed twelve years ago in a car crash. That was the worst day of my life. I loved my parents and I loved growing up with them. I wouldn't have changed a single day of it, Miss Parker, and that's the truth. I had one of those idyllic childhoods that nobody believes when you talk about it. But it's true; we had a lot of fun together, the three of us. I never missed having brothers and sisters, because my parents were always there for me. I had lots of friends; our house was the place where everybody wanted to hang because my parents were so cool. There was always someone for me to play with, I was never lonely or left out. And I have a ton of cousins in the old country, which is what we call Puerto Rico."

He laughed, a soft, self-deprecating chuckle. "Two weeks ago I could call it that because I was Puerto Rican. Now I'm African-American, how about that? Only in America could that happen."

"Doesn't that make you mad? Aren't you angry about all this, John?" Still lost in his thoughts, John didn't hear the warm concern in Nina's voice.

"How can I be, Miss Parker? The man gave me life and he gave me to two people who wanted me more than anything. I've had a good life, no, a *great* life. How can I be upset about that?" A comfortable silence grew and the scent of the night air, laden with honeysuckle, refreshed the interior of the car. The quiet was broken by John's voice in the darkness.

"That was the first thing he asked me, if I hated him for what he'd done."

John's eyes closed as he recalled with photographic clarity the first meeting with his biological father. The first thing that struck John, other than the physical resemblance, was the fact that Big Benny Cochran was nervous.

"Why don't you have a seat, John, and let's talk for a while?" the older man said. John had graciously indicated that Big Benny should be seated and Benny took a large leather club chair with a nod to acknowledge John's good manners. John then seated himself, not on the sofa, where he would have had some distance from the man, but in the matching club chair next to it with only a small magazine table to separate them. Benny was so self-possessed that only the most discerning eye would have noticed his anxiety, but John wasn't a psychiatrist for nothing. He could see as well as sense how important this was to Benny and how much he had at stake.

"I won't be upset if you despise me," Benny said quietly. His eyes searched John's face almost hungrily, assimilating his features and learning him. "Do you hate me? It's the most normal thing, I suppose."

"I don't hate you. I don't know you, so how could I possibly hate you, Mr. Cochran?" John waited to see the effect of his words on Benny. What he said didn't seem to affect him as much as the fact that John had referred to him as Mr. Cochran.

Benny winced a little before giving him a wry smile. "I suppose I deserve that *mister*," he said. "I don't have any right to expect anything else from you."

"I didn't mean it as a censure, it was a sign of respect. And a lack of knowing what else to call you," John said easily. "I don't hate you, nor do I hate what you did. I'm alive because of you. I've had a good life; I'd be a hypocrite if I said I didn't enjoy being here. I don't hate my parents, either. In a strange way this makes me love them more, not less. If they hadn't wanted a child so badly they might have said no, thanks instead of giving me a wonderful home. I'm not sure they wouldn't have eventually told me that I was adopted, had they lived. They might have told me about it, who knows?"

"Would you have tried to find your birth parents if you'd known?"

John didn't hesitate in his answer. "No. Because no matter who planted the seed, the fact is that Nestor Flores was my father and Consuela Flores was my mother. Period. There was nothing missing in my life, Mr. Cochran. No matter why she did it, your sister-in-law found me the best home I could've ever asked for," he said with quiet sincerity.

Ignoring Benny's reaction to his second use of the formal title, John pressed on. "I'd like to know something, sir. My biological mother, what was she like?"

The question caught the older man off guard and he sighed deeply. A sudden sheen of moisture washed over his eyes and he pinched the bridge of his nose tightly, as if to stem the flood. "Cassandra Hightower was a beautiful girl, inside and out," he began. "I was seventeen years old, working in my father's nightclub, the Hacienda. It was a Wednesday morning in late spring and I was cleaning the mirrors. My father said I was going to learn the business from the ground up and that meant doing maintenance and every other thing he told me to do. So there I was, washing mirrors like there was no tomorrow and I heard a soft little voicing asking for Mr. Cochran. I looked up and I could see her reflection all around me. She was standing in just the right spot so she was in every mirror, every single one, it seemed like. She was the prettiest thing I'd ever seen in my life and I knew right then and there I was going to marry her."

He told John all about Cassandra and their courtship, all the way up to the web of lies that caused him to leave home. Even though John had heard a version of these events from Bennie and Andrew, he listened intently, observing and cataloguing Benny's emotions. Benny's eyes were full of sorrow as he met John's gaze.

"I just realized how much Cassandra would have loved you, son. She'd be very proud of you. You're a fine man and a fine doctor. I never thought I'd get to say that to you, but I want to tell you how grateful I am for what you did for Benita."

John's face showed his surprise. For some reason he'd almost forgotten about that connection. He bowed his head slightly in a quick nod. "No thanks are necessary. Benita is an exceptional woman, a very strong woman. It was her determination to get well that made her heal, not my treatment." The two men looked openly at each other, each taking the measure of the man in the other chair.

"I have another question for you, actually two questions," said John. "One, why did you decide after all this time to contact me? You could have continued to ignore my existence and no one would have been the wiser."

Benny leaned back in his chair and slowly moved his head from side to side. "That's just what I couldn't do, son. I'm an old man and I've made a lot of mistakes in my life. Some things you can't do anything about, and some you can try to put right. I couldn't have gone to my grave without letting you know who I am, and letting the family know about you. You might not want to have anything to do with me from now on, or we might end up being friends. But at least you have the whole truth now. I might not be worth your time, John, but you have five brothers and a sister who are worth the world. I'm hoping you'll get to know them. It's important to have family. I know all about that, I abandoned mine," he said bitterly.

John watched the old man struggle with his memories for a moment and then he spoke. "But you connected with them again before it was too late. At this time in your life I think that's more important than dwelling on the sins of the past."

Benny raised an eyebrow and shot John a look that reminded him of just who he was dealing with. "You wouldn't be trying to get inside my head, would you? How'd you get to be so damned wise?" he said gruffly.

"Four years of college, four years of medical school, two years of interning and a residency, lots of postgraduate studies and years of practice, it all comes quite naturally," John said with a laugh.

"You got me there, son," Benny said as he joined him in laughter.

* * *

Next to John in the passenger seat, Nina gave an indelicate snort. He could see her look of disdain in the muted light shed by the street lamps. "What?" he probed.

"You let him off the hook," Nina said incredulously. "You had a chance to tell him off and let him know what you think of him for screwing up your life and you let him off like it was nothing."

John scratched his left forearm and waited for her to wind down. "I didn't let him off the hook, because he wasn't *on* one as far as I'm concerned. He's an old man who's made his share of mistakes in life and I happen to be one of his more colossal errors in judgment. But I didn't suffer for it, it's not like I was languishing in an orphanage or being beaten in a foster home. The man gave me life and I'm grateful. And I'm not alone anymore," he said with finality. "I don't have any relatives in the States. After my parents died it's just been me and the people I count as friends. Now I'm a brother, a nephew, and an uncle, and in a strange way, I'm a son again. Maybe I should be mad as hell and cursing the Fates," he said, scratching his right arm, "but I choose not to. Life is too short, Miss Parker, and I have better ways of spending mine than hating on an old man who never did anything to me except plant me."

John stopped scratching long enough to reach over and give Nina a caress on the cheek with his long brown hand. "Thanks again for coming with me. Drive carefully, well, drive *slowly*, I should say. You've got a heavy foot, girl."

John had exited the car and was about to go inside when Nina's voice stopped him. "What was your second question? The other question you had for him?"

John turned around with a sad smile. "I asked him how my mother died."

Chapter Twenty-three

Although the ride back to Harbortown was quiet, Adam was ready to break his silence when they arrived. He followed Alicia into the living area of the loft with its big twin sofas and collapsed on the first one he reached. Holding out a hand to Alicia, he gently pulled her down next to him. Alicia tucked her long legs under and sat close to Adam, holding his hand tightly. "Allie, I wish I could explain this better. I don't know how to put it into words," he began. "I went to the living room to get something for Martha and the study door opened. They'd been in there talking, Pop and John Flores. I don't know what I expected to happen the first time I saw him, so I'm not sure if this was weird or not."

"What happened, Adam?" Alicia could barely contain her curiosity.

"Not a lot."

When Adam looked at his father and the man who was supposed to be his half brother, he couldn't feel anything. He was both fascinated and repelled by the resemblance he shared with the man. They were equal in height, although Adam had the advantage of a half inch or so. Their coloring was identical, as were the thick moustaches and eyebrows. Adam even felt a slight pang of jealousy that John still possessed a striking mane of hair confined in a thick ponytail. *Yeah, but mine was longer,* he thought grimly. He couldn't deny their kinship, as much as he wanted to. John looked as much like Adam as any of his brothers, and the concept of them sharing the same bloodline became a reality.

Big Benny sensed nothing amiss, or he was pretending he didn't. In any case he introduced John to Adam. "Well, John, this is as good a place as any to start with the introductions. This is Adam, my next-to-youngest son. Adam, this is John."

Alicia's eyes were huge and she was holding her breath. "What did you say, Adam? What did *he* say?"

"I nodded and he nodded and we shook hands, and that was it. I might have said something scathing like 'How's it going, man?' and he said, 'It's all good, bro,' and that was the end of our first conversation." He pretended to wince as Alicia gave him a poke in the chest.

"You didn't say that and neither did he," she protested.

"I know, but what we did say was just about as banal. When the going gets strange, the Cochrans get trite, what can I tell you? I thought I'd say something brilliantly bitter to let him know I wasn't buying into all this instant family crap, but I didn't do it. I couldn't do it, Allie. I just shook the guy's hand and that was it." Adam shrugged, clearly still at odds with the situation. "I thought bile would rise in my throat and I'd be choked with rage or something. Being civilized is actually a huge letdown," he said with a mirthless laugh.

Alicia rose on her knees and leaned closer to cup Adam's face in her hands. "*Mi corazon,* I think you've thought enough about this for the time being." She kissed him gently and stood up, holding her hands out to him. "Come with me." Adam stood up and gladly followed her into the bedroom.

* * *

John walked around the living room with his hands in his pockets. The events of the day were replaying in his head, an endless loop of images punctuated with a sound track of memories. He'd met so many people it was virtually impossible to keep them all straight, but he didn't care. There was something comforting about the sheer numbers of them. They were his people, his new family. He'd met Alan and Andre, the identical twins, and their wives and children. He'd been deeply affected by seeing Angelique with her husband, Donnie; his first memory of her was as a spoiled little princess. He smiled when he thought about the Angelique he'd met that evening. Who could have predicted how well she would turn out? She was now an accomplished photographer as well as being a devoted wife and mother. He tried sitting down but found it uncomfortable and moved into the bedroom. He decided to take a shower in the hopes that it would help him relax.

He'd shed his clothes and was about to step into the bathtub when his phone rang. He picked it up curiously and smiled when he saw a familiar number on his caller ID. He took advantage of the big bed while he answered the call.

"Checking up on me, are you?"

Abe Gold's voice was cheerful and unrepentant. "It's a tough job, but somebody's gotta do it and I thought, who better than me? How are you doing?"

"Where do I begin, Abe? I lived through it, that's the important thing. It was better than I could have hoped in a lot of ways. Theirs is an amazing family, Abe. Smart, good-looking people who all seem to be happy and normal, except for a couple of great-aunts who swear up and down they're not twins." He explained the Daphne and Dahlia story to Abe, who laughed uproariously.

"That's hilarious, John. What else did you find out?"

John pretended he didn't know what Abe meant and continued to talk about his newly met relatives. "There's so many multiple births in that family it might be worth a study of some kind. Andrew is a twin and he has triplets, Benita is a twin with two sets of twins. The other set of twins, Alan and Andre, they didn't have any multiple births, but they have some really nice kids," he said as though there were nothing more important to be discussed.

"They were all great, really welcoming, made me feel right at home. It could have been totally bizarre, but it was nice. Probably the best night I've had since before my parents died."

A poignant silence might have ensued, but Abe wasn't having it. "Cut to the chase. What did you find out? I hate to be blunt, but we only have so much time, John, I don't have to remind you of that, you of all people."

John took a deep breath. "Okay, Abe, this is what I found out. My mother died of liver disease. Benny doesn't remember the name of it, he's not sure he ever knew it, but that's what killed her. Probably the same one that's killing me," he said without bitterness.

This time it was Abe who was silent. Finally he said, "John, as painful as that must have been to hear, it's another big piece of the puzzle. Primary sclerosing cholangitis, although the cause is still unknown, has some genetic factors. It's almost impossible for you to have it and not have gotten the trait from one parent or another, and now we know. The other thing we know is that there's a way you can be cured. This doesn't have to kill you, John, not if we act quickly."

"That's just it, Abe. I can't act. Not quickly, not slowly, hell, I can't act at all. This is just something I'm not prepared to do."

"John, you have to, you have no other choice. You've run out of options and you're running out of time."

* * *

Alicia drew Adam into the bedroom and sat him down on the bed. She stood in front of him, with her hands on his shoulders, looking at him with a look of loving tenderness on her face. She kissed his forehead and knelt before him to remove his shoes, stroking his long feet as she did so. She stood up and went to the wall by the doorway, turning off the overhead lights and illuminating the base of the bed. The warm, mellow light made the room look soft and seductive. Alicia picked up the remote for the stereo and pressed a few buttons, releasing the seductive sound of Ravel's "Bolero" into the room. She returned to Adam, who had already unbuttoned his shirt in anticipation of what was to come.

Alicia took over, removing his shirt and sighing with enjoyment as she looked at his big broad shoulders, his smooth muscled chest, and his tight stomach with the sexy six-pack. She stroked his shoulders and kissed his neck, then his lips, letting her mouth play all over his for maximum impact. She took his upper lip and licked it gently, pulling it into the warm moistness of her mouth to suck it gently, teasing him with tiny little nips of her teeth, then treated the lower lip the same way. His soft sounds of pleasure let her know that he was enjoying it as much as she was.

Suddenly he stood up, which startled Alicia until she realized that he was getting rid of his slacks and his briefs. Smiling in anticipation as his long, muscular legs came into view, Alicia kicked off her own shoes and began unfastening the halter neckline of her dress. After sliding the supple silk dress down her equally supple body, she stood in front of Adam clad only in a black lace strapless bra and a matching lace thong. She didn't stand long as Adam picked her up and deposited her on the bed, rolling over on top of her with a sigh of complete surrender. "Allie, I'm so glad you're here with me," he said in his deep, sexy voice.

"I'll always be here for you, Adam, I love you. You're my heart," she whispered. Her expression changed from loving tenderness to one of determination. "And this is all for you, so turn over, right now. I have something wonderful for you," she purred.

"That sounds serious, should I be afraid?" Adam joked.

"No, you should be grateful," she responded. As he turned over on his stomach, Alicia went into the bathroom and returned with a bottle of massage oil. She changed the music to the beautiful voice of Lenora Herm and climbed onto the bed, straddling Adam's body and smoothing her hands over his back. "You just close your eyes and don't think about anything, sweetheart. I learned a few things when I was at the spa with Roxy." She poured some of the lightly scented oil into her palm and warmed it by holding her hands together, then spread it over the taut bronzed bounty in front of her. She began to treat him to a wonderful massage, stroking his very willing flesh with strong, sure motions designed to both relax and stimulate him.

Adam immediately succumbed to the tender ministrations of his beloved; the feel of her warm hands on his body was lulling him into peaceful lassitude even while he was experiencing a powerful arousal. Alicia didn't miss any part of his body; she caressed his back, his arms, and his neck, and when her hands worked their way down to his buttocks, he entered a dangerous stage of readiness. "Baby, you need to slow down," he groaned. "Or stop altogether, because I can't take much more of this," he admitted.

Alicia didn't relent, she continued to cup and knead the firm mounds to her heart's content. "I can't seem to stop, Adam. My hands just won't let go of this cute behind of yours. I love this behind, it's so sexy." She sighed.

Her sigh turn into a gasp of surprise as Adam flexed his muscles so the object of her ardor moved under her hands. "Oh my," she breathed. The feel of his now hot skin, slick with the fragrant oil, was incredibly sensual, causing her passion to mount to a level that could only be assuaged by the joining of their flesh.

Adam knew the moment the massage stopped and the foreplay began in earnest. He could feel the increasing heat from the soft flesh of her inner thighs as she continued to straddle him, he could sense the growing moisture the thin lace of the thong did little to contain. With a groan he gently dislodged her as he turned onto his back and held his arms out to her, pulling her into his embrace and fastening his mouth on hers, losing himself in the hot sweetness of their kiss. Their hands moved almost frantically over each other's bodies, each needing the feel of the other, the heat and the fire of their love.

He took her mouth again and again, loving her lips with his mouth and tongue, drinking the nectar from her as he ran his big hands over her body. He kissed down her neck, licking and sucking the tender flesh over her collarbones, her shoulders, and running his hot, seeking tongue along her cleavage, gently sucking her nipples through the fragile fabric of her lacy bra. Alicia shivered under the onslaught of his desire and was trying to remove her skimpy undergarments when Adam stopped her. "Leave them on, baby, I love the way you look." He reached for a condom and with her assistance quickly rolled the latex protection on. Now they were ready, there was nothing to stop them from devouring each other with the hunger that consumed them.

Adam moved the thong aside with a skill born of need so keen it was painful. He entered her moist, welcoming canal slowly, trying to be as gentle as possible given the massive erection. He tried to be slow and careful but Alicia wasn't having it. The feel of him entering her body snapped her control and she pushed forward to take him into her yielding heat. Her hips moved urgently, the motions of her body letting him know that she was more than ready for him. "More, Adam," she whispered, "more."

The sound of her voice coupled with her sensuous, undulating movements released the burgeoning passion in Adam. He grasped her hips and plunged into her sweetness over and over, their sweat-slicked bodies coming together with increasing force until the inevitable end to their mating came in a galvanic climax that rocked them both. Adam thrust himself forward as she ground her hips against him, sighing his name over and over. He buried his head in her neck, trembling with the force of the pulsing shocks that convulsed his big frame, moaning words of love as he tried to regain some control. "Allie, I love you. I love you, baby, you've always been mine, all mine."

"And I love you, Adam." She smiled as he collapsed on top of her, pulling her into his arms and rolling over onto his back to cradle her against him.

When their breathing slowed down, she rubbed his chest and suggested they take a shower. "No, let's just lie here and be sweaty. I love being all sticky and wet after we make love," he confessed. "It feels so natural, like we were meant to be without anything between us. I can't wait to be married to you, baby. And I really want to make love to you outdoors, Allie."

"Outdoors? In the wide-open spaces or under the trees somewhere secluded from the rest of the world?" she mused.

"Both," he answered, pleased that she hadn't rejected the idea. "I can't tell you how much I love making love to you, Allie. When I'm with you intimately, touching you, inside you . . . I can't describe how it feels. I feel so close to you, like we're the same person. It's like you're taking my breaths and I'm taking yours," he confessed.

Alicia smiled delightedly. "I have to tell you something. Sometimes when we're together I can't tell if you're inside me or I'm inside you, that's how close I feel to you. It's always like the very first time with you, Adam, but it's also like we've been making love since the beginning of time. Does that make any sense?"

"It makes perfect sense, my love. So let's be real sensible once more before we go get in the shower," he said as he finally released her from her bra and panties in preparation for another sensual assault.

Her only answer was a soft sigh of anticipation as she turned into his arms for more loving.

Chapter Twenty-four

The next morning Alicia awoke to an empty bed and the sound of one of her favorite CDs. Carlos Santana's *Borboletta* was echoing through the loft, filling it with the sensual Latin rhythm. She smiled lazily and enjoyed the feeling of utter contentment that permeated every bit of her body. After making love again and again the night before, she and Adam had spent a long time in the big bathtub, luxuriating in bubbles and each other, before finally going to bed and a long, dreamless sleep in each other's arms. The memory of the passion they shared made her smile again as she rose from the bed.

She brushed her teeth and took a quick shower before changing the sheets and putting the room back to its normal pristine condition. After making sure the bathroom was equally spotless and tidy, she put on one of Adam's old denim shirts. There was an assortment of items belonging to her in the big mahogany armoire, but she liked wearing Adam's clothes. She slipped a pair of beaded thong sandals on her feet and went in search of Adam. She was pleased to find him in the kitchen, putting the finishing touches on a huge breakfast. He was moving with the music and looking like every woman's fantasy come true, wearing an old pair of jeans and a wifebeater.

"*Hola, querida*, you've been busy this morning," she said, greeting him.

"*Hola* yourself, sleepyhead. I was going to bring you this in bed," he told her, giving her a quick kiss.

"You're too sweet to me," she murmured, kissing him back and wrapping her arms around his waist. "It's such a pretty day, why don't we eat on the roof?"

She took a bottle of cleanser and some paper towels to wipe off one of the glass-topped bistro tables and had set two places with the big square pottery plates she'd given Adam some years before. Adam brought the food out and after saying grace, they began eating a marvelous breakfast of eggs Florentine, crisply browned filet mignon, and blueberry scones, made from scratch from a recipe Alicia's mother had given him. The scones had a hint of subtle citrus flavor from a bit of lemon zest; they tasted just as good as her mother's and Alicia sighed with pleasure as she savored a bite. Adam didn't feel that breakfast was worth eating without grits and he made great ones, smooth and buttery.

"If we eat like this every day I'm going to get huge," she warned him.

Adam scoffed. "That's not going to happen, baby. We run three or four times a week. Besides, you need to keep your strength up if we make love like we did last night," he said with a satisfied smile.

Alicia grabbed his hand and leaned over to him for a kiss. "You've got a deal. You just keep feeding me because I plan to make a lot of love with you. And a lot of babies," she said sweetly.

Adam kissed her back and smiled sheepishly. "Allie, I don't know what I'd do without you. You've been the most important part of my life for ten years and it's going to be that way forever. You amaze me, you astound me, you elate me every day, and I thank God you're in my life. I thought last night would be miserable, but it wasn't. I thought I'd hate John Flores and want to stomp him, but I don't. He's a nice guy, Allie, a good man.

None of this is his fault, after all. He didn't ask my father to betray my mother, he's as much of a victim as she was," he said with a touch of heat.

Alicia studied their still-clasped hands, admiring Adam's strong fingers and neatly kept nails. The things this hand could do to her—she blushed and cleared her throat before meeting Adam's eyes. "So how do you feel about the situation now, Adam? Do you think you can at least be friends with John?"

Adam was silent for a long time. "I'm not saying I can't, Allie. I just don't know at this point. I can't harbor any resentment toward him, even though I planned on it. I planned to ignore his existence as much as possible, but that seems kind of impractical since the family has decided to nestle him to their bosom, so to speak." He laughed grimly, recalling the open affection demonstrated last night as the entire clan made John welcome. "I just don't know how I can accept him as a brother or even a friend when I know what the affair did to my mother. I can't blame John for it, but I can sure as hell blame my father and I do. I don't know if I'm going to be able to deal with him, Alicia. Right now I don't know if I can ever look him in the eye again."

John slept heavily and late, waking up feeling just as tired as when he went to bed. He was used to it, this feeling of lassitude and heaviness that plagued him constantly. The malaise was part of his condition, as was the almost constant itching of his skin. He sometimes felt as if there were a thousand insects inside him trying to buzz their way out. He had various ointments to use and they helped, for the most part, but the lethargy and loss of appetite were harder to remedy. He'd lost a considerable amount of weight in the year since his diagnosis and it was becoming a source of concern. If he were at his normal weight he'd look just like his brothers, big and healthy. Now he looked like a slender version of a Cochran man.

A Cochran. Hard as it was to believe, he belonged to them and they were a part of him. He'd been alone in the world and now he had family. It was still hard to get his head around the idea that he was a Cochran, but it was getting easier. He dragged himself out of bed and took a long tepid shower. He liked a hot shower, the hotter the better, but his doctor told him that a tepid one would help ease the itching. He disliked the scent of the special antibacterial soap he was mandated to use, but he had no choice, it was this or suffer even more intense skin irritation. He liked to use regular soap, great big imported bars of scented soap. John was masculine enough to admit that he enjoyed his creature comforts. He finally got out of the shower and patted his skin dry instead of the usual brisk rubdown he preferred, another doctor's order. He dressed in his oldest pair of jeans, laundered nearly white and full of little rips and tears. It was Miss Parker's fondest wish to confine them to the Dumpster, but they were so comfortable he couldn't let them go.

Miss Parker. He'd have to remember to call her Nina, he supposed, but he loved having a pet name for her. On the rare occasions he watched television, he enjoyed watching syndicated reruns of *The Pretender*. There was a character in the show who reminded him of Nina. She was tough and hard and completely intimidating to everyone, but she had the heart of a marshmallow. Admittedly, Nina showed no such sensitivity, but she had everything else down pat, including the sternly sophisticated look of Miss Parker.

His thoughts were interrupted by a knock at his door. He walked into the carefully neutral, boringly decorated room and opened the door to find a nervous-looking young man apparently making a delivery.

"Mr. Flores, I mean *Dr.* Flores, I have something for you," he said hurriedly.

John smiled to reassure the young man. He was tall and slender with sandy brown hair in neat braids and a smattering of freckles. His green eyes looked both intelligent and anxious. "Are you sure it's for me? I didn't order anything."

"Someone sent it to you, sir. I just work at the restaurant. I'm supposed to bring you this," he said, indicating a large bag with the name of a popular restaurant on it, "and this." John took the other big-shopping bag with handles the young man was holding. It contained a big bouquet of spring flowers in various shades of red, their color bright and cheerful in the morning light. There was also a copy of the Sunday *New York Times*, the Sunday edition of the Ann Arbor paper, and two CDs he'd been coveting but hadn't purchased. With a big smile, he invited the wary young man to come in.

"Come on in and let me get you something for your trouble," he said.

"No, sir, absolutely not. It's all been taken care of," he said hastily.

"But I insist. I appreciate all the trouble you went to, I doubt that your restaurant normally delivers."

"They don't, sir, but the person, the woman, the *lady* who set it up, she made it worth my while, really worth it, I mean. And she said if I took any money . . ." His voice trailed off.

John smiled, already knowing who'd sent him the wonderful gift. "What did she say?"

"She said she would personally eviscerate me with a salad fork and feed my entrails to the birds, sir. I think she meant it." He was now bright red with drops of perspiration on his top lip.

John laughed out loud and pulled the terrified college student across the threshold. "Ignore her. Her bark is no worse than a low-level atomic accident, but I'm almost certain her bite isn't as bad."

He left the room and came back to find the young man frozen right where he'd left him. He handed him a twenty-dollar bill and insisted he keep it. "She may be tough but she's not omniscient, she'll never know."

Wordlessly the boy handed him a folded piece of paper. John burst out laughing as he read the words *Take that money back if you don't want to meet the same fate.* It was signed Miss Parker.

"Trust me, she's not going to come after you. You have my word on it. She just likes to act tough, it's a little game we play."

With a shaky smile of relief the youth dashed off to his disreputable-looking car and took off. John took his bounty into the dining area and opened the Styrofoam containers to find a plump, piping-hot omelet oozing cheese and full of mushrooms, onions, and peppers, along with crisp bacon, rye toast, hash browns, sliced strawberries, and two giant cups of coffee. There was also a big piece of apple pie, a particular weakness of his. Only someone who knew him very well could have assembled this meal. Someone who knew him well enough to care that he ate well. He said a quick grace and did his best to do justice to the meal and found that he could consume most of it, unusual for him as of late. He cleared the table and got comfortable on the sofa to read the papers and listen to the first of his two CDs, a mellow collection of love songs by Chet Baker. He attempted several times to call Nina, but she wasn't answering her cell phone. From what he knew of her he figured she would hate being thanked for doing something so special; thus she was avoiding him. Well, she couldn't hide forever. He'd do something spectacular for her the next day, something that would embarrass her no doubt, but might please her as well. *I knew she had a soft heart,* he thought, gloating.

* * *

The next couple of weeks weren't what Adam would have expected. After his initial reaction to *the* revelation he was prepared for a period of hostility and estrangement, but it wasn't to be. In a strange way he was closer to his family than ever and he couldn't quite figure out why. He was sitting in his office at Cochran and Fuentes Design thinking about the events of the past days. He was watching the traffic in downtown Detroit as he went over what had occurred since the big party at Donnie and Angelique's house.

The day after, the same day he'd made breakfast for Alicia, he'd gotten a call inviting him to play a round of golf with his brothers. It was the first time he'd had an opportunity to really talk with them since Benny's big revelation, and he accepted at once. He'd gone to Andrew's house to collect him and drive over to the golf course. While he was waiting for Andrew he had a chance to talk with Benita. She and Clay were going back to Atlanta in a few days and she had a few things to say to him before they left.

"Adam, I want you to know how proud I am of you. I know this isn't easy for you, but you're handling this much better than anyone has a right to expect you to," she said as she gave him a big hug. They had a rare moment alone on the deck to talk and she was making the most of it. They sat next to each other on a wicker settee with Adam's arm draped around her shoulder. She stroked his hand and looked into his eyes with loving concern. "I remember how close you were to Mama. Of all the boys you were her favorite, although she'd never, *ever* say that," Bennie said hastily. "But she just adored you, Adam. She loved all of us, she really did, and we were all her favorites for one reason or another, but you were her heart and that's the truth. I know this must feel like you're betraying her in some way, but you're not.

John didn't do anything to get here, he didn't ask to be born."

Adam was silent for a minute before responding. "I know that, Benita. In my heart I know this has nothing to do with Mama, but in a way it does." He broke his silence of thirty years and told her everything that happened on the day their mother died. "So you see, I've always felt like I did something wrong, like it was my fault she died. And I'm ninety-nine percent sure that somehow Mama found out about John and that's why she was so angry at Pop before the accident. How do I just let that go, Benita? How do I accept John without dishonoring my mother's memory and how do I let go of the fact she knew what Pop had done?"

Adam was dismayed to see big tears rolling down his sister's face after he stopped speaking. He wiped them away and listened quietly as she told him her own story. "I always thought I was responsible for her dying. I'd asked her to bring my science project to school and she fussed and said, 'You're going to be the death of me, Andrea Benita Cochran,' and those were the last words I ever heard from her. I suffered from guilt for years and years about that, Adam. And you know who helped me understand I wasn't responsible? It was John, when he was treating me in California."

They sat in silence for a moment before she continued. "I'm ashamed to say that nothing Daddy did or will do shocks me in any way. I got exposed to his machinations at a very early age," she said with resignation. "I guess if I didn't know John from a can of paint I might be resentful and angry about it, but I *do* know John. He saved my sanity and my marriage, Adam. He's a wonderful man and he's been a good friend to Clay and me over the years. I owe a lot to him and even before I knew we were related I loved him like a brother. I'm just glad you're giving him a chance. Even if you don't become close, you're not shutting him out."

Further conversation slowed down as first Trey and then the triplets and finally the twins came racing out of the house, followed more sedately by little Andie. He did get a chance to say what was really on his mind, though. As one of his nephews made a dive for his head for a bout of wrestling, Adam turned to his sister once more. "I hear what you're saying, Benita, and I'm not holding anything against John. My question is, how do I befriend him and not dishonor Mama? And how do I forgive Pop? Could *you*, if you were me?"

Benita groaned under the burden of three little girls trying to crawl into her lap at once. "I don't know, Adam. I really don't know how I'd do it if I were you. But I do know you have to try. For *your* sake, not for his. I don't want you to end up like he did. Not being able to forgive his own father for what he thought he'd done, that's what makes him the way he is today. I don't want that for you, sweetie." Her head turned and her voice changed as she noticed one of her sons attempting something dangerous. "Boy, if you don't put that down I'm going to put you in time-out until you're thirty! Clay, come get these children!"

That day had been a revelation and a turning point for Adam. He'd heard similar sentiments from his brothers as they enjoyed a raucous round of golf followed by lunch. They didn't try to push the idea of having a half brother down Adam's throat but sounded a lot like Benita as they applauded Adam's willingness to try to accept the situation.

Alan and Andre were pragmatic about it. "I guess if he was a crackhead or an exotic dancer or a Republican or something I'd have some issues. But he seems like a really nice guy, smart, gainfully employed, and most importantly, he has his own bankroll. And there's no denying he's a handsome fellow." Alan preened with an exaggerated adjustment of his collar.

Andre agreed. "Seeing as he has the good fortune to

resemble *us*, there's no denying that he's a stud. He takes after his big brothers, that's all."

Donnie, Adam, and Andrew all groaned and threw their napkins at the twins. Andrew did offer up an opinion, though. "You know, considering everything he's been through, he's very cool and calm about all this. He grew up thinking his parents were his natural parents, he was a different nationality, and then he finds out that he's black, adopted, and illegitimate. That's a lot to pile on one man's plate, but he seems to be taking it in stride," Andrew said thoughtfully.

"Yeah, but he did mention that he was always raised as a black man. His parents were both dark-skinned and they let him know from jump street that they were all of African descent. Black folks live all over the globe, you know that."

"This is true," Andrew said thoughtfully. "But damn, it takes a truly well-adjusted person to accept all that's been dumped in his lap. He must be the most mentally healthy person on the planet."

"Well, he is a shrink after all. He probably is more grounded than most people. He understands all this crazy stuff," Donnie said as he tried to help himself to the rest of Andrew's fries.

Andrew made a half-hearted attempt to protect his food, then shrugged and gave up. "Take them, it's your cholesterol."

Adam stood and said he and Andrew needed to be leaving anyway. "I have a couple of things I need to do for Alicia before tonight's festivities, then I need to get back to the office for a minute."

Each of the brothers had taken a turn entertaining John, having him over for dinner or brunch so he could get to know them and their families. Adam hadn't gotten that far yet, but he wasn't totally rejecting the man, either. In fact, thanks to Alicia, he was going to be playing host to his half brother that night, in a way. The aunts were visiting in Detroit again. They'd gone home the day after the party, but Benny and Martha had urged them to come again soon, which they had, due to the outing Alicia had arranged. Knowing of Emmaline's love of baseball, Marielle had arranged for the aunts to attend a game as a special guest of the Detroit Tigers Organization. It was a good game, too; they were playing the Yankees and the Yankees were out for revenge since the Tigers had recently trounced them in a two-game series.

The whole family would be there, actually both families as the Fuentes men were on the team, and Alicia's mother would be in attendance, too. They would be in a huge VIP suite enjoying the Tigers' hospitality as well as the game. As he drove to the Cochran Building, Adam smiled, knowing how much his aunts would enjoy the outing. Everyone was coming to the loft afterward for coffee and dessert provided by Alicia and Adam, so it should be a memorable day for everyone. And a day when he couldn't avoid his father the way he had been. As he sat at the wheel, Adam's brow creased in deep thought, but his face relaxed into a smile when Alicia opened his door.

She came over to his desk and leaned over for a kiss. "How are you, sweetie? We have to leave in about a half hour," she reminded him. She smiled and it was obvious she was thinking about something other than the game.

"What's so funny?"

Alicia grinned again and said that Rhonda had just asked her if she and Adam were going to share an office once they were married. "Of course I told her no," she said.

Adam pretended to be offended. "Why don't you want to share an office with me?" he demanded.

"Because I'd never get any work done! I'd be staring at you and thinking about things to do to the gorgeous body I know lurks beneath those clothes and I'd be a total wreck. All I'd be thinking about is having sex with you. Not making love, mind you, but having hot, secret, illicit sex right here in the office. Like on the sofa, or bent over that drawing board, or even in the lavatory . . ." Her voice trailed off and she shook her head emphatically. "No way, sweetheart, it just wouldn't work."

Alicia's vivid words ignited the smoldering flame that always flickered when he was around her and his eyes reflected his need. "Well now, you just gave me a great idea. Suppose we just lock that door and try out a few of those things, just to see if they work?" he said, reaching for her with lust in his eyes.

Alicia's eyes grew huge and she began backing out of the office. "Don't even think about it, Adam. We're leaving here in thirty minutes. Since when have you and I made love in less than forty-five?"

"We could try," he said innocently.

His answer was the sound of the door closing as Alicia beat a hasty retreat.

Chapter Twenty-five

Everyone seemed to be having a wonderful time, especially Emmaline, who was thrilled to meet Alicia's and Marielle's father, Jose. She'd been a huge fan of his when he was a player, something she let him know immediately. He introduced her to his sons and several other players before the game began and promised to rejoin the group after the game. Alicia was watching the aunts with a loving smile on her face when she was struck by Roxy's expression. "Rox, will you quit looking at Bryant like he has the plague? I keep telling you he's a nice guy and you're acting like he's Chester the child molester or a down-low brother or something. Cut it out," she said firmly.

The two women were in the kitchen area of the suite making sure that the buffet was still plentiful and anyone who wanted anything was satisfied. Bryant was chatting with Marielle as if she were the last woman on the planet, or at least it looked that way to Roxy.

"Hmmph. So you say. He acts like an ol' player if you ask me. I still can't get over his nerve, pushing up on me not two seconds after he was all over you. No, thank you, I'm nobody's consolation prize," she said, sniffling.

"Look, honey, he's just being friendly to Marielle; she has no interest in men whatsoever. Since than stupid husband of hers left her high and dry she's had more than a few issues with the opposite sex, so there's no hope of her giving Bryant the time of day."

Sure enough, no sooner had the words left her mouth than Bryant joined them.

"Alicia, thanks again for inviting me. You look wonderful, by the way." He gave her his brilliant beautiful smile and then turned a subdued version of the same smile on Roxy. "Hello, Roxy. I don't want to risk your wrath again, but I'd be remiss if I didn't tell you how lovely you look," he said with warm sincerity.

Roxy did look adorable in a perfectly fitting pair of cuffed shorts with a matching blouse and a pair of sexy orange sandals. Bryant tried mightily but he couldn't stop looking at her big, curvy legs that led up to her high, rounded bottom and delectable hips. He tried looking into her eyes, but that was a problem, too, since her golden brown eyes framed by long lashes seemed to bore holes in him, but he didn't care. Her pouty lips and her pretty, round face were enchanting and he wanted to get to know her better; something that seemed impossible since she acted like she hated him.

"Why don't you like me?" he asked suddenly.

She raised an eyebrow and replied coolly, "It's not you, it's your cologne. I don't care for it."

Bryant looked from Alicia to Roxy with disbelief on his face. "My *cologne*?"

"Yes. It smells like Eau de Unrequited Love to me and I don't like it."

Bryant burst into hearty laughter and had the nerve to reach over and pull Roxy into his arms for a hug. "Thank you for the compliment; I haven't had a woman get jealous on my behalf for a long time. Alicia and I were never involved; we're just good friends," he said gently.

Alicia scooted out of the kitchen, as she knew that Roxy was about to go off on Bryant. She also saw the twinkle in her friend's eyes and knew that there were some serious sparks of attraction flying around. Alicia just wanted to make sure that Adam was okay and that John was comfortable with the teeming mass of Cochrans milling around him. For some reason he'd looked a little tired to her eyes when he'd arrived with Nina. She wasn't very reassured by what she saw in the main area of the suite. John still looked tired and rather pale to her. And apparently not only to her as Nina pulled her to one side. "Is it possible for us to have lunch or something? I'd like to talk to you about something," she said tersely.

Alicia agreed at once, suggesting they get together the next day at a place near the office. Nina didn't linger once they made the date; she went back to sit near John. Adam was on the other side of John and he didn't look uncomfortable at all. They looked like they were having a decent conversation, as a matter of fact. Alicia's gaze traveled around the room to her mother, who was deep in conversation with Reba and Daphne. Or Dahlia, those two were still identical to Alicia. Everything seemed to be proceeding nicely; even the children were behaving well, especially her nephew Paco, who was dazzled by Andie. Clearly she was the most beautiful thing he'd ever seen and to Alicia's amusement, he was glued to her side. She smiled as Adam rose from the sofa and came to join her. "How are you doing?' she asked as he gave her a quick discreet nuzzle on the neck.

"Just fine, baby. Being with you makes everything just about perfect. I couldn't imagine a nicer evening."

Alicia kissed him back and told him that Nina had asked to have lunch with her on the next day. Adam raised his eyebrows as he looked down at her. "That's interesting. I thought she was kind of aloof. She didn't seem like the type to make friends, if you know what I mean."

"Well, it seems like you're wrong about that. It looks like she wants to get better acquainted at least."

"That's nice. Let me know how it goes."

"Oh, you know I will. I can't keep anything from you, now, can I?" She smiled up at him and he tightened his arms around her, smelling her fantastic hair as he did so.

"Can we go now? I need to be alone with you in the worst way," he whispered.

Alicia giggled and told him to behave. "It's going to be a long time before we can do any of that, so chill. I promise to make the wait worth your while, though."

Only slightly mollified, Adam agreed to behave. "But when we're alone all bets are off, so get ready, baby,"

Roxy's eyes were huge and full of concern for her friend. It was the day after the baseball game and Alicia had called her in the early afternoon asking if she could come talk to her. "Of course. I'm at home all day today waiting for the movers, so come ahead." Roxy had, with her usual efficiency, procured a lovely condominium that faced the man-made lake in the middle of the complex, and she was in the process of moving in. When Alicia arrived she found Roxy surrounded by boxes and furniture that looked like it had just been taken off a truck and dropped, which Roxy admitted it had. "Their feet were so dirty I didn't want to risk my carpet," she said, indicating the brand-new snowy-white Berber. "So I had them get in and out as quickly as possible."

Alicia nodded distractedly. "How are you going to get everything in place?"

Roxy smiled mysteriously. "Help is on the way. Now what's troubling you, Alicia? I could tell by your tone of voice that something is wrong."

Alicia's eyes filled with tears and she looked around for something on which to sit. She ended up sitting on a big box and wrapping her arms around her middle before answering. "John Flores is dying, Roxy. He has a liver disease that will kill him in a very short time if nothing is done about it."

Roxy went to Alicia at once, dropping to her knees and putting her arms around her friend. "That's awful, Alicia. How did you find out?"

Alicia pulled out of Roxy's embrace and stared at her with big sad eyes that showed the strain of trying not to cry. "I had lunch today with that friend of John's, that Nina Whitney. She's the one who told me. She found out by accident. John doesn't even know that she knows. But the reason she told me is that John can survive the disease if he gets a liver transplant," Alicia said in a voice choked with emotion.

Roxy looked relieved. "Well, that's something. Maybe Andrew can use his pull to get him on a list or something. With both Andrew and John being prominent doctors, maybe something can be done to expedite the situation," she said with hope in her voice.

Alicia was shaking her head even as Roxy spoke. "It's not like that, Rox. First of all, John wouldn't even consider preferential treatment. I don't know him very well, of course, but I can't see him allowing himself to be pushed to the head of a list somewhere; he'd never put his life in front of another person's." She sniffed and took a deep breath before continuing. "The other thing is this, Roxy, it can't be a cadaver transplant. In order for it to work the transplant has to come from a living donor."

Roxy looked both repulsed and fascinated by the information. "But how can you take the liver from a live person?" she asked with a shudder. "I thought that was an essential body organ."

"It is essential, but it will also regenerate. You can take half a liver out of a living person and put it into a person with a diseased liver and both people will end up with a whole liver because it will grow back. The only thing is the donor has to be about the same height, weight, and age as the person receiving the liver. Which makes Adam—"

"The perfect donor," Roxy breathed. "Oh my God, Alicia, is that why she wanted to have lunch with you, to ask for Adam's, Adam's . . ." She couldn't finish the sentence.

"Yes, that's just about it. She wants me to talk to Adam so he'll agree to do it and I couldn't say yes to her. First of all, I couldn't possibly try to influence Adam in something like that. With all he's been through lately, how could I possibly try to talk him into doing something like that for someone he hardly knows? I understand her concern for the man, but dang, that's a little bit much, don't you think?" Alicia wiped her eyes and continued. "She's either crazy in love with the man or she has no sense of propriety whatsoever. But she did do her homework. I now know more about partial liver transplants than I ever cared to know in this life."

"Maybe it's a little bit of both," Roxy said gently. "Maybe she's in love and desperate. You know you'd be doing the same thing if Adam's health was in danger."

Alicia had to agree with her friend. "Girl, I'd not only ask for the stupid liver, I'd be trying to take it out myself with a melon baller if I had to. I couldn't just sit by and do nothing, which I why I feel so bad about the second reason I can't talk to Adam."

Roxy braced herself for the worst. "What's that reason, Alicia?"

"Because I don't want him to do it," she whispered.

Adam glanced at the caller ID on his cell phone and was mildly intrigued to see it was a call from California. "Hello?"

The voice on the other end wasted no time in getting to the point. "This is Nina Whitney and I'd like to talk to you if you have some time."

"Sure, Nina. Are you out of town? My caller ID read a California call," he said with curiosity.

"I'm calling you on my cell phone. Do you mind if I come to your place?"

Adam raised an eyebrow. This woman meant business, apparently. "Sure, when can you stop by?"

"Open your door."

Adam did so and there Nina stood, slim and resolute, her phone still clamped to her ear. "Why don't you come in and have a seat?" he said with his usual dry humor.

Nina didn't lose a bit of her normal aplomb as she accepted a seat in the cavernous living area. She looked around at the majestic space and commented that it was a very nice place to live. "I can see why you're successful, you and Alicia. You made this place into a real home," she said. She'd said something similar the night before when everyone had gathered there after the ball game, but unlike the night before her mind didn't seem remotely on the appearance of his loft. She obviously had something to say.

Gently Adam encouraged her to unburden herself. "You seem to have something to tell me. What is it?" he asked in a quiet, concerned voice.

"You're probably going to think I have no business telling you this, but I don't have a choice. John is dying," she said in a flat, dull voice. "He has something called primary sclerosing cholangitis; it's a disease of the liver. Nobody knows what causes it, other than there are some genetic factors involved. He probably inherited from his biological mother, but that hardly seems to matter now. What matters is he doesn't have long to live. Once the disease takes hold the patient has only a couple of years to live, three at the most. There is no cure; his only hope is a partial liver transplant from a closely matched donor. I think you're an intelligent man, Adam, you know where I'm going with this."

Adam was amazed that he was able to follow what she was saying. After her initial words he'd been so stunned that he couldn't utter a word, he just listened to her dry, unemotional delivery with an odd sort of admiration. She clearly cared a great deal about John and was willing to approach a near stranger and discuss intimate matters if that's what it took to help him.

"Are you listening to me, Adam?" she asked with intense irritation. *God, what a time for him to be daydreaming.*

"Yes, I am. I'm sorry if I looked like I was drifting, but this is a lot to take in. Does John know you're here?"

"Of course not," she snapped. "He has no idea I know about his condition. I found out a few months ago by accident."

"How so?" Adam asked. There was much more to Nina than met the eye, he was beginning to see that.

Nina sighed in resignation. "I'm not really his assistant, you know. I work for his publisher. John is a brilliant man but his writing skills are somewhat lacking. The publishers were so anxious to put out his book they sent me to help him. I'm a ghostwriter, a person who puts other people's ideas on paper. I'm not terribly imaginative, but I'm quite skilled in writing so it's a perfect match. John is so smart it's scary, but he's not the most organized person I've ever met," she said with the slightest hint of a smile. "In order for us to work together I had to get him organized while his real assistant was on maternity leave and it ended up with me doing a lot of things a ghostwriter normally wouldn't do. I was answering the phone for him one day and he picked up the extension at the same time, so I overheard something I shouldn't." She paused, clearly reliving the moment when she found out his prognosis.

"After that incident, I felt no compunction about nosing around and I found what I needed to know in his files. Now, I don't know you or any of his new family well enough to ask you this, but I have to take the chance. I'm sure all of this has been upsetting and made you rethink your life and your relationship with your father and question everything you've ever been taught, but I want you to stop thinking about that for now and answer me one question. If you could stop him from dying, would you?"

Adam stared at her for a minute and was deeply impressed by what he saw. Her passion and intelligence showed clearly, and so did her anxiety. She was nervous, so nervous that her voice was shaking, but it didn't stop her from laying her cards out on the table. He had no idea what made him blurt it out like he did, but the words just leaped out of his mouth. "You're in love with him, aren't you?"

Nina rolled her eyes and gave him a baleful stare. "What *is* it with you people? Are you all just in love with being in love?" Her voice was full of scorn and she waved her hand impatiently. "I've never seen so many grown people drooling over each other the way you Cochrans do. I'm really not trying to be critical, but you all are way too adorable for me. All that kissing and hugging and lovey-dovey stuff you all do is just too much. It's like being in a very long episode of *The Cosby Show*," she blurted, and then blushed from her chest all the way up to her hairline. "I'm sorry, that was really rude of me. Please accept my apologies because I'm not trying to disrespect your family. Y'all are a little too charming for me, but that's my problem. And John's problem is the most important thing to me right now. I'm not in love with him but I care about him. He's a good man, a really good man, and he doesn't deserve to die this young."

"You don't need to apologize, Nina. I don't think I'd be any more diplomatic if I was trying to save my friend's life, either. This is why you wanted to have lunch with Alicia, isn't it?"

Nina nodded. "I thought maybe I could get her to come talk to you, but she, um, she . . ."

Adam finished her sentence for her. "She said she couldn't do it because I was already being torn apart by this. Or words to that effect, am I right?"

Nina nodded again. "I was pretty hard on her," she confessed. "I said some things that were rather harsh. I hope she can forgive me for it."

Adam waved a hand to indicate it was of little importance. "When you get to know Alicia you'll understand that she's one of the most forgiving and understanding people you'll ever meet. It's one of the reasons I love her so much."

"See, that's what I'm talking about," Nina burst out. "You Cochrans and this love stuff, I've never seen anything like it. Y'all make the Huxtables look like the Simpsons, but that's beside the point. What I want to know is if you're willing to help John. He didn't ask for any of this and he doesn't deserve it," she said with a touch of desperation in her voice.

Adam looked at her, her long slender fingers twisting in her lap and an errant piece of hair falling from her normally perfect hair. Before he could utter a word she leaned forward and asked him again if he would help John. "He didn't ask for this, but for God's sake, he's your brother," she cried.

"You're right," Adam said slowly. "He is my brother."

Alicia and Roxy moved boxes and tried to get some semblance of order going in the condo. The conversation they had while doing it helped Alicia; it kept her mind from straying to the huge question that loomed before her, that of how to address the issue with Adam. The doorbell rang and she answered it for Roxy. There stood Bryant Porter dressed in jeans and a beat-up Alpha T-shirt, ready for some hard labor. He was also carrying a big bag from Potbelly, a curiously named deli that boasted the best sandwiches in the world. He'd come bearing extraordinary Italian subs, bottles of soda, and a huge decadent chocolate malt to share for dessert.

"Ha! I see you two came to an understanding last night," Alicia said with a smile.

Roxy tried unsuccessfully to look indifferent, but she didn't do a very good job. "He's on probation. He's trying to convince me that his heart is pure and his intentions are good and I'm going to let him," she said airily, but the smile in her eyes as she looked at Bryant was a dead giveaway. "Come on in, Bryant, and let me give you the grand tour," she said, taking the bags from his hands and putting them on the counter that separated the dining room from the kitchen. She took his hand and proceeded to lead him around the spacious condo, pointing out various amenities in every room.

While they were looking around the place Alicia picked up her cell phone and hit the speed-dial for a familiar number. When her mother's voice came on the line Alicia told her she needed to talk right away. "Are you busy, *Mami?* Can I stop over?"

"Of course, baby. I'll be waiting for you."

When Roxy and Bryant returned to the living room, Alicia picked up her purse and explained that she was going to her mother's house. Roxy walked her to the door of the condo and she and Bryant watched her until she got to her car and got in. Bryant looked down at Roxy from his towering height and asked where she'd like to begin.

"Honey, as hard as I'm going to work you tonight, we'd better start with food. Let's eat," she said cheerfully.

Alicia finally made her way to the loft. She'd stayed away as long as she could, but she had to face the inevitable. She gave the two sharp knocks that were her signal, and then used her key to open the door. She was surprised to find the entire interior lit with scented candles and soft music playing. "Adam?" she called softly.

"In here, baby. Come on back," he invited.

With a bemused expression she walked slowly through the loft until she came to the bathroom where Adam was filling the tub with her favorite scented bath gel and the whirlpool jets were making a huge froth for her to bathe in. "Adam, what are you doing?" she asked inanely.

"I'm making a bath for you because you've had a hard day. And because we have something important to talk about and I want you nice and relaxed when we discuss it. Nina came to see me tonight." He said it as it if were of little importance, but Alicia knew better.

"I can't believe she did that! She has some kind of nerve confronting you like that," Alicia sputtered.

Adam walked over to her and embraced her tightly. "Don't talk right now, baby. Take off your clothes, get in this nice bath, and I'm going to make you a Bellini so fabulous you're going to fall in love with me all over again. Trust me, baby."

And she did, enough to do exactly as he asked.

Chapter Twenty-six

True to his word, Adam made her a wonderful Bellini. The cocktail of fresh peach juice and champagne was just what she needed; she could feel the tension slipping away from her body as she lolled in the tub. She tried to get Adam to join her in the tub, but he demurred. "This time it's all about you, my love. How's your drink?"

"Lovely. It tastes like more, actually," she said with a tiny hiccup as she passed him her flute.

"Be right back," he said as he rose from the floor next to the tub to refill her glass.

Alicia almost dozed off while he was gone, but her eyes opened and she smiled sleepily when Adam's lips touched her forehead. "Are you ready to emerge from your bath, darling?"

"In a few minutes, Adam. This feels so wonderful." She sighed. She sipped the heavenly concoction and looked at Adam with troubled eyes. "Nina told you, didn't she?"

Adam nodded. "Yes, *chica*, she did. She told me all about John's condition."

Alicia took another sip of her drink and refused to meet Adam's eyes for a moment, then she turned the full force of her big, long-lashed eyes on him. "She got a little ticked with me today," she said dryly.

Adam nodded. "She said she was a little harsh. She apologized."

"*A little harsh?* That cow went ziggety-boom on me,

Adam. She called me a selfish high-yellow heifer with a stank attitude and said I was useless. I think that's more than harsh," Alicia said, pouting. "And I am *not* high yellow, I'm darker than she is."

Trying hard not to laugh, Adam said solemnly, "I think she got caught up in the moment. I'm sure you were your usual calm and reasonable self, though, right?"

Alicia had the grace to look slightly abashed. "I so wish I could claim that, but I went right back at her, although I was doing it in Spanish. I know lots of really base things to say in Spanish," she said with another tiny hiccup. "I should have been more understanding. After all, if you had a terminal condition, who knows what I'd be doing? I'd save your life at any cost, Adam, there's no way I could sit by and let you die. I'd cut out my own heart and any other body part you happened to need," she said quietly.

Adam leaned over and gave her a sweet kiss. "It's time to get out of that tub, baby. You're getting all pruny." He stood up and held out a huge heated bath sheet for her, which she stepped into with enjoyment, sighing as he picked her up and carried her into the bedroom.

While he patted her dry and applied body butter to every part of her warm, moist skin, she didn't say anything outside of the occasional purr. Finally she spoke. "You're going to do it, aren't you, Adam?"

"If I can. I have to talk to him first and find out if it's feasible, if I can be a donor. But if I can, I will. I can't let him die, Alicia, knowing that I could have done something to save him."

A lone tear trickled down her cheek as she made a graceful movement to sit up and seek the comfort of his arms. "I know, Adam."

* * *

The next day, John was hard at work in his new office when he got a phone call. "John, it's Adam. I was wondering if you have some time to talk today." John's face reflected his surprise. Of all his new brothers, Adam seemed the most distant, but he wasn't about to question the reason for the call.

"Sure, why not? You want to meet in Detroit somewhere?" he asked.

"Actually, I'm here in Ann Arbor, why don't I stop by your office?"

"Okay, what time?"

"Open your door," Adam said.

Adam had decided to use Nina's method of gaining entry. It had worked for her; he saw no reason why it wouldn't work for him. Besides, he liked the element of surprise. He didn't want to have to think up a dumb reason for a visit and he also wanted to catch John off-guard. He gave John a half smile as he entered his office, looking around curiously at the décor. Nina had done a wonderful job of organizing and decorating the space for John; it was an efficient but warm and pleasant place in which to work. Adam was amazed to see the lacrosse sticks on the wall; he turned to John with a huge smile.

"Don't tell me you play the Little Brother of War," Adam said incredulously.

John's eyes lit up on hearing Adam use the Native American name for the game. "Since I was ten," he admitted. "You too?"

Adam took the seat John indicated and they spent a while talking about the game and their love of it. Adam felt bad about having to change the subject, but it had to be said. After the lacrosse talk gradually ended, Adam looked at John with the utmost gravity. "John, Nina came to see me yesterday. Without going into a lot of details about how she found out, let me just say she knows about your condition, which means

I know about it now. And I think I can help you with it. What do I have to do to be tested as a donor?"

John's too-thin face paled at Adam's words. "How the hell did she find out?" he murmured to himself. He went into a stunned silence for a moment, finally reacting to Adam's words.

"I appreciate the gesture, Adam, but I can't accept. I don't know you well enough to expect you to do something like that, it's too much to ask," he began.

Adam cut him off before he could continue in this vein. "Look, John, obviously we don't know each other, but what better way to start a relationship than by sharing internal organs?" He gave a short laugh at the utter incongruity of the statement. "Besides, you saved my sister's life a long time ago. This is the least I can do for someone who saved the most important person in my life. I'd never have made it to adulthood without Benita. She was more than my sister; she was my friend, my mother, my teacher, she was my *everything* and she still is. My sister means so much to me I can't even begin to tell you about it. If I can do this for you, I'm going to do it, so let's get started on whatever we have to do to make this happen. And let's hurry because I have a woman who wants to get married really bad and I can't put her off much longer," he said drolly.

John's emotions clouded his face for a few minutes and he was finally able to speak. "I don't know what to say, Adam. How can I possibly thank you for this?"

"First we find out if it's possible, then we worry about the thanking. I'm thinking one of those antique sticks might be a start, though," Adam said while giving the stick in question a covetous stare.

John's answering laughter sounded a little strained, even to his own ears. He quickly picked up his phone and dialed Abe Gold's private number. "Abe? I've got news, good news, I think."

* * *

Alicia was dreading the night that stretched before her. It was the last night before Adam and John were to check into University of Michigan Medical Center for the procedure and she didn't want to think about it any more than she had to. In a lot of ways she was resigned to what was going to happen, but on a base, primitive level the thought of her man undergoing this drastic surgery still made her ill. Thanks to a long talk with her parents and a lot of prayer she was ready to put it all in the Lord's hands. She felt like a terrible hypocrite at times because she knew in her heart that if Adam had been suffering from the same ailment she'd have moved heaven and earth to help him. She was also very moved by his generous spirit and proud that he was so caring. But the part of her that loved him beyond reason couldn't stand the thought of him being cut open and part of him being taken away, regardless of the fact it was saving his half brother's life.

She had no logical reason to be in the office anymore. Everyone else had left and she needed to leave, too. It wasn't like she was working anymore. For the past hour all she'd done was stare into space. She wasn't even trying to pretend she had work to do, she was just brooding. She finally stood up and took a deep, shuddering breath. Gathering her things together, she quickly left the office suite and took the elevator down to the parking garage. She balanced her briefcase on top of the Mini Cooper and made a soft sound of surprise when she found a gardenia on her front seat. The sweet, heavy fragrance filled the car and made her smile. *Adam.* He knew how torn up she was about all this and he wanted to make her feel better. There was a note with the flower in Adam's precise penmanship. It read *Meet me at the loft.*

It took only minutes for her to get to the big converted apartment building in Harbortown and she made the drive with a smile on her face. To her utter delight there was a note on the outside door with her name on it. She opened it and smiled again as she read *I've been waiting for you. Hurry.* She entered the elevator and when she exited, she was touched to her heart to see a trail of petals leading to the loft door. Another note awaited her. *Don't bother to knock, come in and follow the signs.*

Totally intrigued now, she eagerly opened the door to find the living room full of flowers, beautiful exotic blooms full of sensual scents and colors. The air was laden with the fragrance of the flowers and the candles that were around the big loft. The candles gave a mellow amber light and the trail of petals continued. A hand-lettered sign on a small table bade her to leave her brief-case, purse, and shoes there. Near the study was another sign that simply read *Drink me*, it was on a carved stand leaning against a single glass that contained a chilled peach Bellini. She took a sip and ventured farther on the trail of petals, captivated by this lovely game. Another sign pointed to the bedroom and the notation simply read *Take off your clothes.*

By now Alicia had completely entered into the spirit of the game, she was completely ready for whatever Adam had in store for her. Whatever it was, it would surely be pleasurable in the extreme. She'd never known his brand of sensuality existed and now she couldn't do without it. Adam had awakened her to love in more ways than one. He'd tapped into the deepest and most profoundly sexual part of her and in so doing had unleashed a sensuality she had no idea she possessed.

Alicia removed every item of clothing and as she was putting her delicate underwear in the hamper, she noticed another note, this one on the giant mirror of the long dresser. *Just a quick shower, baby, I can't wait much longer.* Her anticipation was making her body react with

growing need. She could feel her nether regions begin
to pulse and moisten and her nipples were already hard
as her breasts reacted to her arousal. She showered
quickly and thoroughly, anxious for whatever exquisite
pleasure Adam had planned for her. Wrapped in a fluffy
towel, she reentered the bedroom and smiled in delight
as she found a beautiful short kimono, heavily embroi-
dered ivory lined in pale green, across the bed. A pair of
matching slippers was next to it with a final note. *Come to
my garden.*

Alicia looked in the mirror and was almost embarrassed by what she saw. She looked flushed with eager
passion; she looked, even to her own critical eye, sensual
and ready for love. Her tousled hair and makeup-free
face only enhanced the look. She smiled at her reflection and went out to meet her love.

Adam was waiting for her in a fantasy come true, a
rooftop garden of love. On the wall nearest the French
doors he'd arranged a day bed covered with a deep
rose silk cover and draped with a filmy canopy that
looked like something out of *The Arabian Nights*. There
were big silk pillows in soft colors with sensual fringes
and tassels; incense was burning, and tall stands held
big candles in copper and glass lanterns that enhanced
the mood with their flickering light. The bedroom
stereo had been placed near the bed, as well as a low
table that held an array of fruit, cheese, pastry, and
other delights, all covered with the kind of net thing
used to protect food at picnics. Adam was on the bed
waiting for Alicia. He looked incredibly handsome,
lying on his side wearing a short robe similar to Alicia's with nothing on under it but bare skin. He held
out his hand to her and she came to him at once, joining him on the bed. She looked around at the flowers
that also surrounded the bed and took a deep breath
of the heavy warm summer air. The evening shadows
were gathering and it was almost dark now.

"Adam, this is so wonderful. I can't thank you enough for doing this for me," she said sweetly. Adam kissed her forehead, her cheeks, and her lips before answering. "I did this for both of us, baby. I want us to have something to remember and something to look forward to when this is all over."

He sat up and turned so he was sitting up straight with his legs spread wide so they hung down on either side of the bed. "Come here, baby, let's try something a little different tonight."

He had her sit facing him with her legs open and her thighs resting on his. "Closer, Allie, come closer to me," he whispered. She did so at once, moving so close to him that their bodies were within an inch of touching. "Have you ever heard of tantric sex?

Alicia nodded, bemused. "I've read about it a bit. Is that what we're going to do?"

Adam pressed his lips to her forehead as he adjusted their positions. "Yes, we are, my love."

"Now what?" she asked with wonder in her voice.

"Now we breathe, Allie. We inhale and exhale together and we try to feel each other," he said softly.

Odd as it sounded, that's what they did, looking deeply into each other's eyes they breathed in and out, with the smell of the flowers and the candles and incenses combining in a swirl of heady fragrance that seemed to help transport them to a place where there was nothing but Adam, nothing but Alicia, nothing but their love and their desire. Alicia could feel every beat of Adam's heart in every part of her body and it pulsed through her with a steady rhythm that transcended sex but was more sexual than anything she'd ever known.

Adam felt Alicia's every reaction; he knew when her need for him and her desire combined to transport her out of herself and into him and that's when he opened his robe to reveal his massively hardened body already outfitted with a latex condom. He opened her robe to reveal her perfect body and lifted her forward onto his erection, sliding into her with exquisite slowness as she clutched his shoulders for balance. Instead of the normal movements, the thrusting and plunging that made their lovemaking so fulfilling, he held her, so close that they could fell their hearts beating as one, until their pulses were as one and the love they felt for each other shimmered through their bodies like they were walking through a curtain of stars together. The climax went on and on and it was impossible for Alicia to tell where Adam's body stopped and hers started; they were the same person, a creature of passion and fire and light, consumed by love.

Alicia finally fell forward onto Adam's shoulder, totally sated and completely spent. Suddenly her euphoria turned to tears and she sobbed softly against the man she loved more than her own life. "It's okay, Allie. It's okay. I've got you baby, I've got you." Adam rocked her and comforted her and she knew at that moment that he was right. Everything would be just fine.

Miles away in Arbot, John was also making his final preparations to check into the University of Michigan Medical Center. Nina was helping him get packed with her usual acerbic brand of cheer, but he had her number. He watched her closely as she added a shirt to the garment bag that lay across the bed. He was reclining next to it with a smile on his face. He still couldn't get over the fact that she'd interceded on his behalf. After Adam confronted him about his condition, John had gone to her hotel and knocked on her door. He didn't have to say anything to her; she knew from the look on his face why he was there. Her reaction was typical Miss Parker.

"You can't fire me," she said at once. "I am not on your payroll, I work for your publisher. You can't ter-

minate my employment and there is no basis for a law-
suit because my actions were absent malice. So if you've
come seeking revenge, think again." She crossed her
arms and dared him to say something, a dare he took
with no hesitation.

He crossed the threshold and closed the door behind
him, coming to stand in front of her and putting his big
hands on her slender shoulders. He was pleased to find
out she was trembling just a bit. Miss Parker truly did
have a heart buried beneath her constant flippancy. "I'm
not here to fire you or sue you or anything else. I'm here
to thank you. That took guts, Nina. A lot of people
wouldn't have bothered; they wouldn't have gotten involved at all. You went way out on a limb for me and I'll
never be able to thank you for it."

Nine tried to mask her pleased expression at his warm
words and succeeded slightly by saying "So now I own
you, is that what you're saying? I want that in writing and
notarized."

His chest muffled her words as he had embraced her
tightly. He was about to speak when his cell phone went
off and with an apologetic smile, he answered it, giving
her time to extricate herself from his arms and wander
around the room looking insouciant.

John smiled again at the memory. He liked to amuse
himself by wondering what would have happened if
Abe Gold hadn't called him at that exact moment. Now
didn't seem to be the time to find out, however, as Nina
was displaying her frightening efficiency in getting his
things organized for the trip to the hospital. "I'm not
touching your underwear in any way, shape, or form
so if you don't plan on going commando I suggest you
see to that. We're actually ahead of schedule on the
book so there's nothing to worry about on that ac-
count. I put a couple of magazines in the bag and I'm
loaning you my I-pod. If you want more reading ma-

terial, I can bring it to you, I suppose," she added with a long-suffering sigh.

"Miss Parker, I've never known anyone who goes to the lengths you do to disguise their essential sweetness and generosity of spirit. You are without a doubt one of the kindest people I've ever met and yet you try to pretend you're a harpy. Why is that?"

"Because I'm unique," she drawled. "Now why don't you get up and do some packing because I don't do other people's underwear."

"When this is all over and I'm healthy and hearty again, I'm going to do something wonderful to thank you."

"Put your drawers in the tote bag, that'll be thanks enough," she said without looking at him.

Chapter Twenty-seven

Nina decided she was going to have to take back some of the things she'd said about the Cochrans. They might be downright goofy with love, but they were definitely the ones to have on your side. From the moment Adam had found out John needed his help, he was there for him just like a brother should be. And that other brother of his, that Andrew, he was a big help, too. He was the one who made sure everyone understood what the procedure consisted of and what would be happening in the operating room. He'd had a meeting to explain to the whole family at once, easily the best way with so many family members.

She rubbed her brow and thought about what Andrew had told them all. "It's a fairly simple procedure, actually. Every healthy adult liver has two globes. One is slightly bigger than the other and that's the one that will be taken from Adam and put into John. After that, both John and Adam will start to grow new livers because the liver regenerates itself. In fact, John will have a full-sized organ before Adam will. For some reason the donor's grows back a little more slowly. After a period of recuperation they'll both be fine."

Nina thanked God that Andrew had made it seem so straightforward and that Adam was so caring and generous. And that Alicia hadn't stopped him from going through with the surgery. No one had to tell Nina. One look at the couple let her know if Alicia told Adam she wanted the moon he'd be trying to figure out a way to bring it to her. They were so in love it should be sickening, but for some reason it was just sweet.

She still cringed when she remembered the things she'd said to Alicia, although as Adam said, Alicia was quite forgiving. And very calm, too, she thought, looking at Alicia fingering a rosary as they waited for the surgery to be over. Praying that she was looking at least as composed as Alicia, Nina went back to surreptitiously stroking the thick gold bracelet John had given her the day after she'd sent him breakfast. Her stupid hands just wouldn't stop trembling, no matter what she did. It wasn't like she was going through this alone; all of John's brothers were there in the waiting room, as well as his father. His father's wife, a couple of wives of one brother or another, Alicia's mother and sister, there were so many people in the waiting room Nina couldn't even begin to remember who was who, nor did she care. It was enough that they were all there for John and Adam.

Alicia looked a lot more serene than she felt. Inside she was a mass of raw nerve endings, each one firing off its share of anxiety and tension. She was trying to concentrate on the rosary beads in her hands, but it was futile. She finally abandoned herself to the love she felt in the room and let herself relax in its aura. Her mother had gone off with Martha to get her a cup of tea and she found herself sitting next to Big Benny, who was surprisingly subdued.

Alicia took his hand and held it tightly, giving him all the reassurance she had to offer. "It's going to be fine, Mr. Cochran. Adam is strong and healthy and he and John are a perfect match genetically. It's going to be just fine," she said bracingly.

Benny squeezed her hand in acknowledgment of her words. "God's going to take care of my boys," he said. He didn't speak again for a few minutes. "I don't deserve to have a son like Adam. Or John for that matter. I'm not a bad man, Alicia, but I've made a lot of mistakes. I tried to be a good father, but who knows how I did? If it weren't for Benita and Andrew and Ruth this whole family might have fallen apart after Lillian died. I made so many mistakes," he repeated sadly.

"Mr. Cochran, I think you were a better father than you know. Look at your children; they're all wonderful people. You were a good father," she insisted. "You raised them to be strong, confident adults with beautiful families and they all love you dearly."

"Not Adam. Adam doesn't want to have anything to do with me, Alicia, and I can't blame him. The fact that he was able to do this thing for John, that means a lot to me because he didn't have to do it."

"No, he didn't. But he couldn't turn his back on his brother and part of that came from you, Mr. Cochran. You and Adam will work through this, I know you will."

Martha and Leah returned with cups of hot tea for Alicia and Benny and one for Nina, which Alicia took over to her. Nina accepted it with her usual clipped thank-you, but Alicia wasn't put off by her tone. "Do you need more sugar? I think *Mami* brought some extra back with her."

"No, this is fine. You don't have to be nice to me; I was pretty nasty to you. I had no right to judge you and say the things I did."

"Nina, please stop apologizing! In the first place, I'd have clowned worse than you if Adam had been ill. And in the second place . . ." Alicia took a sip of tea and looked sheepish. "I wasn't exactly genteel myself. I curse quite fluently in Spanish," she mumbled into her cup.

The two women looked at each other and laughed quietly. It was enough that they'd turned a corner in their path to friendship, but the moment was made even more special by the presence of Adam's and John's surgeon. "The procedure went brilliantly. There's every reason to believe that they will have a spectacular recovery." Alicia's eyes closed in a prayer of thanksgiving and she didn't hear too much more of what was said. She did hear the doctor say they could see John and Adam in post-op for just a minute before they went to the recovery room.

Alicia wiped her eyes as she and Nina were taken to the post-operative suite where John and Adam lay on gurneys waiting to be transported to the recovery room. Alicia stroked the side of Adam's face and said his name softly. His eyelids fluttered once, and then he opened them just enough to see her and smile before they closed again. "Allie. I love you, *chica*." Nina stood next to John's gurney and searched his face with her eyes, not daring to touch him or speak, until his head suddenly turned. Her eyes widened in surprise as he mumbled something that sounded like "Miss Parker." She gently touched his hand and was stunned when he returned the touch with a slight squeeze of his fingers. They had to leave the area and were told the patients would be in recovery for a couple of hours and would then be going to their rooms.

Alicia wanted to weep with joy, she wanted to dance and sing with happiness, and instead she did the next best thing and hugged Nina. After a moment of motionless shock, Nina hugged her back.

Adam looked up expectantly as Alicia entered his office. He was back at work for half days now, although he insisted he could handle a full day. Alicia prevailed, however, insisting that he follow the doctor's orders to the letter. Now she looked as though she could use some time off work. She was gorgeous, as always, wearing a chic and sexy slim-fitting wrap dress in navy with a pair of navy shoes that made him want to lock the door and have his way with her. He was staring at the graceful shoes with the low-cut vamp and enticing ankle straps so intently he missed what she was saying.

"Are you listening to me, Adam? I said the wedding is off, I can't do this," she said with true panic in her voice.

Adam rose from his drawing table and locked his arms around her. "Allie, baby, what's the matter? Have I done something I don't know about?" he teased gently.

"It's my aunts, Adam. They're driving me insane with this wedding. Dresses and menus and themes and venues and invitations, I'm losing my mind. I don't want any of this, I really don't." Her face was so unhappy Adam had to kiss her and nuzzle her neck until she felt more relaxed in his arms. He walked her over to the long sofa across from the bank of windows and sat down with her in his lap.

"Tell me about it, baby. Tell me what would make you happy," he said, smoothing her eyebrow with a long finger.

"I guess I don't mind the idea of a big wedding, but it's going to take so long to plan." She sighed. "I don't want to wait that long to get married. Everything doesn't have to be color-coordinated and exquisitely formal—those are Gigi's words, not mine—I just want it to be happy and fun and soon. I want to be your wife as soon as possible. Is that so wrong?"

Adam smiled down at her and kissed her temple, slowly drawing the tip of his tongue gently down to her sensitive ear, lightly tracing its curves and making Alicia squirm with pleasure. "Adam, stop it," she moaned. "You know that drives me crazy."

He relented and tried to look deeply serious. "You know, I'm not opposed to a big wedding, I think it'll be fun. But I'm also all in favor of us being together as soon as possible. So, I propose a compromise, something I think you'll like very much," he promised.

Alicia still couldn't believe they were really going to do it. She and Adam were in the Range Rover heading for

Idlewild with Nina and John in the backseat and Roxy and Bryant following them in Roxy's new Chrysler 300. The only people who knew about this were the aunts and they'd been sworn to secrecy. Adam's idea had been a wonderfully simple one: they were going to elope. As he put it, they could have My Big Fat Cuban Wedding later. Right now they were going to have something quiet, intimate, and simple, just for them.

John and Nina had different reactions to Idlewild and Baldwin. John thought the towns were charming and picturesque, Nina thought they made Ann Arbor, which she considered a backwater, look like Manhattan. "My God, there isn't even a Blockbuster here!" she said in horror.

"Yes, but there's Video Schmideo where you can get a really great pizza *and* use the computer to check your e-mail. You can't do that at Blockbuster," Adam pointed out. Nina gave him a look of disdain but held her tongue. They had a brief tour of the area with Adam taking them to the site where the house was being built. "Next summer, John, we'll all be able to come here for vacations. Actually, the house will be done in time for Thanksgiving; maybe we can all come up here then. What do you think, Allie?"

"I think *yes*," she said happily. "And I think we'd better get ready."

They went back to the Morton Inn, the venerable motel that had served generations of Idlewilders. Nina and Roxy insisted that Adam go to John's room to get dressed because they needed the privacy for Alicia. He agreed good-naturedly and in an hour or so he was ready to concede they were completely correct. The feeling of anticipation was wonderful; it was exciting and humbling all at once. He didn't see Alicia when he walked into the Baldwin Church of Christ, although he looked for her. The women had left the motel before the men and were helping Alicia get dressed at the church. They were going to leave by the back door and come around to the front of the church for her grand entrance.

Adam, John, and Bryant went to take their places at the front of the small church. Roxy and Nina, each wearing a beautiful outfit that didn't match anything but looked perfect on them, walked in next, Nina leading the way and Roxy following. Finally, it was time for Alicia to enter the church. She didn't mind one bit that she wasn't walking down the aisle on her father's arm, because they would do that later. She did mind that her family wouldn't be there, other than the aunts who were already seated. But all she really cared about was becoming one with Adam, right then, right there.

She was looking down at her bouquet when she entered or she wouldn't have been so surprised when she felt a hand on her elbow. She looked up into the face of her father, Jose, who was holding his arm out for her to take. "You didn't think we were going to miss giving our baby girl in marriage, do you?" Her tear-filled eyes also saw her mother, Leah, Martha and Benny, Marielle, and the rest of the Cochran brothers with their wives and children. Raphael and Carlos were missing, but this was a Saturday in August and the Tigers were playing. Her aunts were there, though, all looking fabulous. She was so startled to see everyone she could feel the tears starting, but the deep, sonorous voice of Brother Sims calmed her down.

"There should be no tears on this day of joy. Come forward, daughter, and claim your husband."

Brother Sims was the handsome, articulate, and totally eloquent Minister Emeritus of the Baldwin Church of Christ and a very good friend of the aunts who'd asked him to officiate.

As Jose escorted Alicia down the aisle to meet Adam, a small commotion at the back of the church made everyone turn around. "We object!"

It was Raphael and Carlos, accompanied by a very

large Michigan State Trooper. "The game was rained out and we may or may not have been speeding, it's a matter of interpretation," Carlos said hurriedly as he attempted to put on his sport coat. Raphael agreed. "I'm pretty sure we were somewhat within the speed limit but we had to see Patti get married."

Brother Sims laughed out loud at the spectacle. "I'm sure we can this all straightened out afterwards. If not, I'm sure we can make bail for you. Now, let's get these young people married." He performed the ceremony with tender humor and deep faith. It was a sweet, memorable joining of two people who loved each other completely. As the Church of Christ did not use musical instruments, all the singing was a cappella, which made for lovely, spirited to Sunday services. To everyone's surprise, however, there was a soloist at the wedding. Nina sang "The Lord's Prayer" in a contralto so clear and sweet it was like the singing of angels. If Adam had been facing the audience while she was singing he'd have exploded with laughter; everyone was turned toward Nina with the same look of total shock on their faces.

The only thing Adam was looking at, however, was Alicia, the woman he would love the rest of his life, the woman who knew him better than he knew himself, the woman who made him complete. When she appeared at the back of the church, Adam felt an inexplicable burning sensation in his eyes, something suspiciously like tears. She looked beautiful. Totally sweet, feminine, and almost innocent in the ivory blouse and matching lace skirt he'd bought for her on their first shopping spree. Her hair was soft and sleekly arranged off her face and there was an ivory rosebud tucked behind one ear with a spray of baby's breath. She carried a bouquet of gardenias and white roses and she looked composed, but he could feel her trembling with emotion. She handed her bouquet to Roxy, and Adam took both her hands. His profound joy was obvious. He loved the sound of the vows that united them for eternity.

"Do you, Alicia Evangeline Guadalupe Fuentes, take Adam to be your lawful wedded husband?"

Alicia said, "I do," in a clear, sure voice, even though Adam was mouthing "*Guadalupe?*" with raised eyebrows.

"Do you, Adam Brantley Cochran, take Alicia to be your lawful wedded wife?"

"Yes, I do," Adam said fervently.

As Brother Sims drew the ceremony to a close with some poignantly memorable remarks, Adam and Alicia looked at each other with pure delight.

"I love you," he whispered.

"I love you back," she whispered with her heart in her eyes. "I'm going to make you happy for the rest of our lives, Adam."

"You already do, baby."

When Brother Sims pronounced them man and wife, he didn't mind a bit that they took an unusually long time to seal their vows with a kiss, and, judging from the soft *ahhhs* from their assorted relatives, no one else minded, either.

"I now present to you Mr. and Mrs. Adam Brantley Cochran. What God has joined together, let no man put asunder."

Adam and Alicia smiled at the loved ones gathered to celebrate with them and at each other, then walked down the aisle to start their life together.

Epilogue

The brilliant coral of the setting sun spread its radiance over the ocean as Adam and Alicia lounged on the lanai of their honeymoon retreat. Alicia was looking at the brilliant sunset with a very private smile on her face. Adam was enjoying the sight of his bride's reverie but he felt compelled to discover the source of her joy. They were seated on a big double chaise and he reached for her, pulling her into his embrace and his asked her why she was smiling.

"Because I'm so happy. I'm married to the most wonderful man in the world, I'm having the most marvelous honeymoon imaginable and we had the best wedding I've ever been to. Both of them," she said happily.

Adam gave her a lingering kiss before. "Yeah they were both very special. Your aunts really went all out for us," he said.

Alicia could only agree as she remembered the lengths of Marguerite, Graciela and Gigi gone to so their formal wedding would be a beautiful celebration. They'd picked out her wedding dress and the bridesmaids dresses with Leah's help and consent and the end result had frightened Alicia into hiccups. The wedding dress had huge poufy Gibson girl sleeves and a bustle, as well as a fourteen-foot train. The entire thing was constructed of Chantilly lace and satin and weighed about a ton. The bridesmaid's dresses were also satin with huge puffed sleeves and rows of ruffles in a shade of iridescent orange that was in blindingly bad taste. Alicia was truly horrified by the spectacle, but her aunts were so anxious to make her wedding memorable she didn't have the heart to protest. Or the resources to back her up, as Marielle, Leah and Roxy seemed to think there was nothing amiss about the dresses.

Reminding herself over and over that she and Adam were already man and wife and this was just a formality to assuage her aunts, Alicia went along with the program, albeit with a heavy heart. When the moment came for her to don her dress in the room of St. Cecelia, the church she'd attended since she was a little girl, she almost went into shock when the aunts stepped forward with a sleek, simple and utterly lovely dress devoid of ruffles, lace, giant sleeves or anything else objectionable. It was an elegant, bias cut confection, sleeveless with a deep back that had crossed straps. It was a softly blushed shade of white called candlelight and there was an exquisitely sheer veil held with gardenias to grace Alicia's beautiful and very relieved face.

Gigi crowed, "We got you, *mija!* Those other costumes, they were to pay you back for thinking you could elope. Surprise!"

Alicia collapsed in laughter as she beheld the real bridesmaid's dresses, which were simple and elegant in a sophisticated champagne color. Her attendants carried fantastic bouquets in buttery shades of yellow and gold that complemented Alicia's cluster of gardenias and white and yellow roses. Everything about the wedding was perfect; it was a wedding out of a fairy tale.

She smiled up at Adam and asked him what his favorite part of the wedding was. "Besides the pleasure of seeing how lovely you looked?" He kissed her softly before replying. "Everything was wonderful, baby, I loved our wedding. But I have to say; the reception was my favorite part. I never had so much fun in my life, Allie."

Marielle had arranged to have their reception at Comerica Park and it was the perfect venue for the event. There was lots of music, thanks both to Bump Williams and his band and the outstanding DJ who alternated to provide a tune-filled background. There was an abundance of food, both Cuban and southern cooking graced the tables. There were amusements for the children and dancing for the adults and the atmosphere was pure love and happiness.

Alicia had to agree with Adam, although for a slightly different reason. She was thrilled that Adam had made his peace with his father and had accepted John fully as a brother. John was, in fact, one of Adam's groomsmen. But Adam had come to an understanding with his father the night of his first wedding to Alicia. She reminded him of that fact. "Adam, I think it's so wonderful that you and your dad have come to an understanding. It's really none of my business, but it makes me very happy that the two of you are closer than ever. I just think it's important for you to have reconnected with him."

Adam corrected her. "It is your business. Anything that affects me is your business. You're my wife, Allie, not some disinterested bystander. But you're right, I'm also very happy that Pop and I were able to work it out."

After the elopement in Idlewild, Adam and his father had gone over to the site where the vacation house was being constructed and walked around. Adam showed his father the plans for the house and the guest cottages and they talked about the project for a few minutes. Finally Adam had dropped all pretenses and looked his father in the eye.

"Pop, I can't judge you. I'm not the one to say anything about your life and how you lived it. The fact is, you gave me life and I have no cause to regret a single day of it. I was pretty harsh on you and I regret that. No matter what you did or why, one thing is never going to change. You'll always be my father. And you've always been a good one, Pop, the best."

Big Benny was crying openly, not bothering to disguise the tears that were rolling down his face. "Adam, you had every right to say what you said. I was wrong to cheat on your mother. I was wrong to keep John a secret all these years. I was wrong on so many counts . . ." His words stopped as Adam help up his hand.

"No more regrets, Pop. What's done is done. It's a new day now and we've all had a new start. Let's go back to the party and enjoy this new beginning, okay?"

Now it was Alicia's turn to ask Adam why he was smiling. "Because this has been the best year of my entire life, bar none. I started the year horny and hateful because I was so in love with you I couldn't stand it, I find out I have a whole bunch more family including a new brother, I gave away part of a vital organ and most importantly, I was lucky enough to win your heart and take you for my bride. I couldn't be any happier than I am right now, Allie."

"I feel the same way, Adam, although I'm willing to try on the happiness thing. Let's go inside and see what we can do to be even happier," she said seductively.

By way of an answer Adam picked her up and carried her into their airy, candlelit bedroom. "You've got yourself a deal, baby."